Where Shadows Linger

Where Shadows Linger

Mary D. Brooks

P.D. Publishing, Inc.
Clayton, North Carolina

Copyright © 2007 by Mary D. Brooks

All rights reserved. No part of this publication may be reproduced, transmitted in any form or by any means, electronic or mechanical, including photocopy, recording, or any information storage and retrieval system, without permission in writing from the publisher. The characters herein are fictional and any resemblance to a real person, living or dead, is purely coincidental.

ISBN-13: 978-1-933720-31-9
ISBN-10: 1-933720-31-X

9 8 7 6 5 4 3 2 1

Cover design by Linda Callaghan
Edited by: Linda Daniel

Published by:

P.D. Publishing, Inc.
P.O. Box 70
Clayton, NC 27528

http://www.pdpublishing.com

Acknowledgements

Many thanks to the following people for their help in the production of this novel:

Tee for keeping me on the path; wouldn't be the same without her support, encouragement and dedication. She took these characters into her heart and helped in the birth of this novel.

"The Flower Chicks" for their wacky sense of fun, their love and encouragement. What a great bunch of mates!

Linda Callaghan for her usual creative magic in producing the wonderful cover.

Lucia Nobrega for the use of her artwork of Eva and Zoe on the cover — a very giving soul and a dear friend.

My editor, Linda Daniel, for her dedication and love for these characters and her friendship.

Dedicated To:
Ann — Because You Are You

For every hill I've had to climb,
For every stone that bruised my feet,
For all the blood and sweat and grime,
For blinding storms and burning heat,
My heart sings but a grateful song—
These were the things that made me strong!
For all the heartaches and the tears,
For all the anguish and the pain,
For gloomy days and fruitless years,
And for the hopes that lived in vain,
I do give thanks, for now I know
These were the things that helped me grow!
Tis not the softer things of life
Which stimulate man's will to strive,
But bleak adversity and strife
Do most to keep man's will alive.
O'er rose-strewn paths the weaklings creep,
But brave hearts dare to climb the steep.

~ *Growth* by Unknown Author

Chapter One

October 1947
"The Emerald City" or "The Land of Milk and Honey" — nicknames that the city of Sydney, Australia, had collected over the years evoked images of tranquility and of opportunity. However, tranquility was nowhere to be found as the traffic slowly made its way across the Sydney Harbour Bridge. The sun beat down upon the city, casting a golden shimmer over the waves. Beneath the large grey bridge, sailboats scudded back and forth or bobbed in the calm waters.

Sydney's nickname "The Emerald City" originated from the deep green shimmering waters that surrounded it. To many people, the city was their haven from war-torn Europe and all other places in between. The label "The Land of Milk and Honey" was given to the great southern land by the refugees and immigrants because Australia offered her new citizens a chance for a new life and hope for the future. It was a place to forget and to rebuild.

Eva Muller rested her head against the window and shut her eyes, already feeling claustrophobic on the crowded bus. The sounds of chattering voices, the blaring horns of nearby cars, and the whining of a child who had obviously also had enough of the noise, were fraying her patience. She was tired, hot, and annoyed. Australia might have been the Land of Milk and Honey, but it was not her land of opportunity at that particular moment.

Eva, a tall, dark-haired woman with sapphire-colored eyes, captivated almost anyone who met her, including prospective employers. Quiet, unassuming, and polite with a reasonable grasp of English despite it not being her native tongue, Eva had a gift for languages; she spoke several languages fluently. But she also had a problem. As soon as she spoke, her accent caused many interviewers to decide instantly that they had no positions available.

Eva was German. Her accent was German and her heart was German, although her parentage was Greek. The odd combination was one that was very difficult to explain without going into a complicated story. She found she was either a "wog" or a "dago" — derogatory terms used for Greek and Italian immigrants by the Australian natives — because of her appearance, or a "kraut" because of her accent.

My life has taken a very different turn from the direction I thought it was going, Eva thought, grateful for the coolness of the window glass against her forehead. She thought back to her youth in Germany. *The war was the start of my nightmare. First, my mother's murder on Kristallnacht. I was told at the time that she had been mistaken for a Jewess. Then, my adopted father's cruelties after he discovered I was a homosexual. It was a miracle I survived. Then Larissa, Greece, where I was reborn and began to live again. That's where I met Zoe.* The thought of Zoe put a soft smile on her face until her memories continued. *But it was also during that time that I was told that my adopted father had ordered the death of my mother. I don't know what to believe. One thing I do know — if it hadn't been for Zoe, I wouldn't be here today.*

The Greeks were a proud people. Their land had been overrun by the might of the German army, but their will had never been subjugated. It was in Larissa, a small Greek town, that Eva had met the woman who finally brought light into her darkened world.

Zoe Lambros.

Eva smiled as the image of her lover, the woman who was her best friend and her knight-in-shining-armor all rolled into one petite package, came back to her mind and stayed.

Zoe was a red-haired young woman with emerald-colored eyes. As the bus slowly made its way across the Harbour Bridge, an unobstructed panorama of the harbor came into view. The shimmering waters made Eva smile. The emerald-colored waters reminded her of her lover's eyes. Every time Zoe smiled, her smile lit up her eyes and made Eva's heart melt. Despite being only fifteen at the time they had met, Zoe had been a courageous member of the Greek Resistance.

The diminutive young girl had tragically lost her entire family. First, her brothers were killed defending Greece from the invading Italians. Then upon hearing the news of their deaths, her father suffered a heart attack and died, leaving Zoe and her mother the only two family members remaining. After the Germans advanced into Greece, Zoe's mother was murdered by the German military leader in charge of Larissa, Eva's stepfather, leaving Zoe alone. While Zoe held her dead mother in her arms, she made a promise that her death would be avenged. Zoe had set her sights on Eva, determined that Eva was going to pay for the sins of her father even knowing that killing Eva would have condemned a hundred Greeks to their deaths.

Zoe never made good on that promise, even though she had the opportunity. Instead of killing Eva as she had planned, she fell in love with her. *Now there's something I didn't count on. She got under my defenses. I still don't know how she did that.* It had been as much of a shock to Zoe as it had been to Eva. Despite Eva's vow that she would not allow herself to fall in love with a woman again, she had found herself totally lost when it came to Zoe. She felt awkward, shy, and unsure of herself, and, as Eva soon learned, once Zoe's mind was made up, there was nothing on earth that would or could change it. And Zoe made up her mind to have Eva. So after knowing Eva for over a year, Eva and Zoe shared their first kiss.

Zoe made her feel alive again, gave her hope, and made her laugh. She opened up a part of Eva that lay dormant, a part Eva had thought long dead. Eva began to dream again; the world held new possibilities and maybe, just maybe, there would be a little bit of happiness for her.

Eva took out a photograph she carried in her purse and looked at it. Zoe was sprawled on the grass, laughing. It was Eva's favorite photo of her lover. Eva traced Zoe's smiling face with her fingertip and sighed pensively. They could not declare their love for each other to the world. That would be unthinkable. They had to pass themselves off as sisters. *Even a blind man can tell that Zoe and I look nothing alike, but that's the story we have to maintain. Lies, lies, and more lies.* Eva shook her head and sighed.

Zoe wanted to tell the world of her love for her partner, but Eva knew all too well the cost of such declarations. She was certain Zoe did not fully understand the consequences, did not know the price they would both pay for that admission. Still, Eva often thought that angels would not dare tread where Zoe wanted to go.

Eva smiled. An indomitable spirit was one of the things she loved about Zoe. She looked at the photo again before putting it back in her purse. Signaling to the driver to stop at the next turn, she untangled her long frame from the tiny space it had been crammed into for the trip into the central business district.

Her mind went from her loving partner to her upcoming interview. This would be her last interview of the day. Eva had stopped into The Immigrants' Job Network after her previously unsuccessful interview for a job as a filing clerk, one employment opportunity Eva was glad she did not get. The Job Network had given her the address of a factory where a secretary was needed.

Eva had never been a secretary, but she could type. She did not know shorthand but was assured that the job did not require it. Clutching the address in her hand, Eva found herself outside the Johnson Brothers' Biscuit Factory. A smile creased her lips as the aroma of freshly baked cookies seeped into the air. Taking a deep breath, she opened the door and entered the building.

The cacophony of sounds inside the factory was as deafening as the noise she had endured riding the bus. Machines whirred and a giant fan tried valiantly to cool the place down. Women in white uniforms with little white hats, similar to nursing uniforms, stood at a conveyer belt, placing packets of biscuits into boxes. Eva stood and watched them for a long moment. Men in white pants and shirts or overalls picked the boxes up and carried them away. Eva was used to factory floors. She never worked in one before, but she would often visit her grandfather, Karl Muller, at his factory. He owned one of the largest steel and iron factories in Germany. This factory made some of her memories bubble to the surface.

"Can I help you?"

Startled, Eva turned to find a scowling woman standing next to her. The woman wore a white uniform like the others, but her hat had a pink band across the top.

"I'm looking for Mr. Peabody," Eva explained, and quickly looked at her note to make sure she had remembered the right name.

"Why?" the woman asked. She took out a cigarette and lit it while waiting for Eva's reply.

"I am here for the secretary position."

"That way," the woman said, jabbing her cigarette to the left, and walked away, leaving a very bemused Eva in her wake.

Eva shook her head and went to the door marked "Office". She passed through the doorway and was grateful to find that the noise subsided dramatically when she closed the door behind her. A young woman sat at a desk.

"Yes?"

"My name is Eva Muller, and I have an appointment to see Mr. Peabody."

"For the secretary position?" the young woman asked.

"Yes."

The woman sighed. "I'm so sorry, but Mr. Peabody has already hired someone."

"Oh," Eva sighed. She stood there for a moment not knowing what to do. "All right, thank you," she said and began to walk out of the office.

She had gotten as far as the door when a voice behind her asked, "Do you want a job?"

Eva turned and saw a short, balding man wearing large round spectacles that seemed to take over his entire face. He wore a three-piece suit that looked a size too small.

"Yes, but the young woman said that the position was filled," Eva replied.

The man nodded, took out a white handkerchief, and brushed it over his bald head. "I'm Mr. Peabody, the factory manager," he said. "It's not the office job; I'm looking for process workers."

"Oh," Eva said, nonplussed.

"You look like a strong girl. What's your name?"

"Eva," she told him.

"Eva, do you have a surname?"

"Muller," Eva said, holding her breath as she awaited his reaction.

"That's German, isn't it?"

"Yes sir, it is."

"So you are a kraut?" Peabody took off his glasses and cleaned them with his handkerchief.

"Yes, sir, I am German," Eva replied. She knew how the rest of the script would play out and was resigned to the inevitable response. Eva swallowed her disappointment as she realized that yet another job had been lost to her. She slowly raised her eyes to meet those of the bespectacled manager.

"Well," Peabody said quietly after a moment, "even krauts need jobs." A fleeting glimpse of softness invaded the man's steady stare.

Eva simply nodded.

Peabody dropped his gaze, then loudly cleared his throat. Eva had the impression the man was embarrassed at showing any understanding of anyone.

"So, Eva Muller, what was your last job?"

"I have not been working since coming to this country."

Peabody grunted. "What did you do before coming here?"

Eva licked her lips and sighed. "I was in Egypt for a year after the war ended." Eva deliberately omitted to say she had also been recovering from her own wounds which she had received from her stepfather's second-in-command, Jurgen Reinhardt, during the dying days of the German occupation of Greece.

"Hmm, all that nasty business with the Jews..."

"I'm not Jewish, sir."

"You're not?" Peabody asked with a slight look of surprise on his face.

"No, sir, I'm a Christian," Eva replied and wanted to shake her head. Peabody was quite shortsighted if he didn't notice the gold cross that hung around her neck.

"Ah," Peabody said, as he took off his glasses again. Taking the tip of his necktie, he rubbed his glasses. "Well, many people are displaced. You're not a Nazi, are you?"

"No, sir, I'm not."

"My oldest boy was in Egypt when the war ended."

"I met quite a few Australian soldiers. Very brave men." Eva was fond of the Australian soldiers that she had met. They had not cared that she sounded like a German. She had helped in the hospital where she put her little-practiced English to use. Although she had been taught the language at university, Eva had rarely had an opportunity to use it. In Egypt, Zoe had befriended an Australian nun and quickly learned the language. Eva had joined her and found that the formal English she had been taught was different from Australian English, a lesson that was driven home to her every day.

"Good." Peabody nodded and his double chin wobbled. "So, can you start on Monday?"

Eva stood there for a long moment before she found her voice. "Doing what?"

"You'll take the biscuits off the conveyor and stack them," Peabody replied. "It's good, honest, hard work. You're not afraid of hard work, are you?"

"No, sir," Eva said, shaking her head slowly. This was not what she'd had in mind. A job in a factory was not something she would have chosen, but they needed the money. Eva knew that if she wanted to give Zoe a chance to fulfill her own dreams, then the job was necessary. She had not had much luck elsewhere. "All right," she said.

"Good, good." Peabody nodded, walked over to the door, and yanked it open. He stuck his head out in search of the nearest supervisor. "Where is that woman when you need her?" he muttered to himself. After failing to find who he wanted, he spotted someone else and called out. "Wiggins! Get yourself over here!"

Chapter Two

It was hot, it was sticky, and Zoe Lambros was bone-dead tired. To add to her woes, another stack of pots, pans, and plates had been put on the pile next to her. For eight hours a day, five days a week, the steamy, busy kitchen of Hatton's By The Sea was her own personal hell. She didn't mind hard work, but a dishwashing job was the last thing she had ever thought she would be doing. It was supremely ironic that she should be washing dishes for a living. She had hated doing this chore as a child, and was certain her mother, God rest her soul, must be laughing at how things had turned out.

Zoe sighed in abject misery and brushed away an errant red-gold strand of hair that had escaped from her scarf as she leaned against the sink. The job paid a minimum wage, but with her beloved partner unable to find work, it was left to Zoe to be the breadwinner. What she really wanted to do was paint and draw, but Fate had had other ideas. Instead of working in front of an easel, she found herself in front of a sink.

Eva hated the idea of her working in a kitchen and was even less accepting when she found out it was to wash dishes. Zoe absent-mindedly played with the suds on a pot as she thought of her beloved partner. *Blessings are those special moments when life gives you all that it has to offer, asking nothing in return*, Zoe remembered her mother's saying. And Zoe had been given a blessing by the name of Eva Muller.

Meeting Eva in Larissa was a miracle to Zoe. The fact she had not killed Eva was an even bigger miracle in her eyes. It was ironic that her desire to avenge her mother's death had turned out to be what brought her and Eva together. Zoe thought she had been given an opportunity to inflict the same grief that had befallen her when Major Muller had shot her mother in cold blood. Zoe had wanted to see the man's pain, to be the one to inflict it, to rejoice at the taking of a German life.

Again, it seemed Fate had had other ideas. Instead of killing Muller's daughter, the young Greek had had gone to work for Eva as a maid — by Father Haralambos' insistence. Over the next year she realized that she had fallen in "heavy like" with her. According to Zoe's beloved brother, Mihali, once one fell into "heavy like" there was no hope. Her brother told her that she would know she was going to marry the man of her dreams, if she ever found herself in that frame of mind about someone.

Zoe chuckled to herself. Mihali had been wrong about the man of her dreams. The *woman* of her dreams had come into her life, and Zoe had fallen into "heavy like" very quickly. Even though it was over a year before their first kiss, Zoe knew something was special about Eva long before that moment. However, everything else Mihali had told her was absolutely true. There was no hope. No matter how hard she had tried not to let her heart rule her head, she had soon found herself hopelessly, and without hesitation, in love.

Zoe knew exactly when her heart had begun to overrule her head. It had been May 1, 1943, a day that would remain burned into Zoe's mind for all eternity. Zoe was outside her house when Muller's daughter was walking up the street. Without thinking, Zoe had picked up a stone and when Muller's daughter had gone past her, she threw it with all her might. It had hit the tall woman on the back of the head. When the woman turned around, Zoe saw Eva for the first time — a shy and sad woman, not at all what she had expected. That had been quite a revelation.

Zoe had scoffed at some of the village girls who had fallen for Italian soldiers stationed in Larissa with the Germans. She had been appalled that they would collaborate with the enemy, thinking of them as traitors. What Zoe did not know at the time was that their hearts were controlled by Fate, and they had absolutely no say in the matter. It was so easy to judge them and yet she had fallen for "the enemy" as well.

As her feelings for Eva began to grow, she had tried very hard to understand what she was experiencing. She had never been in love before, and no boy in the village had ever set her heart racing. Even when the village matchmaker had tried to pair her up with the local boys, Zoe resisted; they were too fat, too thin, too short, too dark, or too tall. The real problem was that they were too *male*.

Zoe could not explain it, and she did not want to know why God made her that way. She knew the attitude of the Church towards homosexuality and how it taught the faithful that those who were "that way" would burn in hell. She often heard the old women gossiping about a man who was "that way" or about a woman that they thought was "different". She had not understood it at the time. There were lots of things Zoe didn't understand. Sometimes she wished it would stay that way.

Looking back through the eyes of a grown woman, she knew there were others like her. Like Eva. They lived quietly in the shadows, trying not to make too much noise or attract any attention. In a small farming community like Larissa where getting married early was the norm, there were women who were considered to be "on the shelf" and who sometimes were stigmatized as being lesbians.

Zoe and Eva's relationship was a slow burn — not like it was portrayed at the cinema. They had flirted with each other for months, testing the waters. Each of them was scared of making any type of move, fearing the lost of their friendship. Eva was also scared because of what she had experienced from her father's wrath. Zoe didn't know what she was feeling other than knowing the person who was finally right was definitely not whom she had pictured. When Eva finally mustered up the courage to kiss Zoe, it was as if Zoe's entire world had somehow come into focus. It felt right. She knew in her heart that it was right. When she looked into those sapphire eyes, her heart melted, her knees trembled, and she felt weak. It was a monumental leap of faith on Eva's part. Eva took the biggest risk of her life not knowing if Zoe felt the same way or if it was safe to give her heart away. In the fall of 1944, Eva had trusted Zoe not to betray the gift of her heart.

Zoe had fully expected a bolt of lightning to descend from heaven when Eva kissed her for the first time. It didn't happen but by then it didn't matter because God and lightning were the farthest things from Zoe's mind. She had found her person to fall in "heavy like" with and she was not letting go.

The war which shredded Zoe's life finally gave something back. Yet even when Fate had given Zoe this gift, she had to work hard to keep Eva in her life. Or more specifically, she had to keep Eva alive. Saving Eva's life, by killing the man whom Muller ordered to kill Eva, was the easiest thing Zoe had ever had to do. Eva's death would have been the final nail in Zoe's coffin. Without Eva, she would have not wanted to continue to struggle on alone. They both survived and, with Eva's injuries, were sent to Egypt to recover in an Allied hospital.

When she and Eva ended up in Egypt, they had decided to make the long trek to a new land. It would be difficult. Australia was not Greece, and Zoe found she was often very homesick. She missed the hills, the beauty of the olive trees, and the cotton fields. She missed the smell of her mother's freshly baked bread and the sound of her father's singing. She even missed the sound her shoes made as she walked down the cobblestone streets. She knew it was silly to miss those things, but she could not help it.

Australia was a hot, humid place where there were no olive groves or cotton fields. The people were different, and even the sound her shoes made on the street was different. She had already had more than enough of the flies and mosquitoes biting her, and of the spiders that seemed to like to crawl into her shoes when she left them outside.

When Zoe got really homesick, Eva would find a way to brighten her spirits. She would read her a poem or sing to her. Eva would find something that would bring her out of her gloominess. Eva didn't discuss her family and any attempt by Zoe to get her talking was met with silence. Or when Eva did respond, it was something to cut off the conversation quickly. Usually an "I don't want to discuss it" was all it took to end Zoe's attempt. Zoe had heard that request so many times that she could predict it even before the words left Eva's mouth. Sometimes when Zoe was feeling a little more melancholy, Eva would surprise her by revealing little things about her childhood, little things that gave a brief glimpse into the woman's past. Zoe knew Eva missed her family even though she didn't want to admit it. Zoe believed that Eva couldn't admit she was missing her family, because it might bring a deep sense of loss from her family not wanting her. Somehow Zoe didn't believe that Eva's family would blindly disown her; Germans were not so cold-hearted. At least Zoe hoped they weren't.

"Stop daydreaming, Zoe!" exclaimed a man's voice, breaking into her reverie. "We have a mountain of work here."

Zoe turned to find the chef scowling at her and, before she could retort, he was gone. With a sigh, Zoe wiped the sweat from her brow and took another pan from the pile.

The door to the kitchen opened and Zoe looked up to see Elena Mannheim walk in carrying a tray of empty plates. Elena was a slim woman, a bit taller than Zoe, with caramel-colored eyes and long brown hair that she braided to keep it restrained on her neck. Zoe muttered curse words in Greek as she scrubbed at a stubborn pot stain, causing Elena to stop mid-step. Zoe was sure Elena knew her words were not very complimentary since they both knew the assistant cook always managed to burn something at least once a day.

Zoe and Elena were close friends; in fact, they were kindred spirits.

Elena was a survivor of Hitler's Final Solution for the Jews, and the only remaining member of her entire family — a family that had been big, proud, and loving. The others had all perished in the killing fields of Germany, Poland, and Austria. Elena's childhood had been spent in Bergen-Belson concentration camp. She was lucky that, for a while at least, she had had her mother with her.

Zoe turned back from the pot to see Elena add her tray of dirty dishes to the rest. "Oh no! Not more!"

"It's nearly over, Zoe." Elena put her arm around her and gave her a friendly squeeze. "Come on, I'll help. The lunch crowd has left anyway." Elena put on an apron and joined Zoe, scraping the dishes and stacking them in neat piles. "So how is the job hunting going?"

"I think Evy is going to go mad if she doesn't find something," Zoe replied, as she rinsed a pot.

"I do not understand why they do not give her a job. She's so smart..."

"She opens her mouth and they instantly don't have a job anymore," Zoe replied. It was disgusting the way Eva was being treated because of her accent. This resulted in Eva retreating into her shell. Zoe wasn't surprised by Eva's doubts in her own abilities. Every day she got assaulted by people's prejudices and it was destroying her confidence.

"I still don't get it." Elena washed, then rinsed a plate and set it aside. "I didn't have a problem."

"You're Jewish."

Elena stared at her friend. "Since when is that such an advantage?"

Zoe stopped and turned to her friend. "Eva isn't Jewish, so people assume that if she's not Jewish and is a German, then she must be a Nazi."

Elena scowled. "That's stupid." She attacked another dish with a bit more energy.

Zoe shrugged. "You did, why shouldn't complete strangers?" she gently reminded her friend. Elena had taken a long time to become comfortable with Eva around, even though they were both German.

"Yes, well...um," Elena stammered. "I never thought she was a *real* Nazi."

Zoe smiled. "Eva as a Nazi?" She chuckled at the incongruous idea of her sweet and gentle partner belonging to the death merchants.

"So that's why they don't give her a job?"

"Yep." Zoe nodded and went back to her scrubbing. "She's going crazy in the apartment."

"What job did she have before the war?"

"She didn't."

Elena turned to Zoe with a perplexed look on her face. "She didn't have a job?"

"No, Eva was a university student."

"Wow, must be nice to have wealthy parents."

Zoe remained silent as she continued to wash the remaining dishes. Eva's past was never discussed with anyone else, not even Elena. Zoe had no qualms about revealing her own history to her friend, but she didn't discuss Eva's life. It wasn't something Eva had asked Zoe not to do, but Eva was a very private person. Zoe respected that in her partner.

"Zoe?"

"Yes?"

"Off limits?"

"Yep, off limits," Zoe replied, giving her friend a smile before starting back on rinsing the soapy plate in her hands.

Elena looked at her friend for a long time before resuming her washing. In less than an hour, they had finished the entire load.

Zoe wiped her hands on the dishrag and looked at her fingers. "I'm going to get dishcloth hands."

"Dish*pan* hands," Elena corrected.

"Whatever you call it, I'm going to get it," Zoe muttered. "Come on El, I want to get home and see if Eva got one of the jobs she went for today."

The two women smiled at each other. They went to the time clock, took their cards, and punched out for another day.

Chapter Three

"You do have a slim waist for such a big girl."

Eva looked down at the seamstress who was taking her measurements. Unsure of what to say, she remained quiet. She had been given a tour of the area where she would be working before being taken to the sewing room to get her new uniforms. The room, which was quite small and hidden away at the back of the factory, was a hive of activity. Eva counted four sewing machines being used and noted that there seemed to be three different conversations going on at the same time.

"All right, you're in luck," said the seamstress, bringing out three neatly folded white uniforms. After she had wrapped and tied up the clothing in brown paper, she picked up three matching white hats and gave them to Eva. "These remain the property of the factory. If you lose them, you pay for them."

"Yes, ma'am," Eva replied and took the bundle of clothing before leaving the sewing room and going to another part of the factory. The noise and the heat were overwhelming as she made her way towards the office.

"So let me guess; you're 36-25-35?" asked the man whom Peabody had instructed to escort her on her tour of the factory. His name was Earl Wiggins, and despite his rude question Eva found herself liking the blond-haired, blue-eyed, bearded young man. He reminded her of a childhood friend back in Germany.

"You do not ask ladies that question," she admonished him mildly, and continued to walk away.

Earl grinned and hurriedly walked in front of Eva, making her stop.

"I'm known as the Errol Flynn of the factory," he said.

"I thought your name was Earl?" Eva asked, frowning in puzzlement.

"No," Earl said. "Errol is my nickname."

"Hey, Wiggy! Give the girl a break. She hasn't even started working here yet!" called a strident male voice.

Eva saw four men leaning against a machine and laughing at their mate. She turned back to find Earl stroking his beard, a very smug expression on his face.

"Is this some game?"

"Nah." Earl waved off the men and took Eva by the hand. "I'm the welcoming committee for beautiful girls who start work here." Eva's skeptical look made Earl chuckle. "A beautiful woman such as yourself deserves to have a welcoming committee."

"Uh huh," Eva answered, turning once again to walk away.

"Absolutely." Earl smoothly took the uniform package out of Eva's hands as they walked. "So, Eva Muller, what will Mr. Muller do while his wife is slaving away making biscuits?"

"There is no Mr. Muller." Eva grinned. She was very surprised that he had not commented on her name or her accent. It was refreshing not having to tell Earl the usual "yes, I am a German, and, no, I'm not a Nazi" response to people she first meets. Even though the questions were quite flirtatious, she found Earl endearing.

"Ah, that's even better." Earl waggled his eyebrows. "So what about that ring on your finger?"

Eva looked down at the silver ring and smiled. Zoe had given her the ring on the *Patris* during their voyage to Australia. The memory remained fresh in her mind.

The sun had begun to set over the harbor at Cape Town, South Africa. Shadows formed across the becalmed sea as Eva leaned on the railing and looked out over the serene vista before her.

This was going to be one of the last stops the Patris made before reaching Australia where their new life awaited them. Eva watched the sky turning a reddish-gold and smiled. She felt a hand on her lower back and turned to find Zoe looking up at her. Her young lover put her arm around her waist and they both looked at the sunset.

"Did you have a good time shopping?" Eva asked.

Zoe nodded as she kept her eyes on the scene before her. Eva was slightly surprised not to have Zoe regale her with the shopping news or the latest ship's gossip as had become their sunset ritual. No malice was involved, but Zoe enjoyed telling Eva what some of the other refugees had been up to.

"Evy, let's go inside," Zoe said, taking Eva's hand and leading her away from the deck railing.

"Didn't you want to see the rest of the sunset?" Eva asked, a little bewildered. They both loved sunsets but particularly Zoe as she was fond of painting them. She had often told Eva that no one sunset was the same as any other.

When the two arrived back in their closet-sized cabin, Eva sat on the bunk and patiently waited for Zoe.

"Remember when you were sick and you asked me to spend our lives together?" Zoe asked tentatively.

Eva was not sure where this was going. Without realizing it, she scowled.

"Don't do your scrunchy face," Zoe said, and knelt in front of her. She gently smoothed out the skin between Eva's eyes that tended to bunch together when she frowned.

"What's this about, Zoe?"

"Well, do you remember that day?" Zoe persisted, causing Eva to worry more.

"Yes. It was the happiest day of my life."

Zoe smiled. "It was the best day of my life."

"Yes, it was for me, too, and still is," Eva replied. They looked at each other for a moment before Eva leaned across and tenderly kissed the woman she considered her wife.

"Um...where was I?" Zoe said after the kiss ended, looking dazed. Eva knew the woman's train of thought had been interrupted by her kiss, causing her to grin.

"You were asking me if I remember the day I married you."

"Uh, yes." Zoe cleared her throat. "You know today I went off the ship with Elena?"

"Yeesss," Eva patiently said, but was tempted to ask her to hurry up and say what she was going to say. Normally that wasn't a problem with her young lover. Normally, Eva had to slow Zoe down. For a brief moment, Eva had a terrifying thought. "You haven't changed your mind?"

"About what?"

Eva took a shaky breath. "Zoe, are you trying to tell me that you don't want to...be with me?" she asked, her voice breaking.

"Why would I want to tell you a stupid thing like that?" Zoe sat back, looking bewildered.

"Because you're asking me to remember our vows."

Zoe looked at Eva as if she had grown an extra head. Finally, the younger woman groaned loudly, took Eva's hands, and held them against her heart.

"I would never do that. Never. Do you hear me?"

"I hear you, Zoe, but my heart's about to jump out of my chest here," Eva replied. It was true the organ in question was racing a mile a minute. Zoe put her hand over Eva's heart and looked into her eyes.

"I wasn't going to tell you that I didn't love you anymore," Zoe said, taking Eva's left hand. With her free hand, Zoe reached into her pocket and took out a ring. "I wanted to give you this."

Eva looked down at her hand where Zoe had slipped a simple silver band onto the third finger. She couldn't find her voice as tears began to flow down her face. Zoe tenderly brushed them away.

"It's not what I wanted to buy you, but that can wait for our first wedding anniversary," Zoe said. "I love you, Evy."

Eva stood up on shaky legs and took Zoe in her arms. "I thought..."

"You think too much, Miss Eva," Zoe said, and kissed her tenderly. "And you talk too much," she finished, gently pushing Eva down on the bunk.

Eva brought her thoughts back to the present, blushing at the delicious memory of what else had happened that night in their cabin. She noticed Earl staring at her and stammered, "I...um..."

"I understand. I'm sorry I asked," Earl said earnestly, dropping out of his joking persona. "Too many boys never made it home." He handed the bundle of clothing back to Eva.

"Hmm." Eva nodded, considering what Earl had told her. She felt bad for making him think that she had lost a husband because she felt his sentiment was sincere. The other thing which impressed her was that he clearly knew she was German and that her "husband" may have been the enemy. It had been the first time since she had arrived in Australia that she had experienced a compassionate attitude.

Eva shyly looked up at the broad-shouldered man and smiled when he matched her long strides.

"Has anyone ever told you that you look like Ava Gardner?" he asked.

"It's the dimple," Eva said. In Egypt, Zoe had convinced her to go to the local cinema so they could see an English-language movie. Ava Gardner was an actress in the film that had captured Zoe's attention. Zoe had been mesmerized by the woman, so much so that Eva had been a little worried until after the movie, when Zoe had told her that the actress looked so much like Eva, they could be twins. Eva, however, did not see the resemblance.

"So was I close about your measurements?" Earl leaned in and whispered.

"You ask too many questions, Mr..." Eva replied, stopping when she realized she had forgotten the man's name.

"Wiggins." Earl took off his white hat and held it against his heart. "Earl Edward Wiggins," he said, and bowed.

Eva chuckled at the man's antics. "Well, Mr. Wiggins..."

"Call me Wiggy; everyone else does."

"Wiggy?"

"You shorten the Wiggins."

"Why?"

Earl scratched his beard thoughtfully. "It's just the Aussie way."

"Ah. So I would be called 'Mulli'?" Eva asked gravely, which caused Earl to look at her for a moment, then laugh.

"I like you, Miss Eva Muller," Earl said, putting his arm around Eva's shoulders. "Actually, you would be called 'Muzza.'"

"I'm confused." Eva shook her head and got out from under Earl's arm.

"Ah, don't run away from me, Eva Muzza!" Earl seemed to be hurt, but the twinkling in his eyes told Eva he was feigning. He stood in front of her, causing her to stop once more.

"Are you always this annoying?" Eva asked. She was not offended by the man's banter. She found to her surprise she was enjoying the teasing.

"Only to beautiful girls like you," Earl replied, and knelt on one knee. Eva looked around the factory floor. The women workers were laughing and shaking their heads. "Marry me, Eva Muzza, and become Mrs. Wiggy!" Earl exclaimed.

"Sorry, not today," Eva said with a chuckle.

"Are you sure? We can honeymoon in the shortbread section." Earl went down on both knees with both hands outstretched, begging the now very amused Eva to marry him.

"Wiggins, get up off the floor and leave the poor girl alone." Peabody had come out of the office and stood at the doorway, scowling.

"She was about to marry me, Mr. Peabody," Earl declared, as he stood and dusted the dirt off his white trousers. He put his hat back on his blond head.

"If every girl that was about to marry you did so, we would have to have you carted off as a polygamist," Peabody snickered. "Now go home."

"I was about to do just that, Mr. Peabody. And offer the lovely Miss Muller a ride," Earl said, snatching back the uniform package from Eva and holding it up for his boss to see.

"I would be wary of our factory Romeo, Miss Muller," Peabody advised, winking at Eva before he went back into his office.

"So, Miss Muller, would you like a ride home?"

"My mother always told me not to ride home with strangers," Eva joked back when Earl replaced his arm around her shoulders.

"But since we're nearly engaged, that's all right," Earl replied. Eva looked at him and shook her head.

"Seriously, where do you live?" Earl asked.

"Glebe," Eva said, revealing the suburb as Earl took off his hat and put it inside a large green canvas bag.

"Well, if you really want to go on public transport, it will be crowded and smelly. If you ride with me, I promise we won't get married on the way."

Eva could not help but smile. "All right. Because if we did, my sister, Zoe, would be very surprised," she replied.

"Zoe? Hmm, how old is she? Would she be interested in marrying me?" Earl quipped, and showed Eva the way to his car.

Eva was surprised that she allowed herself to be led to the dark sedan and even more surprised that she had mentioned Zoe to him. "She's too young for you."

"Ah, womanly rivalry," Earl nodded. "I like it when girls fight over me."

Eva laughed out loud as he opened the car door for her and she got inside. She was amazed at how easily Earl had got under her defenses and made her feel comfortable. He hadn't done anything other than joke with her. Eva put it down to his uncanny resemblance to her long-lost childhood friend. When Earl tossed the brown paper package on the seat behind them and climbed behind the wheel, Eva found herself wondering how Zoe was going to like her new acquaintance.

"So who's that?" Elena asked, leaning on the railing of the apartment's balcony and looking down. Standing beside her, Zoe glanced down, too. In the street below them, a car had stopped at the curb. A tall, blond-headed man got out, walked around the car, and opened the passenger side door.

Zoe frowned when she spied a distinctive figure exiting the vehicle. "Eva," she said.

"Getting out of a car with a young man, no less," Elena observed.

Zoe ignored her friend as she watched Eva talk to the stranger. Her partner was holding a package and looking up at the man. "I wonder what that's about? She does look pleased with herself."

"She is? She looks like she's just having conversation," Elena commented.

Zoe smiled. She knew how to read Eva's body language and this was definitely a good mood for Eva. "Oh yes, she's very pleased with herself."

Below them, Eva smiled and waited while the man got back into the car.

"She's relaxed and happy," Zoe continued. "Whoever that man is, he's really made her comfortable." It was not just the fact that Eva was smiling; she smiled at people even if she did not like them. But Zoe knew when her tall partner was upset or happy just by looking at her shoulders. It was an odd way to ascertain how the person was feeling, but Eva had a slight shoulder twitch that manifested itself when she disliked someone or was in a situation that made her uncomfortable. Zoe had noticed it in Egypt but didn't tell Eva, because she didn't think Eva knew about it herself. It was also the perfect barometer for Zoe.

"How can you tell?"

"I know." Zoe smiled at Elena. "It's the little things."

"Well, do you know what's going to happen now?" Elena asked and pointed at their landlady, who was hurrying towards Eva.

Zoe smirked. "I believe it's called a payback."

"Payback?"

"Eva has avoided Mrs. Jenkins for weeks." Zoe saw their landlady, Mrs. Nelly Jenkins, wobbling down the pathway, and then glanced back down at Eva, who had clearly also seen the older woman. Zoe giggled, knowing Eva had decided to face the landlady.

"What's so funny?" Elena asked.

"Mrs. Jenkins wants her nephew to go out with Evy," Zoe explained, catching Eva's eye as she looked up at her. Eva gave her a slight shake of the head. "It's been a real cat-and-mouse game," Zoe continued.

"The cat's got the mouse?"

"Nearly." Zoe smirked. "This is better than the wireless dramas."

"Aren't you going to rescue her?"

Zoe smiled devilishly. "Not yet."

"Miss Muller!"

Eva closed her eyes momentarily and steeled herself for a conversation with the landlady. She had been avoiding Mrs. Jenkins for weeks and had even resorted to getting Zoe to go to the Jenkins' apartment to pay the rent. Eva glanced up at the balcony again and caught what looked like Zoe winking at her before Eva turned her attention back to their landlady.

"Mrs. Jenkins, so nice to see you," Eva said, plastering on a fake smile. She heard guffaws from above, and resisted the urge to look up and stick her tongue out at Zoe. *I'm going to get you for this, Zoe, just you wait,* Eva thought. Aloud, she said to Mrs. Jenkins, "How are you?"

"It's too hot," Mrs. Jenkins said, stating the obvious. "It's not supposed to be hot in October. Usually it gets hot in December, but the weather has gone strange on us."

"Indeed," Eva said, and gave the old woman a smile.

"Eva, can I call you Eva?" Eva nodded her head and the landlady continued. "Eva, I've been meaning to talk to you for weeks!" She fanned herself with an old magazine she was holding in her hand.

"Really?" Eva feigned interest and hoped Zoe was going to come downstairs and rescue her. She knew it was not going to happen because, when she glance back up to the balcony, Zoe was still leaning over the railing, grinning widely. *I'm really going to get you for this!* Eva was feeling desperate.

"Yes, didn't Zoe tell you?"

"Hmm, she did, yes." Eva nodded. "It must have slipped my mind."

"Of course." Mrs. Jenkins patted Eva's hand. "Now, I wanted to ask you if you would like to go to see a film with my nephew, Harry. Harry is coming down from Queensland,

and he doesn't know many girls, so would you be interested in seeing a film with him? He's really very nice and polite."

Eva was stuck. She looked up and saw no one at the balcony railing. She prayed that Zoe had taken pity on her and had decided to come down to rescue her.

"I...um," Eva stammered. She mentally sighed in relief when she saw Zoe and Elena exit the building and come towards them.

"Hey there." Zoe smiled at her partner before turning to their landlady. "Hello, Mrs. Jenkins."

"Hello, Zoe. How are you, dear? Is Mr. Hatton treating you well?"

Zoe said, "Yes, ma'am, he is."

"Good, good, because if he doesn't, tell him Mrs. Jenkins will come over there and have a word with him." She chuckled. "Now I was telling your sister that my nephew, Harry, is coming down from Queensland and he doesn't know any girls here, so..." Mrs. Jenkins paused to take a breath before continuing. "I asked Eva if she wanted to go to see a film with him."

"When is he coming down?" Zoe asked, smiling at the older woman.

"Next Saturday." Mrs. Jenkins put her arm around Eva's waist and looked up at her. "He has problems with the krauts, but I assured him you're a good kraut and not like those nasty Nazis."

Eva smiled down at the landlady, hoping that Zoe knew she was expecting to be rescued from Mrs. Jenkins' bigotry. Zoe leaned against Eva, who began to relax a little in her lover's reassuring presence.

"Oh I'm so, so sorry Mrs. Jenkins, but we've been invited to Elena's for dinner that night," Zoe said. "Don't you remember, Evy?"

"Uhh..."

Elena had been clearly enjoying the charade until her name was mentioned. "Oh, yes indeed, I invited them for that Saturday meal," she said, flushing slightly.

"Oh, what a shame. Harry is going to go home on Sunday." Mrs. Jenkins sighed. "Tsk, I knew I should have caught you earlier."

"Maybe another time," Eva said, hoping she would not be around when the woman was looking for her.

"Oh, absolutely." Mrs. Jenkins smiled. She said her farewells and went inside where it was somewhat cooler.

"Oh boy," Eva exhaled and glanced at Zoe, who was giggling. "Thank you, love."

"You owe me." Zoe patted Eva's behind as she started to walk back inside. Eva and Elena looked at each other for a moment before following her back up to the apartment.

Chapter Four

The two women entered the apartment after parting with Elena. Zoe was still chuckling over Eva's need for a rescue. Eva closed the door and sighed in relief as Zoe went to the kitchen to get them both some cold lemonade.

Eva was home. With the door closed, the outside world remained at the threshold. The apartment was a haven for both of them, where they could safely be themselves with no pretence and no lies.

The small apartment had once been part of a multi-story mansion. Elegant in its day, the mansion had been neglected until it was turned into several small apartments. Eva and Zoe had found the place quite by accident in their hunt for an affordable and clean place to stay, away from the immigrant hostels that housed the majority of new arrivals.

The main door opened into a lounge, from which two french doors led out onto a long balcony with a distant view of Botany Bay. A long yellow and green sofa occupied the center of the lounge. Eva had fallen in love with it when they had been on a furniture hunt. Although the color combination made Zoe wince, the sofa was a rare find and perfect for the room, and it was long enough to allow Eva to stretch out and get comfortable.

The sofa faced a fireplace where they sometimes cuddled in front of a roaring fire. Eva had been disappointed to find that winters in Sydney were very mild compared to the harsh German winters. Zoe was used to mild temperatures and was not at all unhappy to discover that Sydney winters were similar to those in her home town of Larissa. To the right of the fireplace was a second-hand oak bookcase filled with books in English, Greek, Italian, and German. On the other side of the fireplace was a small table on which sat a gramophone. A small, tidy stack of records leaned against the leg of the table.

Two medium-sized bedrooms flanked the french doors. Each bedroom contained a double bed, a very expensive subterfuge designed to cover up the fact that Zoe actually slept in Eva's room and not her own. Zoe's room was furnished with little mementos, her easel, and pieces of her art in various stages of completion. Little dolls and artifacts that Zoe had collected during their journey from Larissa to Sydney were spread around on the chest of drawers, holding court amid the many other small artwork pieces that were stuck on the mirror. The collection included some of Zoe's funny little sketches; pink elephants dancing on the Harbour Bridge, and goats riding a tram.

A bright pink bedspread covered the bed and a doll sat at the center of the headboard. The room appeared to be a typical teenager's bedroom, dominated by Zoe's artistic personality.

Eva's bedroom was more sedate. The double bed filled the center of the room, with a chest of drawers and a body-length mirror completing the arrangement. A desk and chair were positioned under a large window. Eva's camera, tripod, and other photography equipment cluttered the desk, along with her journal and other books. A white *flokati* rug, fluffy as a sheepskin and very popular with Greek immigrants, had been placed at the foot of the bed with smaller matching rugs on either side. At the side of the bed was a table with a clock.

Next to Eva's bedroom was a small hallway that led to the large bathroom. Occupying a place of pride was a huge antique bathtub, another piece of furniture that had caught Eva's attention, mostly because of its unusual length which could accommodate her six-foot-plus height.

The whole apartment had polished wood flooring. To make the lounge appear warmer, smaller area rugs covered the flooring. Zoe did not like wooden floors. Eva knew they put her in mind of the drafty, wooden floors of her childhood home in Greece.

They had been lucky when searching the stores for second-hand furniture. The Greek Orthodox Church had also helped them in acquiring other small items that they had needed. Eva was loath to accept charity, but her pride had to take a back seat to necessity. They were more fortunate than most immigrants; they had a home when the majority of their fellow refugees still lived in government-run hostels.

Overall, it was a cozy apartment and a place that could support the pretence of the two women being sisters.

"I've got just what you need."

Zoe stuck her head out of the kitchen door and met Eva's raised eyebrow. Zoe blushed and her skin color matched her red locks, making Eva laugh. "You know what I mean," Zoe mumbled, as she went back inside the kitchen.

"Would love some." Eva got up from the sofa where she had fallen over laughing after Zoe had disappeared. She went over and stood before the balcony doors, still chuckling at Zoe's response.

Thunder boomed overhead and a streak of lightning flashed across the skyline of the city, briefly illuminating the lounge. The display was typical of summer in Sydney, where the heat of the day was cooled by a weather change from the south so quickly that it was gone as fast as it had arrived.

Zoe came out from the kitchen with two glasses of lemonade. Eva took the offered glass and drank deeply. "Ah, now that is so good," she said, smacking her lips for effect and causing Zoe to giggle.

"Come here, Miss Zoe." Eva took Zoe's lemonade and set both glasses down on the small table beside the couch. She put her arms around the petite woman, leaned down and kissed her. The kiss ended and, still embracing, they smiled happily at each other.

"Now that is some thank you." Zoe stroked Eva's cheek and stared into her eyes.

"I got a job, love." Eva's beaming smile got bigger when Zoe's face lit up. She received a big sloppy kiss at the news. Eva put an arm around her partner's shoulders and brought Zoe into a tighter embrace. "Felt like I was searching for work forever." Eva sighed and kissed the top of Zoe's head.

"So did you get the photographer's assistant job?" Zoe looked up expectantly.

"No." Eva shook her head, still saddened by the disappointment. It was the job she had wanted most and one that they both had thought would be impossible for her not to get. Eva had collected some of the photographs she had taken and put them in a nice portfolio to show her prospective boss. Unfortunately, her efforts had been wasted. "I opened my mouth, and he said he didn't want a kraut working for him."

"Boofhead," Zoe said angrily.

"Boofhead?" Eva asked, bewildered by the new English expression. She pulled back to get a better look at Zoe's expression.

"It means stupid," Zoe explained.

"Who taught you that?"

"I heard Mr. Jenkins yelling at the paperboy this morning," Zoe said. "I asked him what it meant."

"Boofhead." Eva sounded out the word. "I guess we've met a lot of boofheads since we've been here."

"Too many," Zoe agreed. She took Eva's hand and kissed it. "By the way, who was that man that gave you a ride in his car?"

Eva grinned. "Are you jealous, love?" she teased.

"Nah." Zoe tweaked Eva's dimpled chin. "He's not your type."

"Oh? Are you sure?"

"Oh yes," Zoe replied, making Eva laugh. "I don't think blond-haired boys are your type."

"My type," Eva tipped Zoe's chin a little and looked into her green eyes, "has beautiful flame-colored hair," she touched Zoe's long red tresses and continued, "the most beautiful green eyes and is a very beautiful artist," she said as she leaned down, taking Zoe's face in her hands. She slowly leaned over, pressing her lips to Zoe's. The kiss was gentle at first and slowly became more aggressive until Eva could feel the excited response from Zoe. They both parted a little breathless. "That's my type," Eva finished, wrapping her arms around Zoe again.

"So what were we talking about?" Zoe joked.

"You wanted to know who that gentleman was."

"Right. I got a little distracted," Zoe said. "So who is he?"

"He is part of my job story."

"Ah, so tell me the story."

"I have to tell you how I got there first," Eva said. She took Zoe's hand and led her to the sofa. After they sat down, Eva put her arm around Zoe and they snuggled close. She smiled as Zoe looked up.

"All right, I'm comfortable," Zoe announced.

"I was sent to another job as a filing clerk, but it didn't work out."

"You opened your mouth?"

"No, he didn't even see me. He got a call to say I was coming for an interview and he asked what my name was."

"Let me guess; the job was taken?"

Eva nodded. "He didn't even bother to tell the people at the Job Network that the job wasn't available so they could stop me from going to the interview."

"Bastard," Zoe cursed.

"Anyway, I had to go back to the agency office. That's when they sent me to another interview for a secretary job."

"You can type?" Zoe asked, looking a little surprised at this new information.

"Yes." Eva grinned. "I am a woman of many talents."

"You do wonders with those fingers," Zoe said as Eva wiggled her fingers at her. Both women giggled. "So, Miss Talented, what happened?" Zoe asked.

"Job was gone," Eva replied sadly, tired of getting her hopes up only to have a promised employment opportunity snatched away on account of her nationality or because of other people's carelessness.

"Did you have a chance to open your mouth?"

"Yes, but it wasn't like that this time. The job really was taken," Eva explained. "The manager, Mr. Peabody, came out of his office and asked me my name."

"And?"

"And nothing. He just acknowledged I was German and then asked me if I wanted a job."

"Wow, I like Mr. Peabody. What's the job?"

Eva hesitated for a long moment. "Process worker," she finally said. Of all the jobs she thought she would get, this was not it. It was a menial job and did not utilize her language skills. Eva was disappointed and knew Zoe would be as well.

"A what?"

"Process worker...I'll be working in a factory."

"Doing what?"

"Packing biscuits," Eva replied.

Zoe's expression turned into a scowl. "Packing biscuits? Won't that be messy?"

Eva was a little confused until she realized what Zoe meant. "No, love, not the pastries you make."

"I should hope not," Zoe quipped. "So what are they?"

"Biscuits are what we have with tea..."

"You mean like *kourambiethes*? Those butter cookies you like so much?"

"Yes! That's what they call them here. I'll be working at the Johnson Brothers' Biscuit Factory."

"So that's what they're called," Zoe mumbled. "So they want you to pack cookies?"

"Yep," Eva agreed.

"Hmm, you're not going to take it, right?"

Eva already knew what Zoe was going to say when she was told about the job. Factory work was not Eva's ideal job, but when no one else was going to give her a chance, it was the only thing she could do.

"Yes, I am. That's what the package is," Eva explained, pointing to the brown paper bundle. "They even provide uniforms." She did not wait for her partner's reaction but continued in a rush, "Zoe, no one else wants to give me a job."

"Evy, that job isn't for you," Zoe implored. "You're smart. You're educated, and you know four languages!"

"They won't give me a chance, love, educated or not," Eva reminded her. "As soon as I open my mouth, the job is gone. It doesn't matter what skills I have or that I know four languages. I'm German and that's all that matters."

"That shouldn't matter." Zoe's temper was building. She stood up and faced Eva. "A factory isn't where you should be."

"A kitchen isn't where you should be," Eva reminded her. "Zoe, it's the only job I could find."

"Just give it some time," Zoe pleaded. "I know you can get a better job, one that uses your skills."

"I don't have the time to wait," Eva patiently explained. "I've also never had a job before, love, so I don't have a lot of experience in that area. I just can't wait around until someone who doesn't have a prejudice against Germans gives me a job."

"Why not?" Zoe asked. It was obvious that she was not ready to accept Eva's answer.

Eva sighed. "I want you to stop working."

"What?" Zoe's temper reached a new level, her ire evident in the stiffening of her spine "You're too quick to give up and accept a job that's totally unsuitable. Do you think you have to work because you're older?"

"No." Eva shook her head. She knew where this conversation was going and hoped she could stop Zoe's anger from reaching the boiling point. "Zoe, I can't let you work in that kitchen any longer."

"I want to work there," Zoe replied. "I told you that when I started. I have to work there because, Evy, we can't live on fresh air."

"I don't want you to work there," Eva repeated. "Why can't you just accept that?"

"Don't treat me like a child," Zoe said, her eyes blazing. "It's like Egypt all over again."

"I'm not treating you like a child!" Eva said, trying to keep her temper. "Egypt was different. I told you not to go to the market by yourself. What was wrong with that?"

"You didn't tell me why, Evy, you just said, 'Don't go to the market without me.'"

"Yes? Was that wrong?"

Zoe looked at her partner, incredulity on her face. "You still don't understand why I got so mad?"

Eva leaned back on the sofa and let out an exasperated sigh. "Zoe, you don't understand what I went through after I came home to find that you weren't there. I was just so scared that, because you'd gone to the market alone, I might never see you again."

"Not every woman is kidnapped," Zoe said, defending her choice.

"No, but if you were, then the only woman I cared about would have been lost," Eva whispered. The whole incident had made Eva physically sick for days afterwards.

"This is exactly like Egypt," Zoe muttered, as she turned away from Eva, who looked out at the stormy sky that mirrored the atmosphere inside the room. "You're treating me like I don't know what's up from down," Zoe continued.

Eva mentally shuddered at the mention of their argument in Egypt. She knew it was time they discussed the underlying problem that the fight had brought to the surface. Eva did not want to talk to Zoe until Zoe was ready, herself, to verbalize how she felt. Zoe normally had no problems in saying exactly what she thought, but this situation was unique. Eva knew Zoe sometimes felt insecure about their relationship. Not whether Eva loved her — that fact was cast in stone — but their eight-year age difference created some doubts. Zoe was not alone in feeling insecure about their relationship. Eva harbored doubts that Zoe would even want to stay with her once she discovered more of the world and found someone far more interesting than her. *Time to tell her how I feel.*

Eva stood up. She went over to where Zoe was standing and put her arms around her lover. She could feel the slender form shaking from the angry outburst. "You are my equal," Eva whispered. "You are not a child."

"Then stop treating me like one," Zoe said, taking Eva's hands and holding them. Eva smiled at the gesture. Zoe was angry, but she had learned from Egypt not to push Eva away when she was upset.

"I'm not treating you like a child. You are my best friend, my lover, and my wife. You are younger than me, but that doesn't mean I think of you as a child." Eva kissed the top of Zoe's red hair. "Age means nothing, Zoe."

"Yes, it does," Zoe muttered.

"Why?"

"I'm nineteen and you're twenty-seven," Zoe stated the obvious. "Doesn't it bother you sometimes?"

"No." Eva smiled. "I have a younger lover; now that is nothing to be bothered about," she joked, bringing a little smile to Zoe's face.

"Would you want someone who is the same age?"

Eva took a deep breath and exhaled slowly. "Zoe, I was lucky to be still breathing by the time I met you. I don't want anyone else, and your age is irrelevant," Eva explained, hoping she could reassure Zoe by saying just how much the woman meant to her. "I'll tell you what I see when I look at you." Eva put her arms around Zoe. "I see a beautiful woman who, for some unfathomable reason, has fallen in love with me. I see a woman who is mature, thoughtful, and talented. Mostly I see someone makes me deliriously happy." She smiled at Zoe and brushed away the tear that ran down her cheek.

"I'll tell you what I don't see," Eva continued. "I don't see a child. Nor do I need to mother you because you don't need a mother. I'm your wife and your lover, not your parent. I want you as my equal. You have brought joy and love into my life, you give me a reason to wake up every morning, and there is no one in this world that I love more than you." Eva's voice broke with the emotion she was trying to express. "I should have told you this in Egypt, but I was scared."

"Of what?" Zoe wiped her eyes with the back of her hand and waited for Eva's response.

Eva shrugged. "That you would be hurt, or taken from me, and even more afraid that you would run away from me." Zoe's eyes widened in surprise. "I didn't know if you wanted to stick around and be lumbered with someone like me..." Eva stopped and grimaced at her own insecurities.

"I never thought of running away," Zoe replied and shook her head. "Please don't tell me you were worried I would leave you."

"Zoe, you haven't really had the chance to meet different people..."

"Whoa! Stop right there. What does that have to do with it?" Zoe responded tersely. "What do you mean 'someone' like you?"

"Zoe, you know what I mean. I'm moody and I drive you crazy when I don't want to talk, I wake you up at night with my crazy dreams."

Zoe sighed deeply. "With everything that you've been through, Evy, some days I'm surprised you get out of bed. I love you and I don't want anyone else. Sometimes I think you might want someone who is older and more mature. More worldly. Someone who shares your love for opera..."

"I don't want that."

"You don't want me to understand opera?" Zoe gently teased and smiled up at Eva. "Eva, sometimes you just need to tell me what's on your mind. I guess we both had some things we needed to tell each other."

"I'm sorry I left it unspoken for so long. I'm not doing that again. Never have I looked at you and thought you were a child. Please believe me," Eva implored. "In Egypt I knew the markets were a place you could get kidnapped, and there was still a war on. It was dangerous."

"I know." Zoe nodded.

"I spent hours trying to find you, and the more time passed, the more frantic I became. I thought I had lost you." Eva shuddered involuntarily at the memory. "If you were my age, I still would have told you to keep away from the market. It didn't matter whether you were younger or not."

"It didn't?"

"No, it didn't," Eva said. "When I say that I don't want you working at the restaurant, it's not because I want to boss you around."

"Bu-but..." Zoe stammered but was silenced by Eva's fingers against her lips.

"Zoe, God gave you a gift," Eva said quietly, and took hold of Zoe's hands. "Your hands need to be protected. They aren't protected when you wash dishes."

"Evy—"

"I want you to follow your dream," Eva said as she kissed Zoe's palm. "Don't you understand that?"

"I *am* following my dream," Zoe replied. "I'm with the woman that I love."

Eva smiled. "And I love you, Zoe; that's why I want you to go to Sydney College."

"Don't you think I know what I want?"

Eva sighed. "Yes, I do, but you didn't dream of working in a kitchen when we were in Larissa," she teased gently, pleased when Zoe smiled back at her. "You had another dream. Your dream was to be an artist. Do you remember what you told me back then?"

"I told you a lot of things," Zoe replied. Reading the expression on her face, Eva understood that Zoe knew exactly what she was talking about.

"You said you wanted to go back to school, learn the things you missed out on, and that you wanted to travel," Eva said, knowing full well that Zoe had not forgotten. "Dreams should never be buried, Zoe."

"Well," Zoe said quietly, "I have traveled."

"One out of three is unacceptable."

"Eva, I can't go back to school..."

"Yes, you can." Eva grinned. She let go of Zoe and went to her bag. Retrieving a sheet of paper, she brought it back to Zoe. "This is from the Sydney College of the Arts, part of Sydney University," she said, and showed Zoe the flyer.

Zoe held the sheet of paper in her hand and read aloud. "'Sydney College of the Arts invites immigrants to further their studies and to gain Australian...'" Zoe stopped when she came across a word she did not know. She showed the flyer to Eva.

"Qualifications," Eva said in English, then repeated the word in Greek.

"'Qualifications,'" Zoe repeated and then continued. "'Grants given to selected immigrants to be taught at Australia's most prest...'"

"Prestigious — it means important," Eva said, with a smile.

"'...prestigious college,'" Zoe finished reading.

"I want you to go to the Sydney College of the Arts." Eva took the sheet from Zoe. "I want you to become the great artist that you have dreamed you could be. When we were at Athena's Bluff, you told me that you wanted to see what was beyond Mount Ossa." Eva glanced at the paper and then back up at Zoe. "This is what is beyond Mount Ossa."

Zoe lowered her head. "We can't afford it, Eva, even if I wanted to go."

"Yes, we can," Eva replied as she pointed to the sheet of paper. "It says they give grants."

"What's a 'grant'?"

Eva smiled inwardly. Getting Zoe to the point where she could think about the possibility was the most difficult step. She thought the next part was going to be easy. "They pay for you to go."

Zoe scowled. She looked at the paper and then back up at her partner. "They will pay me to go to college?"

"Yes. I spoke to one of the people giving out the leaflets, and he said that immigrants under the age of twenty-five can apply for a grant."

"Applying for a grant doesn't mean I'll get it," Zoe said, although Eva could tell her resistance was wavering.

"Anyone who applies and passes a test gets the grant." Eva repeated what she had been told. "I asked the same question."

"Hmm." Zoe looked down at the leaflet in her hand. "I know you have read this thoroughly, but are you sure that this is for me?"

Eva nodded. "Absolutely. This is *your* dream, Zoe. Jump off the cliff and enjoy the experience — the scary times and the exciting times."

"You want me to leave the best job I've ever had to go to college?" Zoe grinned, her temper tantrum forgotten.

"I know it's going to be a real hardship for you to stop washing dishes, but we all have to make sacrifices," Eva joked, and then turned serious to address some of the real issues that she knew were bothering her partner. "Love, I know that this is going to be scary for you, because you don't know the language so well and you feel out of place."

Eva took Zoe's hand and led her back to the sofa.

"Among other things," Zoe mumbled. "I never finished the eighth grade, Evy."

"That's not because you weren't smart, love," Eva replied. Zoe had a quick, intelligent mind and, had not the war intervened, Eva knew Zoe would have achieved anything she set her mind to. Eva was certain of that.

"Do you think I'm smart?" Zoe asked hesitantly, looking down at her hand which was intertwined with Eva's larger one.

Eva looked down at the flame-colored head for a moment before she gently tipped Zoe's chin up and looked into her eyes. "You are an intelligent woman, Zoe. I'm not sure you understand that."

"The people at the university finished high school." Zoe gave voice to her insecurity.

"Does that make them smart?"

"Yes."

"No," Eva shook her head. "It makes them fortunate. The war didn't come to Australia, love. It didn't interrupt their schooling. The Germans didn't invade their village and kill their family. That's why the college is offering grants to immigrants."

"I have to sit for a test. What if I fail?"

"Then you fail, but at least you will have given it everything you have," Eva said, holding the smaller woman close. "But, my Zoe, you won't fail. When you set your mind on something, you give it all you have." Eva smiled. "It's one of the things I love about you."

Zoe smiled. "You have more faith in me than I do."

"I know you will succeed and that one day your work will hang in the art galleries of the world."

"But there's going to be a test," Zoe reminded her.

"I'll help you study for it. I'm pretty good at mathematics and we will get a tutor for you for the English grammar part of the test."

"I hate mathematics." Zoe winced. "Hated it at school."

"Yes, but did you have a teacher like me?" Eva winked, making Zoe giggle.

"No," Zoe replied. "I would have paid attention just to be the teacher's pet."

"Zoe, I'm willing to work in a factory so you can fulfill your dream. Won't you let me do that? You are going to be a great artist. I can feel it here," Eva said, putting her hand over her heart. "You have to learn to trust your abilities, Zoe."

"You are giving up a lot."

Eva shook her head. "No, I'm not. I don't consider this a burden or some sort of sacrifice. I want to do this."

Zoe sighed. "I love you," she whispered, and kissed Eva tenderly on the lips. "I hope I don't fail."

"You won't fail," Eva stated firmly. "I know you won't fail."

Zoe snuggled back against Eva. After a moment, she tipped her head back, showing a new sparkle in her emerald eyes. "Do you think Elena would want to go to college with me?"

"I don't know. You'll have to ask her," Eva replied, knowing Zoe's mind had gone from "insecure young woman considers college" to the "out of my way, I have things to do". The battle was over, and Eva felt very pleased with herself.

"I still don't like the fact you're working in that factory," Zoe said.

"I promise, if a better job comes along, I'll take it," Eva reasoned. "Being a process worker is not my dream job either," she added, and they both chuckled.

"Evy, what about your back? Did you tell the fellow that hired you about your back?" Zoe asked, and frowned when Eva shook her head. "I worry you might hurt yourself. You know Dr. Mavropoulos said..."

"I know, love," Eva nodded. "It's only going to get worse with age."

"You won't be lifting heavy things, will you?"

Eva shook her head. "No, I don't think so. The women were taking the cookies off the conveyer belt and putting them in a box. Then the men took the boxes away." Eva related what she had seen on the factory floor.

"You will tell them if you have to lift heavy boxes, right?"

"Yes, I'll tell them," Eva agreed, although she was not sure if anyone would care. Factories did not have a high regard for the infirmities of their employees, as far as she knew.

"So who was your new boyfriend?" Zoe asked.

"His name is Earl Wiggins. He wants to marry me."

"Over my dead body he will," Zoe said. "Really?"

"Yes. He proposed to me on his knees. You didn't propose to me on your knees," Eva teased.

"No," Zoe agreed. "That's because you were on your knees to me, Miss Eva. It would have looked very strange if both of us were doing that."

Eva laughed and remembered the day she had asked Zoe to be with her for the rest of her life; the memory was amazingly clear, as though it had happened yesterday. The feeling of anxiety and then the euphoria at Zoe's response were still sharp in her mind. "I'm so glad I did."

"Yeah, so am I," Zoe said, chuckling. "I would have done it, but you beat me to it."

"You would have gone down on your knees and asked me?" Eva asked with a huge smile on her face. It had taken several days for her to pluck up the courage to ask Zoe. She never regretted it, but what she would have liked was not to have been sick with the flu while she had been proposing.

"Yes, but without the throwing up, or the aches and pains," Zoe said, teasingly.

Eva hugged her. "I would have done it in any condition."

"You are such a romantic," Zoe said, and tweaked the dimpled chin she considered very sexy. She gave Eva a quick kiss. "So do you think you've found a friend?"

Eva nodded. "I think so. He's very sweet and I feel comfortable around him. I think there is more to him than the joker he portrays."

"Really?"

"Hmm." Eva nodded again. "I don't know what it is, but there is more there."

"Very interesting, Sherlock." Zoe tried to put on an English accent but failed, causing Eva to laugh at the attempt. Her amusement turned into a tickle fight that landed them both on the floor.

"Did I hurt you?" Zoe asked urgently as she lay on top of her partner. Eva was on the floor with her arms outstretched and a big grin on her face.

"No," Eva shook her head.

"You are so beautiful," Zoe whispered. Eva pulled her down and passionately began to explore every inch of Zoe's sweet mouth with her teasing tongue. Soon both their bodies shuddered as though electrified. Intoxicated by the kiss, Eva was oblivious to Zoe's wandering hands as she unbuttoned her blouse and removed her bra. Only when Zoe pulled away did Eva become aware of the ache in her breasts, as well as the tingling feeling running all over her body. Panting with excitement, Eva looked down at her naked torso. She grinned at Zoe. "How did you do that?" she asked, giggling.

"Evy, you talk too much," Zoe said, and started to remove her own clothes, tossing them over her shoulder. Talking was the last thing on Zoe's mind, and Eva did not mind at all.

Chapter Five

"Hans, you can't sit here all day," Erik Rhimes called as he walked into the small apartment. "Drinking is bad for you. You know what the doctor said." The curtains were drawn closed, and the darkened room smelled of cheap whisky and cheaper cigarettes. "Makes my nose itch," Rhimes grumbled, putting down the bag of groceries he had been carrying and walking to the bedroom.

Hans Muller sat on the bed, surrounded by empty whisky bottles. He guzzled the last of yet another bottle in a few swallows. A record on the gramophone played a melancholy piano concerto, complementing the mood in the apartment. Muller watched Rhimes through the open bedroom door, the whisky burning its way down his throat.

Now in his late fifties, Muller had once been a tall, handsome man. In the past few years, his wavy blond hair had turned prematurely white. His wife has been dead for several years now, and though he had tried to love her, he was more upset that he didn't have a beautiful wife to show off to his commanding officers. A major in the German army, he had had everything he wanted: a good command, prestige, power. The war was the best thing that could have happened to him. It had given him the respect he had always craved. He had been somebody. The world had been at his feet until that October morning in 1944 when his life had suddenly collapsed around him.

Earlier on that fateful morning, he had received the news from his second-in-command that his daughter had reverted to her disgusting deviancy. Then later his command center had been bombed by the Resistance. After the effects of the explosion, he couldn't remember how he had escaped. All he could recall was his friend, Erik Rhimes, hovering above him, yelling orders.

Muller sighed as the last of the music faded away. He turned to Rhimes, who was standing looking at the empty bottle he held clutched in his hand. "What else is there t'do, my friend?" he retorted, slurring drunkenly. "I can't go out. There is a reason I can't go out, isn't there?" Too much drink had made his memory a shoddy thing. He was so drunk, he easily forgot what he was talking about.

"Hans, the doctor told you not to drink. It won't help." Rhimes tried to get the bottle, but Muller moved it out of his reach.

"I drink to forget," Muller muttered.

"It's not over, my friend," Rhimes said, reasonably. "There is a doctor in Argentina..."

"Why do we have to leave again?" Muller asked. He tried to take another mouthful from the bottle of whisky. He had forgotten it was empty.

"Hans, we need to leave Sydney."

"Why would I want to do that? Wait...didn't I just ask that question?"

"I was told by our friends that we are going to be arrested!"

"Arrested for what? That's a joke, Erik."

"They write the rules, my friend." Rhimes sat down next to Muller and finally pried the empty whisky bottle out of his hand. "They are holding a court at Nuremberg. They've already tried Hermann Goering — he killed himself before the Allies could hang him."

"Bastards."

"*Ja* well, they are bastards, we are bastards, and the Jews thrive," Rhimes replied. He looked at the bottle in his hand and threw it through the open bedroom door. It hit the couch and bounced off. Muller suddenly remembered that Erik Rhimes had commanded the German forces in northern Greece. He had been proud of it. He had done his job like Muller and followed orders; then the war turned against them all. Athens fell, Larissa fell, and then Thessaloniki. Both men were lucky to be alive. They had barely managed to escape, and now it was a cat-and-mouse game to try and outrun the Americans.

"I've got news from our friend," Rhimes said. "Hans, I have something to tell you. Eva is here."

"Who is here?" Muller replied, and looked around the room. He only saw his friend. Shrugging, he fell back on the rumpled bed.

"Your daughter."

After a long moment, Muller started to laugh. The sound faded when the import of Rhimes' words sunk in. Muller stared, abruptly sobered. "I should have killed her."

"I know you sent Reinhardt to..."

"No," Muller shook his head. "Not then."

Hans Muller was enraged, and the object of his hatred and revulsion lay at his feet. He held a fireplace poker in one hand and his belt in the other. The belt was covered with blood, as were his hands and his uniform. His "daughter" lay on the floor. He staggered back and fell down, dropping the poker. The sound reverberated around the room. The girl was motionless and quiet. He hoped she was dead so that the shame she had brought to the Muller name would be eradicated.

He was not sure how long he sat on the floor, only that he started to cry. Not for the deviant before him but for his wife, who had been killed earlier that night.

The door opened and a white-haired woman entered the room. Muller heard her shocked gasp and he continued to weep.

"What have you done?" Elise Muller asked, accusingly.

Muller had expected his mother to tend to him and not to the refuse that was his daughter. Instead, she had gone to Eva, who was still crumpled on the floor, beaten and bloody.

"What are you doing?" Muller growled at her.

His mother ignored him as she brushed blood-stained strands of hair from her granddaughter's bruised face. "Call a doctor."

"No." Muller shook his head and stood up, picking up the poker he had dropped on the floor. "Get away from her."

Elise looked back at him with undisguised disgust. "What are you going to do, Hans? Hit me?"

"No." Muller shook his head. "Not you." The man's hands fell limply to his sides, but he retained his hold on the poker.

"You are a disgrace," his mother replied, and turned her back on him to continue to attend to Eva.

"She is a deviant," he yelled.

"Don't yell at me, Hans," Elise warned. "You have done enough damage tonight."

"Mutti..." he whimpered.

"Hush! Put down that poker and help me take her to her room."

Muller hesitated for a long moment, earning another withering look. He reluctantly dropped the poker again and knelt down. "I am doing this for you," he said to his mother, who merely glared at him.

He picked up the injured young girl and, despite everything he had done to her, she moaned and rested her head against his chest.

"She is your daughter," Elise said quietly. She followed him into Eva's bedroom where he laid the injured girl on the bed. "Go and get me some hot water and some rags. I need to clean her up before the doctor gets here."

"No, no doctor."

"Hans, don't be an idiot. She will die if you don't call a doctor."

"Then she dies." Muller shrugged.

He did not expect the slap, the sound of which reverberated around the room. Elise had hit him, and he put his hand over his cheek in shock. "Mother!"

"You are behaving like an animal," his mother told him, and once again turned her back on him. Reluctantly, he left the room to get the water and rags. When he returned, he found Elise had removed the bloodied clothing and had wiped most of the blood from the girl's back using previously unstained parts of Eva's clothing.

"Did you call the doctor?" Elise asked.

"No. He will report me for this."

"So he should."

"General Krieger hates me," Muller whined. His superior truly despised him. He was not about to tell the general what had happened, even if it was for the right reason. "Krieger will send me to some god-forsaken hellhole."

His mother shook her head and took the water and rags from him. "Call your brother."

"I thought..."

"Don't think, Hans. Just call your brother and bring him here. He's at home on leave from Austria."

Muller left the room without another word. Despite it being late at night and obviously having been sound asleep, Dr. Dieter Muller immediately became lucid upon hearing the news that he was needed.

Half an hour later, Hans stood back while his brother assessed the damage he had done. After he had finished, Dieter wiped his hands and turned to Muller with a look of utter contempt on his face.

"What?" Muller asked, suddenly feeling as if he were the monster, not Eva.

"You didn't have to do this, brother," Dieter admonished.

"She's a lesbian, Dieter, it's, it's..."

"I know; Mutti told me. But you could have killed her."

Muller threw up his arms in frustration. "That's what I was trying to do!"

"Shooting her would have been less messy," Dieter replied, drolly. He looked down at the blood-stained towel in his hands. "But I think I can help you."

"You can? How?"

"I am working with a team trying to eliminate certain behaviors. I think Eva would be a good candidate for the experiments."

"She will be made normal?"

"Yes, I believe so."

"Can you do it tonight?"

Dieter shook his head. "We have to heal her first, Hans. I will take her back to Austria with me."

"What do I have to do?"

"I think you have done enough." Dieter gently slapped his brother's cheek and put an arm around his shoulders. "I will do the rest."

Silently, Muller agreed. The last thing he saw that night was his mother's cold, disdainful glare.

Muller brought himself out of his thoughts and back to the present. He scoffed, "Ja, sure, Dieter said it would cure her."

"Hans, I haven't asked you this before, but what happened to Eva?" Rhimes asked.

"She wasn't cured." Muller shook his head and began searching for another bottle of whisky. "Reinhardt should have killed her. W-w-what happened to Reinhardt?" Muller slurred, frowning. He had forgotten about his second-in-command. In his drunken fog, he remembered that he had decided Reinhardt was an inept fool.

"Why?" Rhimes asked.

"Why what?"

"Why did Reinhardt try to kill Eva?"

"Oh. She wasn't really my daughter, you know." Hans turned to his surprised friend. "Yes, that's true. Daphne...oh, my Daphne...well, Daphne; you remember my wife?"

"Yes, I remember Daphne," Rhimes replied. "She was a beautiful woman, Hans."

"Well, Daphne was a bad girl. Sh-sh-she got cozy with some Greek peasant that her father didn't like so he shipped her off to Austria. She had the baby — Eva — and I married her."

"Why?"

"Why did I marry her? Ah, my friend, that is a very good question...a very good question," Muller replied. He tried to smile but with half his face scarred, he could only manage a grimace. "I needed a wife. A good German officer needs a wife, with a baby. A family, every good German officer needs a family..." He trailed off, trying to remember what he had been saying. Muller turned to his friend. "I can't have children, Erik."

Rhimes was shocked. "You can't have children?"

"So here is this Greek peasant, with a daughter and here I am. I need a wife and a child...too bad she wasn't a boy. Ah...yes, then it would have been perfect. Well, she sure acted like a boy!" Muller chuckled at his own crude joke. "She was strange, that one."

"She is a beautiful young woman, Hans."

"*Ja*, I suppose...but she is a lesbian, Erik."

Rhimes looked Muller in stunned silence. Finally, he said, "Surely you jest! My son, Heinrich, went out with Eva."

"You don't believe me, eh?"

"It's not that I don't believe you, my friend, it's just that..."

"That's why I sent Reinhardt to kill her. The fool didn't do his job again...that's why she had to die." He shook his head to clear his mind of the wandering thoughts. *Eva*. He sighed. "Do you remember Franz's daughter, Greta?"

"*Ja*, but what..."

"Greta and Eva were lovers. *Ja*! Can you believe that?"

"Greta? A lesbian?"

"*Ja*, she was. A disgusting, deviant les-lesbian."

"What happened to Greta?"

Muller shrugged. "I don't know, Franz never told me. Whatever happened to Franz?"

"He died at the Russian Front," Rhimes replied.

"Ach, *ja*, that's where I would have ended up. The Russian Front. ... Reinhardt should have killed her, you know."

"Why? Because she was a lesbian?"

"Of course! That fool Reinhardt brought the whore to her, and they had sex in my house sp-spec-special delivery! My house, Erik! Can you believe it?" Muller found a half-full bottle and took several long drinks. "My hous-s-se," he hissed. "Did you see Reinhardt?"

"I don't know. We were in a slight hurry to get out of there that day."

"I 'member Thessaloniki. They had nice *ouzo*. Wish I had some..."

"Come on, my friend, I think you need to sleep this off."

"My face hurts, Erik," Muller moaned. His head rolled to one side and he promptly fell asleep. Rhimes watched him for a moment and shook his head. Finally, he took the bottle out of the prone man's limp hand and quietly left the bedroom.

"I need to get us out of Sydney quickly, or we'll be arrested," Rhimes whispered, and closed the bedroom door behind him. Semi-conscious, Muller grunted and rolled over, then fell back asleep.

Lightning streaked across the sky in the distance as rain continued to fall. It was midnight and Eva's favorite time to sit outside. Her insomnia wasn't caused by her nightmares, this time, but her nervousness about her new job. Coming from a wealthy family, Eva never worked other than helping at her grandfather's factory and those were half-hearted attempts at earning some pocket money to see a favorite opera. Eva sat outside on the balcony watching the rain tumble down, enjoying a glass of wine and a cigarette. Would she be accepted? How would they treat her? She took a drag off her cigarette and exhaled slowly.

Eva smoked and enjoyed it. Cigarettes, beer, and a fondness for wine: as vices went, these were rather harmless, she often thought to herself. On the other hand, Zoe did not smoke and had no tolerance for alcohol. One glass of wine was enough to make her tipsy.

The balcony door opened and Eva turned in her chair to find Zoe standing there, looking sleepy and rumpled, her hair sticking up in all directions.

"It's midnight, love, what are you doing up?" Eva asked.

"It's midnight, Evy. What are you doing out here?" Zoe yawned and shook her head. She took a seat across from Eva, away from the smoke. "I was just wondering where you were."

"Couldn't sleep."

"Your back hurting?"

Eva shook her head. "No, just a little bit nervous about tomorrow."

Zoe rubbed the sleep from her eyes and stifled another yawn. She spied Eva's wineglass next to her and took a sip. "They'll love you," she said a little hoarsely. "This is nice."

"Want a drag?" She offered the cigarette to Zoe, who still looked half-asleep.

"No." Zoe shook her head. "I vowed never to do that again."

"You smoked?" Eva asked, taken aback by the revelation.

Zoe giggled and shifted to sit cross-legged on the chair. "Not exactly."

"Are you going to tell me the story?" Eva asked.

"If I tell you a funny bedtime story will you come to bed and stop worrying about something you can't control?" Zoe gently admonished her, "You're going to get ulcers worrying about stuff."

"I don't think you get ulcers that way," Eva said.

"Yes, you do," Zoe disagreed, and tried to stifle another jaw-cracking yawn. "Do we have a deal? I want to go back to bed and I can't do it with you out here."

"Yes." Eva stubbed out her cigarette. "So tell me."

Zoe smirked. "When I was eight or nine years old, we were celebrating Easter at my uncle John's farm," she related, getting more comfortable. She looked out at the rain and her smile broadened. "It was a big gathering with all my uncles and aunties, my grandmother, and all my cousins. The men were outside smoking and doing what men do."

"They often do that," Eva said with a chuckle.

"Me and my cousin Maria—"

"Which Maria was this?"

"My uncle John's Maria," Zoe replied. She smiled at Eva's befuddled look.

"How many cousins did you have called Maria?" Eva asked. Zoe had often related stories about her childhood, and it seemed to Eva that every other cousin was named Maria.

"Six," Zoe replied, "all with the same name."

"Why?"

Zoe shrugged. "Every son in our family wanted to name a child after their mother."

"But not your father?"

"No, Papa didn't want another Maria Lambros in the Lambros clan. I was named after my mother's mother."

"And how many cousins named Zoe are around?"

"None. There's just one Zoe and I'm it. My mother's sister, Aunty Stella didn't have children as far as I know..." Zoe moved the ashtray from the low table next to Eva, went over, and cuddled next to her partner. "Now *this* I like," she said before stealing a quick kiss. Eva knew her mouth tasted like wine even before Zoe continued, "Mmm, this stuff is much better on your lips than in the glass."

Eva laughed and kissed Zoe again, emboldened by the darkness. They were unlikely to be seen by anyone on the street or from the other balconies at that time of night. "So what happened with Maria?"

"I'm not quite sure who suggested it, but we wanted to smoke as well. I knew where Uncle John kept the papers that he used to roll up his cigarettes so we snuck into his room and we took a couple." Zoe laughed. "We couldn't find the tobacco he used, so we decided to make our own."

"Uh oh..."

Zoe gave Eva a gentle poke. "I thought tobacco looked like hay, but Maria said that it smelt like cow poop."

Eva burst out laughing and slapped her hand over her mouth. Regaining her composure with difficulty, she said, "Go on."

"Well, Uncle John didn't have a cow, but he had horses and he had hay, so we went into the barn. I got the hay and Maria got the poop."

Eva lost control again and started to laugh until tears streamed down her face. Zoe laughed as well.

"Um, well," the younger woman stammered through her laughter, and took a deep breath. "We went behind the barn and we rolled the hay and the poop into the cigarette paper. I knew how to do it because I had seen Papa do it many times."

"Did you smoke it?"

"Uh huh. We had a cigarette each and we took a puff at the same time. Ended up coughing and spluttering so much, Mihali came rushing over to see what we were doing."

Eva wiped the tears from her eyes. "Then what happened?"

Zoe grinned. "We explained to Mihali what we had done and he couldn't stop laughing. That brought Thieri and Leftheri over to see what the commotion was about." Zoe rocked back and looked up at the ceiling, trying to stop more giggles from bubbling out and preventing her from finishing the story. "Papa heard the boys and next thing we knew, he came over to see what the trouble was."

"Oh, no," Eva squeaked.

"Papa couldn't believe it and he really tried not to laugh, but I knew he wanted to because his eyes were going crinkly."

"What did he do?"

"He rolled and lit a proper cigarette, gave it to me and told me to smoke it."

"He didn't! Did he?"

"Yeah. I took it and took one puff, inhaling deeply like he told me to. My eyes watered, my throat burned, and I began coughing." Zoe snickered. "When I could talk, I told him I wasn't going to smoke ever again."

"Smart man, that Papa Lambros," Eva said, grinning.

Zoe nodded in agreement. "Very smart man. Just the thought of smoking makes my stomach churn. So that's why I don't smoke."

Eva chuckled at the story. "I don't blame you for not wanting to take up the habit, but are you sure you don't mind if I smoke?"

Zoe smiled. "I know it relaxes you, so I don't mind. Why would I? How did you start?"

"Willie got me started on cigarettes...well actually it was cigars?"

"Cigars?"

"My grandfather used to smoke these great big cigars." Eva smiled as the memory of the smell of cigars and of clandestine meetings she shared with her best friend, Willie, returned to her. "Willie really wanted to try one, but he was scared he might get caught. So he convinced me to go with him. If we got caught, I would say I was there to see my grandfather." Eva stopped, looked out in the darkness, and chuckled.

"Did you get caught?"

Eva looked down at her partner and smiled. "We got caught with our hand in the cigar box," she said, then laughed.

"What happened?" Zoe asked.

"Well, my grandfather came in and caught us. We tried to stammer our way out of it. Willie was terrible at lying—"

"And you are good at it?" Zoe interrupted, with a big smile to soften the sting of her words.

"Well," Eva smiled, "I was better at it than Willie."

"Did your grandfather believe you?"

"No."

"Well, you weren't better than Willie."

"Ha ha." Eva shook her head. "*Opa...*"

"Opa?"

"Grandpa," Eva translated the German word into Greek. "He gave us a cigar, each, and taught us how to smoke it."

"You're joking!"

"No, he said if we were going to smoke, we should do it right."

"Did you enjoy it?"

"Oh yes," Eva nodded. "I made the mistake of going home and being so excited that I told my grandmother. She was furious with my grandpa!"

"How old were you?" Zoe wondered out loud.

"Fifteen. I miss him," Eva said with a sigh, then took Zoe's hand and kissed it. They both fell silent watching the light rain fall. "What happened to Maria?" Eva asked.

"Uncle John moved to America just before the war," Zoe replied. "She's probably married to some American boy."

"So you have family in America?"

"Maybe. Evy, I want to go to sleep," Zoe announced, getting up from her cozy position. Eva put her glass down and got up herself. They closed the balcony door and quietly made their way to their bedroom.

"That was a nice story," Eva said as she put her arms around Zoe. "Thank you."

"You're welcome," Zoe replied, and took off Eva's robe. She took her hand and they both got into bed, immediately snuggling together. "Evy?"

"Yes?"

"Stop worrying. Everything will be all right."

Eva smiled. "I hope so."

"I know it will. Now hush and go to sleep."

"Yes, Mama," Eva joked. She got a quick kiss as Zoe settled next to her. Eva looked up at the ceiling and smiled. "Zoe?"

"Hmm," Zoe mumbled.

"I love you." Eva kissed the top of Zoe's head and closed her eyes.

Eva scowled at herself in the mirror. The white uniform they had given her fit well enough, but that wasn't the problem. It reminded her too much of a nurse's uniform. The white cap added to the illusion. Eva held the cap in her hand and sighed. She did not like hats, especially crisp, white ones.

Zoe was leaning against the door jamb, watching her.

Eva turned away from the mirror and focused on Zoe. "I know you want to say something."

Zoe smiled. "You look gorgeous," she said.

Eva returned the smile but shook her head. "I look like a nurse."

"Have I told you I really like nurses?" Zoe said. Pushing away from the door jamb, she came over to where Eva was standing. "You do look beautiful. I like white on you," Zoe said, and put her arms around Eva, looking up at her.

"I'm not wearing anything underneath this tunic." Eva jiggled her shoulders a little.

"Hmm, that's not a bad thing," Zoe said, putting her hands on Eva's backside. "Not a bad thing at all."

Eva smiled. "I didn't mean it that way."

"Drat," Zoe said. "What did you mean?"

"I can't wear anything to hide..." Eva stopped for a moment and glared at herself in the mirror. "To hide the scars on my back," she concluded, still glaring.

"They won't show," Zoe said. She took Eva's hands and led her to the bed where they both sat down. Eva looked down at the cap in her hand and sighed once more.

"It's a light fabric, Zoe," she said. Eva was very self-conscious about the scars that marred her skin.

"I know but you told me it gets awfully hot in the factory, so wearing something underneath is going to make you uncomfortable. You know how much you hate the heat," Zoe replied.

"I know." Eva got up from the bed and put on her cap.

"Maybe when we come back we can play doctor and nurse." Zoe giggled, getting up from the bed and resting her head against Eva's back.

"Who's the doctor?" Eva asked.

"Me, since you already have a nurse's uniform on," Zoe said.

Eva turned around and looked down at the young woman. "How do you do that?"

"Do what?"

"Make me feel special?"

"It's a gift, but it's not hard," Zoe replied, tweaking Eva's dimpled chin. "You *are* special."

Eva was heartened by the love she saw reflected in Zoe's eyes. She leaned down and kissed her quickly. After they parted, Zoe said, "And if you don't get going, I'm going to be tempted to play doctor and nurse right now."

Eva grinned. "I hate being a grown-up."

"Oh, I'm loving it," Zoe said as Eva gave her another quick kiss before going to the lounge to collect her bag.

Chapter Six

"Muller! I thought krauts moved quicker than that!"

Eva looked up in the direction of the voice and grimaced.

The booming voice of a short, dark-haired man standing on the steps leading up to a small office reverberated around the factory floor. Jack "Bean" Stalk was the one-armed, short-tempered, and irritatingly rude shortbread section supervisor, the master of his little domain. He was also a man whom Eva wished she could belt across the head with a two-by-four.

Added to his insolence were his racist taunts. From the moment he had met her, he called her "kraut" and took great delight in finding her the most menial jobs to do. Eva learned quickly not to annoy him, but somehow it appeared Stalk had been annoyed with her since she had first walked in the door. Eva wondered if the man had been born angry.

Not satisfied with yelling at her loudly enough for the whole floor to hear, Stalk stormed down the steps to Eva's position at the conveyer belt. He angrily took the packets off the belt, showing her how he wanted it done.

"That's how you do it. Do — you — understand?" he said slowly and loud. "Or do I need to learn kraut to get through to you?" The furrow between his eyes got deeper. "Didn't I tell you to move those packets quickly?" he yelled.

"Ease up, Bean." Earl came round the corner and put his arm around the supervisor's shoulders. Stalk shrugged him off.

"Aren't you supposed to be somewhere else?" Stalk asked.

Earl grinned and took a deep breath. "No. I'm on a smoke break," he said, and showed his unlit cigarette.

"Well, go and have your bloody smoko so I can have a word with Muller here." Stalk turned his back on the big man, then spun around when Earl didn't move. "Are you still here?"

"Yep." Earl winked at Eva, who stood uncomfortably with her back to the machine. "I came to get Muzza."

"Who?"

"Miss Muller," Earl corrected himself.

"Well, she can't have a smoko..."

"Yes, she can. She's been working without a break since she came in."

"She had a tea break..."

"No, she didn't," Earl cut him off. "She was with Mrs. Higgins."

Stalk let out a frustrated groan. "Ten minutes," he growled.

"Actually, Mrs. Dunning wants her in the Flossy Flute Fingers section." Earl chuckled. "I just love that name," he said, putting the cigarette into his mouth.

"Fine! Get your bloody arse out of here and take the kraut with you!" Stalk retorted as he stormed off, muttering loudly to himself.

"Wanker," Earl swore and gave the retreating man a single-finger salute. "Absolute bloody wanker."

Eva sighed and moved out of the tiny cul-de-sac she had created with boxes of biscuits, wiping the sweat from her brow. "*Blödes Arschloch,*" Eva muttered, scowling in the direction of Stalk's retreating back. She had spent most of the morning in the room with no fresh air. The windows were shut and with the roaring whir of the machines, she had been feeling quite distressed. Eva had quelled the rising panic that threatened to overwhelm her, but control had not come easily. Earl's appearance was a godsend.

"Come on, Muzza, let's go for a smoko. I need one," Earl said as he guided Eva out of the section. They walked silently up the stairs where a blast of cooler air hit Eva like the answer to a prayer. She stopped for a moment and enjoyed the blessed relief.

Earl looked a little worried. Eva shut her eyes and leaned back against the railing. "Hey, are you all right?" he asked.

"Yes," Eva nodded. "It was too hot in there," she said, and started up the steps. Her hair was damp with sweat. All she wanted was to go home, have a bath and lie down.

"No kidding. That blasted fan has been broken since yesterday." Earl opened the door and waited for Eva to go past him, then joined her outside. He took out another cigarette and offered it to Eva, who took it gratefully.

"So, how come you didn't go for your tea break?" Earl asked as he lit Eva's cigarette.

"My what?"

"Oh, strewth, woman." Earl shook his head. "Didn't Bean tell you about tea breaks?"

"He told me a lot of things, mostly at the top of his voice," Eva replied, taking a long drag off the cigarette. She cast a shy glance at Earl. "What's a wanker?"

Earl grimaced. "I'm sorry, I don't usually swear in front of women," he apologized. "Um...well, it's something men do."

Eva looked at him blankly. "I do not understand."

"Um..." Earl sighed. "It's an Aussie saying."

"Yes, I figured that out." Eva grinned. "So it's an...impolite word?"

"Yes, it sure is."

"Ah." Eva took another drag off the cigarette. "And," she said to Earl, "I shouldn't call Mr. Stalk a wanker to his face?"

Earl stopped for a long moment. Noticing the mischievous glint in Eva's eyes, he smiled and said, "You already knew what 'wanker' means, didn't you?"

Eva blew out a perfect smoke ring. "Yes, I knew," she said, chuckling. In the short time she had been working at the factory, she had heard the word used more than once, and it was usually associated with Jack Stalk. The hand gestures that followed had given her a good indication of the word's meaning.

Earl laughed and gently slapped Eva on the shoulder. "You have a great poker face, you know that?"

"Too bad I don't play poker." Eva smirked. "So what's wrong with Mr. Stalk?"

"He needs a good fuck," Earl replied, obviously without thought. He paused midway through a drag off his cigarette, looking at Eva in embarrassment.

"Hmm, that could help," Eva said chuckling. "But I meant with his arm."

Earl grinned. "You have a wicked streak in you, Miss Muller," he said playfully. "Ah, Stalk...his arm was hacked off by a Jap."

"Ow." Eva grimaced.

"Yeah, well sometimes I think something else was hacked off, too." Earl grinned. "Bean has a lot of problems up here," he said, tapping the side of his head. "I guess we all do."

Eva studied the man's handsome face for a moment. "You were in the war?"

"I was a guest of the Emperor for a while," Earl replied. "Fought in North Africa before going to Singapore where I was captured." He stopped, watching the smoke rise. "Spent the rest of the war in hell."

"I'm sorry," Eva said softly. Earl was looking away and she knew he was trying to compose himself. Eva understood the posture, the strength it required not to let the outside world know the storm that was raging inside. "Your soul was rendered," she quietly remarked.

Earl blew out more smoke before turning to Eva, gazing at her for a long time. "You understand. Don't you?" he asked, his voice soft. "Being a guest of the Emperor..."

Eva looked at the cigarette she held and watched ashes float downward. "I understand," Eva replied. "I..."

"Don't," Earl responded as he put his hand on Eva's arm. "You don't have to."

Eva looked at Earl for a moment and let him see the truth behind her steady gaze, a glimpse of the pain-filled horror that she usually managed to keep locked away.

They both fell silent and watched the trees sway in the breeze, lost in their own memories.

"So you came home?" Eva asked, finally breaking the silence.

"I came home and started working here," Earl replied. "It's the right job."

"Did you work here before?"

"No. I was a high school teacher."

Eva's eyebrows lifted. She continued to study the tall, blond man.

"Why this place?" she asked him.

Earl smiled. "I needed mindless, numbing work that didn't require me to think."

"Well, this qualifies," Eva replied, and they both chuckled.

"How about you?" Earl returned her question.

"I studied languages at university before the war," Eva explained, and smiled shyly. No one had asked her about her studies before, apart from Zoe.

"Really? What languages can you speak?"

"Italian, German, and Greek," Eva replied.

"I can speak a little German." Earl puffed on his cigarette. "Guarded some krauts for a bit in North Africa."

"And you learned German from them?"

"I got tired of hearing '*Affenschwanz*' all the time."

Eva put her hand over her mouth in surprise but could not stop the giggle that escaped. Earl looked at her, his amusement apparent. "So you understood what I said back there?" Eva asked.

"Stupid asshole," Earl translated. He smiled when Eva's face turned bright pink.

"I went to one of the interpreters and he gave me some useful phrases," Earl said. "So, *Fräulein* Muller, why this place?" Earl mimicked Eva's accent and they both smiled.

"I needed mindless, numbing work," Eva replied, her heavily German-influenced attempt at an Aussie accent making them both laugh.

"Hey, that was good."

"I have a gift for languages — and usually for accents, too." Eva shrugged.

"So, really, why work here? You could get a decent job with all the immigrants around and stuff."

"No one would give me a job," Eva replied. "I also want to help my...my sister with her education."

"Younger?"

"Yes," Eva replied, a broad smile creasing her face. "Zoe. She's an artist."

"So you're willing to work here to get Zoe into school?"

"It's what she has always dreamed about."

"She must be one very special girl for you to do that."

Eva smiled. "She is. She lost all her family."

"I thought you said...?"

"Different mothers, long story," Eva said quickly, covering her slip.

"Daddy got around, eh?" Earl guffawed. "The krauts are a randy lot."

"He was Greek," Eva said, happy to be in easier territory. She was a lousy liar and always failed miserably when she tried to alter the truth.

"Your mother was German?"

Eva shook her head. "She was Greek too. My stepfather was German."

"So how did you find out about each other?"

Eva scratched her ear and mentally winced. She liked Earl and hated to lie to him, but until she could trust him with her secret, she would have to be very careful about what she said. "The war. It tore families apart, and it brought us together." Eva sighed. *Well, it was the truth — somewhat.*

"That was a neat trick," Earl said. "So it's just the two of you?"

"Just the two of us." Eva looked at her watch. "Um, how long is this tea break?" she asked, not wanting to talk about Zoe further, just in case she said something that would cause her problems.

"It's in our union rules that you have to take a break for ten minutes in the morning and ten minutes in the afternoon."

"Ah," Eva nodded. "Well, I think we have been gone for half an hour."

"Actually, it's closer to forty minutes." Earl shrugged. "But it's okay, this is union business."

"Union business?"

"Yeah. So did you join the union?"

"No," Eva replied. "I don't like unions."

"Why not?"

"I just don't like them," Eva replied. "I'm not a socialist." She dropped the stub of her cigarette onto the pavement and ground it out with the heel of her shoe.

Earl frowned. "What?"

"Unions are formed by socialists," Eva patiently explained.

"You *are* confused," Earl said. "It's not that way here."

"So they don't want you to belong to a political party?"

"Not unless they've changed the rules and I wasn't told," Earl said, grinning. "I'm the union rep."

"Union rep?"

"Yes, I take care of the workers for the Whole Workers United Union." Earl took out a card and gave it to Eva. "If we have a union, we can get better conditions and don't have to put up with working in an atmosphere like you had to endure this morning."

"And I have to join this union?"

"Well, if you want to be protected, yes."

"But I don't have to join a political party?"

"Nope. Interested?"

"As long as you don't make me wear a funny uniform and salute," Eva said smiling, and slipped the card into the pocket of her white coat.

"Now there's a great idea." Earl stubbed out his cigarette and held the door open. They went back into the stifling heat of the factory.

The afternoon dragged on as Eva tried to keep pace with the rest of the women in the processing line. At least she was a lot cooler in the Flossie Flute Fingers biscuit section than with Jack Stalk in his hell-hole. She was now working in an area that was more welcoming to her. The majority of the women were Greek and Italian. Eva's responses to them in their own languages surprised them and made them less suspicious of the new worker. It was gratifying, since Eva did not make friends easily.

She looked up at the clock and sighed. A few more hours until she went home and then she could lie down. Her body was aching in places she had never felt aches before. Eva put another packet into a box and closed it.

"Take that to the pallet." Mrs. Higgins had stopped at Eva's station and motioned to a large pallet. The older woman moved on after issuing the order.

Eva looked down at the box which she had packed. She looked around for Earl; he had been on the floor carrying boxes and moving pallets, but he was nowhere to be found. Eva decided to lift the box herself.

Not a good idea. Immediately her back began screaming at her. She managed to get the box full of biscuit packets onto the pallet and grimaced as her back continued to protest loudly. She knew she had overdone it; that had been made very clear, very quickly.

Eva took several deep breaths before going back to her station. The sciatic pain radiated down her spine and into her legs, which now began to feel rubbery.

"Are you all right?" a woman asked her.

Eva smiled and nodded at her co-worker, Maria Spiropoulos. "I just need a minute."

"You know, I told Earl that we are going to have an accident if we don't get more of the boys down here..."

"I'm okay, Maria," Eva repeated, and smiled. "It's just a twinge."

"Hmm." Maria gave Eva with a dubious look. "If it's a twinge, why are you looking so pale?"

"I'm fine." Eva smiled. "I'll just take these to the storeroom." She picked up some empty boxes and slowly made her way out.

Maria watched her leave and shook her head. "I know a bad back when I see one," she muttered to herself, just loudly enough for Eva to hear.

The factory door opened and Zoe popped inside. She was early, but she did not care. She had managed to get off work a little ahead of her normal time and catch the bus. Zoe wanted to go home with Eva, and was more than a little curious about Eva's new workplace. She was not happy with what she saw. A large metallic fan whirred, increasing the noise to a level that hurt Zoe's ears. The smell of the biscuits gave her an odd feeling and the heat of the factory made her wince.

"Oh, Evy, this is a hell-hole," she muttered. Going deeper into the factory, she looked around at the large machines and the women who operated them. All the women wore white and they continued working without glancing up at the stranger in their midst.

"Excuse me, miss. Members of the public are not allowed here." A young man stopped and motioned to a sign that said the same thing. He turned and left without looking back.

"Funny place to put a sign if no one is here to read it," Zoe muttered, looking back over her shoulder, hoping to catch a glimpse of Eva. With a sigh, Zoe left that section and was about to leave the building when she caught sight of a very familiar figure in the storeroom just outside the area she had been in.

"Evy!" she cried, and walked quickly to where Eva was standing. Zoe noticed that Eva looked tired, but on seeing her, the tall woman's face lit up in a smile.

"What are you doing here?" Eva asked, glancing around in an obvious attempt to see if any of her supervisors were nearby.

"I wanted to see you."

"You are a sight for sore eyes," Eva said, and took Zoe's hand. She closed the door and led her to the back of the storeroom.

Without a word, Eva embraced Zoe and kissed her tenderly. "I missed you," she whispered, melting into Zoe's arms. "It's so good to see you."

"How was your first day?" Zoe asked, already knowing the answer just by looking at her lover's exhausted expression.

Eva sighed. "Hell."

"I believe you," Zoe said. She put her arms around Eva's slim waist and hugged her. "I was only in that place for a minute and it made me sick."

"That was the nicer place," Eva replied, clearly too tired to censor herself. "One of the fans was out and it's stinking hot."

The two women sat down on a pallet, still holding hands. "Are you all right?" Zoe asked. Already Zoe could tell this new job was not going well. Eva was not even trying to hide her disgust.

"Yeah," Eva nodded. "My back hurts and I'm cranky."

"Evy, are you sure..."

"Zoe." Eva closed her eyes for a moment and sighed again. "Are we still having this debate?"

"I saw the hell-hole, Evy."

"It won't be forever, love," Eva pleaded, and got up from the pallet. "Let it die."

"Okay, okay, I'm going to let it die." Zoe shook her head and got up herself. She went over to Eva and put her arms around her. "You also smell..." Zoe sniffed at Eva's uniform, "you smell like those frosty pink things."

"Flossy Flute Fingers." Eva smiled. "I was there this afternoon."

"Flossy Flute Fingers," Zoe repeated. "Sounds like a disease."

Eva smiled even wider. "I love you," she said, caressing Zoe's cheek. "I'm so tired. All I want is to go home and sleep."

"How about," Zoe took Eva's hands and held them, "you have a bath and I'll give you a nice," Zoe kissed Eva's hands, "long massage?"

"You have a deal." Eva kissed her tenderly.

"Hey, Muzza, are you in here?" Earl yelled, walking into the storeroom and grabbing a pallet.

"Over here, Earl," Eva said.

Earl came around the corner. From her position on the pallet, Zoe smiled at him.

"Earl, this is Zoe...my sister. Zoe, this is Earl Wiggins."

Zoe hopped off the pallet and looked at the man who towered above her. "Evy didn't mention how tall you were. Hello," she said, and stuck out her hand. "Zoe."

"Wiggy." Earl smiled and shook Zoe's hand.

"Wiggy." Zoe giggled. "So what do you do around here, Wiggy?"

"Oh, this and that — and I'm Eva's protector." Eva gave him a dark look and a subtle shake of her head. Zoe caught the movement out of the corner of her eye.

"Huh?" Zoe was puzzled and looked back at Eva, who sat down.

"One of my supervisors is a Nazi in training," Eva quipped, earning a very surprised look from Zoe.

"What the hell is going on in here?" Jack Stalk shouted as he stomped around the corner. "Wiggins! Muller! Who the hell are you?" he asked, spotting Zoe.

"*Blödes Arschloch*," Eva muttered loudly.

Zoe was dumbstruck at Eva's comments. *She's going to explain that when we get home*, she thought.

"What the hell did you say in that kraut talk?" Stalk growled.

"She said that you are...her supervisor." Zoe smiled, turning on the charm. "Hello, my name is Zoe."

"Members of the public are not allowed in here." Stalk continued to growl but softened a little when Zoe smiled at him. "You have to get out."

"I will, Mr..."

"Jackson Stalk." He gave his full first name, which seemed to surprise both Eva and Earl. "You can call me Jack."

"Jack," Zoe said. "I came here to see my sister."

"Who's your sister?"

"Eva." Zoe indicated her partner. Eva seemed bemused at how easily Stalk had been tamed by the attention Zoe was paying to him.

"*You* don't sound like a kraut," Stalk said.

"That's because I'm Greek. Long story, different fathers," Zoe replied, making Eva look at her in surprise. Zoe realized she had slipped up on their rehearsed story and avoided looked at Eva. Out of the corner of her eye she noticed Earl was leaning against a pallet, fiddling with a cigarette.

"Oh, well...all right...you saw her?"

"Yes."

"You have to wait outside then," Stalk said, a little less gruffly. He smiled at Zoe before turning his attention to the other two. "Another smoko?" His voice was heavily laden with sarcasm.

"Not now," Earl muttered, slipping the cigarette into his shirt pocket. Eva and Earl both left the storeroom, quickly followed by Stalk, while Zoe headed toward the exit from the factory.

Zoe waved at her partner before disappearing through the front door.

The rest of the hour dragged on as Eva and Earl worked together to pack boxes in the storeroom. Nothing was said about Zoe's slip-up. Eva hoped Earl had been distracted enough not to have understood the significance of what he had heard.

She closed a box with tape and straightened up, letting out a small groan as her back protested again. The storeroom was quite stuffy, and both of them were sweating. Earl's solution was to take off his heavy white shirt and work in only his undershirt and trousers. It was not company policy, but he did not seem to care.

Eva looked up and smiled. "You know that's a great idea."

"What?"

"Taking your shirt off."

"You can do it too." Earl laughed, and jumped down from the pallet. "So how long have you had back problems?"

"How do..."

"Maria told me." Earl shrugged, taking out his cigarettes from his pocket.

"Since I was eighteen years old."

"Uh-huh." Earl offered Eva a cigarette and lit both of them with a match. "Accident?"

Eva looked quizzically at him, then dropped her gaze and stood for a long moment staring down at her feet. She sighed. "No, not an accident."

"Deliberate?"

"Very."

"With what?"

"A poker and a heavy leather belt," Eva replied, and took a drag off her cigarette. "Long story."

Earl winced. "Sounds painful. I know what it's like to be beaten." He paused, then brightened somewhat. "Everything seems to be a long story..." Earl quipped, which earned him a scowl from Eva. "Come here," he said, beckoning with a crooked finger.

"Why?"

"I've got a trick to show you."

"What trick?"

"A trick." Earl pulled Eva to him, relieving her of her cigarette before dropping it, together with his own, to the floor. "I learned this at the Jap Ritz," he said. He put Eva's arms around his neck. "Hang off me."

"Hang off you?"

"Yeah, I'm tall enough." Earl grinned. "Go on."

Eva put her arms around his neck and lifted her legs. She rested her cheek on his shoulder and Earl's fingers began to massage her lower back. The tightness began to fade and Eva smiled as the pain receded. A relieved sigh escaped her.

"I bet Zoe doesn't know how to do this," Earl teased as he held Eva close. Then they both heard Jack Stalk's voice drifting in.

"Eva, trust me on this all right?" Earl said quietly into her ear.

"On what?"

"Just trust me. Kiss me."

"Kiss you?" Eva's eyes went wide and she started to move away from him.

"Please, just kiss me. I promise to explain," Earl pleaded. He seemed hugely relieved when, after a moment, Eva's lips met his. At that instant Jack Stalk, Mr. Peabody and Mrs. Higgins entered to find the two of them in an apparently passionate embrace. To add to the illusion, Earl lifted Eva's uniform skirt up a little to show off her shapely leg.

"Mr. Wiggins!" Mrs. Higgins was the first to react to the scene before them. She scowled at them both. "This is not the place to do whatever you are doing!"

Earl disentangled himself from Eva, who pulled her uniform skirt down. "I couldn't help myself," he said.

"Wiggins, I know you are the company Lothario, but please, not on company time!" Peabody admonished.

Earl pulled Eva towards him. Eva played along. "We're going to get married, Mr. Peabody," he said.

"That's what you say about every girl," Stalk grumbled.

"Nah, she's the real thing," Earl replied, taking Eva's hand and kissing it.

Mrs. Higgins stormed out of the storeroom muttering to herself, closely followed by Stalk and Peabody. After the door slammed shut, Earl collapsed on a pallet. "Oh man, that was great! Just absolutely perfect. I give it five minutes before it hits the rest of the factory."

Eva scowled at him. "Would you like to tell me what's going on?"

Earl took out another cigarette and offered it to Eva. "How would Zoe feel about you marrying me?"

Eva frowned. "I'm not marrying you."

"No, not really, but how would she feel about it? Do you think she would like to be one of those gals who..."

"Bridesmaids?"

"Yes, one of those."

Eva shook her head slowly. "Not much."

"By the way, you're a great kisser." Earl grinned. "I guess Zoe knows all about that, eh?" he asked. Eva stared at him, trepidation making her legs wobbly. "I saw you both here earlier," he continued. "You were a little too friendly to be sisters."

"Oh." Eva sat down hard.

"You really have to co-ordinate your stories," Earl said. "It's either the same mother or the same father."

"So, what are you going to do?"

"Marry you," Earl replied seriously. "Well, if Zoe doesn't kill me first for pulling a stunt like that," he said, grinning.

"So you're not going to tell Mr. Peabody?"

"Nah," Earl shook his head. "Tell him what? That you like kissing in the storeroom? You really do have a thing about this area."

"Really, Earl, what are you going to do?" Eva stood and walked over to him. "You know..."

Earl's expression turned serious. He took her hand. "I wouldn't betray you, Eva," Earl said, putting his arm around her. "We're family."

"We're...what?"

"Family. You and I...we have the same...instincts."

Eva stared at him, totally confused.

Earl groaned. "Oh for goodness' sake! I'm a homosexual."

"You're a...?" Eva asked, still a bit shocked.

Earl shrugged. "So you see we are both in a bit of a predicament."

"Is that why you go after all the girls?"

"Yes," Earl replied. "I had to be the factory Romeo."

"And you were nice to me so you can bolster your image?" Eva tentatively asked, playing with the silver ring on her finger.

"When you came for your first meeting with Peabody, I did," Earl replied, honesty in his voice. "Not today. I like you, Eva. You are a smart, charming, witty woman and I prefer friends like that."

Eva smiled at him, feeling shy. "So how did you know that Stalk was coming?"

"I heard him, and I figured that if I kissed you, the news would travel faster than any telegram ever could."

"So now we're together?"

"It seems so," Earl said. "Well, you have to tell Zoe."

"Oh, no." Eva shook her head giving him an evil grin. "You're going to do that," she said, and chuckled at his surprised look. "I'm not telling her."

"Are you scared of that slip of a girl?" Earl teased. His gaze was fixed on Eva's face. "I'm glad you've stopped being so afraid of me," he said, smiling. "So tell me about the woman...is she a better kisser?"

Eva grinned broadly. "Hate to deflate your ego, but you are not anywhere near Zoe's league," she said. She loved the feel of her partner in her arms; Zoe's perfume, her softness and her absolute passion. "She is the best."

"Oh, that hurts." Earl put his hand over his heart and feigned deep pain, then laughed. "How did you two meet?"

"Long story," Eva quipped, getting a groan from her friend. "It really is a long story, and one that I think you should hear over dinner."

"Are you sure?"

"Yes, I'm sure."

The sound of the end-of-shift buzzer made the two grin at each other. "Zoe's waiting," Eva said. "I think I'd better tell her when we get home."

"Is she the jealous type?"

Eva laughed as she left the storeroom with Earl at her side. "You have no idea, my friend. No idea at all."

Chapter Seven

"So, you're a little quiet," Zoe said, setting the table for dinner. The bus ride from the factory had been subdued, far too much for Zoe's liking. There was the usual banter with Eva telling Zoe about the people she had met and other general news, but Zoe felt that Eva was holding something back. She was not going to press the issue. She knew she would find out in time, but that did not stop her from being extremely curious.

Zoe's curiosity had climbed higher when Eva had suggested that they eat one of her favorite dishes — eggplant with potatoes and peppers. When they had stopped off at the grocer's shop on the way home, Eva had purchased more items than usual. At the time, Zoe had not said much about it, but now Eva came out of the kitchen and set the table with an extra place setting.

"Are we expecting company?" Zoe asked as Eva came around the table and took her into an embrace.

Eva looked up at the clock, then back to Zoe. "I have something to tell you."

"I knew it."

"Knew what?"

"You were giving me the *Daily News* version of your day," Zoe replied. "So give me the real version."

"That was the real version," Eva said. "Well, with a little bit of editing." She laughed when Zoe stuck out her tongue. "Now, now, patience is a virtue."

"I have patience."

Eva rocked back and laughed heartily. After a moment, Zoe joined her, knowing that finding patience and herself in the same situation was a rare event. Eva took Zoe's hand and led her to the sofa. "Everything I told you happened."

"Stalk doesn't like you," Zoe said, stating the obvious. "I don't understand why."

"He's a veteran," Eva replied. Zoe gave her a knowing look.

"I feel sorry for him, but he's still a boofhead," Zoe said, interspersing the Greek they spoke together with Australian slang. "So spill it."

"You remember Earl?" Eva asked, smiling when Zoe nodded. "Well...he kissed me."

Zoe stared open-mouthed at Eva, whose face was contorted as she clearly tried to hold in her laughter. "He kissed you?" Zoe asked incredulously.

"Yes."

"And you let him?"

"Yes." Eva nodded and pressed her lips together. She took a deep breath. "We were in the storeroom..."

"That storeroom sees a lot of action," Zoe said.

"We were in the storeroom," Eva continued, "and he showed me a trick for my back."

"Uh-huh," Zoe muttered, her irritation growing.

"Well, I was hanging off him and he asked me to kiss him," Eva finished in a flurry and sat there frowning, not making eye contact.

Zoe stared incredulously at her lover. Her irritation was turning into anger at Eva's nonchalant retelling of what happened in the storeroom. "You kissed him?" Zoe's voice rose. "You actually kissed a man?"

Eva nodded and tried to avoid looking at Zoe. "Yes, I kissed him."

Zoe ran her hand through her hair in absolute frustration, then palmed the back of her neck, feeling the tension that made her muscles wire-tight. "Then what happened?" she asked, through gritted teeth.

"He asked me to marry him," Eva said.

Zoe let out a frustrated groan. "Did you tell him you were off limits?"

Eva looked up at her partner with a very slight smile. "You are *so* jealous."

For a moment, there was absolute silence except for the ticking of the wall clock. It did not last long. Zoe pounced on Eva and they fell backwards against the sofa amidst peals of laughter. "You are such a lousy liar!" Zoe said, tickling Eva who eventually held up her hands in surrender.

"Uncle!" Eva said, tears running down her face. She grinned up at Zoe, who was sitting on top of her. "Got you going there, huh?"

"That wasn't nice, Miss Eva," Zoe gently rebuked her lover.

"I know," Eva admitted. "I'm sorry I teased you."

"So which part was true?"

Eva grinned. "The kissing, the marriage proposal..."

"And the back problem," Zoe added.

"I thought I would slip that in and hope you didn't notice it," Eva said.

"Hmm, what did you do?"

"Picked up a box to take to the pallet and it was a little heavy," Eva confessed. "It was just a twinge."

"Right." Zoe gave Eva a look that said she did not quite believe that.

"Earl showed me a trick he learned from when he was a POW."

"Earl was a prisoner of war? Wow."

"Japanese," Eva added. "He massaged my back and then the pain was gone."

"Don't you mean the twinge in your back was gone?" Zoe tweaked Eva's dimpled chin.

Eva chuckled. "Yes, the twinge was gone. Anyway, while he was doing that he asked me to kiss him and said that he would explain."

"Very odd man."

"While he was kissing me, Mr. Peabody, Mr. Stalk, and Mrs. Higgins walked in and found us," Eva continued, smiling at Zoe's reaction.

"So does that mean they're going to sack you?" Zoe asked eagerly.

"No, sorry, you don't get your wish," Eva said.

"Rats." Zoe sighed.

"They told us to get back to work and left."

"And then what happened?"

Eva's beautiful face sobered a bit before she continued. She looked directly into Zoe's eyes. "Earl is family," Eva told her.

"Earl is family?" Zoe asked, perplexed.

"He's a homosexual."

"Oh," Zoe nodded, frowning. "He must be a very confused homosexual if he's kissing you."

Eva put her arms around Zoe and laughed softly. "Oh, Zoe, you are priceless."

"Well, is he confused?"

"No," Eva stroked Zoe's face. "He was protecting himself — and us."

"And now *I'm* confused," Zoe admitted plaintively.

"If they find out that he's a homosexual, they will fire him," Eva explained. "He acts like the factory Lothario so people will think he's just after everything in a skirt."

"Oh, that must be horrible. But how did he know he could trust you?"

Eva smiled. "He caught us," Eva motioned to herself, then to Zoe, "kissing in the storeroom."

"Oh." Zoe's frown deepened. "So he is blackmailing you into doing this."

"No, no, no, Zoe, it's not like that. He said that when I first went for my interview at the factory, he played up to the role he had created for himself. Today he told me that he really likes me and he wasn't playing any games this time, and besides, it helps us as well. Now they think he and I are a couple."

"I don't want him hurting you, Evy," Zoe replied. "I'm not sure I like him."

"He doesn't want to hurt me, love."

"I don't know, Evy. How much can you trust him? You hardly know him."

"How did you know you could trust Elena?" Eva asked.

Zoe took a moment to think about that. Finally, she said, "I just felt like I had known her all my life."

Eva smiled. "That's how I feel about Earl. I've only known him for a few days, but I feel so comfortable around him. I consider him a friend."

Zoe looked surprised. "I have to get to know this Earl much better since he's now family," she said, very aware of Eva's shyness with people she did not know. Anyone who had managed to get through her partner's shy exterior was a person that Zoe wanted to know better, even if he did dole out confusing kisses. She would have a chat with him about that very soon.

"You will," Eva replied. "He's coming for dinner shortly."

"Ah!" Zoe looked at the extra place setting. "So that's our mystery guest."

"You don't mind, do you?" Eva asked a little belatedly.

"No, I have to meet the man who wants to marry you," Zoe replied. "You really think we can trust him?"

"Yes, love, I do. I think he has a lot to lose by trusting me."

"You'd never betray a trust."

"He doesn't know that," Eva replied. "He reminds me of my childhood friend, Willy."

"Is that why you like him?"

"No, not just that," Eva said. Her brow furrowed. "I feel safe when I talk to him; he..." Eva hesitated for a moment, her gaze cast down to her hands. It was clear that she was having difficulty expressing her thoughts. "He was a POW and went through hell."

"Did you tell him...?"

"No," Eva shook her head. "But I think he figured it out. I don't know how but he did."

"Then you do have something in common with him," Zoe said, holding Eva's hand. "That's why Elena and I are friends; we both lost our families and we know how the other feels."

Eva smiled in response. "Yes, something like that."

"I've never really asked you if you minded that Elena is my second best friend," Zoe said.

"I don't mind," Eva said. "So, who is your first best friend? Do I know her?" she teased.

"Not sure. She's tall, has a gorgeous figure, dazzling blue eyes, a beautiful soul, and answers to Eva Muller. Now do you think you know her?"

Eva did not reply but gently touched Zoe's face and pressed her lips to Zoe's mouth. The soft kiss intensified, becoming passionate. Zoe moaned in pleasure, which encouraged Eva to become a little more aggressive. They were both breathless when they parted.

"Oh my, yes, you do." Zoe fanned herself after they broke away from each other. "What were we talking about?"

Eva brought Zoe to her for a quick hug. "I'm going to change," she said, moving to her bedroom. "Earl should be here any minute." A few minutes later she re-emerged, dressed in a casual outfit. Zoe gave her partner a bright smile.

"I promise to be polite to your boyfriend," Zoe said seriously, causing Eva's blue eyes to widen.

A knock on the door alerted them that their dinner guest had arrived. Zoe crossed the room and opened the front door to find Earl standing outside, flowers in one hand and a bottle of wine in the other. He wore a dark blue suit with a matching tie; a fedora hat was pulled down over his eyes.

"Flowers for the lady of the house," he said, thrusting the bouquet at Zoe. "And booze for the other sheila," he quipped, giving the wine to Eva.

Earl took off his hat and held it in his hands. He was obviously feeling a little shy with Zoe staring at him. "Should I be scared?" he asked Eva, who had stepped back and leaned a hip against the sofa.

"I'd be protecting your knees..." Eva said.

"It's not my knees I'm worried about," Earl said, and put his hat in front of him at groin level. That garnered a very tiny smile from Zoe, who was doing her level best to remain serious.

"Hello again." Zoe shook Earl's hand. After she pulled him into the apartment and shut the door, she stopped the man with an imperious look. "Stay right where you are," she instructed. Zoe walked away and came back a moment later, carrying one of the dining room chairs.

"Is there a whip around here, too?" Earl asked, his expression betraying his worry.

"In the bedroom," Eva said and indicated the room with a gesture.

Zoe smirked at the comment. She positioned her chair and climbed up on it, which made her a little taller than Earl's six-foot-four.

"So, you kissed my Eva," Zoe said, crossing her arms and giving him a stern look.

Earl looked around Zoe to glance at Eva, who had sat down on the edge of the sofa. Eva held up her hands and shrugged. He turned his attention back to the woman in front of him. "Yes." Earl nodded. "And it was *very* good," he added. "She's not a bad kisser."

"She's the best," Zoe said with a forced scowl. She was still slightly annoyed that the man in front of her had kissed her partner. She knew why it was done but doubts still niggled at her. For Eva's sake she decided to try and like the man. Her father used to say that humor covered up many transgressions or something equally profound. Zoe could not quite remember, but she was certain the sentiment was good. "So what are your plans for my Eva?" Zoe demanded, becoming serious again.

"Well, I have to survive meeting her jealous lover. Have you seen her?"

Eva guffawed from the sofa, clearly enjoying the scene as Zoe and Earl exchanged light-hearted banter as though they had known one another for years.

"Eva tells me that you have plans to marry her," Zoe said, continuing her interrogation.

"Want to be a bridesmaid?" Earl asked, giving her what he clearly considered to be his best hopeful expression.

"Great idea!" Zoe agreed, and they all started to laugh. "Welcome to the family, Mr. Wiggins." She held out a hand and Earl took it into both of his.

"You can call me Wiggy."

"And you can call me..."

"Stretch," Earl said, giving Zoe a friendly nickname as he scooped the petite woman up and carried her to where Eva had fallen over on the sofa, laughing. Zoe let out a yelp and protested until she was put down on the sofa where she collapsed next to Eva.

Chapter Eight

Oh, how Eva hated the graveyard shift! Six weeks on the job and half her time had been spent working from ten at night until six in the morning. The only good thing about it was that it was cooler inside the factory at night, but not by much. As a result of the nighttime hours, Eva's internal clock went haywire, causing Zoe to stay awake at odd times too. It was always bedlam whenever Eva switched to working nights.

Earl passed Eva and blew her a kiss. Eva smiled shyly and continued to work, listening to her co-workers joke about her "boyfriend".

So much had happened in the past few weeks. Earl kissing Eva in the storeroom had become legend and cemented Earl's reputation as the factory's "lover boy". Eva had found that she got a lot of jealous stares from some of the women, but she and Earl had become fast friends. They shared long chats about their lives and their experiences, and Earl had dinner with her and Zoe more and more often.

Eva smiled, putting another packet of biscuits in the box. One of the subjects that she, Zoe, and Earl had explored was Zoe's wish to go to the university and study art. Not wanting to take advantage of their budding friendship, Zoe had been reluctant to ask Earl to help her with the entrance exam. Eva had mentioned the situation to Earl in passing. A few evenings later, Earl had shown up with a stack of textbooks. He told Zoe it was settled; he was helping her. Zoe was ecstatic and, between Earl's tutoring and Eva's patient help, she was making great progress. Her English was improving by talking to their new friend, and also because Eva had convinced her to speak English instead of Greek at home. *At least until she passes her exams*, Eva thought.

"Hey, Muzza." Earl tapped Eva on the head as he passed.

"Wiggy," Eva replied, accepting a kiss on the cheek.

"There's someone waiting outside for you," Earl whispered in her ear.

"Oh, don't tell me…" Eva shook her head and looked out of the window. Opposite the main entrance to the factory was a small brick wall. Sitting on top of the wall was a diminutive figure wrapped up against the weather. "I told her not to."

"Uh huh."

"She's got a cold," Eva told him, watching Zoe with some annoyance. "She's already had to take two sick days from her job at the restaurant." She continued staring out of the window. "Zoe, will you *ever* listen to me?"

"Apparently not." Earl gave Eva a wave, took his timecard and punched out.

"Apparently not," Eva repeated to herself, shaking her head over Zoe's stubbornness.

Earl buttoned his jacket and lifted the collar to keep his neck warm as he walked outside into the early morning cold. A light rain fell as the city began to come to life.

"I hate the night shift," Earl muttered. He wanted to wait to see Eva off, so he made his way to the brick wall. Usually at that time of the morning the entrance area was deserted. Earl decided to have some fun with Zoe, and went over to where the young woman was perched. He could not make out her face. All he could see was two legs, two arms, and a bomber jacket. The beanie on her head almost covered her face completely. He smiled at the sight.

Earl had found himself feeling very protective of both women, but in particular of Eva. He had soon discovered Zoe had an underlying steel resolve, despite her slight frame and her youth.

"G'day. Are you waiting for anyone?" Earl asked, pretending Zoe was a stranger.

She nodded.

"It's cold, huh?"

She nodded again.

"You must be freezing out here."

"Oh, yeah, it is rather chilly," Zoe said, deepening her voice to artificial gruffness in an attempt to disguise it from Earl.

The fact she attempted the disguise was something Earl found rather humorous. He forced himself not to guffaw. "Who are you waiting for?" Earl asked.

Zoe lifted the beanie and exposed her face. She gave the big man an impish grin. "It's me, Wiggy."

"I know, Stretch." Earl laughed, using her new nickname. "Eva's punching out in a few minutes."

"Oh, gud." Zoe sniffled, took out a handkerchief and blew her nose loudly.

"Oh, that's nice." Earl ruffled her hair. "You're in big trouble, missy. You shouldn't be out here."

"Where do you want me to be?"

"In bed," Earl replied seriously. "Eva's not very happy with you."

"I'll go to bed." Zoe winked at Earl before her glance fell on the woman who had just exited the factory door. Earl followed Zoe's gaze. "Here I thought you were waiting for me," Earl teased. "I think both of you should go to bed."

Zoe lifted her beanie and stared, open mouthed at Earl. It took a few moments for Earl to realize what he had said. "I didn't mean that. Eva looks as tired as I feel, so I figure..." Earl stopped as soon as Eva reached them.

Earl kissed Eva on the cheek. He then bent down and kissed the top of Zoe's head.

"Hey." Eva ruffled Zoe's hair. "What did I tell you last night?"

"You loved me," Zoe's mucus-muffled reply came back.

Eva sighed. "Come on, let's go."

"Can we go to the park later?" Zoe asked.

"Only if you're good and stay in bed for the morning," Eva replied, getting a snort from her partner.

"That's what Earl suggested," Zoe said and looked innocently at Earl.

"Know what I think? I think I should drive you both home before Zoe's cold gets worse," Earl said as he noticed their supervisor exit the building. He moved in between the two women and put his arm around Eva's shoulders. "Let's go," he said. The trio strolled down the alleyway to Earl's car.

It was close to five o'clock in the afternoon. That morning, the clouds had parted to reveal another beautiful day, but the two women had been oblivious to it as they both fell into bed. They woke to find gorgeous sunshine streaming through the window.

They decided upon a picnic at their favorite spot as the order of the afternoon. Zoe's cold had been proclaimed much better, and now she was sprawled on the grass on a hilltop overlooking the harbor, her sketchpad open in front of her. She brushed away yet another fly buzzing around her head and sighed. Flies. She hated flies, and she had quickly discovered that Australia had lots of them. Zoe surmised that Australia was the fly capital of the world and had soon perfected what the Aussies called the "Great Australian Salute", which was the hand motion of shooing flies away from the face while carrying on with normal activity. After a while the action became second nature to Zoe and she did not consciously think about it very much.

The flies did not bother Eva, who was sitting in her chair, face to the sky, with her eyes closed. Her long legs were spread out in front of her and she had her head tilted back to catch the final rays of the setting sun. Zoe grinned as she noticed that Eva's skin had become bronzed. Zoe had more difficulty in getting a tan; her fair complexion easily burned a lobster red by the sun, a look she did not particularly like. She sighed again and glanced up at the sky where soft, fluffy clouds drifted lazily by.

She loved this vantage point because it gave her an unrestricted view of the beautiful harbor. They had found the site when they were strolling one day, and both women promptly fell in love with the hilltop. Zoe considered it their "special place". Although Eva had pointed out the Municipal Council signs prominently displayed around the place, it had not stopped Zoe from claiming it. They regularly had picnics at the lookout, as they were doing now.

Eva, her dark hair neatly combed back, got out of her chair and sat cross-legged beside Zoe on the cool grass and asked her about the envelope tucked into the sketchpad. Zoe took out the requested envelope, having tucked it there as they had left their apartment earlier.

"Have you already read this?" Zoe asked, pointing to the envelope as she turned her head to see Eva.

"No, not yet," Eva replied. "I was waiting for you to wake up so we could read it together." Zoe's grin reappeared. Eva had gotten out of bed and prepared breakfast, which despite Zoe's illness, had been well received. Afterwards, the postman had delivered letters, one of which was from Greece in their friend Thanasi's familiar handwriting.

"Oh, that's sweet. No wonder I love you," Zoe replied and leaned forward to kiss Eva before returning to her place on the grass.

"I knew there had to be a reason," Eva said, grinning. "Are you going to read it or just stare at it?"

"Alright, hang on." Zoe opened the envelope, laid the letter flat on the sketchpad in front of her, and began to read it aloud.

> *My dear sisters, I hope this letter finds you well and happy. I want to thank you for the food package you sent over to me. Some of it was quite tasty. I do have a question about one thing you sent; this jar of Vegemite. Am I supposed to eat it or use it to grease my truck? I tried it, but I think you left out the instructions on how to use it on my truck. I did anyway and the truck goes really well now! Ha, ha, ha.*

They both burst out laughing. Zoe could imagine the look on their friend's face when he had tried the Vegemite. She had learned to love the spread, which was really a yeast extract, while in Egypt. Zoe enjoyed the salty flavor, but Eva could not stomach the taste and was horrified every time Zoe spread the black substance on her toast. When they had both stopped chuckling over Thanasi's new-found truck grease, Zoe went back to the letter.

> *Despina sends her love and tells me to let you know she misses both of you and wishes you all the happiness in the world. Paul wanted to know if you ride kangaroos. Well, do you? Everyone wishes you the best in The Land of Milk and Honey.*
>
> *The news from here is not that good. Greece has descended into anarchy. We've had the Turks, the Italians, and the krauts, and now we are our own worst enemies. Brother is fighting brother. I don't know what this country will become, but at the moment Greek blood is being spilt by our own countrymen. I am so glad I listened to Father Haralambos and got you out of here. I'm quite sure Zoe would have found even more trouble to get into, Eva.*
>
> *I am well. I was wounded in the leg the other day, but I'm still going strong although hobbling a bit. Dion was killed in the fighting. He was a very*

brave boy. The monarchists killed the little man. When is this madness going to end? Petracles was captured but we got him back, a little worse for wear than when we lost him, but he is a strong boy and he will come through.

I will leave you now, and again I want to thank you for the parcel, but please, next time no more Vegemite. If I have trouble with the truck, I may use it again. May God bless you, my sisters, and know I am thinking of you every day. One day I will emigrate to The Land of Milk and Honey and be with you, but my place for now is here, fighting for my homeland.

Love, Thanasi.

The women sat in silence. Zoe's thoughts and prayers went out to the man they both considered a brother. Athanasios Klaras had been with the Greek Community Party (known as the KKE), functioning as the leader of the communist resistance cell. Their friendship with him had been born from their mutual love for the village priest, Father Haralambos. The cleric's death had bound them together and allowed that friendship to grow.

"We'll go to church tomorrow and light a candle for Dion," Eva said quietly.

"Oh, I almost forgot. The letter from the Immigration Department also came today." Zoe held out another letter.

Eva took the envelope, not opening it, just staring at it with a sort of fascinated horror, as though she expected it to bite her.

"Evy, I know you've been waiting to get this letter; shouldn't you open it?" Zoe prompted.

"I will," Eva said and turned the envelope over, staring at the flap on the back.

"Father H would be so proud." Zoe took the letter out of Eva's hands. "Do you want me to open it?"

"No...I mean yes."

Zoe suppressed the urge to tease her partner and simply tore the envelope open. She removed the letter without reading it and gave it back to Eva. Zoe watched her lover's face, trying to discern whether the news was good or bad.

"What did they say?" Zoe asked impatiently.

"I need to go for an interview," Eva said as she scanned the letter. "They want identification and a picture of me for my new passport."

Good news! Zoe flashed a wide smile and rolled onto her side to hold Eva as they laughed together at the good news. "Father H would have loved that," Zoe said and proceeded to tickle Eva until she squealed and fought against Zoe's hands, trying to tickle Zoe back at the same time.

Their playfulness ended with both of them sprawled on the grass. Eva sighed and took a quick look at her watch. "Zoe, I need to get going, and you need to get inside. The night air won't be good for you."

"I know," Zoe answered ruefully.

They packed away the picnic basket. While Zoe was folding the blanket, Eva stood and looked around, causing Zoe to stop. "What's the matter?" she asked.

"I feel like someone's watching us," Eva said. She glanced around even more studiously. The picnic area was surrounded by shrubs and the area was quiet. "It's odd."

"Hmm." Zoe could not see anything.

Eva's apprehension was obvious as they walked away from the picnic area. Occasionally, her suspicious gaze would dart here and there. "I used to get this same feeling back in Austria," Eva said aloud.

"Was someone following you?" Zoe asked, keeping pace with Eva up the small hill.

"Yes," Eva replied. "My uncle had someone follow me all the time. I guess it was to keep me safe."

There was an edge of sarcasm in her tone as she emphasized those three words which told Zoe that the guards' function had been anything but safeguarding Eva.

"And it was the same feeling?" Zoe persisted.

"The same."

Zoe did a complete turn as she tried in vain to ascertain what the problem was. She did not see anything out of the ordinary. A woman with a baby stroller was slowly making her way up the road, children were playing street cricket. It was quiet and nothing seemed out of the ordinary. "Maybe you're tired from working nights," she said.

Eva sighed. "It might be that."

They fell silent and were still quiet as they entered their apartment block. Zoe saw Eva look back again. It was clear that her partner was unable to shake the feeling that they were being watched.

"You really think someone is watching us?" Zoe asked.

"Yes," Eva nodded as she entered their building. Zoe took a final look around, shrugged and joined Eva inside.

Two days later, Eva was singing as she got out of the shower. After wrapping one towel around her body and another towel around her head like a turban, Eva entered the bedroom still singing, and found Zoe stretched out on the bed, smiling up at her.

"Are you going to get dressed for church or go naked?" Eva broke off her song to ask.

Zoe did not reply. Instead, she got out of bed and pulled Eva's towel off her body.

"You like the view?" Eva asked.

"Oh, yes, very nice."

"You have way too much energy, young lady," Eva replied. She did not move when Zoe wrapped herself around her waist.

"Are you complaining?"

"Me? Noooo." Eva drew the vowels out in an exaggerated drawl. "But we do have to get dressed, because we will be late for church."

"If I must," Zoe sighed. She stole a quick kiss from Eva before leaving the room to go to her own wardrobe, which was in the other bedroom.

Eva watched her naked partner leave and shook her head. She turned to her reflection. "She is so damned gorgeous," Eva said aloud. She started to get dressed and was soon joined by Zoe, who was now attired suitably for church.

Zoe perched on the bed and watched her. "How is it that I can get dressed quickly and you take forever?" she asked.

"There's less of you to dress," Eva quipped, easily ducking the pillow thrown at her. "Hey, watch the hair," she said, chuckling. Eva chose a light yellow shirt and was about to button it but was stopped by Zoe.

"Let me," Zoe whispered and slowly began to button the shirt. She stopped just below the collar and pulled the fabric back to reveal a small scar on Eva's shoulder. "Does that still hurt?" she asked as she used her fingertip to trace the scar left by the bullet that had nearly killed Eva. She gently brushed her lips against it.

"Sometimes, when the weather changes," Eva replied, holding the smaller woman. Eva was all too aware of how close each had come to losing the other, and she saw that knowledge reflected in Zoe's steady gaze. She leaned down and kissed Zoe, putting every bit of the love and tenderness she felt into the kiss.

A knock on the door interrupted any further romantic thoughts. Zoe let out a frustrated groan, reluctantly letting go of Eva and flopping down on the bed. Eva grinned at her as she finished dressing, then walked out of the bedroom to answer the door.

Elena was standing in the corridor with a large bowl in her hand.

"Your timing is really lousy," Eva said, motioning for the woman to enter.

"Yeah? Why?"

"Zoe was teaching me how to cook." Eva walked into the lounge, chuckling.

"Did I hear my name?" Zoe asked, coming out and closing the bedroom door behind her.

"You were teaching Eva how to cook?"

"Cook? Eva can't cook to save her life," a bemused Zoe replied, her brow crinkled in obvious thought. Eva recognized the expression that crossed Zoe's face when understanding dawned, and she grinned. Zoe started to laugh.

"What's funny?" Elena asked.

"Nothing," Zoe said quickly. "What's that?"

Elena put the bowl down. "I bring gifts!" She flipped off a tea towel covering the dish to reveal coconut balls.

"Beware Greeks bearing gifts," Zoe murmured. She snatched a couple of the small balls and sat down at one end of the sofa.

"Yeah, but I'm not Greek, Zoe," Elena replied, slouching down next to her friend.

"Honorary Greek," Eva replied and turned to the door again when another knock resounded through the room. "We are popular this morning." Eva crossed to the door, opening it wide. A man stood there, his cane in one hand and his overcoat neatly slung over his other arm. A smattering of black was scattered through his white hair. His clear blue eyes sparkled with a hint of mischief. He was clean-shaven and wore a smart suit. Eva did not recognize him and thought he must be a salesman. "Zoe, it's for you," she said as she turned away from the open door. Eva always let the younger woman handle salesmen, knowing they would never return once Zoe finished with them.

"Aren't you going to invite your father into your home?" the man said.

Shocked, Eva stood stock-still, then very slowly turned back around. She knew that voice. Out of the corner of her eye, she saw Zoe rise from her seat on the sofa.

"Fa-Father H?" Zoe was the first to speak. Eva was rooted to the spot, unable to move.

The man smiled broadly and winked. "What does a man have to do to get a kiss from his daughters?"

Zoe squealed, ran over and jumped into Father Haralambos' arms, nearly bowling him over. Eva hung back, not fully believing that the man standing in front of her was indeed her father — a father she had thought was lost forever. Zoe hugged and kissed the big man on the cheek while Eva continued to hesitate.

"You're going to kill me with kindness!" Panayiotis cried, laughing as he was almost dragged through the doorway and into the lounge by an exuberant Zoe.

Zoe looked back at Eva, her grin showing her sympathy for the situation. She caught Elena's attention. "Okay, Elena, my dear, I think this is the perfect moment to go into the kitchen with me and tell me how you made those coconut thingies." She took Elena by the arm and steered her into the kitchen, closing the door and giving Eva and Panayiotis some much-needed privacy.

Father and daughter stood for a moment looking at each other. Tears ran down Eva's face as she closed the space between them and melted into her father's embrace.

"I'm not dreaming this, am I?" Eva whispered, hoping that she was awake. "Please tell me I'm not."

"No, you're not dreaming," her very-much-alive father replied hoarsely, his voice breaking. He held Eva in his arms, wrapping his arms around her and squeezing her tightly.

Eva looked at the clean-shaven man, tears streaming down her face. "I can't believe you're here. You're really here."

"I'm really here." Panayiotis looked at Eva and tenderly kissed her on the cheek. "I prayed to God to help me through and to find you; He listened. I love you, my child,"

Panayiotis said, holding the sobbing Eva close. "Here, let me look at you." He held Eva at arm's length. "You're a bit skinny; is Zoe not feeding you?"

Eva laughed through her tears and brushed some of the wetness away. "I thought you were dead," she said, her voice breaking as emotion overwhelmed her once more. "I prayed so hard that somehow you would have been able to survive."

"God was looking out for me, my child. And He was watching out for you and Zoe. Just like I asked Him," Panayiotis said and kissed her on the forehead. "Can we sit down?" he asked, gingerly making his way to the couch. He stretched out his bad leg, which was a reminder of the train crash that many believed had killed him. Eva sat beside him on the couch, still not believing her eyes. Her father was sitting in her lounge room. Alive!

"You don't believe it, eh?" he said, his eyes sparkling with happiness.

"D-d-does Thanasi know? He didn't say anything about it in his last letter. You went back to Greece? How did you escape? Were you on the train when it blew?"

"One thing at a time!" Panayiotis put his hands up at the volley of questions. "Before I answer, tell me about yourself." He hugged Eva's still-trembling shoulders. "Are you happy, my child?" he asked.

She looked down at her hands, which were entwined with her father's. "Well, I don't like the heat and the people are sometimes very strange." She looked into her father's eyes and a beatific smile lit up her face. "But yes, Father, I'm very happy!" She lifted her arms to encircle his neck and placed a kiss on his cheek, then rested her head on his shoulder with a contented sigh. "Having you here makes me even happier."

"That's all that matters," he said. Panayiotis stroked her head, running his fingers through her hair, which had been cut into a bob that gently framed her face. "I like your hair cut short. It suits you. Your mother had her hair like that," he said, smiling.

"Do you really like it?" Eva asked and ran her hand through her short hair.

"You look so much like your mother," Panayiotis whispered and tenderly stroked her cheek. "The last time I saw Daphne, she had her hair the way you have it now. I thought she was the most beautiful woman. Now I have a beautiful daughter."

Eva took her father's hands and kissed them. "I can't believe you are here."

"Oh ye of little faith," Panayiotis joked. "Now, do you think you can call Zoe back in from the kitchen, so I can greet my other daughter properly?"

Eva wiped away her remaining tears, then cupped her father's face in both her hands and gave him a loving look. "Zoe, get out here!" she called. Zoe and Elena came out of the kitchen; Zoe was carrying a plate full of cheese, olives, and bread.

The former cleric took a moment, a smile creased his face, and he started to laugh and slapped his thighs in joy. Eva started to laugh herself at Zoe's joke. The German occupation of Larissa had been brutal and many families were left starving whilst the Germans ate quite well. Cheese, olives, and bread were the staple diet for many Greeks. Zoe had often joked that she was never going to eat them again if she survived the war.

"Ah, my little Zoe, you remembered!" Panayiotis clapped his hands. "Come here, little one."

Zoe put the plate down and melted into the man's arms. Eva could not believe the sight before her. Zoe was now sobbing against him. Eva caught her father's eye and he winked.

"My little Zoe," Panayiotis repeated and kissed Zoe on the forehead. "I missed you so much."

"I love you, Father H," Zoe replied and looked up at him. "I'm so happy you're not dead."

"So am I," Panayiotis said dryly.

After a long moment, Panayiotis opened his arms and both women hugged him. "So, my daughters, are you going to introduce me to your friend here?" he said.

"Hello. Since these two are quite rude," Elena joked and her smile broadened at the sheepish looks both women were giving her, "I'll introduce myself. My name is Elena Mannheim," she said, extending her hand and grinning.

Panayiotis took Elena's hand in his own. "Pleased to meet you, Elena. You may have guessed that I'm Eva's father."

"Would not have guessed that at all." Elena shook her head and put her arm around Zoe. "Mr. Haralambos, I think I'd better leave you with your girls." Elena smiled at the man, giving him a little wave as she was led out by Zoe. The corridor light bulb flickered on and off as Zoe closed the door, leaving Panayiotis and Eva together in the lounge.

"Thanks for the coconut thingies, El," Zoe said.

"You know, Zoe, I would say that you two are very lucky." Elena smiled sadly. "I'm a little jealous."

Zoe gave the other woman a hug. "If I could wish you anything, El, it would be to see your family again."

"I know, my friend, I know." Elena wiped her eyes. "I would give anything in this world to see my family again."

"You can share him with us if you like," Zoe offered. "I love this man so much. He took care of me after my mother died. He was there for me even though I gave him so much trouble..."

"Trouble? You?" Elena teased. "I don't believe it."

"Ha ha." Zoe bumped her friend with her hip. "I love him so much."

"Father H? Is he a priest?"

"Yes, a priest; it's a very long story which I'll tell you tomorrow."

"Does everything with you two have to be different?" Elena wiped her eyes. "Are we still going out tomorrow?" she asked, referring to their usual weekly excursion to Farmer's department store in the city.

Zoe had discovered that she and Elena both loved to shop; they spent many hours window-shopping. It had brought them closer together in a strange kind of way. To their mutual amusement, the two young women had also discovered that Eva passionately hated shopping.

"I would love to but not in the morning," Zoe said. "Can we go in the afternoon? I want to spend some time with Father H tomorrow."

Elena nodded. "Of course. I didn't think you would just abandon him and go shopping right away."

"Thank you. Are you sure you don't want to stay? Get to know Father H a little bit?"

Elena took Zoe's arm and held it. "I think this is a special time for the both of you. You'll tell me all about it tomorrow," she said and gave Zoe a kiss on the cheek before walking away, heading towards her own apartment.

Zoe watched her friend leave and sighed. She opened her apartment door and went inside where she found Eva nestled in her father's embrace. Eva had her eyes closed and a look of pure contentment on her face. Her expression made Zoe feel warm inside and she sighed again, this time in happiness that the two people she loved most in the world were here, safe and together at last.

"Ah, Zoe, come sit." Panayiotis tapped the seat beside him. Eva made room for Zoe to sit between her and her father.

"So, Father H, what happened with the train?" Zoe asked, choosing the most obvious question first.

"Ah, the train. Well, we left the station and I'm not sure how long we traveled, and then I heard an explosion and that was it. I don't remember much of it. I woke up in a tent with people speaking bad Greek." Panayiotis laughed. "*Very* bad Greek. It wasn't until a few days later that I realized it was the Americans. I asked them to forward a note to you."

"We didn't get a note," Eva replied, looking at Zoe, who shook her head.

"Oh! I gave the note to the young medic and he told me he was going to send it on. I guess they had more pressing matters than playing postman."

"Eva was hurt too," Zoe said, taking her partner's hand. "Muller tried to kill her."

"What happened?" Panayiotis asked. Concerned, he glanced to Eva, then to Zoe.

"Reinhardt found out about us and Muller ordered him to kill me. He would have succeeded if Zoe hadn't appeared with half the Resistance," Eva said, smiling proudly at Zoe. "Reinhardt shot me."

Panayiotis exclaimed, "Oh, my dear child! Are you all right now?"

"Perfect," Eva replied and took Zoe's hand. "I've got Zoe and now I have you."

"So what happened after you woke up? Why didn't you come and find us?" Zoe asked, wanting to know how the priest had managed to stay alive.

"I got moved to a hospital ship. I didn't know about it until I woke up again. That's when I met my angel."

"You died?" Eva asked, alarm evident in the rising tone of her voice.

Panayiotis laughed. "No, I met Ally. She was my nurse, Alberta Fisherman." He looked at Zoe's expectant face and grinned. "My wife."

Eva and Zoe looked at each other and then back at their father. "Your wife?" Zoe asked, not quite believing what she had heard. Greek Orthodox priests did not marry. "You're married?" She shook her head, certain that she had heard incorrectly.

Eva was too surprised to respond. She tried to say something but a squeak was all that came from her mouth, so she decided to be quiet and wait for the initial surprise to subside.

"Yes, I fell in love with her," Panayiotis said. "She is my angel."

"Where is she?" Eva exclaimed, once she had command of herself again. She was overjoyed that her father had found happiness, but the way in which he had done so was very unexpected. Eva was shocked, as she had never thought he would leave the priesthood. "Is she Greek?"

"No. She's an American, but she speaks fluent Greek, German, and Spanish. She's at the hotel. She wanted me to come alone today and surprise you," Panayiotis replied. "I was quite nervous about coming over, you see, and she thought I ought to have some time alone with my beautiful daughters."

"You should have brought her with you!" Zoe gave him a ferociously mock scowl. Panayiotis' laughter reverberated around the tiny apartment.

"Why didn't you come back to Larissa?" Eva asked.

"The war in Greece was heating up and the Americans wanted the hospital ship out of harm's way, so we sailed away. I thought you would have got my note," he added, looking annoyed. "I'm so sorry that they didn't tell you. I thought you knew. I married Alberta when we arrived in America, and we made our home there. When you didn't reply to my letter, I didn't know if you were still alive. I hoped you had gone back to Germany because I didn't want to think the other option, that you…"

"You thought I had died," Eva whispered, her heart clenching in empathy at the agony her father must have suffered.

"Yes, I waited every day to hear from you. Every time they passed out the mail and I didn't get anything from you, I thought I had lost you again." He swallowed hard. "I cried like a baby. I lost hope that you were still alive and I damned Muller to hell. I know I should have prayed for him, but he took my little girl and I wasn't ready to forgive…or forget."

"Oh, Father," Eva said, kissing him. "I'm so sorry. I was in an American hospital unit in Larissa until I was well enough to travel. Then we went to Egypt because you told Thanasi to take us away. We spent a year in Egypt before sailing to Australia."

"How did you know we were here?" Zoe asked.

"Thanasi told me."

"You saw Thanasi? When? He didn't say anything in his last letter!" Zoe said, her face alight with excitement.

"I asked him not to. We went back to Greece and we were in Athens. One day Alberta and I ran into a friend of his. You remember Constantine's younger brother, Alex?" Panayiotis paused to take a sip of tea. "I was going to the bakery to get those little cakes Ally loves so much and when I turned the corner, I bumped into Alex."

"Did he recognize you?" Eva asked.

"Not right away; I had shaved off my beard. I introduced myself and the poor boy nearly fell over."

"I'm sure he did," Zoe said and glanced at Eva.

"The best part was when he told me both of you were alive and living in Australia," he explained. "He told me you were living in 'The Land of Milk and Honey'. As you know, the civil war is still going on in Greece, but we managed to get a message to Thanasi. He wrote back and gave me your address."

"That little sneak!" Zoe added. "Next letter, I'm going to give him a piece of my mind for keeping the news to himself."

"Go easy on him, Zoe. I asked him not to tell you. I wanted to surprise you both."

"You surprised us," Eva replied and put her hand over her heart. "Any more surprise and I think my heart would have stopped. So my stepmother is at a local hotel," Eva stated.

"Yes. She thought one shock was enough for the day. Since today is Sunday, I thought we might go to church together."

"We were about to leave when you arrived."

"I always had good timing," the former cleric smiled. "Tomorrow you will meet Ally."

"Where are you staying?"

"At the Grosenor Hotel. It's a nice little—"

"Father, I meant long term. Are you returning to America?"

"Ah, well, Allie and I have talked and we want to stay here in Australia. You are my family and God has blessed me by finding you. I want to spend whatever time God grants me close to you. As to specifically where, I'm not sure yet, but I'm sure we will find something close by."

"How about here?" Zoe glanced at Eva who smiled at the suggestion.

"With both of you?"

"Yes," Eva replied. "I can't have my father living in a hotel."

The former cleric gazed at his daughter for a moment. "Well, I would like that, but on the way here I spotted a To Rent sign outside this building—"

"Mrs. Olivet's apartment!" Zoe exclaimed. "The poor lady died last month!"

"Yes, Mrs. Jenkins did mention that."

"You spoke to Mrs. Jenkins?" Eva asked. She was surprised by her father's quick action.

"Indeed, she told me the apartment was available tomorrow. We don't have a lot of luggage and I believe it comes furnished."

Eva beamed at the news; something she wasn't expecting, to say the least, when she woke up that morning. "Tonight you're sleeping here. You can sleep in Zoe's room tonight."

"I can't wait to tell Alberta about all of this," he said and then stopped. "You have your own room?" he asked Zoe.

Zoe grinned. "Oh, yes."

"You're not together?" he asked, frowning.

"She's married, Father," Eva said, suppressing the laughter that was threatening to explode.

"What?" His eyebrows rose with his voice, and he half stood in surprise.

"Yep, see?" Zoe showed off her ring.

He took her hand. The simple band was on her ring finger and his frown deepened. He looked at the women in shock. "The last time I saw you, Eva, you confessed your love for Zoe. What happened? Did you change your mind?"

Eva began to feel a bit sorry for her father. She let her mouth stretch into a grin. "Yes, Zoe fell in love on the ship. She was asked and she said 'yes.'"

"Hey, I was in love long before then; I just got married on the ship. Seems it took *somebody* a long time to pluck up the courage to ask me!" Zoe said, teasingly.

"Where is he?" Panayiotis asked. It was apparent that he had decided to be supportive, no matter how bizarre the situation had become.

"Who?" Zoe asked, an innocent expression on her face.

"Your husband."

"Right here," Zoe replied, hugging Eva.

"I'm confused," Panayiotis complained.

Eva burst out laughing, as did Zoe.

"Gotcha!" Zoe exclaimed. "That will teach you to surprise us!" She hugged him. He blinked, then playfully swatted Zoe's behind, matching her mischievous look with his own.

"You always were a scamp," Panayiotis told her.

"I asked Zoe on the ship if she wanted to be with me for the rest of our lives and she said yes," Eva confessed, sitting down at her father's other side. She chose her words carefully, not wanting to use the word "married" in case her father found it unpleasant.

"'Be with you'?"

"Well, as you can see, I gave her a ring," Eva said a little shyly, "and I pledged my love to her."

"I see." Panayiotis nodded. "And did you say vows to each other?"

"Yes," Zoe answered.

"Are you living up to those vows?" he asked, his tone and expression serious.

"Yes," Eva replied. "You don't approve?" she asked, her happiness wavering suddenly. What if he did not approve? What if he insisted that she and Zoe be separated? A sick feeling spread outwards from her stomach, and she tried to quell her apprehension by remembering who he was — a father who loved her.

Panayiotis put an arm around her shoulders. "Do you remember what I said to you in Larissa, after you told me how you felt about each other?"

"You didn't care what the church said, you were going with your heart," Eva replied quietly.

"I know what the church says, but I lost you once before and I'm not going to lose you again," Panayiotis stated. "I don't understand it but if that is what you have chosen..."

"Does it make you love us less?" Zoe asked in some trepidation.

Panayiotis closed his eyes and shook his head. "My dear, dear, Zoe," he said, pulling her closer to him. "I can't love either of you less. It would mean denying my flesh and blood and that is something I vowed before God never to do."

"We love you so much," Zoe smiled. She leaned over and brushed away the tears that were falling down Eva's cheeks. "And I love your daughter very much," she told him.

"And to think, once you wanted to kill her." Panayiotis cupped Zoe's cheek in his palm. "You are a blessing to Eva," he said. The three of them huddled together. Panayiotis put his right hand over Eva's head, and with his left touched Zoe's head. "You have my blessing."

Eva and Zoe broke down and sobbed together as they hugged him. Having her father acknowledge her love for Zoe and approve of their relationship made everything that had happened to Eva in the past with Muller just melt away, the heartache and hurt dissolving in a flush of happiness. Her *real* father loved her unconditionally.

"Come on now, this isn't supposed to be about tears," Panayiotis said, gently rubbing Eva's back. "Let's get to the important part. I won't have any grandchildren?"

"Not unless Earl gets Eva pregnant, you won't," Zoe said, wiping her wet face with the heel of her hand.

"Who is Earl?" Panayiotis asked sharply. It was clear that Zoe's comment shook him.

"Eva's boyfriend," Zoe quipped, earning herself a swat on the arm from Eva.

Panayiotis' confusion was reflected by his puzzled frown. "You have a boyfriend?"

Drying her tears with a handkerchief, Eva said, "It's a long story, Father, but no, he's not my boyfriend. Not in that sense. He's a very dear friend to us, but that's all."

"I see." Panayiotis' expression relaxed in relief. "Does he know you two are...?"

"Lovers," Eva supplied.

"I was going to say 'married'," he said. "Vows are said when one is married, isn't that correct?"

"Yes." Eva smiled at him.

"Then if that is the case, you are married."

"Yes sir," Eva replied obediently. She looked at Zoe, who was grinning at her. "We are married," Eva said, and it was spoken as much to Zoe as to Panayiotis.

"All right then, does this Earl know you are married?"

"Yes, he does."

"Hmm, I have to meet this man," Panayiotis stated. "Now tell me all about life in Sydney."

Eva sat back and let Zoe fill her father in on what they had been doing since they had arrived in this new country. She smiled to herself and sighed contentedly.

Things were looking up at last.

Chapter Nine

"Father!"

The former cleric smiled at the exasperated cry from his daughter. "Yes?" he asked, knowing full well what had caused his daughter's outrage. Panayiotis sat at the dinner table with Eva seated to his right and Zoe to his left. Across the table sat Earl and Elena. He was certain that Eva had not mentioned her part in the war to her friends; Eva was reluctant to talk about herself and her past. He deduced that since Earl and Elena were very much aware of Eva's relationship with Zoe, then revealing a little about their past wasn't such a bad thing.

Panayiotis smiled at the glare he was getting from Eva. His morning surprise visit and going to church with Eva and Zoe, had led them to introduce him to their local priest, Father Gregorios.

Before long the two men were deep in conversation. Eva hadn't been surprised to find out that Father Gregorios offered him a job as the church's Psaltis or cantor. He had a good singing voice and he rather enjoyed that part of the service. It wasn't his old profession, but Panayiotis had resigned himself to the fact that he couldn't be a priest.

"Don't stop, sir, I'm enjoying this," Earl said. His quip was rewarded with one of Eva's glares. "You really are not scaring me," he said to Eva mockingly, eliciting a low growl from Eva which only made the young man laugh.

"Father..." Eva tried once more to stop her father from continuing with his tale.

"No." Panayiotis took his daughter's hand and held it. "I'm going to guess that Earl and Elena haven't heard how the two of you helped the resistance during the war."

"I haven't heard any stories," Elena said.

"I'm sure you haven't," Panayiotis went on. "My two daughters worked side by side, forging documents and delivering them to me."

"Who was the forger?" Earl asked, winking at Zoe.

"Eva," Zoe pointed at her partner. "She forged Muller's signature and I delivered the papers to Father H."

Elena smiled at Eva, who was looking down at the table self-consciously. "You helped Jews escape?"

"I did what I could do," Eva replied modestly and looked over at Elena with a shy smile.

"She did more than that, El, she saved some soldiers when they were hiding in Larissa..."

"Zoe..."

"Will you stop? These are our friends and they should know."

Elena reached out and touched Zoe's hand. "I'm such a busybody, I just want to know everything about my friends."

"We were lucky we didn't get caught."

"How did you forge Muller's signature?" Earl asked.

Eva played with the hem of the tablecloth for a moment before she looked up. "I sat in my room and practiced his signature. I would then burn the papers so no one could find them."

"I don't think I ever asked you how you could forge his signature so well," Zoe said, glancing at Eva.

"It took some practice, but I managed to fool everyone. I wasn't alone in helping the resistance. Zoe was the one who took the papers from me and delivered them to my father, which was actually more dangerous if she had been caught."

"How did you two meet?" Earl asked.

"Ah, that was my doing." Panayiotis pointed to himself proudly. "It wasn't easy to get these two together."

Eva turned to her father, a mock scowl on her face. "Now can we please talk about something else? Tell us about Alberta."

Panayiotis laughed at his daughter's attempt to deflect attention away from herself. "All right. What would you like to know?"

"How does a priest get married?" Zoe asked.

"You go to church, the priest marries you," he said, his grin broadening at the exasperated look he was getting from Zoe. He had seen that look many times and it never failed to make him smile. "I found myself falling in love."

"Is she pretty?" Zoe asked.

"She is very beautiful," Panayiotis replied. He took out his wallet and opened it to show them the photograph inside. "This is my Ally."

Eva took the black and white photograph and held it carefully. The woman in the photo was seated on a bench, looking at the camera with a wide smile. Her dark hair was up in a bun and she had a fan that she held to her chin. "She *is* beautiful," Eva said.

"She is indeed," her father said proudly. "She has auburn hair and hazel eyes."

Zoe spoke up. "So when are we going to meet her?"

"Soon," Panayiotis replied, ruffling Zoe's hair. "Now enough about me," he said, turning to Earl. "So, young man, tell me about yourself."

"The apple didn't fall far from that tree," Zoe quipped.

Earl flashed a charming grin. "Not much to tell, sir."

"There isn't?"

"No, sir," Earl replied.

"Hmm, so what is this I hear from my Eva that you want to marry her?"

Earl looked at Eva, who merely shrugged. "I...um," he stammered helplessly, frowning in puzzlement.

"You haven't asked me yet," Panayiotis said, feigning seriousness and scratching his ear. "You have to do that first."

"I do?"

"Yes, that is the Greek tradition."

Eva smirked and winked at the dumbfounded man. "Rules are rules."

"But I don't want to marry you," Earl told her with trepidation, obviously feeling that Eva had not explained their unique situation.

"You don't want to marry my Eva?" Panayiotis asked, scowling at him outwardly, but inwardly laughing at the young man's predicament.

"Uh, no sir," Earl said, sparing a quick look at Eva and then turning back to Panayiotis, who was hiding his glee.

"Hmm," he murmured and stroked his chin. He could see Eva was enjoying the little "interrogation", although Earl was looking a little alarmed. He liked the young man and could see why his daughters liked him. Earl was a decent young man who appeared to have won Eva's and Zoe's trust, a trust that wasn't easily given. "Do you want Zoe?"

Earl's frown turned into a crooked smile. "I don't think so! And now I know where Eva gets that evil streak," he said as everyone started to laugh.

"I don't have an evil streak," Eva protested.

"A mile wide and five miles deep," Zoe said cheekily as she got up from her seat and stood behind Eva's chair, flicking Eva's head with her fingers. Eva caught Zoe's hand and held it.

"Takes one to know one, eh, Zoe?" Panayiotis quipped before turning his attention back to Elena. "Zoe tells me you're an artist."

Elena smiled shyly at the compliment. "Not as good as Zoe."

"Don't be so modest," Zoe said as she went back to sit in her chair. "Don't believe her, Father H. She draws so beautifully."

"Is that so?" Panayiotis smiled. "And you are both studying to get into this art college?"

"Yes sir," Elena nodded. "Earl and Eva are helping us."

"That's very generous."

"I was a school teacher before the war," Earl replied. "I haven't taught in such a long time, but Zoe and Elena are great students."

"Ah, yes, the war." Panayiotis took a long, assessing look at the young man and decided not to pursue his next question about what Earl had done during the war. "You now work in the same factory as Eva?"

"Yes, sir."

"You are wasting your talents, young man." Panayiotis turned to his daughter. "You too," he added, pointing his finger at his daughter.

Eva shrugged. "For everything there is a season."

"Quoting Bible texts at me won't change my opinion," the former cleric said, ruffling his daughter's hair. Eva smiled, then caught his hand and kissed it.

Earl watched and after a moment, caught Zoe's attention. Zoe gave him a knowing smile.

"I keep telling her that," Zoe said, only to be on the receiving end of Eva's mock glare.

"Stubborn. You didn't get that from me," he added and chuckled anew when Zoe let out a peal of laughter and nearly fell off her chair. "You're going to hurt yourself," he warned Zoe.

"Can I ask you something?" Earl asked.

"Absolutely."

"How do you pronounce your surname?"

Eva smirked. "Getting into practice?"

Earl turned to Eva and rudely stuck out his tongue at her before turning back to Panayiotis, his attitude now earnest. The former cleric was a little perplexed by their antics, but he undertook to answer Earl's question.

"You break it up into two words; *hara* is one word and *lambos* is the other. *Hara* means happiness and *lambos* means..." He paused for a moment to find the right word in English. Alberta had worked hard to teach him, but he picked up the language a little more slowly than he wanted. He spoke to Alberta in English whenever he could but always reverted to Greek when he could not find the right word. After a moment's mental groping, he continued, "*Lambos* means a shining bright light."

Earl put his arm around Eva. "Muzza, you're going to get a new nickname."

"Muzza? I don't know what that word means." Perplexed, Panayiotis looked at Earl and then at his daughter for an explanation.

"The Australians have a nickname for everything, Father. I don't know how it works but he takes Muller and turns it into Muzza," Eva said.

"Very strange. Earl, why do you ask about my name?"

To his surprise, Eva answered the question; her unmistakable joy was infectious. "I know this news will make you as happy as it makes me. I've put in an application to have my surname changed to Haralambos."

Her father's smile widened until the muscles in his face protested. He opened his arms and gathered his daughter into his embrace. Eva kissed his cheek tenderly. "I wanted to honor your memory," she said.

"Thank you. You have greatly honored me," he whispered and returned her kiss, pressing his lips against her soft cheek. "When is this going to happen?"

"As soon as I'm interviewed by the Immigration Department," Eva replied. "I got the letter a couple of days ago."

"So you go from Muzza to Huzza," Earl guffawed.

"As much as I would like to sit and talk to you all, I need to get some sleep." Panayiotis pushed away from the table and got up from his seat, holding on to the back of the chair for support. His bad leg had started to ache and he hoped a good night's rest was going to be better than taking pain pills, which he hated. "Thank you for your company, Earl and Elena."

"Thank you, sir," Elena and Earl said in unison, smiling.

Panayiotis followed Eva into Zoe's bedroom. He was tired but happy that he had met his daughter's friends, and that both she and Zoe seemed to be thriving in the new life they had made together.

"What a nice man," Elena observed.

"He is the bravest man I know," Zoe replied. "He worked secretly, with Eva's help, to get Jews out of Larissa. Eva would supply the travel documents and he would smuggle them out somehow."

Earl whistled in amazement. "How many?"

"Don't know." Zoe shook her head. "Evy doesn't know because she didn't keep track but just did the paperwork and passed it on."

"It was safer that way," Eva said as she came back to the dinner table and stood behind Zoe, resting her hands on Zoe's shoulders. "If I got caught, I wouldn't give anything away."

"They didn't know that," Elena said. "You could have been killed."

Eva smiled sadly. "Yes, that's true," she said. Zoe gazed up at her. Eva continued, looking down and meeting Zoe's gaze, "We all could have been killed."

"You were in the Resistance too?" Earl asked Zoe. He did not seem surprised when she nodded.

"Zoe's mission was to kill me," Eva said matter-of-factly, and returned to her place at the table. "But I had ways of changing her mind," she observed, sitting down.

Further talk was curtailed as a knock on the door made Zoe jump up to answer the summons. She opened the door to find two men standing outside. One of the men was short with close-cropped brown hair and brown eyes. His black pin-striped suit looked quite severe for a young man. Adding to the look, he wore glasses with thick black frames. He held his brown briefcase in front of him like a shield. His partner was blond with green eyes, and was taller than his colleague. This man also wore a black suit but with a red tie.

"Hello. May we speak to Miss Muller?" the brown-haired man asked, smiling.

Zoe stood still for a long moment with her hand on the doorknob. She had never seen two salesmen come to the door together. "How do you know I'm not Miss Muller?"

The brown-haired man looked at his partner, then shifted his gaze back to Zoe. "We know you're not."

Zoe smiled. "How?"

"Look, Miss Lambros—"

"How do you know my name?" Zoe was taken aback at the recognition. She scowled at the two men. She knew salesmen's tricks, but this one was a little too much.

"Maybe we should introduce ourselves," the blond man murmured.

Zoe was on the verge of shutting the door in their faces when the brown-haired man said hastily, "My name is Friedrich Jacobs, and this is my partner David Harrison. We're from the Immigration Department."

Zoe's scowl turned into a delighted smile. "Oh, wow, that was quick," she told them. Over her shoulder, she called, "Evy, the Immigration people are here."

"On a Sunday?" Eva asked as she came up behind Zoe. "I thought I was supposed to come to you."

The men exchanged glances. "Well, we thought it would be best if we came today," Friedrich said.

"All right then," Eva shrugged. "I'm Eva Muller."

"Yes, we know," David replied. He smiled charmingly as they were led inside.

"I think I'd better get out of your hair," Elena whispered to Zoe. "The short one is cute," she added, low enough for only Zoe to hear. Zoe nudged her with an elbow before giving her a hug and walking her to the door. She came back just as the two men sat down in the lounge.

"This is my friend, Earl, and my sister, Zoe," Eva said.

"Pleased to meet you and your sister," David said, trying without success to hide a smirk. He caught Zoe staring at him and returned his attention to Eva.

Alarm bells began jangling in Zoe's mind. These men made her feel uneasy.

"I didn't think Immigration made house calls," Eva said as she sat down. "So what paperwork do you need to see?"

"Paperwork?" Friedrich asked.

"Aren't you here for the interview to change my surname?" Eva asked, clearly puzzled.

"No," Friedrich replied. He unlocked his briefcase, which was balanced on his knees. "We're here to talk to you about your father."

Eva glanced at Zoe, who smiled encouragingly at her. "We already know," Eva said.

"You do?" David asked, sounding puzzled himself. He glanced at Friedrich before turning back to Eva. "You know about your father?"

"Yes."

"I see. How do you know?"

"He's sleeping in the bedroo—" Eva did not have a chance to finish the sentence before both men jumped up and drew pistols from shoulder holsters concealed beneath their jackets. Eva took a step back when she saw the guns, her hands flying to her mouth. Before anyone in the room had a chance to react, David headed in the direction of the spare bedroom, the only closed door off the lounge, his partner at his heels.

Eva, Zoe, and Earl stood transfixed by shock for a moment before they followed the two strangers. Zoe was concerned for Panayiotis' safety. Were these men Nazi sympathizers who wanted to take revenge for the old man's Resistance work? Her heart pounded at the thought that they might harm Eva, too. Zoe was determined that would never happen, not as long as she drew breath.

"What are you doing?" Eva yelled at them.

"We have a warrant for your father's arrest," David said. "Didn't think it would be this easy," he added beneath his breath.

"You're here to arrest a priest?" Earl asked, in disbelief.

"He's not a priest. He's a war criminal," Friedrich replied. He nodded, holding his pistol in a two-handed grip. David drew back his leg and kicked in the door, putting his weight behind it. Unfortunately, the door was unlocked and the latch not engaged. Like a scene from a Laurel and Hardy film, the door banged open and David stumbled into the room, unable to regain his balance as momentum carried him forward. He fell across the bed, waking the older man. Zoe was hard-pressed not to laugh at David's predicament, and the disgusted expression on his face as he lay sprawled over and on top of the priest, although he had retained his grip on his gun and was aiming it at the older man.

"What is going on?" Panayiotis asked, his voice thunderous and his scowl impressive despite the fact that his hair was sleep-mussed and he was wearing a nightshirt.

"You're not Muller," David said. From his tone, Zoe surmised that the man was displeased. Then he began to snigger.

Friedrich sighed and shook his head. "I think we have made a mistake," he said and put his gun away, clearly feeling very foolish. Eva was staring open-mouthed at them. Zoe started laughing hysterically. The men had jumped to the wrong conclusion and they both looked stupid, their dignity hopelessly shattered. Panayiotis had sat up in bed and was staring at Friedrich and David, slowly shaking his head in disapproval.

"This is my father, Panayiotis Haralambos," Eva said. "I'm not quite sure who these men are, Father, but they say they are from the Immigration Department."

David slid off the bed. His face was red, and he was laughing loud enough to drown out Zoe's own hilarity.

"Well then. How about you leave me to sleep and you all can talk in the lounge without causing too much more fuss."

Zoe's eyebrows rose in astonishment as David passed her, still chuckling to himself. It had been such a comedy of errors that Zoe wondered if these men were truly agents of the Immigration Department or if they were Keystone Cops in disguise. Zoe closed the door to the bedroom and followed the rest into the lounge, shaking her head.

Chapter Ten

Eva picked up a chair from the dining room table that had fallen over in the melee, and brought it into the lounge. She sat down on it, crossed her legs, and waited for the two men to start explaining why they had turned into raving lunatics only moments earlier.

Zoe sat on the end of the sofa next to Eva. Earl had decided that he wanted a cigarette after all the excitement. He had opened the balcony doors and was perched half-way inside the room while holding his cigarette outside, to avoid offending Zoe with the smoke.

Friedrich and David seemed more than a little mortified by their behavior. Friedrich tried to hide his embarrassment by going through some files in his briefcase. David chose to gaze at Eva with an embarrassed smile, just a faint curvature of his mouth that was met by her steely glare.

"So, do you want to start this again?" Eva asked tersely. She glanced at Earl and wished for a cigarette herself. The two Immigration officers were making her nervous.

Friedrich cleared his throat. Eva stared at him until he stopped rifling his files and looked at her. "I am Friedrich Jacobs and this is my colleague, David Harrison," he said.

"At least they still know their names," Zoe quipped.

Friedrich ignored the comment. He took a file out of his briefcase and set it face down on the coffee table near him. He sighed before looking directly at Eva once more. "We are War Crimes Investigators with the Immigration Department—"

"What does that have to do with us?" Eva asked.

"I'm getting to it," Friedrich replied. He picked at the edge of the briefcase with his thumbnail, clearly nervous.

"Get to it before my next birthday," Zoe said irritably.

"We need to confirm a few things first..."

Earl guffawed, which made Eva stifle a smile as she continued to stare at the two men.

"You are Eva Theresa Muller?" Friedrich asked.

"Theresa?" Earl yelped as Eva looked over her shoulder and gave him a small grin. Turning her attention back to Friedrich, she resumed her stoic glare.

"Yes," Eva replied.

"According to official records, you were born on the twentieth of July, 1920, in Vienna, Austria, to Daphne Muller and Hans Muller?"

Eva glanced at Zoe and sighed, tired of the bureaucratic errors that continued to plague her. She said to Friedrich, "My mother was not married when I was born."

"Do you know a Hans Albert Muller?" Friedrich asked.

"I knew a Hans Albert Muller," Eva replied quietly. "He was my stepfather."

"Not your father?"

"No," Eva shook her head. "You interrupted my father's sleep just moments ago."

A broader smile creased David's face. "We will apologize to—"

"Father Panayiotis Haralambos, a Greek Orthodox priest," Zoe said. "Well former priest, but that's only because he got married and can't be a priest." Zoe stopped when Eva's hand touched her knee to stop her from continuing.

Friedrich asked Zoe, "You are Zoe Lambros?"

"Yes," she answered.

"What is your relationship with Miss Muller?" Friedrich asked, making a point of looking through the file in his hands.

"Sister," Zoe replied without hesitation. She stared a challenge at Friedrich, silently daring him to contradict her.

Friedrich glanced at Zoe over his thick, black-rimmed glasses and took out a photograph from the file. He held it for a moment before giving it to Zoe. She took the photo; a long moment passed while she stared down at it, then she smiled grimly and passed it to Eva.

Eva saw herself and Zoe at the park, captured in a clearing that they had thought was secluded. There was no mistaking the fact that the two women were not sisters. They were both on the grass, Eva leaning over Zoe and kissing her.

"Told you someone was there," Eva said to Zoe in Greek before she returned her attention to the photograph.

"In Greece, sisters kiss like that all the time," Zoe said matter-of-factly in English to the investigators.

Friedrich and David exchanged incredulous glances.

The balcony doors rattled closed as Earl stepped outside and pulled the doors closed behind him; he had been coughing and spluttering at Zoe's ludicrous response. Eva could hear his booming laughter as he tried to compose himself without much success. Zoe herself looked as if she could not quite believe what she had said in the face of the evidence before her.

Eva did not say a word but kept her head down, studying the photograph.

Friedrich's response was to take another photograph out of his file and hand it to Zoe. The second picture was of Eva and Zoe fishing at a lake. Eva had her back braced against a tree trunk and Zoe sat between her long legs, leaning back against her chest. Eva was nuzzling Zoe's neck, while Zoe was trying to hang on to the fishing pole.

"Oh," Zoe said quietly. "That was such a nice day." A soft smile came to her lips.

"It is a crime to lie to a federal agent," David said, a grin taking the sting out of his words. "We have been following you for over a month. You tend to find out a lot about someone when you do that."

"The photographs didn't give you enough of a clue?" Zoe asked and met David's gaze.

"So you know we are lovers," Eva finally said, glancing up from the photographs. "Is that why you are here?" She handed the photos back to Friedrich.

"No, Miss Muller, we don't think homosexuals are war criminals," he told her.

"Not unless you happen to be Rudolf Hess," David joked weakly. The attempt was met with stony looks from both women. "We are aware that you are lesbians," he said, sobering.

"Then why the charade?" Eva asked. "Why have you been following us? We haven't done anything wrong."

"We know you haven't. That's why we are here." David paused and took a short breath. "We need your help."

"With what?"

Friedrich glanced at David and sat back, allowing him to continue. "Miss Muller, we have been tracking several war criminals in several countries. We have intelligence—" David was interrupted by Earl's chuckle coming clearly through the balcony doors. He stopped for a moment, then continued. "We have intelligence which tells us that Hans Muller is in Sydney right now."

Eva shook her head. "Hans Muller is dead."

"He's burning in hell as we speak," Zoe muttered.

"Are you quite sure of that?" David asked.

"He was in a building that was blown up by the Greek Resistance," Eva patiently explained. "You tend to die when the building you are in explodes," she added with a shrug.

David smiled at Eva's reply. "So you are certain he is dead?" he asked, removing another photograph from the file in front of them. He showed it to Eva.

"You do like your photographs," Zoe said. She leaned across to see the photo that Eva held.

Eva stared at the image for a long moment. She sighed and showed it to Zoe, who swore in startled but vehement Greek. It was indeed Hans Muller in the photograph. Half his face was scarred and he wore a black eye patch, but he looked as menacing as ever. There was no mistake; this was the monster who had terrorized Greece and brutalized Eva to her core, and he was very much alive.

Eva found her hands shaking as she held the photograph and tried not to let the fears that were bubbling to the surface overwhelm her. Zoe took the picture out of her hand, then crumpled it up in disgust and threw it on the table. Eva put her arm around Zoe's shoulders and brought her close, wanting to have her near.

"We won't let him hurt you," David said in Greek, surprising both Eva and Zoe. "I can speak Greek and German," he added in explanation. "Look, Miss Muller, I know what this man has done to you."

"No, you don't," Eva replied, her voice breaking at the realization that her tormentor was still alive.

"He will pay for his crimes," David said. "You have to believe me. I know you don't want to trust me, and there isn't any reason for you to do so."

"Why *should* I trust you?" Eva asked.

"Because I want to catch him as much as you want to see him punished for his crimes," David replied, and leaned forward. "I know what was done to you, Miss Muller. I know you have suffered at this man's hands."

"What do you want?" Eva's question was barely a whisper.

"We want you to help us catch him," David replied.

Eva's expression went from shock to disbelief. Zoe, on the other hand, was visibly shaking with rage. She stood up and faced the two men.

"Do you know what you are asking of her?" Zoe screamed at David in Greek. "Get the hell out of our home!"

Earl rushed back into the lounge. "What's the matter?" he asked, moving over to Zoe, who looked ready to kill someone.

Eva stood up and put her arms around Zoe. She whispered reassurances into the smaller woman's ear.

"No, Evy, I won't let them," Zoe replied, gazing at Eva.

At that moment, the bedroom door opened and Panayiotis came out. "What is going on out here?" he demanded, putting on his glasses.

Eva stood and went to her father. "These men are from the Immigration Department and they want my help in catching Hans Muller."

Panayiotis was taken aback by the news. "Isn't Muller dead?" he asked as he put an arm around Eva's shoulders. His expression was concerned and alert.

"No," Zoe angrily replied.

David looked at Friedrich. "This is going well," he whispered *sotto voce*, but loudly enough for everyone in the room to hear him before he turned his attention back to Panayiotis and Eva. "Miss Muller, believe me," David began in a more normal tone of voice, leaning forward to address Eva, "we can capture this man without your help, but it would be easier if you helped us."

"If you can do it on your own, go and do it," Zoe said tersely.

"We are a small unit, Miss Lambros, and we are chronically understaffed," David patiently explained. He stood and paced next to the sofa. "There are four of us trying to bring these people to face justice. I know what it means to—"

"How do you know, Mr. Harrison? How do you know how we are feeling?" Eva asked.

David sighed and closed his eyes a moment before opening them again and focusing on the men and women who awaited his reply. "In 1945, I was a German translator in the British army. We were the first to enter the Bergen-Belson concentration camp."

"Elena was there," Zoe whispered. "That's my friend, Elena Mannheim. She was in Bergen-Belson."

"I saw what these animals did, Miss Lambros, and if your friend survived, she lived through hell on Earth first."

"Elena has never spoken about what happened," Zoe replied.

David closed his eyes and swallowed audibly. "I doubt she will want to remember it, Miss Lambros," David said, and paused. "Bergen-Belson was what I assume hell to be. Thousands were sick, they were dying, they were dead. I was there." David paused and took out his cigarettes. "May I?"

Eva nodded despite the rule they had in the apartment about not smoking. She found she needed one herself. Earl had the same idea and produced a lit cigarette for her. Zoe held onto her, quietly watching as Eva brought the cigarette to her lips, her hand shaking a little.

"I vowed to spend my life in catching these fuc— ... I'm sorry, but this isn't just a job for me. It's not just a job for Friedrich, either. He lost his entire family in Auschwitz."

"I'm sorry, my son," Panayiotis said quietly as he held Friedrich's gaze with his own.

"Father, it's something we have vowed to do, to catch these animals," Friedrich stated, his normally quiet voice firm. "We can't let these murderers live a quiet life in the countryside. I can't do that," he added.

Eva stubbed out her cigarette in the ashtray Earl had brought in from outside. "I need to talk to Zoe privately," she said and got up from the sofa. She took Zoe's hand and led her into their bedroom. As the two women left the room, Eva glanced over her shoulder and saw Panayiotis raise a firm hand to the two men facing him. David and Friedrich wordlessly accepted the former priest's silent admonition.

Once inside the safety of their bedroom, Eva closed the door and melted into Zoe's embrace. They stood in the middle of the room holding each other, gaining strength from their bond.

"Evy, I know what he said is right, but I don't want you in that bastard's firing line." Zoe led Eva to the edge of the bed and pushed her down, then put her arms around Eva's neck and looked into her eyes. "I made a vow, too."

"Which one?" Eva asked with a tiny smile.

"I vowed to kill anyone who hurt you again," Zoe replied. "They want you as bait."

Eva stood up and gently brushed away the hair from Zoe's eyes. "I know, love. I want to run far away from here and never look back," Eva admitted. Her heart was still beating so hard, she was afraid it might jump out of her chest at any moment. The news that Muller was not only alive, but in Australia, left her feeling sick and cold, as though someone had sunk a knife into her gut.

"Zoe, my head is telling me to run, but my heart is telling me Mr. Harrison is right. We have to help."

"Am I a coward for wanting to keep you safe?"

Eva smiled, leaned down, and kissed Zoe tenderly. When they parted, Eva brushed her fingertips over Zoe's cheek and looked deep into her eyes. "You don't know the meaning of that word. I'm scared, too."

"I'm always here for you, Evy," Zoe gently reminded her. "Always."

"I know, love," Eva pulled Zoe into a hug. They stayed that way for a few minutes. "Let's go and tell them."

"Evy." Zoe hesitated.

"Yes?"

"Next time you want to feel adventurous outside, remember someone might be looking," Zoe said. She got a blank look from Eva. "The pictures," Zoe reminded.

"I did like the one of us fishing."

"You weren't paying any attention to the fish."

"I was busy," Eva pulled Zoe in for another hug. "Zoe, we are going to get him," she whispered into Zoe's ear before kissing her.

They left the bedroom and returned to the lounge where everyone was waiting for their decision. David and Friedrich stood up as the two women entered the room. Earl was leaning in the doorway of the kitchen. It was obvious he had put on the kettle while they were inside. Eva caught his attention and mouthed, "Thank you."

"Mr. Harrison, we're in," Eva announced. The two Immigration agents beamed.

"Call me David," David said, taking Eva's hand. "Thank you, Miss Muller."

"Eva."

"Thank you, Eva." The four of them sat down again, Eva and Zoe on the sofa, David and Friedrich in the two chairs they had occupied before. Panayiotis was sitting in the kitchen chair that Eva occupied earlier. Earl remained standing. "Do you know an Erik Rhimes?" David asked after a nod from Friedrich.

Eva glanced at Zoe. "General Rhimes."

"Yes, he is with your fa—" David stopped. "I'm sorry, Eva, I meant your stepfather."

"They have been friends since their school days," Eva said. "I'm not surprised. How are you going to get them to come here?"

David and Friedrich looked at each other before turning back to Eva. "He knows you are here."

Eva forced her panic aside. "He knows I'm here? In this apartment?"

"Not exactly where you are, but he knows you are alive and in Sydney."

"It was just a matter of time, wasn't it?" Eva sighed. "How did he find out?"

"We have an informant who leaks information. We don't know who it is yet but—"

"I don't like the sound of this," Zoe muttered to herself, but loudly enough to be overheard.

"Yes, but we can control the information," David said. "We can put it out on the Nazi grapevine that you will testify at Nuremberg against him."

"There's a Nazi grapevine?" Eva asked skeptically.

"There is," David replied.

"That isn't true, is it?" Zoe asked. "That Eva would have to..."

"No. We have enough witnesses in Greece and Germany. We don't need Eva to testify," Friedrich took his turn in the conversation. "But Muller doesn't know that. It will also be leaked that you can testify against Rhimes and others, since you were close to them."

"I wasn't *close* to them," Eva responded. "I was a witness to their brutality, but I wasn't *close* to them." She held on to Zoe, who seemed ready to pounce on the hapless man. Eva needed to control the younger woman's anger at Friedrich's comment, as well as fight back her own fears. She knew she had to do this. Hans Muller could not be allowed to roam free, but the trouble for her and Zoe that she suspected loomed ahead weighed heavily on her heart.

"Miss Muller, I seem to be putting my foot in my mouth. Please excuse me for the poor choice of words. I meant you were close in the sense that you were *with* them...I meant you...*knew* them." Friedrich tried to explain himself. "I didn't mean that you were close to them in the sense that..." he said, struggling to get out of the verbal mess he had made for himself.

"I understand what you meant," Eva said, trying to settle her aching back against the sofa cushion. "Now tell me exactly what you want of me."

She took a breath and listened to what the two investigators were hoping would happen in their hunt for Muller and Rhimes.

"The best-laid plans of mice and men," Panayiotis muttered, as the two men talked. Only Eva heard his comment and was chilled.

The air around her was hazy and foggy. Zoe turned around slowly. She was in a field and then, inexplicably, in a room.

"Oh no, not again," Zoe kept repeating to herself as she walked down a long corridor. She knew the way; she'd traversed it many a night but that did not stop her from making her way down the hallway to a closed door.

Her sweaty hand clasped the doorknob and turned it. She pushed the door open and the gloom of the corridor gave way to a brightly-lit room. She gasped in shock at the tableau of horror before her.

Standing in the middle of the room was Muller, dressed in his Nazi uniform and holding a gun. At his feet was Eva's lifeless, battered, and bleeding body. Muller was laughing, and Zoe knew he laughed at the sight of Eva's blood splattered on his clothes. In fact, blood was everywhere, on their clothes and the walls.

"You! You killed her. See!"

Zoe turned around and everything was covered in blood. The walls, the floor, her hands. Everything.

Zoe could not move no matter how hard she tried. She willed herself to scream but nothing came out of her mouth. All she could do was watch Muller...

Zoe gasped and bolted upright, freeing herself from the bonds of the nightmare. Her heart ached at the slowly fading images of her battered and bloodied lover lying at Muller's feet. Her breath came in shallow gasps, and she wiped the sweat from her brow. She shook her head to try and get the images out of her mind. Zoe took a deep breath and exhaled slowly, but the sight of Eva's bloodied body was seared into her brain.

She glanced at the nightstand and grimaced. The clock displayed one o'clock and, as had happened several times before, even in Greece and Egypt, the same nightmare had invaded her sleep. This time it had been caused by the news that Muller was still alive, and it was obviously not going to stop until the madman was caught.

Eva, my precious Eva, she thought. She looked at her lover.

Eva was contentedly sleeping on her stomach, the thin sheet pooled around her waist, exposing her scarred back. The moon's soft beams illuminated her broad shoulders, highlighting her silken hair in such a way that Zoe sighed at the sight, her heart melting with tenderness.

Lying back to watch Eva sleeping, Zoe propped herself up on one arm and gently traced the faint scars put on the other woman's body by Muller's hand. She caught her breath, touching the exit scar from the bullet that had shattered Eva's collarbone and almost taken her life. If the bullet had gone just a little lower, it would have killed her. Zoe shuddered involuntarily at the memory; a cold shiver ran down her spine.

When she closed her eyes, Zoe could still see the blood-spattered white shirt and Eva's pale face as she lay silent and still on the floor. Muller's henchman, Reinhardt, had nearly succeeded in killing the woman she loved. It was ironic that just a little over a year prior to Eva getting shot, she would have cheered gleefully to see Reinhardt or anyone else kill Eva, but Fate had had other plans in store for her. She was glad she had arrived in time to save Eva.

Zoe shook her head vigorously, trying to get the image out of her mind. She leaned down and softly kissed the scarred shoulder, reaffirming to herself that she never wanted to lose this special, wonderful woman.

After a few minutes of staring at her sleeping lover, Zoe sighed and snuggled next to her, her head rested slightly on Eva's shoulder. She tried to go back to sleep but every time she closed her eyes, the nightmarish images would resurface.

"Oh, damnation," Zoe muttered to herself. She knew she would toss and turn, and wake Eva in the process. That was the last thing Eva needed as she was switching back to the day shift after weeks of working nights. Zoe leaned across and brushed Eva's hair away from her face, smiling her lover's peaceful face, half-buried in the pillow. She kissed Eva very softly on the cheek before throwing off the light blanket and getting out of bed.

Mindful that Eva's father was sleeping in the next room, and would get quite a shock if he saw her in her bright pink baby-doll nightie, Zoe put on a robe and slippers. She stood in the doorway watching Eva sleep for a long moment before turning and walking out of the bedroom, closing the door quietly behind her.

Zoe padded silently into the lounge where bright moonlight filtered through the balcony doors, providing subdued illumination. She picked up the lamp that sat next to the sofa and nearly tripped. The lampshade wobbled a little, causing Zoe to hold on to it to stop it from falling and making a noise and waking everyone. She brought the lamp next to the coffee table and plugged it in. The soft glow gave her enough light as she curled up onto the sofa with her sketchpad and a pencil.

Zoe found this was the only way she could manage to banish the nightmare visions if she could not curl up in Eva's arms and be comforted. The pencil in her hand flickered across the page, seemingly of its own accord, and Eva's face came into view. Zoe smiled and traced the illustration's cheek with her fingertips.

Some time ago, Zoe had found that drawing her favorite subject was a way of dealing with her own demons. Sometimes talking to Eva about her nightmares was painful; she did not want to relive them by retelling them. Eva understood completely and was very patient and supportive.

The drawing complete, Zoe put it down and curled up on the sofa with her gaze locked on the paper. The artwork depicted Eva looking over the top of her camera, a gleeful expression on her face. Zoe's eyes slowly closed. Her breathing evened out. The nightmare banished, she slipped into sleep, starting awake when a beloved voice called her name. Someone was shaking her gently. Zoe opened her eyes to find a very disheveled Eva looking back at her. Eva was on her knees on the floor, leaning against the sofa. "Hey," Zoe said.

"Why are you sleeping out here?" Eva asked, her fingers brushing Zoe's hair. "Was I snoring?" she asked as Zoe made room for her on the couch.

Eva sat down and put her arm around Zoe, who smiled and said, "You don't snore."

"Well, if it's not that, why are you here?" Eva gently teased.

"I wanted to finish a drawing," Zoe replied. She showed Eva the sketch.

Eva took the sketchpad and gazed down at her image. "This is really nice," she said. "You have a photographic memory, love."

"That's half my problem," Zoe muttered, getting a puzzled look from her lover. "I had one of those dreams again."

Eva nodded, put the sketchpad down, and snuggled next to Zoe. "Why didn't you wake me?" she asked, putting her arm around Zoe's shoulders. Zoe settled into Eva's embrace and smiled at the feeling of utter security she felt whenever Eva held her.

"I can't wake you every time I have a nightmare," Zoe said.

"Yes, you can." Eva's eyes misted over and she kissed the top of Zoe's head.

"It was my turn this time," Zoe said with a slight shrug. She shuddered involuntary, thinking of the nightmares both of them suffered. She would wake up screaming, and Eva would sit and hold her in her arms until she fell back asleep. Some nights, the roles were reversed and Zoe would spend the night holding Eva. Knowing Muller was alive and in Sydney was not conducive to a restful sleep for either of them. Zoe thought that only his capture and the subsequent knowledge that he could never harm them again might help lessen the bad dreams that made their nights a torment.

"Is it the same nightmare?" Eva asked.

"Yes." Zoe tightened her hold on Eva and rested her head on the other woman's chest. "Why doesn't that bastard just die?"

"He will," Eva reassured her.

"I hope so."

Eva gently rubbed Zoe's back. "I know a sure-fire way to banish those nightmares." Eva nuzzled Zoe's neck and untied Zoe's robe. She paused in surprise when her hands were stopped from their exploration.

"Shhh!" Zoe whispered loudly, holding Eva's hands immobile against the front of her nightie. "We can't make love."

"We can't?" Eva asked. "Why?"

"Because your father is in the next room!"

"I didn't say we had to do it here," Eva said and kissed Zoe on the lips. "Our bedroom."

"No." Zoe shook her head stubbornly.

"No?"

"He will hear us," Zoe reasoned, earning a very bemused look from Eva.

"We will be very quiet?" Eva suggested, her expression hopeful.

Zoe laughed, then slapped her hand over her mouth to stop herself. "I love you," she said once she had regained control. "I love you more than anything." The idea that they would be making love with Eva's father in the next room made Zoe very uncomfortable, and she said so.

"I can be very quiet," Eva said with a mock pout, which earned her a kiss. "I really can."

Zoe smirked, got up from her spot on the sofa, and took Eva's hand. "Let's go cuddle," she whispered, and led Eva back inside their bedroom.

"Can I kiss you?" Eva whispered.

"Only if you don't make a lot of noise," Zoe quipped. She shut the door and the two women snuggled back in bed together, still giggling.

Eva yawned. She was hot, tired, and wanted to go back to sleep. She had returned to the day shift, and had not had much sleep after she had awakened to find Zoe wasn't in bed with her.

She smiled to herself. They had kissed and cuddled for quite some time; Zoe's nightmare had been banished, but Eva's half-hearted attempts to make love to her had been thwarted because of Zoe's adamant refusal. It had been quite a morning that did not include much sleep.

Eva glanced up at the large clock in the staff cafeteria and sighed. There were another six hours to go before quitting time.

"Hey, Muzza," Earl greeted her with a gentle pat on the head. His white uniform was marred with black smudges, as was his face, making him look like a commando getting ready to drop behind enemy lines. "You look tired," he said, leaning over to give her a peck on the cheek.

"Hey, Earl," Eva said and yawned again. "Have you been kissing your machines again?" she kidded him, reaching out to clean a smudge off his cheek and displaying the dirty fingertip.

Grabbing a rag from his back pocket, Earl scrubbed at his face with it, then shifted closer to Eva. "Did Zoe keep you up all night?" he whispered in her ear.

She caught one of the technicians looking at them out of the corner of her eye. It seemed Earl did, too, because he kissed her on the cheek again in a show of simulated ardor.

"Will you two just go to the storeroom already?" Harry, the technician, bellowed across the room, much to his friends' amusement.

"You're just jealous, mate," Earl retorted. "Let's go outside," he said to Eva. He put his arm around her waist when she stood.

"That man only has one thing on his mind," Eva said, disgusted.

"You have to forgive him. His mother dropped him on his head repeatedly," Earl replied, getting a chuckle out of her.

The two of them walked outside, where a gentle breeze made the temperature more bearable. Earl pulled out a cigarette and lit it, gave it to Eva, and then lit one for himself. They crossed the street to sit on the low brick wall that overlooked the factory.

"Why are you so tired?" Earl asked.

"Woke up at three o'clock in the morning and couldn't get back to sleep," Eva replied, yawning until her jaw cracked.

"Zoe keep you up?"

Eva smiled and took a drag off her cigarette. Exhaling, she watched the smoke rise before she turned to a smirking Earl. "Yes and no."

"Yes and no?"

"Yes, Zoe kept me up but no, we weren't doing anything you wouldn't do," Eva replied and gave Earl a shy smile.

"I don't have sex with women!" Earl said and received a slap on the shoulder from Eva. "I guess you didn't either," he continued and let out another belly laugh at his own cleverness.

"You're a funny man, Mr. Wiggins," Eva said, flicking ash at him.

"So how come you're not getting any?"

"What kind of question is that?" Eva said and shook her head. "My father was in the next room."

"Aren't you lucky he's not staying with you for a long time," Earl said.

"Ha, ha." Eva smiled and puffed her cigarette.

"So why couldn't Zoe go to sleep?" Earl asked earnestly.

Eva sighed, her good mood gone. "She had a nightmare."

"Oh." Earl looked sympathetic. "Poor kid."

Eva held the cigarette and watched flakes of ash fall to the ground. "I hate it when she's hurting," she said quietly.

"There's not much you can do, mate."

"I know." Eva hitched her shoulders in a gesture that was not quite a shrug.

"It has to do with Muller, right?"

Eva shuddered as the memories of that May afternoon came back to haunt her, the memories of standing in the rain and watching people die around her. Eva arrived in Larissa on one of the town's darkest days. She bowed her head and said a quick silent prayer for those who had fallen that day at her stepfather's murderous hand.

Earl snapped his fingers in front of Eva's face, startling her out of her reverie. "Hey, where did you go?" he asked.

Eva shook herself out of her grim memories and took a drag off her cigarette, the acrid smoke soothing her jangled nerves. "Sorry, I was a million miles away and in a different time."

"Yeah," Earl looked up at the sky, which was a bright blue and cloudless expanse that stretched endlessly from horizon to horizon. "I go there, too."

Eva turned her head and regarded him steadily. "Muller killed Zoe's mother."

Earl whistled in surprise. "He killed her?"

"Shot her in front of Zoe." Eva involuntarily shuddered at the recollection. "We were standing out in the rain and I couldn't bear to watch people dying, so I looked away."

"I don't think anyone can bear to watch someone die, Eva," Earl told her, putting his arm around her shoulders. "Why were you there?"

"Muller wanted me there. I guess he figured it was a way to show me what he would do to me if I had a relapse." Eva shrugged, got up from the wall and stubbed out the cigarette on the ground before sitting back down.

"Son of a bitch!" Earl spat. "Did you know Zoe at that stage?"

"No."

"How old was she?"

"Fourteen," Eva replied. "Her father had died the year before, her brothers were killed fighting the Italians, and then the Germans murdered her mother and many others in the town square."

"Fucking bastards," Earl muttered. "How the hell did she survive?"

Eva smiled despite the nature of their conversation. "Zoe has an unconquerable spirit," she said with undisguised pride. "I met her a year later. She was so full of hate, but there was something about her that just made me admire that fire in her."

"Was it instant love?" Earl teased, his mood lightening a trifle.

"For Zoe, it was instant hate." Eva felt pensive when thinking back to the early times with Zoe. She had been quite a contrast to the loving woman she had held in her arms just that morning. "For me, it was just someone else who hated me."

"You were German so Zoe naturally hated you."

"It wasn't that simple when it came to Zoe. I was Muller's daughter, and Zoe believed in an eye for an eye."

"What did she want to do?"

"Kill me, to get at Muller for murdering her mother." Eva sighed, omitting the part about Zoe thinking she had laughed as Zoe's mother lay dying. "Only problem was that if Zoe had succeeded, Muller would have given her a medal," she added with a shrug. "My death would have solved a problem for him."

"How did you convince her not to?"

"I didn't convince her. Father H told her I was his daughter and that she couldn't kill me."

"I bet she was spitting chips at that," Earl said.

"Spitting chips?"

"It means she was very angry," Earl explained.

"Yes, she was very angry," Eva said. "She was still determined to hate me even though she couldn't kill me."

"What changed her mind?"

Eva looked up and smiled. "She fell in love with me," she said.

Earl laughed. "Now that would put a spanner in the works for sure," he added.

"'Spanner in the works'?" Eva asked, not being familiar with the saying.

"It means that something ruined the plan," Earl explained.

"Yes, a spanner in the works," Eva replied, mimicking Earl's accent. They looked at each other and smiled.

"Hey, you two! Would you like a personal invitation to come back to work?" Stalk yelled from across the road.

The two friends looked at each other again and jumped off the wall. Earl stubbed out his cigarette and took a hold of Eva's hand as they walked across the road and back into the factory where work awaited them. Eva would have another colorful Australian saying to share with Zoe when she went home. Life had taken a turn for the better when she met Zoe and Eva was certain divine intervention was responsible.

Chapter Eleven

The department store was crowded with shoppers moving about, browsing and chattering. It had been a lean few years during the war and money as well as goods had been scarce, but with the ending of the hostilities in Europe and the Pacific, products were becoming available again, and people began to spend some of their hard-earned money.

"Good morning, ma'am," the saleslady said as she smiled broadly. "Can I interest you in some aftershave for your husband?"

Zoe looked at Elena and grinned. Elena saw the twinkle in Zoe's eyes and started feeling sorry for the poor saleslady. She wondered if warning her that Zoe was in the mood to play would do anything but decided that she would rather see where the situation might lead.

"Sure," Zoe said, giving her bags to Elena as though divesting herself of unnecessary accoutrements before entering a battle.

"Were you looking for a gift?" the saleslady asked.

"Yes, a birthday gift. I already bought some clothes." Zoe sniffed at the aftershave, crinkling her nose. Elena smiled. Their morning's shopping had been very fruitful, with Zoe finding a few inexpensive items. Both women had a day off from the restaurant, which had closed to allow some painting to be done. It was a chance for the two of them to go shopping and have fun together.

"Oh, how wonderful! I'm sure your husband is a lucky man," the saleslady gushed.

Elena turned away and rolled her eyes, disgusted by the woman's sycophancy.

"I'm the lucky one," Zoe replied.

"Of course, of course. Now, how old will your husband be?"

"Twenty-six."

"Ah, a young man, with a beautiful wife! Any children?"

"No, none, we can't have any," Zoe said, giving the saleslady a sad look.

Elena coughed loudly to cover up her chuckles as Zoe played with the woman. She moved further away from her friend, trying very hard not to lose her composure, although she was afraid that she might rupture something important if Zoe's mischief continued too much longer.

"Oh, I am so sorry! You have your husband, though. That's the main thing," the saleslady sympathized, patting Zoe on the shoulder. "We have an excellent range of aftershaves and colognes for men."

"Hmm..." Zoe sniffed at the various bottles. "Hey, El, come over here."

Elena returned to her side, a grin threatening to split her face as she struggled to control her expression and not give the game away. "Yes?"

"Do you think Eva would like aftershave for her legs? Hmm, no, I don't think so." Zoe turned to the saleslady and Elena attempted unsuccessfully to strangle a snort of amusement. "My lover doesn't shave; well, except for her legs of course," Zoe said.

The saleslady's face had turned a bright shade of crimson which only increased in color when Zoe started giggling. Elena was torn between wanting to laugh at Zoe's antics and being concerned about the scene Zoe was now creating. Elena gave up the fight, finally bursting out laughing. The saleslady had such a look of total shock and horror on her face.

"You said you were married!" said the saleslady, finally, after opening and closing her mouth a few times, clearly having difficulty articulating her disbelief.

"I am married," Zoe replied, still chuckling. "My lover is the most wonderful, loving woman on the planet, and she loves me, too. Isn't that great?"

"Utter filth!" the saleslady huffed angrily, lifting her chin. "Get out of my store!"

"Was it something I said?" Zoe asked Elena, who had regained her composure at last. "Come on, El," Zoe continued, "I hear food calling my name."

"You're a wicked woman," Elena whispered after they were a short distance from the saleslady.

"Oh, yeah!" Zoe replied, steering Elena out of the perfume section. Elena glanced over her shoulder and saw the saleslady chatting to another person and casting dirty looks at their retreating backs. Zoe stuck out her tongue in the woman's direction and said, "Cow."

"You know, it is the way most everyone thinks in today's world. Though, for you and Eva, it doesn't matter," Elena said, placing an arm around her friend's shoulder as they exited the store and began walking down the sidewalk together.

"Yes, it does," Zoe replied. Reaching their destination, the women settled into the booth of a little teahouse just up the road from the department store. "It matters. That lady can't see past her snout."

"If that woman was accepting, would it make your love for Eva any stronger?"

"No."

"See? It doesn't make a difference. She's a narrow-minded old cow."

"Elena, it's not that simple. I can walk down the street holding Evy's hand like we're girlfriends and having a gay old time, but I have to censor myself from saying how much I love her." Zoe sniffed. "She's not my girlfriend. She's my lover. She's my wife for God's sake!"

"But you didn't censor yourself, you just told half the department store about your love for Eva!"

"I wish I could tell the entire world about it."

"Do you *want* people to hate you, Zoe?" Elena asked.

"No, of course not," Zoe replied, sounding sullen. "Why should they hate me for loving a woman, El? That's so stupid. Why does that cow instantly have to think I'm married to a man?"

Elena shook her head slowly. "She thinks you're married to a man because that is what girls marry."

"Well, she's wrong."

"I don't know what to say, Zoe. I don't know why you are getting upset at the saleslady. She just wanted to help you," Elena said. "I don't think you should go around declaring you are a lesbian."

"I don't."

"Well, you did back there." Elena indicated the store's direction with a jab of her thumb. "People are going to hate you, Zoe, and I'm sure you don't want that."

"Of course I don't," Zoe replied defensively. "It's hard, El. Husbands and wives can shop for their spouses, but all I can do is talk in riddles in case someone gets upset."

"There have to be people who are like you—"

"Lesbians." Zoe smiled wryly. "So I have to go looking for a lesbian department store or lesbian glee club?"

"Are there such things?"

"I don't know." Zoe shrugged. "I'm quite sure Evy and I are not the only lesbians in Sydney."

"I know you're not," Elena said cryptically.

Zoe looked curious. "Really, how do you know that?"

"You know Maggie in apartment two?"

"Yes."

"*She's* a lesbian," Elena whispered.

"Sounds like we belong to some club already." Zoe grinned. "How do you know?"

"I have eyes and I can see," Elena said and laughed. "So you're not the only ones." Elena was pleased with her ability to spot a lesbian like Maggie. She had often wondered if she could tell if a woman was a lesbian; Zoe and Eva did not seem any different from ordinary girls when she had initially them. She and Zoe had had a discussion once on the subject. Elena was not quite sure how the conversation had started but she had told her friend that Eva did not look like a lesbian, whatever that meant at the time. She had got a few giggles out of Zoe for that observation.

"How does that help the fact that I can't kiss Eva out of our apartment?" Zoe asked.

"It doesn't, but you alone can't change the world," Elena said reasonably. "It's just the way things are."

"That's defeatist, El."

"No, Zoe, that's being a pragmatist. Being a lesbian isn't normal—"

"Oh, that sounds great, thank you, Elena." Zoe glanced at Elena and shook her head. "What is normal? Because society tells us something is normal, then it's normal?"

"Zoe, you know I didn't mean..."

"I love a woman; that is normal to me." Zoe's hackles were clearly rising. "I'm sick of people saying that what I feel is a sin against God. I'm sick of people saying I'm a deviant, Elena."

Elena held up her hands in surrender. "Whoa, Zoe, I didn't mean to upset you."

"It makes me awfully mad, El. Everyone says it's wrong, but I know it's not. You're my friend and it hurts to think that *you* think it's wrong."

"I didn't say I thought it was wrong, Zoe. All I said was that it wasn't normal." Elena tried to reason with Zoe, who was becoming agitated by her comments. "You know what I mean. Men marry women, they don't marry men. Or women don't marry women. It's not going to change no matter how much you try to change it."

"That's because everyone is afraid to," Zoe replied as she looked through the tea store window at a man and woman holding hands and talking animatedly. "One day, Elena Mannheim, homosexuals and lesbians are going to be accepted. Just wait. One day they are going to walk down the street and they would be able to kiss their lover out in the open."

"Would you do it?" Elena asked and inwardly groaned. She already knew the answer to the question. Zoe was bold enough and impulsive enough to do anything she wanted, and nobody would be able to stop her once the notion took root.

"Why can't I show the world how much I love Eva? Mrs. Jenkins is organizing a dance soon, and I bet if I took Eva on the dance floor and held her, then kissed her, it would be a mortal sin and everyone will be scandalized. What rot!" Zoe said.

"That didn't answer my question, Zo."

"Yes, I would, if I thought no one was going to stone me for my shocking behavior," Zoe replied bitterly.

"Zoe, I didn't mean to upset you." Elena reached out and touched Zoe's hand. "You know I love you, don't you?"

Zoe nodded. "You don't think we are sick, do you?"

"No!" Elena exclaimed, wishing she had not said anything because her words had hurt her best friend. "Zoe, I just meant that your relationship with Eva isn't what the world sees as normal. I didn't say you were abnormal."

"All right," Zoe said quietly.

Elena wondered if she had hurt their relationship by saying what she did. "Are we still friends?"

Zoe smiled and nodded. "Of course we are, silly."

"So you're going to the dance with her nephew?"

"No, I don't think so. I think Mrs. Jenkins has her eye on Eva for that boy. Earl will be probably be my date. I'll probably find an excuse to dance with Eva and keep her at arms length so no one can be the wiser," Zoe replied and let out a frustrated groan. "I want to dance really close and cuddle. Why can't I?"

"Because Eva is not a man," Elena replied.

"Are you telling me that, fifty years from now, people will still hate me for being a lesbian?"

"They will still hate me for being Jewish, so yes, that's what I'm saying," Elena said.

"I don't think so." Zoe slowly shook her head. "Fifty years from now, El, things will be different. I bet you that when we are old we are going to marvel at how people's attitudes have changed."

"You're an eternal optimist, Zoe, and sadly you're going to be disappointed."

"This is not cheering me up, El," Zoe said, pointing a finger at Elena in mock rebuke.

"I'm sorry, Zoe." Elena patted her friend's hand. "Let's talk about something else."

"Yes, you're right. So who *is* taking you to the dance?"

"No one." Elena smiled triumphantly; she had managed to avoid seeing Mrs. Jenkins and had not been invited. "I'm not going."

"Oh, you sneak!" Zoe exclaimed. "How did you manage to get out of that?"

"Ah, young Zoe, you have much to learn about the art of avoidance...rather like our waitress," Elena grinned, and waved to summon the waitress to take their order.

At a table in the teahouse, Friedrich Jacobs and David Harrison were drinking their morning tea. David spied Zoe in the company of another young woman as they entered and took seats in a nearby booth.

"Hey, Freddy, look who's here." David tapped his friend and nodded towards the two women. He recognized the face of the one who was sitting with Zoe; he had seen her briefly at Zoe's and Eva's apartment, but he had not been introduced to her and did not know her name.

"She's beautiful," Friedrich said, sipping his tea.

"Zoe's a lesbian," David reminded his friend.

"Not her." Friedrich scowled. "The other pretty lady."

"Let's go meet her." David got up and pulled a reluctant Friedrich over to where Zoe was sitting with the other woman.

"Well, good morning, ladies," David said. Without waiting for permission, he slid into the booth next to Zoe, who scooted over to give him room. Friedrich stood next to him, looking stiff, awkward and uncomfortable.

"Good morning, Miss Lambros," David said, extending his hand to Zoe.

"Hello." Zoe seemed caught by surprise. She gave David a very lukewarm smile. He supposed Zoe did not feel as if she could trust him yet, but she was polite enough to take his hand and give it a quick shake.

"I saw you last night," Elena said smiling, her attention directed towards Friedrich. "I'm Elena Mannheim."

"This is Friedrich Jacobs," Zoe supplied.

"I'm pleased to meet you, Mr. Jacobs."

Friedrich looked stumped. "Ah, yes...uh..." He stuttered as a blush colored his face and ears. Elena looked up at him and smiled. David hid a smile of his own. Friedrich did not know how to speak to women; even though David had coached him, the man was still hopeless in social situations involving the fairer sex.

"What my friend is trying to say is that it's a pleasure to meet you, too," David said, sighing. He was going to have to work on opening lines with Freddy again.

"Would you like to join us?" Elena invited Friedrich, since David was already seated. Zoe shot daggers at her friend but Elena ignored her.

"I'm sorry, Miss Mannheim, but we really have to get back to the office—" Friedrich pointedly kicked David's leg, making him wince.

"Oh, that's a shame," Elena said. She sounded as if she was truly regretful, which gave David an idea.

"You know, I was just saying to Friedrich how there's a dance coming up next week and we have no dates. Isn't that sad? Two eligible bachelors and no dates. Would you two like to join us?" David asked. Friedrich appeared to be stunned, and David hoped the man would not blurt out anything that would make them both look silly.

"We would love to," Zoe said. A spark of mischief lit up her eyes. A muffled thump from underneath the table and Zoe's grimace of pain told David that Elena had probably kicked the other woman's shins. *She and Friedrich ought to get on like a house on fire*, he thought, wishing he could rub his own aching leg.

"You would? How wonderful!" David said aloud, waving a hand at Friedrich. "I'm quite sure that Freddy would love to take you to the dance, wouldn't you, mate?"

Friedrich was obviously captivated by Elena. He smiled shyly at her, oblivious to David's attempt to get him a date until David finally smacked him in the stomach with the flat of his hand. "Ah, ye-yes," he stammered.

"Excellent! Come on, Freddy. We have things to do, places to go, and people to see. It's been a pleasure." He got up, put his arm around his friend and steered Friedrich toward the door. He had a great deal of work to do to get Freddy ready. His friend's shy-boy routine was not going to work for this date with the pretty Miss Mannheim. *No rest for the wicked*, he thought to himself and grinned.

"That was a date!" Elena said, turning to Zoe excitedly.

"Really? Well, what do you know," Zoe replied, chuckling. "You like Mr. Jacobs?"

"He's cute."

"Not my type," Zoe replied with a smirk. "I like them taller."

Elena smiled then abruptly sobered. "Oh, no!" she cried, anxiety making her shrill.

"What?" Zoe exclaimed.

"I don't have a thing to wear!" Elena cried. A solution occurred to her and she relaxed somewhat, letting her happiness show. "Come on, I want to go and buy a dress and some shoes and maybe some new perfume! I hope I can afford all that!" she said.

"Hey, let's go terrorize that saleslady again!" Zoe said, getting up and pulling Elena out of the booth.

"I don't know if she'll serve you now," Elena said. She paused as another thought crossed her mind. "I've never been on a date before."

Zoe sighed. "Don't ask me. I've never been on a date with a boy either. This will be my first one as well."

"I thought you said you were going to go with Earl?"

"Change of plans," Zoe replied. "If I didn't go, you wouldn't, so now you have to go because Friedrich asked you to."

Elena looked at Zoe and they both started laughing as they paid for their tea and left the small teashop to search of a dress.

Alberta Haralambos *née* Fisherman looked at her reflection in the mirror and sighed. She was a tall, beautiful woman with auburn hair sprinkled with strands of grey. Bright grey eyes stared back at her as she appraised her appearance. She wanted to make a good impression on her husband's daughter, Eva, when they met.

"You look beautiful," Panayiotis stated as he wrapped his strong arms around her and kissed her tenderly.

"You're biased."

"Is there something wrong in that?"

"No, but—"

"No 'buts'. You look beautiful. Eva will love you."

Alberta sighed again. "I'm not so sure, Pany."

"What do you mean?" Panayiotis said, leaving her to sit on the edge of the bed.

"I don't know if she'd like another mother in her life at the moment..."

"My darling Ally." Panayiotis took her hands and held them to his cheek. "Eva doesn't need a mother; she needs a friend."

"She has a friend, Pany," Alberta replied. She pulled her hands free and held her husband's face between her palms. "Remember?"

"Yes, yes, I know. But sometimes you want to talk to someone who isn't so close."

Alberta gazed at him and shook her head. "That doesn't make sense."

"You know what I mean."

Alberta still felt some insecurity but decided not to press the issue. "Yes, I know what you mean," she said. "Now tell me about this Muller person. I can't believe that man is still alive." She had been shocked when her husband had told her the news about the evil Nazi. "After all this time, it must be difficult for Eva."

"It is, but she has Zoe, and now she has us, too," he said, smiling.

"What's Zoe like?" Alberta was genuinely curious.

"Zoe is...well, she's a force of nature. She can be courageous and strong, and then turn right around and surprise you by her naivety. She gives of herself completely, unconditionally. She reminds me of Saint Peter. So headstrong." He chuckled again. "Yes, that's Zoe. She lives life to the fullest. I'm surprised she survived the war."

It was obvious to Alberta that her husband loved this young woman as much as he did his own daughter. *To have a friend like that must be comforting to Pany's daughter*, she thought. Aloud, she asked, "How old is Zoe?"

"Nineteen."

"She's so young! They must be very special friends with the age difference."

Panayiotis' smile turned secretive, sharpening Alberta's curiosity. There was something not being said here, something being concealed behind her husband's slightly guarded expression. Rather than insist on being told, Alberta elected to be patient and let matters become clear with time.

"She is indeed," he said. "The war didn't allow her to have a childhood. Zoe's father died after getting the news that her brothers had been killed following the Italian invasion. Her mother was killed by the Nazis. She had no one after they died."

"She had you."

"Hmm, she had me, yes, but she suffered greatly the first few months after her mother died. We got through it, though."

"How did they decide to come here?"

"Why don't you ask *her* that question?" Alberta gave him a glare. He continued, shrugging, "You can't ask me all the questions and have nothing left for them."

Alberta was a little put out at her husband's behavior, which was odd to say the least. He was normally very open and honest with her. Her thoughts turned away from her husband to his daughter. If she was going to impress Eva, that meant she would have to impress Zoe as well. "Which one is the easier to get to know?" she asked.

"Zoe is very easy to get to know; she will tell you all about herself without much prompting. Eva is shy," Panayiotis answered. "Don't worry. The girls are going to love you!"

"I hope so," Alberta whispered. Still nervous despite her husband's reassurances, she got up and went to her wardrobe to select another shirt.

Eva got out of the car, careful to shut the door quietly. Earl had winced every time she had banged the car door shut in the past. The white Holden sparkled in the afternoon sunlight; it was Earl's pride and joy. Though the Holden cars were a beautiful design—something Earl had mentioned well over a dozen times—Eva still could not understand the man's love affair with what was, after all, just a vehicle. However, she had heard enough about it from Earl to have an idea of just how much he adored the automobile. She grinned when Earl gave his car a pat on the hood.

"I heard on the radio that driving a good car is like being with a good woman," Eva quipped, leaning around the man and patting the car's hood herself.

"You know, you are funny when you don't get any sleep." He took off his jacket and threw it through the open car window. "It's much better than any woman."

"Is that so? The car doesn't do anything for me." Eva shrugged. "How would you know if it was better than a woman, anyway?"

"Ever been with a man?"

Eva looked at her friend, startled by the unexpected question. "Um, why are you asking?"

"Being with a man is different from being with a woman."

"I don't believe we are having this conversation." She blushed.

Earl smiled. "Well, isn't it true?"

"I would say so, yes."

"So, I would know if driving a good car is better than being with a good woman."

"I'm sorry I said anything now." Eva laughed, her blush deepening.

Earl put his arm around his friend. "It's much, much better than being with a good woman," he whispered in Eva's ear. "Now if you said if it was better than being with a bloke, I would say no."

"Now I'm *really* sorry I mentioned it," Eva said, chuckling. They went together up the walkway. "Vroom, vroom," he added, making Eva laugh as they went up the stairs.

"Hey, is Zoe cooking tonight?" he asked.

"She cooks every night."

"Oh, yeah, I forgot, you even burn water!" Earl ducked a swat, still laughing.

Eva gave him a dirty look and bolted up the stairs to find the apartment door wide open with blaring music spilling out into the corridor. She entered and spotted Zoe sprawled on the floor, listening to a new record. Eva froze in place, staring at her partner, her eyes wide with shock.

Earl followed Eva in. He also halted, staring at Zoe in surprise. "Whooee!" he cried after a moment.

At his exclamation, Zoe rolled over and saw Eva. Her mouth stretched in a cheeky grin. "Looks like yours, doesn't it?"

Eva swallowed. "You cut your hair."

"It was a spur-of-the-moment decision," Zoe said and ran her hand through her shortened hair. "Elena was surprised, too. Do you like it?" Zoe demanded.

Eva was stunned and quite speechless. She had loved Zoe's long, thick, red hair but the more she looked at Zoe, the more she started to like the shortened version. "Wow," was all she could manage. She let her bag fall on the floor. "Wow."

Zoe laughed. "I think she likes it, Wiggy."

"I love it." Eva bent over and tangled her fingers in Zoe's cropped locks. The hair waved around Zoe's finely boned face, lending an elfin aspect to her appearance that Eva found very appealing.

"You look beautiful." Eva tilted Zoe's face up and kissed her.

"Hey, now...take that to the bedroom, you two!" Earl shielded his eyes in mock horror.

Ignoring him, Eva and Zoe ended the kiss and looked at each other, smiling. Eva offered a hand, which Zoe took, and she helped the other woman to her feet. Zoe turned to the big man beside her.

"Hey, Wiggy!" She beamed as she gave Earl a hug.

"Hi there, Stretch. What's for dinner?" Earl replied, picking up the petite woman easily and engulfing her in a bear hug.

"Wiggy, I need to breathe!" Zoe laughed, trying to extricate herself from the embrace. Earl ruffled her short hair as he gently set her back on the floor.

"Love the new look," he whispered in her ear, just loud enough for Eva to overhear.

Eva had turned down the volume of the gramophone, still marveling at Zoe's haircut. She went into the kitchen and looked into the oven where a roast with potatoes and vegetables was cooking. "Hey, Earl, you want to stay for dinner?"

"Nope, can't. I'm meeting my folks tonight," Earl said from the kitchen door. "It sure smells nice, though."

"Of course it does," Zoe said. She brushed past him, giving him a slap on the behind.

Earl complained loudly. "Hey, now! Eva! Zoe slapped me on the bum."

"Lucky boy," Eva said. She passed him, heading to the bedroom to change, and saw Earl stick his tongue out at her in reply.

"Hey, Eva," he called out. "I gotta go and pick up the folks from Central. Spending the week with them is going to be lots of fun."

Eva returned to the kitchen after she had changed her outfit. Earl was about to leave. "Thanks for the ride home," Eva said. She escorted Earl to the door, held it open, and slapped him on the bum as he passed.

"Watch it, woman!" Earl growled, giving her a wink.

"Hey, you rode in The Beast?" Zoe asked Eva, who nodded. Zoe had nicknamed Earl's car as soon as she had seen it, when he had first brought it over to show off to them. Zoe loved cars and Eva knew she could not wait until she was ready to get her license.

They said their goodbyes to Earl, who waved jauntily as he disappeared down the corridor. As soon as Eva closed the door, Zoe pounced and wrapped herself around Eva in an embrace. "Hi," Zoe said.

Eva smiled down at her partner. "Hi. The food smells nice."

"So do you," Zoe said, grinning. "I made some *galaktoburiko* for dessert."

The two women moved to the sofa and sat down together, Zoe snuggled up against Eva. "So, you really like my hair?" Zoe asked, glancing up at Eva from beneath her eyelashes.

"Yes, I do. You look gorgeous, Zoe," Eva replied. "It's going to take time to adjust to you with short hair, but yeah, I like it."

"I was passing this hairdresser and they had a special on, so I did it."

Eva laughed. This was just like the impulsive Zoe that she loved so much. "Well, it suits you."

"Thank you," Zoe said. She stole a kiss, which Eva did not mind at all. "Guess who we met up with at the shops?"

"Mrs. Jenkins?"

"No, our friend Friedrich Jacobs."

"Oh, great. I wouldn't describe him as 'our friend'. What did he want?"

"Nothing. He was having tea with David Harrison. El and I were shopping and we stopped off to get a cup of tea, and he saw us as they were leaving."

"That's nice," Eva said, relaxing back as Zoe settled against her.

"Hmm. You know that dance Mrs. Jenkins is organizing?"

"Yep, how can I forget?" Eva grimaced. "She wants me to go with her nephew."

"Elena is going with Friedrich Jacobs. Her eyes nearly popped out of her head when they met. She wasn't going to accept without some help so I agreed to go with Mr. Harrison."

"Elena and Jacobs?" Eva asked. "Really?"

"Yep. He stammered and hem'd and ah'd. El went all shy and demure."

The kettle began to whistle. Zoe got up to make some tea. Eva followed her into the kitchen. She put her arms around Zoe's waist, her chin propped on the smaller woman's head as Zoe was putting the tea pot on the stove.

"Did you say you are going with Mr. Harrison?" Eva asked.

"Yes. Do you think I shouldn't have agreed?" Zoe asked and turned around in Eva's embrace to face her. "Are you jealous?"

Eva smiled shyly and nodded. "A little bit. I'm going to be stuck with going with Mrs. Jenkins' nephew."

"Not unless you say you already have a date."

"I don't have one."

"Yes, you do."

"I do?"

"Yes, you are going with Earl."

"I am?"

"You are. Earl doesn't know that he's going with you but that shouldn't be a problem," Zoe said, with a mischievous look in her eye. "Don't you want to go with Earl?"

"Of course! And it would get me out of the dating thing with Mrs. Jenkins' nephew." Eva laughed lightly. "You are a genius," she said and kissed Zoe on the lips.

Zoe gave her a smile, then turned to take the kettle off the stove. While she was doing that Eva watched absently, her thoughts shifting from the dance to her father's new wife. Zoe glanced back at Eva and put the kettle down before she poured the water.

"What's on your mind?" Zoe asked.

"Who says anything is on my mind?" Eva replied.

"You've got your worried face on," Zoe quipped. She gently smoothed the furrow between Eva's eyebrows. "It scrunches up when you worry."

Eva gazed at Zoe for a moment. "You are right. I am a little nervous," she confessed.

"About?"

"What do you think this Alberta is like?" Eva asked.

"I don't know. But she loves your father, so she must be a nice lady if Father H loves her, don't you think?" Zoe reasoned as she poured out the tea. "You are worrying for nothing," Zoe said as she poked Eva in the stomach on the way out of the kitchen. Working together, they finished putting the last few items on the kitchen table, which had been set for dinner.

"Why are you nervous?"

"What if she doesn't like me?" Eva asked, sitting down on the couch and taking a sip of her tea.

Zoe sat beside her on the edge of the couch, grinning. "What's not to like? You're gorgeous, you're intelligent, and you're talented. Did I mention gorgeous?"

"You're biased," Eva said, settling back on the cushions after putting her cup of tea on the coffee table in front of the couch.

"Hmm. Yes, I am. Wouldn't you be in a pickle if I didn't think you were gorgeous, intelligent, talented, and, let's not forget, a fantastic lover!" Zoe settled herself on Eva's lap, fluttering her eyelashes flirtatiously.

Eva laughed. "Have I told you today how much I love you?"

"Yes, this morning," Zoe replied. "Have I told you lately how much you mean to me?"

"Yes, this morning," Eva said.

Zoe slipped her hands around Eva's neck and hitched herself even closer, pressing her body against Eva's.

"You're going to wear me out before my time," Eva whispered, using her lips and her tongue to weave a sensual path of pleasure along Zoe's neck.

A small whimper escaped Zoe's lips. She tangled her fingers in Eva's hair. "Mmm...that feels so, so good," the young woman murmured.

"You're right, love, it does," Eva's lips whispered against silken skin. Eva kissed Zoe's ear, lightly running the tip of her tongue along the edge. She loved the feel of the beautiful young woman in her arms. Eva closed her eyes as pleasure ran through her body, delicious sensations that made her desire grow more demanding. She wanted to stay this way forever. Knowing that could never be, she decided to take her time and explore her lover's body, choosing a slow seduction guaranteed to drive Zoe to the brink of pleasure-glutted madness.

"Relax, my love," she whispering, feeling Zoe's muscles twitch in anticipation of her touch.

"I'm relaxed. Boy, am I relaxed! Stop talking," Zoe responded impatiently.

"Yes, ma'am," Eva replied. She knew her breath was warm against Zoe's ear, doing much more to the young woman than Zoe could anticipate. Goosebumps rippled along Zoe's skin when Eva chuckled, and Zoe let out a low moan that caused intense warmth to circle out from Eva's belly, settling between her legs. Eva felt Zoe's nipples harden, and she sighed, "Oh, yes." Zoe's eager response made the tide of desire swell within her.

"Oh, stop," Zoe breathlessly whimpered, clearly despite her better judgment.

Eva stopped her ministrations. Frustration cut through the pleasurable fog. "What?"

"Bedroom, now," Zoe ordered but remained on Eva's lap. Eva continued kissing her. "Please, Evy," Zoe cried out, sliding off Eva's legs and heading for their bedroom.

Eva let out a wicked chuckle and followed Zoe into the bedroom.

Chapter Twelve

A light breeze whipped Eva's hair around as she leaned over the railing of the balcony, gazing off at the distant horizon and feeling very content.

The sun had set just moments ago, leaving the sky still suffused with a slowly fading golden hue. She was distracted by a movement below. Eva tore her attention away from the sunset to see a neighbor wave at her as he left the block of apartments. Giving the person a quick wave back, she tried to recollect if she even knew his name, only having met him once or twice in the hallway. Leaving the railing, she lowered her tall frame onto a cushioned wrought-iron chair that sat against the back wall of the balcony. Her thoughts were interrupted by the sound of soft footsteps behind her.

Zoe came out onto the balcony carrying a cup of tea and settled beside Eva, leaning against her slightly as she raised the cup to Eva's mouth. "Sip of tea?" she asked. Eva moved slightly to press her lips against the rim of the cup for a small sample.

"Mmm, that's good, love." Eva gave Zoe a smile.

"It sure was," Zoe said and tweaked Eva's dimpled chin.

Eva captured her hand and held it before kissing the fingertips one by one. "You were right, you know," she said.

"About what?"

"My father would have been awakened from his sleep if we had..." Eva let her voice trail off and winked. She laughed when Zoe waggled her eyebrows at her.

"Told you," Zoe answered, returning Eva's smile. She looked over the top of her teacup. "How's your back?"

Eva looked at Zoe and grinned devilishly. "Next time, warn me you are going to do that," she said. Their lovemaking had taken a surprise twist when Zoe had turned the tables on her and taken a more dominant role. That did not happen very often but when it did, Zoe's innovative lovemaking brought her to new heights of ecstasy.

Zoe smiled. "I could give you a back rub later."

Eva rocked back and laughed, nearly spilling her tea over herself. "Just a back rub?"

"I promise." Zoe made a cross over her heart. "*Just* a back rub."

Eva kissed Zoe, despite the two of them being in plain view. "I would like that."

"Too bad we're expecting company." Zoe nibbled Eva's ear. "I could give you the back rub now."

"Don't tempt me." Eva quickly gave Zoe another kiss. She straightened when she spotted her father and his wife turning the corner and coming up the sidewalk. "They are here."

Eva got up from her seat, pulling Zoe with her. She took Zoe's hand and led her back into the apartment. She looked at the table and smiled at the bottlebrush, the red plant sitting squarely in the middle. Zoe was fond of the plant, which was native to Australia, and she took every opportunity to cut two or three fronds from the tree outside their building.

Zoe loved the color red. She had set the table with a white tablecloth and red and white napkins. The kitchen cupboards were painted red and white, and they had tried to find dinner plates to match. Finally, they had found red and white plates during a bargain hunt several weeks before, and a delighted Zoe had immediately bought them. These added to the festive atmosphere.

"Okay, everything looks great," Eva said, taking a final look at the settings and the state of the lounge.

"You look great, too," Zoe said, and reached up to give Eva a quick kiss.

Eva had changed into a stylish black trouser suit with a baby blue silk shirt, while Zoe wore a white shirt with her favorite pink trousers. Both women went to the front door, opening it just as Eva's father and his new wife reached the top of the stairs. Eva's heart pounded as her father and Alberta moved down the corridor.

Panayiotis smiled broadly when he and Alberta entered the apartment. Eva took their coats and Zoe ushered them into the lounge.

"Alberta, these are my daughters, Eva and Zoe." Panayiotis introduced his wife. "The other important women in my life."

Alberta shook Eva's hand and was about to shake Zoe's, but Zoe surprised her with a brief hug. Eva grinned at Alberta's bemusement. Everyone settled into the lounge, Panayiotis sitting down on the couch with a sigh. Zoe took his cane and leaned on it, giving the older man a smile as Alberta sat down beside him.

"I'm pleased to meet you finally, after all the stories your father has told me about you," Alberta said in an obvious attempt to break some of the tension.

"I bet he left out a lot," Eva said, and grinned at Zoe. "He told us you're a nurse?" she asked Alberta.

"Yes, that's how I met your father. I was going to be shipped back home, but things didn't pan out and I stayed on the hospital ship," Alberta explained. She turned her head and gazed lovingly at her husband. "It was God who brought us together."

"I woke up, and there was this angel. I thought I was dead," he said, squeezing his wife's hand.

"I had the same reaction to a certain someone," Eva quipped, giving Zoe an affectionate glance.

"Yes, your father told me you were shot?" Alberta asked, almost as if she had a hard time believing it was true.

"Yes. Shoulder," Eva said, putting a hand over the old injury. "Zoe saved my life."

Alberta smiled. "No wonder you're friends."

Eva glanced at her father who was grinning back at her, shaking her head slightly when she realized Alberta did not know anything about her true relationship with Zoe.

"What do we call you?" Zoe asked, apparently not understanding the look of silent communication that Eva was giving her. Eva stifled a groan.

Alberta looked at her husband and then back at Zoe. "Whatever you want to call me, Zoe."

"How about Mother H?" Zoe suggested slyly.

Alberta's surprise showed on her face. "Sure, if you want to…"

"Hey, I never had a mother-in-law before!" Zoe said with glee.

"Mother-in-law?"

"Don't you have them in America?" Zoe asked seriously at the woman's confusion.

"Aren't you supposed to be married to have a mother-in-law?" Alberta said, raising her eyebrows.

"Yes," Zoe agreed. "Is it done differently in America?"

Alberta smiled nervously. "No, but usually one needs a man and a woman."

"Uh oh," Zoe muttered. She glanced at Eva, who almost cheered when it finally registered with Zoe why Eva was giving her warning looks.

"Alberta, there's something my father didn't tell you," Eva said, motioning for Zoe to come and sit next to her. Eva took Zoe's hand and held it. "Zoe and I are lovers."

"You're lesbians?" Alberta asked in surprise. "No, your father didn't mention that at all. I think he may have forgotten about that," she said and gave her husband a glance that promised a long uncomfortable talk in his future.

Eva nodded. "I'm not sure why my father chose not to tell you, but—" Her speech ended abruptly. "Excuse me. I'll go make some tea." Eva got up from her seat and went into the kitchen. She was angry that she had been put into a position where she had to explain to a perfect stranger about her private life. Yes, it was her father's wife, but she felt as though her father was ashamed of whom she was. It was bad enough that she had to hide her love for Zoe from the outside world, but when it came to the only family she had other than Zoe, it was like a slap in the face. It stung. The kitchen door was closed, but she could still hear everything that was going in the room she had just left.

"Pany, that is disgraceful," Alberta said.

"Who are you calling disgraceful?" Zoe asked, her tone betraying her upset.

"Oh, Zoe, I'm not talking about you. I'm talking about my non-thinking husband here," Alberta said, clearly annoyed. "I'm talking to someone who didn't stop and think. You could have told me, Pany!"

"Oh," Zoe replied. "Excuse me, I have to go and check on the tea." She sounded much less angry.

Eva left the door and busied herself at the stove. Nevertheless, she could catch Alberta's voice rising in exasperation. "Panayiotis Haralambos, you should be absolutely ashamed of yourself! Why on earth didn't you tell me?"

"I said they were friends. They are best friends, I didn't lie," Panayiotis said. "I thought it best if you heard about their relationship from them."

Zoe came into the kitchen, the door swinging shut behind her. Eva put a finger to her lips, motioning the other woman to silence, then turned back to the kettle.

"Men!" Alberta continued, her frustration clear. "Go and talk to your daughter."

"I didn't cause any damage—"

"Pany, your daughter thinks you are ashamed of her," Alberta admonished him. "Now, go."

Panayiotis sighed heavily. His footsteps were loud as he crossed the floor. Although Eva was waiting for it, she still jumped when she heard a rap on the door. Panayiotis came into the kitchen and stood still a moment, watching them both.

Eva leaned against the stove, waiting for the water to boil. She glanced at him out of the corner of her eye. Zoe was giving the man a look that spoke volumes. Panayiotis cleared his throat. Zoe patted him on the shoulder and left the kitchen, sensitive to their need for privacy.

"Can I have a word with you?" Panayiotis asked Eva.

"Sure," Eva replied, feeling a little better than when she had first gone into the kitchen. She was angry but the depth of her anger had dissipated somewhat now that she had overheard Alberta's reaction to her father's thoughtlessness.

"Firstly, I want to say that I'm not ashamed of you, Eva," he said, walking over to her and putting his hand on her shoulder. "I am proud you are my daughter."

Eva took a deep breath and let it out slowly, also allowing a bit of her resentment to drain. "You should have told Alberta about me and Zoe."

"It is not my place to tell anyone what you do behind these doors," Panayiotis replied.

"Alberta isn't just anyone, Father, she's your wife," Eva said. "I'm not asking you to stand up in the congregation and tell everyone you have a lesbian daughter, but she *is* your wife," Eva said and looked at her father. "Father, I know having a lesbian for a daughter isn't what you want, but it's who I am. Hiding that from your wife tells me you didn't want to tell her because you're ashamed of me. I'm tired of having to hide who I am and what Zoe means to me."

"I'm not ashamed of you," her father replied sincerely. "I *am* proud of you. Proud that you're my daughter. I thought you would want to tell her yourself," he said. "I know it sounds foolish and it is. I'm sorry."

"Father, what was I going to tell her? 'Hello, I'm Eva, your new step-daughter and I'm a lesbian'?"

"It's a good conversation starter and certainly an ice-breaker." Despite the serious discussion, Eva smiled back at him. "Come here," he said, pulling Eva into his arms and kissing the top of her head. "I could never be ashamed of you."

Father and daughter hugged each other. The kettle began to whistle. Eva gave her father a kiss on the cheek before he left the kitchen. Zoe came back inside, avoiding a collision with the man as they met in the doorway.

"All fixed?" she asked, joining Eva at the stove.

"Yes," Eva replied as Zoe picked up the kettle and poured the water for the tea.

"Zoe." Eva put her arms around the petite woman. "Do you think we can impress Mrs. Haralambos?"

"I don't care," Zoe said. "All I'm interested in is impressing *Miss* Haralambos," she said grinning as she used Eva's new surname. "You know, I really like the sound of that."

Eva took her partner's face between her palms and kissed her.

Someone coughed loudly behind them. "I'm sorry to intrude," Alberta said, smiling. Eva tried to pull away, but Zoe had a different idea and held on, forcing Eva to stay where she was.

"We're bad hosts leaving you two out there alone. I'm sorry...um..." Eva stammered.

"Isn't she cute when she's shy?" Zoe said to Alberta, her eyes twinkling.

"How about we take the tea in the lounge so we can talk?" Alberta asked, taking the teacups out. She was quickly followed by the other two women. She set the cups down and Zoe poured.

"So, Mrs. H, what *do* we call you, apart from Mrs. H?" Zoe asked, giving Panayiotis a cup of tea.

"Well, you can call me Ally if you like. That's what my friends call me."

Zoe glanced at Eva, who had put on her most stoic expression. "So not Mother Haralambos?" she asked.

"I prefer Ally," Alberta said, beaming at both young women. "Mother Haralambos makes me feel very old."

"Ally it is." Zoe clapped her hands together. "So, this hasn't been a very good start, has it?"

After a moment of stunned silence, everyone began to laugh. After their chuckles died down, Alberta turned to Zoe.

"Tell me about Zoe and Eva," she said, making herself comfortable on the sofa.

Zoe glanced at Eva again. "Eva and I made vows to each other on the ship coming out here. Sort of like being married. I know it's not like actually *being* married in the church but—"

"To us it is," Eva interrupted. "We are together, and nothing anyone says will make any difference," she added a little more forcefully than she had intended, surprising herself. Zoe merely smiled and sat back.

"I don't understand it, but I'm sure there are a lot of things I don't understand," Alberta admitted.

"Does that mean you don't approve of us?' Zoe asked.

"Do you approve of my marriage to your father?" Alberta asked Eva.

Eva smiled back. "I have no reason to say no to that."

"And I have no reason to say 'no, I don't approve to your relationship'. It's none of my business what you two young ladies do in your own home," Alberta replied, clearly believing she had given the best answer possible under the circumstances.

Zoe was the only one with a frown on her face. "That isn't a real answer."

Eva put her arm around her partner. "Zoe—"

"No, Eva, she's right that's not an answer," Alberta replied. "I can see this issue is important to you, but does my opinion really matter?"

"It does matter because you are married to my father," Eva said quietly. She found herself wondering why it mattered. She did not know this woman, but somehow Eva felt Alberta's opinion of her was important. It was an unsettling feeling. Eva had only ever wanted to impress one woman and that was Zoe.

"I see that, but you just said that whatever I say won't matter because you love Zoe," Alberta said.

Eva pursed her lips in thought for a moment. "You are my stepmother, so it matters. It won't change how I feel about Zoe, but your opinion is important to me." Eva looked at Zoe and then back at her stepmother. "It's important to *us*."

Alberta nodded. "For me, I can't love a woman the way I love your father. It's not natural for me. I'm going to guess that it's natural for you two, and I can't be judgmental about how you live your life. Am I making sense?"

Eva noticed Alberta was watching them closely. Her own expression remained guarded — Eva knew she could be a difficult person to read when she chose — but Zoe's face was very expressive and instantly showed her approval of Alberta's answer.

"I love Eva," Zoe told Alberta, glancing up at Eva.

"Then that is right for you," Alberta said.

"It's no different to how you love my father," Eva said. "You are my father's angel, and I have my own angel. You saved my father's life and Zoe saved mine."

"I would like to hear that story some day," Alberta said. Eva gave her a very small nod and relaxed a trifle, feeling a little more at ease. "So, Eva, where do you work?" Alberta continued, obviously hoping to change the very sensitive subject.

"I work in a factory," Eva replied. "A biscuit factory, to be precise."

"That must be a very good job. So you work in the office?"

Eva shook her head. "No, I'm a process worker."

Alberta was taken aback at the news. "Your father told me you went to university in Berlin. I hope you don't mind my asking, but why are you working in a factory when you have such a high level of education?"

"I couldn't find anyone to hire me, and I want Zoe to go to art school," Eva replied. "It's a small sacrifice."

Zoe smiled at Eva.

"Ah, I see. So do you like it?" Alberta asked.

"No," Eva replied. "But there weren't any other jobs for me, so I do this one."

"Maybe I can help you there. I've been told by the Immigration Department that they are looking for translators to help with the influx of refugees. You can speak several languages, can't you?"

"She speaks fluent German, Greek, Italian, and of course English," Zoe said, glowing with pride at Eva's accomplishments.

"Excellent. Why don't you join me? I can speak Greek and rusty German. I've got an interview scheduled with them for tomorrow. Would you like to come with me?" Alberta asked expectantly. From her expression, it was clear to Eva that the woman hoped this offer of help would not be rebuffed.

"Yes!" Zoe jumped up and accepted Alberta's offer before Eva had a chance to say anything. "That would be perfect, Evy. You could leave that factory and the night shifts," Zoe told her, trying to convince Eva of the benefits of quitting a job that she hated.

Eva liked the idea of using her language skills to help others assimilate into their new homeland. "I think I would like that," she said shyly, and smiled at her stepmother.

Friedrich leaned back in his chair. A smile played about his lips as he looked up at the ceiling. He replayed the scene from the teahouse in his mind. The young woman had caught his attention even though he had been too tongue-tied to give her any indication of his interest.

At least David had been there to help him out and get him a date. "Oh, damn!" he muttered, realizing something about the dance that had not occurred to him before.

The door opened and David walked in, carrying some files. He set them down on Friedrich's desk. "What's the matter, Freddy, old boy?" he asked.

"Um, I can't dance," Friedrich said, feeling rather dejected.

"Can you kiss?" David asked as he removed a file from the filing cabinet. When Friedrich did not a reply, he turned around. "Oh, don't tell me you haven't kissed a girl yet!"

Friedrich frowned. "Of course I have but, um..."

"But what?" David asked. He opened the file and began scribbling notes, which he inserted among the pages in the folder.

Forgetting David's question for the moment, Friedrich asked, "What are you doing?"

"I'm working on this file."

"I can see that. Why are you adding notes to my file?"

"For our friend," David replied. He knew his short, uninformative answers were annoying Friedrich.

Friedrich sighed, trying not to betray his impatience. "Which friend?"

"Our janitor."

Friedrich looked at him, confused. "David, did you have too many beers at dinner?"

David laughed. He brushed back his sandy blond hair and returned to writing. "I found out our janitor has ties with the Nazis. I thought it was a brilliant strategy for him to work for the government agency that dealt with Nazi criminals. He knows our every move, Freddy. That's why every time we find out where these rodents are, they leave before we get there. I didn't know who it was before, but I suspected that we had an informer inside the office."

"How did you find out?"

"Remember a couple of nights ago when Daniel told us where one of the houses was?" David asked, glancing up from his work. Friedrich nodded.

"Well, the next day when the Feds went to the house — nothing. The landlady told them that her tenants had left town. We have been working for months with those rats knowing our every move. I've suspected the janitor for some time, but I didn't have any evidence linking it to him conclusively."

"How can we use that to our advantage?"

"I'm not only a good-looking bloke, but a smart one. Behold what I'm doing."

"You are writing in my files," Friedrich repeated in puzzlement, stating the obvious.

David handed him one of the papers he had written on. It detailed Eva's testimony against Rhimes and Muller.

"Do you think they'll buy it?" Friedrich asked, impressed by the ruse.

"Of course. They already know Eva is alive. Our friend told them. I let it slip in the corridor with Daniel when Janitor Man—"

"Marko," Friedrich supplied. "'Janitor Man' makes him sound like a comic book hero."

"All right, then, Marko. When Marko finished work, I followed him. I couldn't see who he was talking to, but it must have been about Eva."

"Why Eva?"

"Wouldn't you pass on such a juicy piece of information as soon as possible?" David grinned. "Of course you would."

"So you're going to give him the file?"

"No, I'm going to give him what I want them to see." He pulled out a file that had been sitting in the pile he had brought with him. "I've taken out information about Miss Lambros and certain other details."

Friedrich watched David continue to alter the file. When the man had finished, he slipped the folder with the altered information into the filing cabinet drawer and buried the real file in the pile of paperwork on his desk.

"Come on, Freddy, I want to get out of here," David urged, picking up the rest of the files. "I'll teach you to dance as well."

They turned off the light and David waited while Friedrich locked the office door. They walked down the corridor, a single light on the ceiling creating shadows down the narrow hallway. Stopping near the fire exit, they paused in the shadows for a few moments.

"Maybe he isn't..." Friedrich started to say, then closed his mouth when he saw Marko, the janitor, stop in front of their office door; he was carrying a mop and bucket. He looked down the darkened hallway for a moment before choosing a key from the key ring attached to his belt, unlocking the door and going inside.

"Okay, let's go, Freddy my boy. Are you sure you've kissed a girl before?" David teased as he ushered an embarrassed Friedrich down the stairs, and shut the front door behind them.

Chapter Thirteen

Zoe was tired. She yawned again and tried to snuggle deeper under the downy comforter, even though she knew she had to get up soon to get ready for work. Eva had gone with Alberta to the Immigration Department earlier that morning after calling in sick to the biscuit factory. It was not something she had wanted to do, but it was the only way she was able to get time off for the interview.

After Panayiotis and Alberta had called it a night and left the apartment the previous evening, Zoe and Eva had cleaned up and gone to bed. It was around midnight when Zoe had awakened to find Eva thrashing about, enmeshed in a nightmare. The events of the past few days had finally caught up with the woman and her anxiety over Muller had caused her stoic attitude to shatter. It had taken all of Zoe's patient soothing to get Eva to quiet down and go to sleep once more.

The doorbell interrupted Zoe's futile attempt to sleep a while longer. She let out a theatrical groan before getting out of bed and putting on her robe.

"This had better be good, or else," Zoe muttered. She opened the door to find Earl standing there in his white overalls. He did not bother to be asked in; he barged past Zoe and started looking around the apartment.

"Earl, what are you doing here?"

"Where's Eva? Stalk is chucking the biggest dummy spit today," he said.

"Dummy spit?" Zoe asked, yawning.

"He's really angry," Earl explained.

"Stalk can go and jump off the Harbour Bridge," Zoe mumbled sleepily. She went into the kitchen to put the kettle on. Earl followed her.

"Zoe, this is important. Eva could lose her job," he said.

"Good."

Earl stopped and scratched his head, clearly confused. "You two didn't have an argument, did you?"

"No. We're fine."

"Hey, are you making me a cuppa?"

"No, you woke me up, but since you're here and I'm awake, I can make you one," she said. For the first time since he had arrived, she gave Earl a grin. *I know something you don't know*, Zoe thought, feeling a little more alert now that a chance for mischief had presented itself.

"Thanks, mate, I need it. I really need a beer, but it's too early in the morning for that. So, what's up? Where's Eva?"

"Why?"

"I need to find Eva," he repeated.

"Why? She's off sick. They do allow her to take sick days, don't they?"

"They do, but I guess she didn't call in since they sent me after her. So is she in bed?" Earl started for the bedroom and stopped. "Is she decent?"

"She's not in bed." Zoe wondered what the fuss was about hoping Eva wasn't going to be in any sort of trouble. She forced herself to be casual, "So what's the problem?"

"No one knew she was taking a sick day."

"Huh? Eva told me she called in."

Earl lifted his shoulders in a half shrug. "I don't know for sure. Stalk came up to me and asked me where she was and I said I didn't know," Earl replied. "So here I am, in search of my missing best mate."

"Stalk is a *malarka!*" Zoe cursed. She was tired of Eva being abused by the moronic supervisor. No one deserved to be treated like dirt. It angered Zoe when Eva came home from work and she could see how drained the woman was, both emotionally and physically, from working in that factory.

"Zoe, I love it when you talk dirty," Earl said. He ruffled Zoe's already disheveled hair. "Come on, so where is Eva?"

Zoe sighed at Earl's persistence. "She's gone to the Immigration Department with her stepmother to apply for a translator job."

"Hey, that's great, Zoe!" Earl exclaimed. "So, what's the old lady like?"

"Very nice, once she got over the shock of finding out we are lesbians," Zoe said and smiled at the surprised look on her friend's face.

"She didn't know?"

"She didn't know. Father H thought it would be better for us to tell her."

"Fair suck of the sav!" Earl exclaimed and smacked his hand against his forehead.

"Fair suck of the what?" Zoe asked, not quite understanding the Australian slang. The phrase Earl had used was the strangest she had heard. "What am I going to suck?"

Earl shook his head. "It means 'I don't quite believe it'."

"Well, fair suck of the sav it was," Zoe said and giggled at the nonsense slang. "It started badly with her finding out we were lesbians, then Eva getting upset with her father, and Ally telling Father H how silly he was for not telling her. Then we all sat down and got to know each other," Zoe said and tried to stifle another yawn.

"Sounds like it was quite a night. What does Eva think of her?"

"You know Eva; she takes a bit of time to warm up to strangers, but Ally put her at ease and got her talking, which I must say was quite a challenge last night. Father H was his usual funny self."

Another knock sounded at the door just as she finished speaking.

"What is it around here today? Did they make this Central's new sub station?" Zoe grumbled. She went over to open the door, finding Elena standing with two dresses in her hand.

"Morning, sunshine! I need your advice," Elena said as she came in. She caught sight of Earl and waved with her free hand. "Morning, Earl."

"Morning, Elena. Nice dresses."

"Thank you, but I can't decide," she said. Elena turned to Zoe. "Saw Eva this morning, told me not to wake you until eight o'clock."

"It's not eight o'clock yet," Zoe protested as she looked at the clock on the wall.

"You are such a grouch in the morning! Earl's here, so I thought it was safe to knock." Elena held up two dresses. "I can't decide. Do I wear the blue or the red?"

"Didn't we have this conversation at the store?" Zoe asked plaintively.

"We did, but you didn't give me an answer."

"I dunno, ask Wiggy," Zoe said, walking back into the bedroom to change her clothes. When she had dressed and combed her hair, she came back outside to find Earl trying to teach Elena how to waltz to the polka music coming from the radio.

A solitary fan whirled around in a futile attempt to cool the room which was packed with people eager to join the Immigration Department. Eva watched the fan blades go round and round as she tried to calm the butterflies quivering inside her stomach. She hated interviews. Eva had been fidgeting quite a bit as she and Alberta sat waiting for their turn. The hard wooden chairs felt as though they had been manufactured for school children rather than adults.

"These are certainly uncomfortable," Alberta groused, shifting in her chair. "Does your back hurt? I know mine does. I can't find a comfortable position."

"It's all right," Eva replied as evenly as possible, not wanting to give too much of her discomfort away.

Alberta kept quiet until Eva shifted again. "How did you hurt your back initially?" she asked.

Eva sat silent for a long moment, not sure what to reveal about herself. "How do you know I hurt my back?"

"I was a nurse," Ally reminded her. "Hard wooden chairs make any back sore but for someone with a bad back, they're murder."

Eva nodded her agreement. After a bit of a pause, she admitted, "You're correct. I do have a back problem."

"How did you hurt yourself?"

"My father didn't tell you?" Eva asked, feeling a bit shy. She was wary of allowing people to know her private life. A part of her wanted to hide and not let anyone know how much she hurt. She knew that was impossible, but she guarded her privacy nevertheless. Eva saw Alberta shake her head, no. Out of respect for her stepmother, though, she decided to tell the woman something about her past.

"It happened when I was a teenager," Eva finally said. "My stepfather's legacy."

"Oh, your father told me you and Zoe had gone through some very rough times with your stepfather, but he didn't tell me anything else. Your father believes that I should ask to find out anything, and if you want to tell me, you will."

Eva was not surprised to learn that her father had not told Alberta about Muller and how he had mistreated her or about their time in Greece. Eva liked Alberta a great deal for the way she was handling the obvious emotional minefield. Once she considered the matter, Eva realized that her father understood her better than she thought. He knew her need for privacy and respected it, even if it was done a little awkwardly. "It's a long story," Eva said.

"Well, after we finish here, we can go and have some lunch and talk, if you'd like," Alberta offered.

"I would like that," Eva said, smiling at the older woman.

"Miss Eva Haralimbis?" a middle-aged man asked aloud, calling Eva to her interview. Eva shook her head at the way her new surname had been butchered. She was still getting used to her name being mispronounced.

"Eventually they will get it right," she mumbled under her breath. She sighed in relief as she got out of the uncomfortable chair and followed the interviewer into the room.

Erik Rhimes was not in a good mood. He had spent the morning trying to get in touch with his contact at the Investigations Bureau, although he had been told not to communicate with the man unless it was extremely urgent. Regardless, he thought that his current concern was pressing enough. Having had no luck in locating the man, Rhimes decided to go to the station and return home. He watched dourly as several trains sped past the platform. He had just missed his train and there would be a long wait until he could get another. Resigned, he sat down on a hard bench and lit a cigarette.

"Looking for me, Herr Rhimes?"

Rhimes jumped, startled, as he turned towards the voice. Marko was standing there with his hands in his pockets, grinning. He was a middle-aged man with thin, greying hair, of middling height and sporting a ridiculously thin mustache that made him look quite comical. Rhimes disliked the man but he would deal with the Devil himself if it meant his safety and the continued well-being of his friends.

"Where have you been? I've been trying to contact you," Rhimes snapped.

"My day off today. Thought I would take a leisurely walk. It's quite fortuitous I ran into you, isn't it?" Marko asked as he sat down next to Rhimes on the bench.

Rhimes frowned. "What do you have for me?"

"Well, from reading her file, I would say you are in a heap of trouble," Marko answered, taking out a cigarette of his own and lighting it. He took a drag and exhaled the smoke, watching as it drifted upwards.

Rhimes tried to control his rising temper. "Do you have a copy of the file?"

"You know that's against the law, Herr Rhimes," Marko replied with a smirk.

Rhimes closed his eyes and counted slowly until he had regained control of himself. He could not afford to kill this idiot, not until he had what he wanted. "How much is this going to cost me?" he asked when he could trust his voice again.

"I have a figure in my head. Maybe we can get some coffee and discuss it."

"Fine, whatever. Lead the way."

Rhimes followed the man from the subway into a coffee house across the street. Marko led him to the table at the far end of the room then sat down. The man waited until a waitress took their order before reaching into his pocket and retrieving a piece of paper. "Before we discuss our little business transaction, why is this woman so important?" he asked.

"None of your business, Mr. Berckett. I paid you well for the information you have supplied to us, but I don't think it's in your best interests to ask so many questions."

Marko retained the irritating little smirk on his face until the waitress came back with their order. "Herr Rhimes, I have something you want desperately and I can't figure out why. Was she your mistress or something?" Marko asked impertinently.

Rhimes refused to rise to the bait, but his patience was wearing thin. "No."

"Okay, so you don't want to discuss it. How about we discuss how you will make me a happy man and then I can make you a happy man? How does that sound?"

"Fine," Rhimes spat out.

"I'm assuming you don't have this much on you?" Marko asked, handing Rhimes a note.

Rhimes' eyes bulged at the figure written on the piece of paper. "No, I don't carry that kind of change on me," he verified, and returned the note.

"A Nazi with a sense of humor!" Marko said, just loudly enough for Rhimes to hear. He smiled and watched Rhimes over the top of his coffee cup. Taking a sip, he went on, "How about I meet you someplace and then we can exchange gifts?"

Rhimes sighed. He would indeed give Mr. Berckett a gift, but he doubted the man would enjoy it. He needed that file, then he would deal with this trash. "Fine." Rhimes took a pen from his jacket pocket, scribbled an address on a napkin, then folded it and gave it to Marko. "Meet me there at seven o'clock tonight. I will have your gift."

"Excellent. It's been good doing business with you, Mr. Rhimes," Marko said. He got up and left the coffee shop, leaving Rhimes alone with his coffee.

"Indeed," Rhimes said and shook his head. He waited a few minutes before returning to the train station.

The interviews had gone on for some time. By the time Eva had filled out the myriad forms required, the process had become an exercise in patience, a commodity she was beginning to exhaust. Finally, her labors were over and she sat patiently in the waiting room while Alberta finished. There were only a handful of candidates who had fulfilled all the necessary criteria, and they were also waiting. Eva spent her time flicking through a dog-eared copy of *Women's Weekly* that was on a table. She stood up when Alberta came out of the office, followed by the interviewer.

"Well, congratulations ladies," the tall bespectacled middle-aged man announced as Alberta joined Eva. "You are all successful candidates. Now everyone has filled out their forms, which is good. From here you will go for a medical examination before you join the

Public Service." He glanced down at his clipboard and looked back up, light flashing on the lenses of his spectacles. "After that, you will be told where you will be assigned."

Eva glanced at Alberta, who shrugged. Everyone trooped out of the office and headed across the road to another building, where they were treated to more waiting on more uncomfortable chairs. Eventually, both women had completed their physicals, and they left the Immigration Department and headed for a nearby teahouse.

"How did it go?" Alberta asked, crossing the road with Eva.

Eva kept pace with Alberta. "It went well. He asked me a few questions about my back."

"Why?" Alberta asked. "My physical was very quick."

"The doctor prodded my back a bit. He said my duties didn't involve lifting or anything that would aggravate my back problem, so he didn't see it as a cause for rejecting my application."

"That's good — isn't it?" Alberta asked.

"Oh, that's very good! I don't mind not lifting heavy boxes or working night shifts," Eva replied with a chuckle. "Zoe is going to be so happy that I'm quitting the factory."

Alberta held the door open as Eva preceded her into the teahouse. Eva had found this small teahouse during one of her many job hunting forays into the city. Since the lunch rush was over, the place was nearly empty. A waiter showed the two women to a corner of the room where he seated them at a table with comfortable seats, then offered them menus.

"Can we please have some water?" Alberta asked the young man, who nodded and went to fill her request. She pulled a bottle of aspirin from her handbag, opened it and shook out two pills into her palm. "Now I want you to take these," she said after the waiter had brought them two glasses of water. "Those hard chairs gave me a backache, so I can't imagine what you're feeling like."

Eva smiled at her stepmother. She accepted the aspirin and popped the pills into her mouth, washing them down with a long drink. "Thank you, Ally. That's sweet of you."

"Nothing sweet about it. If I returned you to Zoe with a backache, she might be a little miffed that I didn't take care of you."

"My back problem is a constant worry to Zoe, so thank you."

"I know it's difficult for you to trust someone you just met. I like you as well. I'm sorry about last night; your father did mean well."

"I understand." Eva nodded.

"What I would like is for us to become friends."

"I would like that, as well," Eva agreed shyly. She found herself wanting to get to know her father's wife but feeling awkward and hesitant about putting herself forward. *I'm trying too hard*, Eva thought. *I very much want her to like me.* Not that she ever wanted people to hate her but for some reason she craved this woman's approval. Eva mentally shook herself and looked at the menu.

Alberta's grey eyes twinkled. The tip of Eva's tongue stuck out as she tried to decide what to eat. "Did they tell you where you'll be working?" Alberta asked.

"George Street Immigration Center. They have enough Greek translators, but they don't have many for Italian and German."

"Excellent! That's where I'll be as well. I thought I would be going to the Circular Quay office, but I'm so glad we'll be working together." Alberta took a sip of her water and gave Eva a more serious look. "Your father was going to speak to Mrs. Jenkins today to see how soon we can move in. Does it bother you that we might live so close?"

Eva was momentarily startled by the question. The thought of her father and his wife living close to her and Zoe gave her a warm feeling, and she smiled. "No, of course not. I want you there. I know Zoe will like that very much, too. I haven't had much family around since my mother died."

The waiter came back to take their orders. When he had finished and walked away, Alberta looked at Eva. "How old were you when your mother passed away?"

Eva looked down and fidgeted with her napkin. "She died a little over three months after my eighteenth birthday. The 9th of November, 1938," Eva said quietly. Her mother's death had signaled the start of the darkest period in her life, one she had never believed she would survive. She had not been given time to grieve her beloved mother, since her stepfather had placed the blame for the woman's death at Eva's feet. The burden of that guilt was somehow worse than any of the physical cruelties unleashed by Muller or her other tormenters.

Alberta was shocked. "I'm so sorry. If you don't want to talk about it—"

"No, that's all right. I was first told she was killed on *Kristallnacht* by someone who thought she was a Jewess."

Alberta nodded. "I heard stories about that night. Tragic," she said, touching Eva's wrist.

Eva grimaced and kept her head down, staring at the napkin. "I participated in it," she mumbled. She was quite sure the revelation would sicken her stepmother, who would not be so quick to like her anymore. She was still disgusted with herself for taking part in Germany's night of shame and the start of a nightmare for many European Jews.

"You still hate yourself." Alberta took Eva's hands and held them tight in her grasp. "How did you participate?" she asked. "What did you do?"

Eva continued to hang her head. "I went with my friends and we burned down a synagogue," she whispered.

Alberta nodded at the waiter, who had returned with their order, and waited until he had left. She sat looking at the young woman. "You didn't...?" She left the question hanging.

Eva glanced up, unshed tears burning her eyes. "I did nothing to save the rabbi or the synagogue."

"We all do things that in hindsight would seem to be extremely wrong, but you have to think of what you were like when you were eighteen and not look at the past through the eyes of a twenty-six-year-old. The woman I see before me is gentle, kind, and loving. I don't think that eighteen-year-old Eva would have been any different. But the eighteen-year-old young woman was doing what her peers wanted her to do."

"If I had not gone with my friends, my mother would still be alive," Eva said quietly, staring at the lunch in front of her. The plate and contents were blurred by tears.

"Eva, look at me for a moment." Alberta reached across the table, lifted Eva's chin, and brushed the wetness from her cheeks. "If you had been in the house, you would have lost your life, too. I don't think your being at home would have stopped whoever killed your mother."

"I'm sorry," Eva said. She took out a handkerchief, wiped her eyes, and blew her nose. "I haven't talked about my mother in a long time." Eva took a deep breath and sipped her tea.

"You have nothing to be sorry about," Alberta said. She scooted her chair over and gave Eva a hug. "You're not responsible for your mother's death."

"My stepfather thought so," Eva whispered.

"That man is a heartless brute. Is that when you hurt your back?"

Eva nodded. "He beat me," she said. "He didn't care that I was out on *Kristallnacht*, but he found out that same night that I was a lesbian. It didn't sit well with him that a German officer would have a deviant for a daughter," Eva said bitterly. "Some things were unforgivable in his eyes."

"Eva, you are not a deviant. Anyone who loves as much as you do isn't wrong."

Eva smiled grimly and wiped away an errant tear. "Not many people think like you do, Ally."

Alberta sighed. "Yes, you are right. People think homosexuals have an illness, we both know that, but you love Zoe and you traveled to the other side of the world to make her happy. You provide for her. You were even willing to work in a factory to support her. There is absolutely nothing wrong in that. Nor do *I* think you have an illness, and neither does your father or your friends."

Eva smiled. "Zoe was my saving grace. She saved my life."

"I'm sure Zoe would say the same thing about you," Alberta replied and gently brushed her fingertips through Eva's bangs. "That young woman worships you. I've only just met you both, but I could easily see the love she has for you."

"I never thought I could love anyone so much," Eva whispered. "Ally, I know you don't understand us, but—"

"I know enough about love to understand what you mean. When I met your father, I thought I knew love, but getting to know him and being with him gave me a new understanding. How did you meet that little minx, anyway?" Alberta asked, clearly wanting to steer the conversation back to a happier topic.

"Well, it was a little difficult at first, what with her wanting to kill me," Eva said, and her grin broadened at the pole-axed expression on Alberta's face.

Chapter Fourteen

Zoe was slumped on the sofa, her feet up on an armrest, as she found a comfortable position to listen to Aliki Manolas, one of her favorite singers, on the gramophone. She loved listening to Greek music and closed her eyes to let the beautiful strains of the song wash over her. Eva had given her a love for jazz and opera but listening to Aliki took her back home. She could close her eyes and be instantly transported back to Greece; to lazy summer days. She could not believe how fortunate she had been to find Aliki's records in a small Greek store that sold a little bit of everything from her native country. As the song ended, she glanced at the clock and wondered when Eva was going to be home. Zoe's own day had ended early because the restaurant was still in the throes of painting and cleaning.

As if on cue, the door opened and her partner walked through with some shopping bags in hand, followed closely by Alberta. Zoe jumped up and ran the few steps necessary to greet Eva with a kiss and a hug. "Hey, you're back! How did it go?" Zoe asked, wrapping herself around the taller woman.

Eva grinned, trying to hold both Zoe and the shopping bags. "We both made it."

Zoe squealed with delight and kissed Eva in celebration. "Thanks, Ally!"

Alberta beamed. "My pleasure, Zoe."

"So did you behave yourself?" Zoe asked as Eva attempted to put the bags down.

"I always behave myself," Eva replied.

Zoe snorted. "Oh yeah, like the time..." Her story was cut short by the arrival of Mrs. Jenkins and Eva's father at the still open door. Eva let go of Zoe as soon as she noticed Mrs. Jenkins and went over to the sofa. She tried to act nonchalant, but Zoe could read the stiff set of Eva's shoulders and other signs of concealed anxiety.

The lies and deception were getting to her lover, as they were to Zoe. At some point the true nature of their relationship was going to become crystal clear to the landlady. Zoe knew what would happen then. They would get evicted. It was just a matter of time, and the thought made her feel simultaneously sad and angry.

"Nelly, I would like you to meet my wife, Alberta," Panayiotis said to Mrs. Jenkins, who had apparently taken an instant liking to the older man.

"So, Eva, you're going to get new neighbors!" Mrs. Jenkins exclaimed. "Your father is quite a charmer."

Eva smiled at him. "You're right, he *is* quite a charmer."

"And such a handsome man, too," Mrs. Jenkins cooed. "I can see where you got your good looks from," the older woman said, oblivious to the ill-concealed smirks that were directed at her by Zoe and Eva. "Oh, Eva, I nearly forgot. Can you ask your Earl if he can help Timmy in setting up for the dance?" Mrs. Jenkins asked.

"I'll let him know you could use some help," Eva answered.

"Thanks much," Mrs. Jenkins replied. "So nice to meet you," she said to Panayiotis and Alberta as she walked away.

Eva closed the door and rejoined her family.

"Who's Earl?" Alberta asked.

"Eva's boyfriend," Panayiotis said, laughing at Alberta's confusion.

"Eva's boyfriend?" Alberta asked. She glanced at Zoe, who shrugged unconcernedly and went to the kitchen with some of the groceries. She kept the door open, though, and was still able to see what was happening in the lounge.

"Come on, wife, and I'll tell you all about it." Panayiotis took his wife by her hand and left the apartment. Eva joined Zoe in the kitchen with the remaining groceries.

Eva put her arms Zoe. "How would you like to go with me to the factory?"

"What are we going to do?" Zoe asked, turning around to face her lover.

"I'm going to hand in my resignation and my uniforms," Eva answered, smiling.

"You bet. Can I tell Stalk...?"

Eva shook her head. "No. Jack could make life difficult for Earl if you do that."

"Boofhead. I had this all planned out. We were going to go down there and tell him to shove the job right up his backside," Zoe muttered.

Eva shook her head again. "Nope. Sorry, Zoe; can't do that."

"Can I kiss you in front of them?"

"Nope. Can't do that either," Eva said.

Zoe let out a heartfelt sigh, somewhat disappointed. "All the fun things are not allowed," she complained, and pouted when Eva just grinned.

The traffic noise hit them as soon as the two women jumped off the streetcar. Eva took Zoe's hand, leading her through the afternoon crowd towards the biscuit factory. Eva held the resignation letter in her other hand. When they entered the building, they were both nearly overwhelmed by the oppressive heat and noise.

Zoe frowned. "I hate this place," she muttered as they walked through to the main office. A moment later, Jack Stalk rounded a corner, heading straight for them. "Oh, poop," Zoe said.

"Well, well, well, if it isn't Miss I-Hurt-My-Back. Good afternoon Fraulein Muller. So nice of you to join us."

Zoe stood next to Eva, fuming while Eva kept a calm expression on her face. She handed the resignation letter to Zoe and took a step forward to confront the man. Eva would have loved to tell him off but knew if she did, Earl would feel the repercussions.

"You do know how to use the telephone, don't you?"

"Oh yes, I know how to use it."

"This is your first strike, Muller. If you don't..."

Eva smiled at her now former supervisor. "You won't have to worry about the kraut anymore," Eva told him. She stepped forward until her face was inches away from Stalk's. "I quit. Do — you — understand?" she chanted slowly. She waited a moment, enjoying the man's look of amazement. Giving him a knowing smile, she took the letter from Zoe and turned, heading for the office and leaving Stalk staring at her in shock.

"So too much hard work, eh? I knew you krauts are all the same." He shouted after her.

"She's leaving for another job — better pay and better supervisors," Zoe said very slowly, as if speaking to a slow-witted person.

"She can't quit!" Stalk exclaimed. "I am... We have... She can't do that."

"She just did." Zoe smirked and followed Eva into the office, giggling the entire way.

Hans Muller sat on the sofa and watched Rhimes glance at the clock yet again. He had been watching his friend for over an hour as the man paced back and forth in the small apartment that was their refuge, wearing a path in the cheap carpet.

"You can't do it here," Muller finally said.

"Why not?"

"You're going to get blood on the carpet, and Mrs. Neiler will be upset," Muller replied with a grin. Despite the seriousness of the situation, Rhimes grinned back at him.

"Hans is right, Erik. Mrs. Neiler is none too happy if we just get *beer* on the carpet," their hired thug, Klaus, piped up from the corner, waving the gun he had been busy cleaning.

A knock on the door prevented Rhimes from replying. He pulled out his own gun and looked through the spy hole. Unlocking the door, he opened it to reveal Marko Berckett standing outside. Rhimes quickly ushered the man into the room.

"Gentlemen, I'm pleased to meet you," Marko said.

Klaus grunted and continued cleaning his weapon. Muller nodded as Marko sat down.

"So, do you have what I asked for?" Marko asked.

Rhimes shrugged. "It all depends. Do you have the file?"

Marko smiled and produced a file from his briefcase. He handed it to Rhimes, who flipped through it, then handed it to Hans.

"Well?" Marko asked, twitching nervously.

"The bitch is alive. That's her," Muller muttered. He stared at the photograph of his stepdaughter, hatred burning inside him.

Marko's smile turned ingratiating. "Does that mean I get my money?"

"You're going to get something better," Rhimes said, sitting down next to the janitor.

"W-what?" Marko stammered.

"Actually, I'm going to give you a choice," Rhimes said. He held his gun to Marko's head. The man went pasty white. "Okay, choice number one is that I kill you here," Rhimes said matter-of-factly.

"Mrs. Neiler doesn't like blood on the carpet," Klaus muttered from his corner.

"Bl-blood...on the ca-carpet?" The sharp scent of urine blossomed in the air as a terrified Marko wet himself, a stain spreading across the front of his trousers and a yellow stream running down his leg onto the floor.

Muller looked at the stinking puddle with disgust. "She doesn't like that, either." He smirked, the expression pulling at his scarred face. They were toying with the man, who had realized by now that he had walked into a trap and was probably not going to get out alive.

"Choice number two would be for Klaus to take you on a nice scenic trip to the Blue Mountains. Would you like that?" Rhimes asked, still holding the gun to the man's temple. "Since Mrs. Neiler isn't going to be happy with us getting blood on the carpet, I think option number two is best, don't you?" He looked over at the man who was still cleaning his gun in the corner of the room. "Klaus, please escort Mr. Berckett out."

Klaus unfolded himself from the chair. He was a mountain of a man who towered over the much shorter janitor. Klaus grabbed Marko roughly by the arm and yanked him to his feet. Marko whimpered, hanging limp in Klaus's beefy grasp.

"Oh, before I forget. Thank you so much for the file," Rhimes said pleasantly as Klaus dragged Marko out of the door.

Muller stared down at the photograph in his hand. Eva's smiling face drew his attention. *So beautiful and yet that beauty is a lie,* he mused. *One would never guess that beneath that lovely exterior is a loathsome abomination.* The photo also showed a blond-haired man laughing and holding Eva closely.

"She doesn't look like a lesbian to me," Rhimes remarked, glancing over Muller's shoulder at the photograph.

"This is a fake," Muller said, confident that he was correct.

"Hans, why are you so quick to believe she is a lesbian? Who told you?"

"Reinhardt told me."

"Both times?" Rhimes asked, making no attempt to hide his skepticism.

Muller nodded.

Rhimes continued, "Could it be he simply didn't like being spurned?"

"No. When I confronted Eva with the accusations Reinhardt made, she didn't deny them."

"Was she conscious at the time?" Rhimes asked with only a hint of irony.

Muller glared at him, his confidence not faltering in the least. "This is a fake," he repeated. "I know my own daughter, Erik."

"Not well enough if she is a lesbian, my friend," he replied, softening his jibe with a little smile. "What does the rest of the file say?" he asked, picking up the folder. Rhimes looked through the statements and shook his head. "We need to get out of here."

Muller sat silent with the picture in his hands and his head down, lost in his own thoughts about his treacherous daughter and the disgrace she represented.

Rhimes raised his voice. "Hans, did you hear me?"

"*Ja*, I heard you," Muller snapped, his focus returning to the present.

"Well?"

"I want her dead," Muller replied, scrunching up the photograph in his fist.

"Hans, listen to me. They won't catch us if they can't find us. I'll get Klaus to—"

"No! I want to do it this time. I sent Reinhardt the last time and the fool got himself killed. I need to do it myself," Muller insisted. One of his arms had been badly burned and he had limited use of that limb, but he was determined that his deviant stepdaughter must die.

Rhimes sighed in resignation. "I suppose you won't leave until you have your own way," he said to Muller. "All right, my friend. So be it."

"Good," an irritated Muller replied. His gaze returned to the crumpled photograph. "I am going to kill her."

Rhimes exhaled loudly. "Hans, this is a trap," he said, in an apparent attempt to convince Muller to drop his plan. "It's a trap," Rhimes repeated. "Can't you see that?"

"I see this," Muller pointed at the photograph, a black tide of hatred rising until he could have choked on it. He controlled himself with an effort. Erik Rhimes was his friend and had his best interests at heart, even if the man could not comprehend how Eva's continued existence was a blot upon everything good and decent, everything the glorious Third Reich had stood for.

"Hans, they want you to try and kill her," Rhimes pleaded. "It's a trap. Berckett was set up and we are being set up. I can smell it."

"You need to calm down, Erik," Muller replied. He retrieved the photograph and smoothed out the creases, then took out his lighter and set it on fire. He watched as Eva was consumed by fire, holding the photo by the corners until the heat became too much for him and he dropped it into the empty trashcan.

"I can't support you—"

Muller gave Rhimes a lopsided smile. "I know it's a trap my friend."

"You do?"

He nodded. "They are rank amateurs if they think they can fool me. I *will* kill her, Erik. I will!"

Rhimes sighed. "If you kill her, then will you listen to me?"

Muller smile turned menacing. "When she is dead, I will go wherever you want."

"Fine." Rhimes shrugged. "Such a waste of a beautiful girl," he added beneath his breath.

Muller merely returned his gaze to the ashes of the photograph. *I should have killed her when I had the chance. I was too soft-hearted*, Muller thought to himself. *I let Eva get away with her deviant behavior too long, and then I trusted someone else to take care of her. Now I'm going to do the job properly. She won't get away again!*

Eva got out of bed quietly, not wanting to disturb the soundly sleeping Zoe. She picked up her robe and threw it over her shoulders, put her slippers on, and went to the wardrobe to take out a towel.

As she left the bedroom, she caught sight of a damp towel that had been flung through the door previously. Earlier, Zoe's bath time had taken an amorous turn and towels had got in the way, only to be summarily dealt with in Zoe's exuberant fashion. Grinning, Eva picked up the towel, detoured to the laundry and put it in the basket. What she wanted was a nice cold bath. The hot evenings were tiresome for her and she found that by having a cool bath she was less tired and cranky in the morning.

Eva watched the bath fill, then poured some perfume into the water. When they had moved into the apartment, she and Zoe had scoured the department stores looking for a bathtub that would be big enough to accommodate her long frame. The tub that was already in the apartment when they arrived was so small that even Zoe had problems stretching out in it. The one they had settled on was long and wide, big enough to hold both of them at the same time.

She stretched out her legs, slid down until the water covered her chest, and sighed. Closing her eyes, she rested her head on the rim, letting the cool water relax her.

Eva heard a click. Her eyes flew open in alarm and she sat up, perfumed water sloshing over the rim of the tub, to find a grinning Zoe holding their camera.

"Zoe!"

"Eva!" Zoe grinned, unrepentant.

"Oh, Zoe, that wasn't fair!" Eva cried, sitting up further.

"Oh, nice view there, Mrs. H.," Zoe said cheekily, taking another photo. "You looked so peaceful that I want to paint you, and I can't do that without a picture. You don't want to pose for hours in the water; you'll turn into a prune."

"You have a photographic memory, my sneaky wife. You don't need photographs, you have painted me plenty of times," Eva responded. She sank back in the water until it lapped at her chin.

"Yeah, but you're my inspiration," Zoe said as she put the camera on the chair, dropped her robe to the floor and climbed naked into the tub to join Eva.

"Oh, nice view, Mrs. H," Eva mimicked Zoe's previous comment.

"Hmm," Zoe said. She sat back between Eva's long legs and leaned back onto Eva's chest. Eva put her arms around her. "This is nice, but the water is a little cool," Zoe said.

"Want to heat it up a bit?" Eva whispered suggestively, nibbling Zoe's ear and letting her hands roam the other woman's body. The action soon elicited a low moan from Zoe.

Zoe turned her head and looked at Eva; her pupils were so dilated by pleasure that there was the merest rim of green around the black. Her fingertips stroke Eva's face, then she ran her index finger along Eva's lips and chin, stopping to tease the small cleft. Zoe's mouth stretched in a lazy seductive smile, as if she was enjoying a private moment.

"What are you grinning so devilishly about?" Eva asked in a near whisper.

"This," Zoe replied. Once again, the tip of her finger teased the pronounced dimple in Eva's chin. "It's very...very..." Zoe stammered, clearly unable to think as Eva continued to caress her skin, "sexy," she finally said, breathlessly, almost shyly.

Eva graced the young woman with a tender, lopsided smile and placed a gentle kiss on her sweet lips. Opening her mouth slightly, she ran the tip of her tongue along the edge of her Zoe's upper lip before capturing her mouth once again in a slow kiss that was filled with the promise of desire. When the kiss ended, Eva continued tenderly caressing her lover's body. Although sensual, the caresses were also relaxing for both of them. Eva leaned back against the tub, her long arms resting around the petite woman in front of her while Zoe lounged contentedly against Eva's breasts.

After a little while, Zoe let out a particularly satisfied sigh and turned around to gaze up at her lover. She was rewarded with one of Eva's most dazzling smiles, which Eva knew made Zoe's heart race. They sat in the cool water for a few more moments.

"Evy."

"Hmm?"

"I'm getting cold."

"Okay," Eva responded, pulling the plug with her toe, which made Zoe giggle as the water drained away. "How about we continued this in bed?"

"You read my mind," Zoe crooned. She stole a quick kiss, got out of the bathtub, picked up a towel and wrapped it around herself. "Don't go away," she ordered, racing into the bedroom, and picking up another towel.

Eva watched with a bemused smile as Zoe padded back into the bathroom with the towel, and opened it up in invitation. Zoe wrapped the towel around her after Eva got out of the bathtub.

They walked back into the bedroom arm in arm. Eva removed hers and Zoe's towels, leaving them at the foot of the bed as they snuggled up together beneath the covers.

Brilliant sunlight poured into the bedroom, causing Zoe to open her eyes and then shut them again. She had left the curtains open, much to her disgust. She had wanted to sleep in and cuddle with Eva since it was Saturday.

She moved closer to the sleeping woman beside her and rested her head on her arm, watching Eva sleep. A smile played on Eva's slightly parted lips, which made Zoe grin. She loved to watch Eva's face as she slept. Zoe lightly traced Eva's high cheekbones and Eva stirred at the touch. Slowly, the woman's drowsy blue eyes opened. Zoe smiled more broadly when those eyes focused on her.

"Hey," Eva said, her voice roughened by sleep.

Zoe replied with a soft, loving kiss. "Hey, sleepyhead, how's your back?"

"Back? Oh, no back pain," Eva replied, now fully awake. She scooped Zoe closer. "I think you found a cure to my back problems."

"Dr. Zoe to the rescue. You're staying in bed today."

"Can't. I have to..."

Zoe leaned back, giving Eva a scowl. "You most certainly are. Well, at least for the morning. It's Saturday and that means I have a day off. So I'm going to pamper you," she said and nuzzled her partner's neck. "And, you're going to enjoy it," she concluded, kissing Eva passionately to emphasize her words.

Eva smirked when they finished the kiss. "Oh, this is nice."

"So you're staying in bed?" Zoe asked, hoping Eva was going to do what she was told and not be stubborn.

"All right," Eva said, uncharacteristically meek.

Zoe was taken aback. She had expected Eva to offer at least some resistance. "Who are you and what have you done with my Evy?" she asked playfully. Zoe rose up on an elbow and brushed a stray sleep-tousled lock of soft dark hair off Eva's forehead. She sobered. "You need to rest, love. All this work is really tiring you out. I hated it when you came home and were just so tired. I hated it when Stalk treated you like a pack mule. I hate it when your back hurts, because when you hurt, I hurt," Zoe said, caressing Eva's cheek. "I love you so much."

A tear escaped and slowly tracked down Eva's face. "I love you, too, Zoe."

Zoe gently wiped away the wetness. "Hey, I didn't mean for you to cry. I just want you to relax today. I'll make you the biggest, juiciest breakfast and then I'll give you another massage."

"But my back doesn't hurt now," Eva interjected.

"Who said anything about your back hurting?" Zoe replied in a sultry voice. "I read about some new relaxation techniques that involve a lot of kissing," she said, leaning down and again kissing Eva's sweet lips. "Lots of exploration of skin." She nuzzled Eva's neck while sneaking her free hand down to gently rub circles over the flat stomach below her, drawing a little moan from her partner. "And lots and lots of loving," Zoe finished as she moved up for a long sensuous moment of exploring her partner's lips while her fingers continued to stroke fire over Eva's belly.

"Oh, I *like* that," Eva purred a little breathlessly.

Zoe grinned. She watched Eva close her eyes and sigh contently. "Then it's settled; you stay here all nice and relaxed," Zoe told her and gave the woman a quick kiss before scooting out of bed. "I'll get breakfast."

Eva watched Zoe pick up her robe, put her slippers on, and pad out to the kitchen. "Whatever I did to deserve her, thank you," she said, loud enough for Zoe to overhear.

In the kitchen, Zoe's heart ached with tenderness, and she smiled, not minding at all.

The two women spent the morning eating breakfast in bed while Zoe read the newspaper to Eva. Afterwards, they spent a long time exploring Zoe's new relaxation techniques. By the time the afternoon rolled around, both of them were quite relaxed and enjoying their day together.

It was mid-afternoon when they heard a knock on the door. Zoe put on her robe and answered the summons. She opened the door to let Elena in; the woman was dressed up and ready for the dance and her date with Friedrich Jacobs.

"El, why are you dressed already?" Zoe asked, moving aside to let her friend pass.

"I was nervous," Elena said, coming into the lounge. She frowned at the sight of Zoe and Eva in bathrobes despite the late hour, and shook her head at them in disapproval.

"What's the matter, El?" Zoe asked, smirking. She thought she already knew the answer to the question.

"Nothing," Elena replied, moving to the sofa. "I'm just so nervous," she repeated. "I've tried on six dresses since this morning and nothing seems right. I'm down to two possibilities, but I can't make up my mind."

Eva gave Zoe a grin and sat down next to Elena. "You're *really* nervous."

"Does it show?"

"Not too much," Eva replied, still grinning. Zoe went to the kitchen, while Eva got up and disappeared into the bedroom.

Zoe came out of the kitchen to find that Eva had also returned to the lounge. She whistled at the sight of Eva's long legs, exposed by the tan shorts she had change into. The outfit was completed by a white shirt. "Nice view. Where are you off to?" Zoe asked, keeping her attention fixed on Eva while she gave Elena a glass of orange juice.

"Going to Earl's place to pick up some stuff I forgot from work," Eva explained. She walked over and gave Zoe a kiss before she left.

Elena inhaled, then let out the breath in a sigh. "Zoe, can I ask you a question?"

"You just did," Zoe grinned at her own joke.

"How did you know you were in love with Eva?" Elena asked.

Zoe smiled broadly. "Wish I could say I knew the minute I saw her, but that's not true. I think it was a gradual thing. It's not like in the magazines or the movies where people fall in love when they see each other across the room."

"So it was a very gradual thing?"

"Very. And it took Eva a lot longer, I think," Zoe replied. "She really didn't want to."

"Didn't want to fall in love?"

Zoe shook her head. "No, she resisted but in the end I got under her defenses," Zoe said, buffing her nails on her shirt and giggling. "It was meant to be."

Elena giggled with her. "So seriously, when did you fall in love with Eva?"

Zoe took a deep breath, becoming serious. "I fell in love with Eva in Egypt," she said. "I was watching her sleep one morning and I found myself not wanting to lose her."

"Not in Greece?"

"No, that wasn't love." Zoe shook her head. "That was what my brother called 'heavy like'. There's something that happens to you when you look at someone and know that whatever happens, you want them there with you."

"That's *love*?"

Zoe smiled. "*That's* love," she said.

"Is lesbian love the same as...you know?"

"I don't know, El, I've never been in love with a man," Zoe admitted. "I'm guessing it is."

"You mean you never had a crush on a boy?"

Zoe shook her head. "No, never."

"So how do you know that you're a lesbian if you have never fallen in love with a man?"

Zoe thought about it for a moment. The question was something she had asked herself, but no one had directly asked her that question before. "I guess I know because I never had *any* romantic feelings for *any* man."

"So when Eva shows up, you just knew?"

Zoe shook her head. "No, when we first met, I wanted to kill her. I was in the Resistance and she was the enemy. I can't tell you how it happened, but it was a gradual thing. We were friends for almost a year before we finally told each other how we felt."

"So this 'heavy like', is it nice?"

Zoe nodded vigorously. "Oh yes. You will know when you're in the heavy like stage."

Elena played with the fringe of her dress as she contemplated Zoe's words. "Do you think I will find someone like that?"

"Are you telling me you're a lesbian, El?" Zoe grinned. She got a shy smile from her friend. "You will find someone."

"How can you be so sure?"

"Because I'm all knowing," Zoe joked, earning a snort. "Haven't you ever been in love?"

Elena shook her head. "If I had been, I wouldn't be asking you now, would I?"

"I guess not."

"Exactly," Elena said. "So how do you know?"

"You just know." Zoe fingered the ring she wore and glanced at Elena. "I can't put it into words. I knew I never wanted to wake up and not find her there, you know what I mean?"

"Sort of."

"Eva is the most important person in my life, and when you find that person...well, I think that's what love is." Zoe shrugged.

"If he is as loving to me as Eva is to you, then I really hope I find that special someone soon," Elena said. "Eva just loves you so much and I want that for myself."

Zoe smiled. "You can't have her, she's taken."

"You're a goof; you know what I mean." Elena tapped Zoe lightly on the shoulder. "I want what you have."

"You'll get it," Zoe assured her friend. "Could be that nice Mr. Jacobs."

"From your lips to God's ears," Elena said, and gave Zoe a grin.

Amused, Zoe leaned on the doorframe and watched Eva as she got dressed. Eva had put on a trouser suit made of apricot rayon with sequins and beaded trim on the jacket that Zoe loved her to wear. Eva hated shopping, but when Zoe had caught sight of the suit, she had known instantly it was perfect for Eva and no amount of argument had deterred her. A determined Zoe had almost dragged Eva into the store to try it on.

Eva looked into the mirror; her reflected gaze met Zoe's. "How do I look?"

"Gorgeous," Zoe replied, moving over to give her a hug. Zoe had finished dressing herself moments earlier. She normally did not wear dresses, but she had finally agreed (after hours of searching and testing Eva's patience) on a black silk faille and white organdy dress with a dropped waist. Zoe would have preferred wearing something more casual, but it was a dance and, therefore, she was required to "dress up".

"You look great, too," Eva said, holding Zoe and kissing the top of her head. She smiled and pulled Zoe's body closer. "Nice perfume. I love that scent on you." Eva sighed, clearly savoring the moment and rested her chin atop Zoe's head. "Thank you for today."

"I didn't do anything special, just got you to relax a bit," Zoe mumbled into Eva's shoulder. "We can do my special relaxation techniques again tomorrow, if you like."

"Hmm, let me think on that," Eva said. Zoe could feel the other woman's grin on the top of her head. "Do you still have some cherries?" Eva asked.

"Oh, yeah!" Zoe grinned as well, patting Eva's side. "Lots of them." She had found some new season cherries and fed them to Eva in bed in increasingly creative ways until the snack had turned into a rather interesting and delightful game.

"You have yourself a deal," Eva said quietly. She leaned back a little, taking Zoe's face in her hands and tilting it back. Gazing into Zoe's eyes, she slowly closed the distance and pressed her lips to Zoe's. Eva tasted sweet, and Zoe let her body melt against her partner's warmth. Eva's kisses slowly became more aggressive. Zoe slid her arms around Eva's neck, tangling fingers in her hair.

They both groaned when a knock at the door resounded through the room.

"I'm going to kill whoever is outside that door," a flushed Zoe muttered, following Eva out of the bedroom.

Eva opened the door to reveal a grinning Earl leaning casually against the frame.

"Don't you look handsome!" Eva said as she gazed at Earl, who wore a black tuxedo with a red bow tie and matching red cummerbund.

"Of course," Earl said. He leaned down and gave Eva a kiss on the cheek, then spared one for a red-faced and scowling Zoe. "What's the matter with you?" he asked.

"Nothing," Zoe mumbled. Earl chuckled as he took a seat to wait for his friends to finish dressing.

Eva returned to the bedroom followed by Zoe, who pinched Earl's cheek as she passed him by. Earl half-whined an "Ow!" and gave the retreating Zoe a mock glare. Zoe responded by sticking her tongue out at him before joining Eva.

"What did Mrs. Jenkins want?" Eva called from the bedroom.

"You are looking at Mr. Security Man," Earl replied. Zoe re-emerged from the bedroom in time to see him strike a Superman-like pose. He waggled his eyebrows at her. His comic actions made Zoe start giggling. Eva exited the bedroom as Earl continued, teasing Zoe, "You clean up nice!" He got a hard poke in reply, but that did not seem to deter his good humor. "So, Miss Zoe, you're going out with David, the super-spy."

Eva rolled her eyes. "Keystone Cop Number One," she said, smirking. Any further comments were forestalled by a knock on the door. Eva answered it. The caller proved to be David Harrison, his blond hair neatly combed. He held a bouquet and shuffled his feet under Eva's steady gaze. "Hello. I'm here to escort the lovely Miss Zoe to the dance," he said.

"Mr. Harrison, please come in." Eva held the door open and David entered, clearly feeling a trifle intimidated with three sets of eyes on him.

David shifted nervously and toyed with the bouquet of flowers in his hand.

"Zoe, your date is here," Eva called out. "Would you like to put those in some water?" she asked sweetly.

Zoe gave Eva a quizzical look, which Eva seemed to ignore purposely as she gestured David to follow her out of the room.

As soon as David entered the kitchen, Eva closed the door quietly behind him and turned to the surprised man. David leaned against the kitchen bench and crossed his arms across his chest, a casual pose that did not fool Eva for a moment. "You want to tell me something?" he asked.

"What gave you that idea?" Eva asked as she found a vase and filled it with water.

"We're alone in the kitchen. I'm going to assume that you didn't call me in here just to check out my suit," David said.

Eva glanced back at the blond man and smiled. "So you really are an investigator."

"Guilty as charged."

Eva arranged the flowers in the vase. "Do me a favor?" she asked in German.

"If I can," David replied in the same language.

"Twirl Zoe around the floor a couple of times this evening. She loves to dance," Eva confided.

It was obvious that David had not expected to hear Eva say that. "Is she a good dancer?" he asked after a pause.

"She is," Eva said.

"That's not really what you wanted to ask me, is it?"

"Well, it was one reason." Eva put the vase down on the bench and turned to the Australian man. "What are you doing to track Muller down?"

"He is going to surface. We haven't been able to pin him down because they move from one place to another nearly every day."

"Are you sure he will come after us?"

"Yes." David nodded. "He has unfinished business."

Eva sighed. "I hope you and your partner will be ready for him."

"I give you my word that we are both committed to catching these bastards." He stopped speaking for a moment and looked at Eva, his gaze clearly assessing. "My wife was murdered by these swine and I aim to make them pay."

"I'm sorry. You were married? You can't be older than twenty!"

"I'm thirty years old and my good looks come from my mother," David responded, his face warming in a slight smile. "I lived in Germany for a few years and I married this beautiful girl. Her name was Winola and she was the most extraordinary woman I had ever met."

"That's a beautiful name."

"She was a dark-haired beauty with blue eyes," David said, still smiling. "Although she wasn't as tall as you are."

"How did you lose her?"

David looked out of the kitchen window, where city lights blazed against the darkness of the night. His smile vanished. "She was taken away and sent to a concentration camp," he said quietly, a muscle in his jaw working.

Eva sighed and closed her eyes. "I'm sorry," she said. So many good folk had lost their lives. There were times when she was ashamed of her native country.

"I tried to find her, but it was futile." David stopped and ran a hand through his blond hair. "I escaped from Germany and fled to Britain. I joined the army as an interpreter and when D-Day rolled around, I was in the thick of it."

"Did you ever find out where she was sent?"

David nodded. "Bergen-Belson," he said. "She was murdered a month before we liberated the camp. I found Anna, her sister, but she was so sick with typhus that she didn't survive."

Eva wiped the tears that tracked down her face with the back of her hand. "Elena was also in Bergen-Belson. You can ask her if she knew Winola."

"There were so many people, I don't think—"

"She might remember her, David. You never know."

David smiled sadly. "I'll ask her."

The two remained silent until the door opened, startling them both.

Zoe came in with a quizzical look on her face that soon turned to a deep scowl when she saw Eva's tear-stained cheeks and slightly swollen eyes. "Are you all right?" she asked Eva, shooting David a dirty look.

"I'm fine," Eva replied. She stepped closer and put an arm around Zoe's shoulders. "We were talking about the war."

Zoe glanced at David again. "You're only depressing yourselves, and tonight is supposed to be fun."

Eva kissed the top of Zoe's head. "That's true."

"While you two depressed each other with talk about the war, Elena and Friedrich arrived. I'm having a hard time keeping the conversation going out there. Elena is so shy around Friedrich and Friedrich is looking away every time Elena turns to him." Zoe threw her arms up in exasperation. "Those two won't say 'boo' to each other all night."

"Friedrich is a little shy around women," David observed.

"Well, can you two stop your war talk so we can get going to this dance?" Zoe shook her head and left the kitchen, quickly followed by Eva and David.

Chapter Fifteen

Once the group was finally ready to leave, they headed off to the two cars. Earl and Eva went in Earl's car, followed by David, who drove with Zoe, Elena, and Friedrich in his car. When they arrived to the site of the dance, they parked the vehicles under a stand of jacaranda trees. Exiting their cars, Zoe and Eva smiled at each other once they heard the music coming from the building.

"It's a beautiful night, isn't it?" Zoe said to David as they walked along.

"Yes, very beautiful," David replied. "Eva tells me you like to dance."

Zoe nodded enthusiastically. "I love it."

"Would you dance with me?"

"Aren't you my date?"

"Yes," David said with a chuckle.

"Well, then who else will I dance with?"

"I'm quite sure your dance card will be rather full," David said. "They'll be standing in line."

"Really?"

"Really," David told her as Elena joined them.

"Hey, Zoe, this looks great!" Elena said, coming up behind them. She was quickly followed by Friedrich.

Zoe and Elena bumped into each other and smiled. They entered the big auditorium filled with people. The band was playing waltzes to warm up before getting into the swing of things. Streamers hung from the rafters, and a few couples were already on the dance floor.

Elena took Zoe's hand as soon as they entered and dragged her into the ladies' bathroom.

"El, I don't need to—" Zoe protested.

"I can't dance," Elena said. She twirled around in the tiled bathroom and looked at herself in the mirror. "I bet Friedrich is a great dancer."

Zoe rolled her eyes. "Friedrich can't even talk to you, let alone dance."

"Maybe he doesn't like me…"

Zoe let out a frustrated groan. "Elena, you are being silly. He likes you."

"How do you know?"

"I've seen that shy look before. That means he really likes you."

"Where have you seen it before?"

Zoe smiled. "On Eva, silly," she said. "You should have seen Eva when we first met."

"You tried to kill her, Zoe. I don't think that's the same thing."

"I meant after that," Zoe said, dismissing her friend's statement with a wave of her hand. "She was really so shy, getting her to talk was like drawing blood. Just like Friedrich is behaving. She would look at me when she thought I wasn't looking, and I saw that she would have this really sweet smile…" Zoe stopped as Eva's image sprang to mind. They had flirted with each other for so long, testing the waters. Zoe wasn't even aware that she was flirting, and Eva was ever so careful not to be too obvious. It was quite transparent to Zoe, now, how Eva felt about her back then. Zoe mentally shook herself from the memories.

"All right, so what do I do?"

"You don't have to talk, just go dance with the man," Zoe said. She leaned against the wall, heedless of her dress.

"I can't dance!"

Zoe put down her purse with a sigh of resignation. "Come here," she said, tugging Elena's hand. "I'll show you."

She took Elena in her arms. "Okay, look at my feet and follow me," she said. The two of them waltzed around the bathroom with Elena stepping on Zoe's toes a few times. A couple of women came in and laughed good-naturedly at the friends' efforts.

After a short time, Eva entered the bathroom, where Zoe was still trying to guide Elena in the steps of the waltz. "I think the dance is supposed to be out there," she suggested.

Zoe turned and stuck out her tongue. "I'm teaching Elena how to dance."

"Well, David wants to dance with you and Friedrich thinks Elena left."

The two friends giggled and passed Eva on their way back to the dance floor.

Friedrich looked very relieved when Elena joined him again. She smiled shyly at her date. "Do you want to dance?"

"I'm...uh...I'm..." Friedrich stammered.

"Yes, he does," David interjected, slapping his friend on the shoulder. "Don't let him talk your ear off."

Elena and Friedrich joined David and Zoe on the dance floor. Apparently feeling very awkward, Friedrich held Elena at arm's length as they moved about.

"Dear God," David muttered under his breath. "Excuse me for a moment," he said as he guided Zoe around to get closer to the couple. "Hold her close," he whispered in Friedrich's ear before twirling Zoe around and heading in the opposite direction. This was not to Zoe's taste, so she nudged David until he guided her back within listening distance of the couple.

Friedrich took a deep breath and gently pulled Elena to him. "I don't know how to dance all that well."

Elena smiled. "You're pretty good."

"Yo-you think so?"

"Yes."

Friedrich smiled broadly and held Elena a little closer as they danced. "Um...are...you enjoying yourself?"

"Very much so," Elena replied. She caught Zoe's gaze. The two friends looked at each other and Elena winked, making Zoe grin. Satisfied that matters were well in hand, Zoe allowed David to lead her to the opposite side of the room where they continued to dance.

"So what did you say to upset Eva?" Zoe asked him matter-of-factly.

"I talked about my wife," David replied. "She was murdered in Bergen-Belson."

"Oh." Taken aback, Zoe did not offer another word for the rest of their dance.

Finally, David asked, "Zoe?"

"Yes?"

"This is supposed to be fun, so let's not talk about the war, all right?" David smiled down at her.

"Deal," Zoe replied. She looked over David's shoulder and spotted Eva dancing with Earl. She took a moment to admire Eva's elegant style before concentrating on her own dance partner's movements.

The evening wore on and to Zoe's delight, Friedrich and Elena began talking to each other and appeared to be having a very good time. In the meantime, Zoe found the punch bowl and downed a few glasses before realizing that the drink was spiked with alcohol. David had proved to be a good dance partner, but he had also been distracted, keeping an eye on Eva. He had just joined Zoe at the punch bowl when a strange man came up and spoke to him. From his manner and the irritated way that David greeted him, Zoe knew the stranger must be a colleague.

"Berckett's dead," the man said without preamble.

"Are you sure it's him?" David asked.

"Very sure, according to the police. They found his body in the bush."

David sighed. "Oh, that's just bloody perfect. All right, I'll go and get Jacobs."

David beckoned to Friedrich, who abandoned Elena and came over in answer to the summons, his face like a thundercloud.

"What is so important that you have to drag me away?" Friedrich asked angrily. Zoe did not blame him for his annoyance. From what she had observed as the evening had progressed, Elena had joked with him until he had got over his stammering and nervousness. Zoe knew that Elena was interested in getting to know Friedrich better, and she wished them both well.

"Daniel just told me the police found Berckett," David said.

"And?"

"He's dead, Freddy."

"Oh. Damn!" Friedrich replied tersely.

"We have to go stake out the apartment."

"*Now*?" Friedrich asked, his tone incredulous.

"Well, I don't think they're going to wait until the dance finishes, do you?" David said, sounding more irritable than before. "We're close to arresting the Nazis and there's no way I'm going to miss the opportunity to get those rats. Look, since the girls are here, they won't be in the way. They'll be safe in the crowd."

"Okay, okay." Friedrich muttered. He cast a final look of longing at Elena and followed David, his heels dragging in a show of reluctance.

Wondering who Berckett was, Zoe absent-mindedly took another sip of the spiked punch and almost choked. By the time she finished coughing, the two men were gone.

Rounding the corner, the car slowed down and pulled over to the curb. Klaus stopped the car and shut off the lights. The night was dark and quiet except for the ticking of the engine as it cooled.

"Wait here," Muller ordered the driver as he opened the back door and got out.

Rhimes got out on the other side of the car and followed Muller up the path. Both men wore jackets and kept the collars up and their hats pulled down low to reduce their chance of being identified. Once they got closer to the building, Rhimes pulled a piece of paper from his pocket. "The report says she lives in number five," Rhimes said.

They casually walked down the corridor and stopped at the door to number five. "Won't she be surprised?" Muller muttered. He rapped on the door with his knuckles. Not hearing a sound after a minute, Rhimes looked down the darkened hallway and was just about to kneel to start picking the lock when a woman popped her head out of her door.

"Can I help you, gentlemen?" Mrs. Jenkins asked and came out into the corridor. "I'm Mrs. Jenkins, the landlady."

"Good evening, um...we're looking for Eva Muller," Rhimes said.

"Why?"

Rhimes smiled at the woman while Muller stood silently by, fuming. "We're her uncles," Rhimes said.

"Oh!" Mrs. Jenkins came out of her apartment. "I didn't know she had uncles living in Australia."

"We just arrived from Germany," Rhimes replied. "I'm Erik and this is my brother Hans."

"Oh, how nice!" Mrs. Jenkins enthusiastically replied. "*Kali nikhta*," she said in Greek, feeling rather proud of herself.

Rhimes' smile widened, although Muller read the puzzled tilt of his eyebrows. Why was the stupid woman speaking Greek to them instead of German? "*Kali nikhta,*" Rhimes repeated. "Do you know when Eva will be back?"

"No, you know young people these days, staying out 'til all hours. I was at the dance earlier, but I just couldn't stay out any longer. You understand, don't you?"

"Yes, I do. We aren't as young as we used to be. Hans and I have traveled a long way to see our favorite niece," Rhimes hinted.

"Oh, you poor things. I'm sure Eva wouldn't mind if I let you into their apartment. Just let me get the master key. It's a shame you missed your other brother, he was here just half an hour ago. I don't remember his name, though."

Mrs. Jenkins was still talking when she re-entered her own apartment. Rhimes looked at Muller. Both men shrugged. Muller kept his face blank, although he privately wondered if anyone would miss the woman if he shot her, and where might be a good place to hide the body of an inconvenient witness. Mrs. Jenkins emerged a moment later and slowly trudged up the stairs, followed by the two men. She stopped at number twelve and opened the door for them.

"Eva doesn't live in number five?" Rhimes asked.

"No, that apartment has been empty for a few weeks now." Mrs. Jenkins shook her head. "Well here you go, please rest after your long travels. I can't wait to tell Eva when she comes back—"

"NO! I mean, no, please don't do that. We wanted to surprise her," Rhimes said hastily. He took Mrs. Jenkins' hand and kissed the back of it in the gallant continental fashion. "Thank you kindly, madam, for your help tonight." After the kiss to the hand, Rhimes and Muller entered the apartment.

The plump old woman blushed. "Oh, you Greek men are so gallant! Think nothing of it. Have a good night!" She waved coquettishly at them both before leaving the apartment, closing the door behind her.

Muller watched the door close and could only shake his head at their good fortune. *Finally some good luck,* Muller thought to himself. *I will be rid of the burden of my inconvenient daughter once and for all.*

"This is just horrible," Elena muttered under her breath. "Isn't it?" she asked Eva who was watching Zoe on the dance floor. "Eva?"

Eva spared the young woman a glance, and offered a sympathetic smile. "Where's Friedrich?"

"He had to leave with David," Elena replied. "This is so boring!"

Eva frowned, watching Zoe dance. She would have to step in soon and take her partner home, but Zoe did look as though she was having a good time. *Perhaps too good a time,* Eva thought, taking in the woman's heightened color and the slightly manic edge to her laughter. The young man dancing with her held Zoe's hand and was looking a little too friendly for Eva's liking. When he leaned down and whispered in Zoe's ear, Eva's eyes narrowed. She watched intently and rose from the table when she noticed Zoe head outside, followed by her dancing partner.

"Oh, yes, I know what you're after," Eva muttered to herself. She caught Earl's eye and cocked her head in the direction she had seen Zoe and the young man leave the dance floor. Earl glanced in the same direction, nodded his agreement, then headed towards the door that led to the terrace. After a moment, Eva quietly followed, having a feeling that she would be needed soon.

Zoe looked flushed, and that only meant one thing. Eva was certain Zoe was drunk or, at least, on the brink of intoxication. Her partner could not hold liquor very well. The young man became more amorous in his attentions, which infuriated Eva even more.

"Hey, Zoe, how's about a kiss?" the young man asked, grinning.

Zoe looked at him blankly. "No."

"No?"

"No."

"C'mon, just a little kiss..." He caught Zoe and pushed her against the brick wall, using his body to hold her in place despite her struggles. He was moving to kiss her when he was grabbed and thrown backwards.

"She said 'No,'" Earl growled. Stupidly, the young man tried to charge Earl but the bigger man took hold of his collar with one large hand and dragged him away, taking him to the door and tossing him bodily back inside the auditorium.

Eva went to Zoe. "Boys! They think with their dicks," she angrily said in German, as she put her arm around the smaller woman.

"You said 'dicks,'" Zoe giggled, then frowned. "Evy, that wasn't a nice boy."

"No boys are nice," Eva replied, still angry with the fool who had tried to attack Zoe, and angry with herself for not stepping in sooner.

"Wiggy is nice." Zoe looked up at Eva. "You're not a boy."

Eva looked down and smiled. "No, I can't say I am," she said, remembering a different time and place when Zoe had uttered that same observation. Zoe was sober then, although she had been dripping wet from being in the rain.

"That's good because..." Zoe paused and looked up, "...I don't like boys."

Eva smiled. "I know," she said her anger dissipated by the loving look she was getting from Zoe, even though her partner was clearly drunk. "I think we need to go home."

"I don't feel so good, either," Zoe mumbled, her complexion suddenly green-tinged.

"You've had a little too much to drink, love," Eva said. She kissed her lover's sweaty brow.

"Is everything all right?" Earl asked as he returned.

"Zoe is a little tipsy and I want to take her home. Can you drive us back?"

"No worries. I'll just tell Tim that I'm leaving." Earl turned to go inside, but paused when Eva spoke.

"Thanks, Earl."

"Anything for you, you know that. I'll let Elena know we're leaving," Earl replied and went to arrange for his absence.

On the way home, Eva sat in the backseat with Zoe, who was still not feeling very well, while Elena rode in the front seat with Earl. "Hey," Eva whispered to the suffering young woman.

"I hate punch," Zoe whined.

Eva smiled, although she knew Zoe would not see her in the dark. "Don't drink it next time."

"Bleh." Zoe rested her head on Eva's shoulder.

"How's she doing back there?" Earl asked. Eva saw his concerned gaze reflected in the rearview mirror.

"I think she's a little sick to her stomach at the moment." Eva kissed the top of Zoe's head. "It was the punch."

Considerately, Earl parked the car in the closest open space, but she and Zoe and Elena would still have a little walk to their apartments.

It was a clear night. Eva smelled the jasmine in the air as they went up the walkway, Earl acting as an escort. They climbed the stairs and bade goodnight to Elena at her door. Finally at their apartment, Eva put the key into the lock, opened the door, and entered, half-carrying Zoe in her arms.

A grinning Earl said good-night and turned to go, only to halt and let out a choked exclamation when, without any warning whatsoever, all hell broke loose.

Friedrich sighed, disgusted. Here he was, sitting on a wooden crate in the dark and empty apartment number five. He did not want to be here; he wanted to be back at the dance with Elena. Exhaling loudly, he glanced over at David, who was also perched on an empty milk crate. They had managed to get into the vacant apartment without anyone noticing; the number to this apartment, knowing it was empty, was fed to their informant as being where Eva lived. David had not wanted Rhimes and Muller to show up at Eva and Zoe's actual apartment. They decided to wait there, in the bedroom area of the apartment, with the lights off, in case the Nazis decided to kick the front door in and surprise the supposed occupants. The space was shadow-filled and gloomy, which suited Friedrich's mood just fine.

Friedrich wondered how Elena was getting along. He had been enjoying the company of the young woman very much before he had been dragged away. Tonight had been the only time he had ever enjoyed himself at a dance. He grimaced, thinking about Elena giving up on him and allowing another man to take her home. His annoyance grew. Turning to the person responsible for his current state of mind, he gave David an angry glare.

"All right. I know you're mad at me," David said quietly. "No need to stare daggers."

"I'm not just angry with you; I'm so furious, I could shoot you!" Friedrich whispered back vehemently.

"I'm your mate; you wouldn't do that," David replied. He suddenly looked unsure. "Would you?"

"Shut up!" Friedrich replied.

"Tell you what, Freddy," David put an arm around Friedrich, who tried to shrug him off, "when this is all over, you and the lovely Elena will go out to dinner at the most expensive place in town — my treat," David said.

"Just shut up, David. They probably aren't even going to show up tonight," Friedrich retorted.

David looked at him and sighed, then released him from the unwanted embrace. Friedrich knew his partner was desperate to apologize, but he was in no mood to listen. David took his flashlight out and shielded most of the glare as he pointed it at his watch. "Come on, where the hell are you?" he muttered as he shut off the flashlight.

The two men spent the next half hour in silence, sitting and listening, while David also kept watch on the front door from his position near the bedroom door, which had been left cracked open. Tension tightened to a fever pitch several times when they heard footsteps pass by in the corridor, but no one stopped at the door to number five. Both of them were growing increasingly impatient and still nothing was happening.

Friedrich broke the silence at last. "Tell me something, did you have to give Berckett the file yesterday? Couldn't it have waited?"

David frowned. "Friedrich, as much as I want to improve your love life, I don't think waiting until the dance ended would have been a good move."

"It would definitely have helped my love life since I didn't have one before tonight," Friedrich muttered. "I don't think they're going to turn up any time soon, David. It's already getting late."

"Let's wait a little longer."

Friedrich snorted, crossed his arms over his chest, and tried to direct his thoughts more positively towards Elena and David and the whole stinking situation. He did not have much success.

It happened so quickly that no one had time to react. As soon as Eva pushed open the door to the apartment, Muller yanked Zoe in by the front of her shirt, pulling her towards him.

Before any of them knew what had happened, Muller had the muzzle of a gun pressed to Zoe's temple, so tightly the skin turned white.

Eva was horrified by what she saw in the dim light — the only light in the apartment was coming in from the hallway behind her. Her constant nightmare became reality right before her eyes, and all she could do was stand there like a statue. Her beloved partner was being held in a death grip by the man she despised more than any other on earth. Eva's heart began to pound so relentlessly she thought her ribs would shatter under the strain. Transfixed by terror, she remained where she was. Someone — not Muller, but she could not identify the man in the dark — flipped on the lamp next to the sofa, flooding the room with light that burned Eva's eyes. She blinked to clear her vision. Muller motioned for Earl to close the front door, leaving the five of them inside the apartment.

Since the room was well lit now, Eva could clearly see General Rhimes sitting on the sofa pointing a gun at Earl, who also stood stock-still. She was well aware of how quickly the former soldier could begin shooting; Rhimes had no respect for human life. She sighed, frustrated by her own helplessness.

She turned her full attention to her stepfather trying not to look into Zoe's eyes. Muller's once blond hair was now nearly white and wispy, and the left half of his head was scarred from his neck to his hairline, though it was partially covered with an eye patch. His once strong bearing had turned into a round-shouldered stoop, giving him the appearance of a frail old man. Eva knew better; the man's malevolent aura had not diminished one whit. Within Muller's wrecked frame, the blackest evil still dwelled; pure menace shone out of his good eye.

Eva now watched Zoe carefully. Zoe was looking at her, beseeching her silently to remain calm, but Eva was far from calm. She was consumed by dread. Her knees trembled and her heart jack-hammered in her chest. A thin film of sweat coated her skin. Every nightmare she had suffered since learning Muller was alive had ended like this. Staring at her tormentor was terrifying and yet she noticed a new strength settling within her.

"Why aren't you dead?" Muller rasped. He released Zoe and stood in front of Eva, shoving the gun barrel under her chin.

"Why aren't you?" Eva answered, surprising herself by the steadiness of her voice. She was so glad to know Zoe was temporarily safe — she'd much rather have the gun pointed at her. She watched his good eye squint and she tensed, expecting to be hit, but to her astonishment, Muller controlled himself and merely sneered.

"Aren't you going to introduce your friend to your father?" Muller asked, shifting his focus to Earl.

"You are not my father," Eva replied, enunciating each word slowly and clearly.

"Ah, how soon they forget," Muller said over his shoulder to Rhimes. "Who do you think gave you all the nice things you had when you were an Austrian whelp?" Muller growled. He grasped Eva's chin and turned her face towards him when she looked away. "That's right, girl. I did."

"I'm Eva's fiancé, Earl Wiggins. Who are you?" Earl asked, knowing exactly who he was confronting.

"Fiancé, eh? Well, then, I'm your future father-in-law." Muller let out a broken wheeze of a laugh. "So, isn't this cozy?" he went on, grimacing in what Eva supposed was a smile limited by the scar tissue that disfigured his face.

"I wouldn't say cozy," Earl muttered.

Muller looked at Eva and then at Earl. He snickered crudely. "So, Earl, you are her boyfriend? You look like a good Aryan boy."

"My mother's Jewish," Earl replied, baring his teeth in a defiant smile.

The comment was surprising, and not only to Eva. Zoe, Muller, and Rhimes stared open-mouthed at him. Despite Earl's unexpected claim, Eva's gaze remained riveted to her partner.

Rhimes began to laugh. It was an ugly sound. "That will make it easier to kill you."

"You can try, but I won't make it easy." Earl looked directly at Rhimes, any semblance of a smile having disappeared. "The Japs tried and they couldn't do it."

"You are a foolhardy—"

"Enough!" Muller screamed. He took the few steps necessary to bring him back to Zoe, and took her neck in a tight grip. "Enough with the comedy! You," he said, motioning to Earl with his free hand. "I don't know who you are, I don't *care* who you are, but you are going to die."

"So you're that Nazi bastard Eva's told me so much about," Earl spat.

"Yes, I'm that Nazi bastard," Muller sniggered, his quicksilver mood changing.

"Appropriate for the bastard child, yes?" Rhimes said as he got up from his seat.

"Hold her for me, Erik." Muller roughly pushed Zoe towards the former general. Rhimes grabbed Zoe by the collar of her dress and held his gun to her head.

Very slowly, Muller approached his stepdaughter. His expression made Eva's blood run cold. His remaining icy blue eye bored into her eyes. Muller's presence and the hatred in his expression triggered every horrible memory she had.

Frozen to the spot, Eva tried desperately not to let fear consume her. She glanced at Zoe who, despite her own predicament, mouthed, "I love you", which somehow gave Eva the strength to be defiant. She turned her attention back to the monster in front of her.

Muller raised the gun and stroked Eva's cheek with the barrel. "I'm going to kill you," he said very softly. "I should have killed you myself instead of letting that fool Reinhardt fail at such a simple task. I should have killed you and not let your grandmother stop me."

Her stepfather's words about her grandmother made her stop and she briefly wondered how her beloved grandmother was involved. She didn't remember her *Omi* being there. "You didn't have the balls," Eva heard herself say, somewhat shocked by her new boldness. It was the response no one appeared to have expected, least of all Eva herself. Muller only sneered at the comment before striking Eva with a doubled-up fist, causing her to fall backwards. There was a loud thud as her head connected with the wall. Blood dripped from her split lip onto her apricot colored jacket. Earl went to her aid, heedless of Rhimes' and Muller's threatening frowns. Eva struggled to get up, holding onto Earl's strong grip. She was dizzy and that, adding to the pain in her face, made her nauseous.

Zoe was enraged. She tried to break free but was held in place by Rhimes. "You're a cold-hearted son-of-a-bitch," Zoe growled.

Muller turned towards her. "I should have killed you when I killed your mother," he taunted, ignoring the outraged look he got from Zoe. He drew closer, coming to within inches of her face. "Pop," he said, snapping his fingers for emphasis. "I did enjoy that."

Zoe was outraged, her green eyes blazed with anger. Reacting without thought, she spat in the man's face. He reached up and touched the spittle on his cheek. Eva flinched, expecting violence. Instead, Muller laughed and turned away.

"Such a spirited *Fräulein*," Rhimes quipped, striking Zoe's head with the butt of his gun. Eva was horrified as she saw Zoe's knees go weak. Zoe would have collapsed to the floor had she not been held up by Rhimes.

Muller focused on Earl. Gesturing with the gun, he motioned for Earl to move away from Eva. Earl took one step to his left and stopped, glaring at Muller, who had already directed his attention back to Eva.

"You are nothing, Eva. You have no family since you spat on your grandfather's grave with your filth. How could you do this to me, to him, to your grandmother!" Muller ranted, spittle flying. He stepped closer to Eva and looked into her eyes. Eva tried to swallow the lump in her throat as sweat slowly dripped down the side of her face. "You are dead to me. You died ten years ago."

"Don't listen him Evy, don't!" Zoe found her voice and yelled in Greek. Rhimes grabbed her tightly to hold her back.

"Shut up!" Muller turned to Zoe and leveled the gun at her. "Shut up!" Muller cocked his gun and appeared on the verge of shooting.

"You always were a coward," Eva yelled at her stepfather to get him to turn away from Zoe. It worked as he turned towards Eva, angry at her words. "Before, you would send Reinhardt to do your dirty work. Even now you are need someone else's help."

"I'm a war hero!" Muller screamed at Eva and pushed her backwards. Eva backed away but found only the wall behind her. Muller, only inches from her face, ordered, "Get down on your knees."

"No," Eva said. She defiantly stood her ground, her chin held up proudly. Unfortunately, she could not see Zoe because Muller was blocking her view, and Eva desperately wanted a last glimpse of her partner. She knew this was the end for both of them and, if she had to die, she wanted to see Zoe's face as she let God take her soul into His care.

"No? My, haven't we grown bolder?" he asked. Muller turned and went to Zoe's side, putting the muzzle of his gun against her chest as Rhimes stepped away. The sound of the weapon cocking was very loud in the stillness of the room. "You decide, daughter. You obey me or you see this deviant die."

The two women stared at each other for a long moment. Eva wilted, then very slowly stepped forward and sank down on her knees. Her gaze was still locked onto Zoe, who, she could tell, was still feeling the effects of being hit in the head.

"I love you." Eva declared her love for Zoe knowing it was going to infuriate Muller.

"I love you with the breath, smiles, tears of all my life," Zoe replied, quoting one of Eva's favorite poems, fearlessly following Eva's intention.

"You both disgust me." Muller shook his head as if trying to clear an unwanted vision from it. He stood in front of Eva, grimacing. "Apologize before you die."

"Why?"

"Why?" Muller asked. He seemed absolutely dumbfounded that Eva would even ask the question. He grabbed her by the chin and peered into her eyes, as though seeking an answer there. "Why? *You* are a disgrace. You disgraced *me*. That's why!" he raged. Droplets of spit flew into Eva's face, but she did not flinch at the man's rage or the spittle that wet her cheeks. "You are nothing but filth!" Muller screamed. "Apologize to *me!*"

Eva smiled, causing the man's good eye to widen. "I'm sorry—"

"No, Evy..." Zoe cried out not wanting her partner to give in to Muller.

Eva started again, still with the smile on her face. "I'm sorry that you're not dead," Eva said. She used to cower whenever Muller raised his voice to her, afraid that if she even looked at him, he would become enraged and strike out. That was in the past. She was no longer a cowering teenager, desperate to avoid her father's wrath. Eva looked at Muller and realized what a truly pathetic figure he was — an arrogant creature who had no basis for his pride, a thing of sound and fury that signified nothing.

Muller growled, "That wasn't the apology I was looking for." He tried to hit her. Eva swayed out of the way, allowing Muller's fist to brush past her.

"Kill her and let's get out of here," Rhimes said. "I'm getting tired of the charades, Hans. We have a boat to catch."

"Shut up!" Muller angrily replied to Rhimes, then turned back to Eva. "Kiss my boots!" he demanded.

Eva glanced down at Muller's black boots and then back up at Zoe, who was giving her a sympathetic look. *I'll kiss your boots, you son of a bitch.* Muller stood in the perfect spot and Eva's heart was racing. *Just where I want you.* Eva lifted an eyebrow and gave Zoe a barely perceptible nod. Zoe followed Eva's gaze, which fell on the *flokati* rug that Muller was standing on. Zoe's eyes widened when she finally understood what Eva was about to do. Her expression went blank as she tried not to give the game away.

"Do it!" Muller screamed, looming over her with his feet planted apart.

Very slowly, Eva bent down and placed her hands on the rug between Muller's boots. Bending forward as if to comply with his demand, she instead clasped both hands together, locking them tightly into a double fist. In one continual movement, she leaned back, sweeping her hands upward, bringing her fist into sharp contact with Muller's groin, and putting her weight into the blow. She enjoyed a moment of triumph when he crumpled forward, his face scarlet, his mouth opening and closing in a soundless protest against the agony in his privates.

In the confusion, Earl picked up the nearest thing to him — Zoe's cricket bat that had been left near the door. He threw it at Rhimes, causing the man to yelp in surprise. Rhimes' reflexes were quick enough to help avoid the blow, causing the bat to strike the wall harmlessly. Nevertheless, Earl had created a distraction.

In the same instant the bat was flying across the room, Eva bent back to the floor and pulled hard on the rug under Muller's feet. The well-polished wooden floor allowed the rug to slide forward easily. Muller, already unsteady on his feet, fell backwards as the gun flew out of his hand. The weapon hit the floor butt first, discharging loudly. Plaster dust snowed down from the ceiling where the bullet had lodged.

Never one to hesitate, Zoe took the opportunity, after the cricket bat was swatted away by Rhimes, to stomp hard on Rhimes' foot. The man cursed and instinctively reached for the injured appendage. Earl jumped Rhimes and took him to the floor, getting in a punch to the stomach on the way down. Earl's movement unintentionally caused Zoe to be shoved aside. Unable to control her movements, she stumbled, eventually falling to the floor. The force of the push continued her momentum until her back hit the stand of iron implements, beside the fireplace, which clattered across the tiled hearth. A moment later, Zoe covered her head and curled into a ball when Rhimes' gun went off. The bullet hit the nearby wall. Earl tried to wrench the weapon away, but Rhimes hung on determinedly and got to his feet.

Eva scrambled away from Muller, who appeared to be disoriented. He groped for his gun — tears of pain rolled from his good eye and curses streamed from his mouth. Heeding Zoe's wordless scream of warning, Eva ducked a flying stool, propelled by Earl and Rhimes' battle. The stool crashed into the wall near her and broke apart, showering her with wooden splinters. Earl's fist connected with the general's cheek and Rhimes staggered, still keeping hold to the pistol.

Hearing her name, Eva looked up to see that Zoe had stood up and was holding the fireplace poker like a sword. "Catch!" Zoe yelled and hurled the poker at Eva, who caught it easily, adrenaline lending her speed and strength. Eva turned her attention back to Muller. The man was on his knees, reaching towards her ankle.

Eva kicked Muller in the face, sending him sprawling to the floor and clutching his bloody mouth. She raised herself to her full height and held the poker in both hands. She stopped and looked down at Muller for a moment, then lowered the poker until the tip dented the soft flesh of the man's scarred throat.

To Eva's surprise, she could see fear in his visible eye. Eva took a deep breath and looked down at her tormentor. The poker, one of the two instruments with which her father had beat her to near death, reminded her of the pain he caused her. The desire for vengeance was screaming inside her. She wanted to push the poker through the man's neck, but she hesitated. Despite all the dreadful things he had done to her, all the torments of mind, body and soul, a part of Eva recognized the man who had been her loving and beloved father so long ago. She was also very aware of Zoe's presence; the Greek woman would have celebrated Muller's death at Eva's hands, considering it vengeance well paid, but Eva could not do it. She refused to let him taint her soul any longer. His blood would not be on her hands. Let others deal with Hans Muller; let the greater justice be served in the name of his many victims. She had overcome him at last. This personal victory was enough for her.

Muller sneered and seemed about to shove the poker aside when Zoe came to stand beside Eva.

On her way over to Eva, she had found Muller's gun and was now squatting in front of him and pointing the gun at him, her aim unwavering in spite of her recent tumble. "I killed Reinhardt to save Eva, you won't take her away from me. I will blow off the rest of your face and I'll enjoy it," Zoe said coldly.

Still locked together in battle, Earl and Rhimes crashed through the balcony doors onto the terrace. Earl connected his fist to the German's jaw, knocking Rhimes unconscious and leaving him on the balcony floor amongst the broken door and splinters of glass. Earl raced over to Zoe where she stood aiming a gun at Muller. "Bloody hell," he muttered and wiped the blood from his nose. "I'll take that." He plucked the gun from Zoe's hand and didn't notice Zoe's aggrieved look.

Eva stood on wobbly legs, not quite believing what she had done. It had only been moments ago since she was helping a drunk and sick Zoe into their apartment. She took a few steps away from Muller and leaned against the nearby wall, close to the door, for some much-needed support. Zoe walked closer, put her arms around Eva, and squeezed tightly. The two women held onto each other, Eva stroking Zoe's back. Both of them relieved beyond words that they were still alive.

Just then, the door burst open causing Eva to instinctively raise the poker again. She was ready to defend herself and her partner against this new threat. Too shaken to recognize friend or foe, Eva saw only a gun and swung the poker down. The poker struck Friedrich's wrist hard enough to cause him to drop his gun. Thankfully it did not discharge. David, following his friend into the room, had to duck as Eva took a swipe at the next intruder she saw. Fortunately, the poker missed him and crunched into the doorframe, taking a small gouge out of the wood.

"Wait!" David yelled, raising his hands in surrender.

Elena appeared in the doorway, gaping in amazement while Eva stood with a poker in her hand, breathing heavily. "I think I missed something," Elena said, her eyes wide. Friedrich, who ended up on his knees in pain, was holding his injured wrist and swearing in heartfelt German. When Elena focused on Friedrich, it only took her a second before she cried out his name and dropped to the floor to comfort him.

Panayiotis and Alberta came rushing into the apartment in their nightclothes, clearly having been awakened by the fracas. Alberta made her way to Eva. "Are you all right?" she asked, touching Eva's arm. "We heard a gun shot along with the other sounds of a ruckus. I imagine your other neighbors did, too."

"We're all right now," Eva said, reaching out to her partner. Zoe, who had been dislodged from her initial hug when Eva went back into her defensive mode, wrapped herself around Eva again. They slid down the wall, both of them trembling in shock. "I think Friedrich needs some help, though." Eva indicated the young man lying on the floor a few feet away now being comforted by Elena.

Panayiotis surveyed the assorted bodies and looked down at Eva, who now was cradling Zoe in her lap. "Are you all right?" he asked, going to one knee. Eva nodded. He gently stroked her head. "Who is that?" Panayiotis asked, pointing at Muller.

Eva smiled grimly. "Father, you remember Hans Muller."

Astonishment warred with a certain implacable satisfaction in his expression. His eyes gleamed unpleasantly. "Well, if it isn't Major Muller. Remember me?"

Muller looked at the man for a long moment. When he spoke, his voice was thick; blood droplets sprayed out of his mouth. "No."

"Father Haralambos," Panayiotis smiled serenely and introduced himself.

"Father Haralambos?. You're supposed to be dead."

"So are you," Panayiotis replied. "You see this beautiful woman here?" he asked and took Eva's hand in his own. "This is *my* daughter."

A look of total shock registered on Muller's face. "Your daughter? *You and Daphne?*"

"Me. You knew Eva's father was in Larissa, that's why you took command. You wanted to punish her even more. Didn't you know a village priest knows about everyone and everything in the village? Eva knew where to look for information, and she found her father, all right. She found me."

"Father," Eva said quietly, a half-hearted admonition because she felt her father's controlled rage; she could see what control cost him in the rigid set of his shoulders. "He doesn't deserve to know about us."

Panayiotis bared his teeth at the fallen man. He was about to move away but glanced back at Muller, his contempt clear. "This time, I will not turn the other cheek. May God forgive me, but I hope the fires of hell torment your soul for the rest of eternity, Hans Muller."

Eva understood it was not the former priest who condemned Muller, but the father filled with anger against the man who had fractured his daughter's soul.

"Bastard," Panayiotis said, still glaring at Muller, having to release the last of his anger. He turned back to his daughter with a sheepish grin and put a hand over his mouth.

"Father H!" Zoe exclaimed and started to laugh.

Eva shook her head as she reached out and grabbed her father's hand and tightened her other arm around Zoe, still in her lap. She needed the connection with her father but realized the move helped calm her father. She lovingly pulled his hand to her face, giving it a kiss before placing his hand against her cheek. "Thank you."

Eva felt like her world was beginning to return to a norm she hadn't felt in some time. She glanced around the room. Alberta and Elena were helping a grimacing Friedrich slowly sit up. The man cradled his injured wrist to his chest and was clearly in pain. Eva could see David handcuffing a very dazed Rhimes. She spotted Mrs. Jenkins standing at the door looking stunned.

"Eva, what is going on here?" Mrs. Jenkins exclaimed, gazing around in disbelief at the damage in the room.

"Um..." Eva blew out a shaky breath and tried to find a good excuse for the two Nazis and two government investigators in various states around the apartment. She could not find an explanation to offer the older woman except the truth. She was about to speak when her father interrupted.

"Come with me, Nelly, we need to have a little chat," Panayiotis said as he came up behind Mrs. Jenkins and steered her out of the apartment. He winked at Eva, who was very relieved to have been spared the landlady's histrionics.

Eva turned her attention to the woman in her arms. Zoe was sporting a developing bruise just under her eye. "I so enjoy these quiet evenings," she quipped. The two women started to laugh in slightly hysterical relief until they were both breathless, and their hilarity turned to murmurs of mutual comfort and thankful tears that they were both still alive.

Chapter Sixteen

The curtains fluttered and a stiff breeze rattled the windowpane. Lightning illuminated the darkened bedroom where Eva lay staring up at the ceiling with a smile on her face. Thunder boomed in the distance a few heartbeats later. She put her hands behind her head and sighed contentedly.

It had been quite an evening with Muller and Rhimes ambushing them in the apartment. The man responsible for all her pain had stood before her and she had not backed down; she had found the strength to look him in the eye and confront him, even defeat him and end his threat forever. The fear that gripped her heart when she first saw him was something she was acquainted with, but the strength to stand up to him was a new revelation.

A laugh bubbled out and Eva tried to stifle it because she did not want to wake the sleeping Zoe, but she could not control herself. For many years, she had dreamed of the time when she would be able to stand up to Muller, to say "no" to him, and openly defy him. Now she had.

She had known she had to overcome her fear of the man. Even when she thought he had died in Larisa, she still carried a fear that wouldn't go away. Years of abuse had made Eva doubt her own abilities and doubt her strengths, and had stripped her of all dignity. All those doubts and fears had melted away when she saw the love and absolute faith that her beloved partner had shown. The fact that Muller had hit her had only strengthened her courage, but it was Zoe's faith that had truly made the difference.

Zoe had galvanized Eva into making a stand, one she was sure would be her last, but she had found the courage to defy Muller for both their sakes. It had been a surprise to him as well, when the words had come out of her mouth. Her fears had been all-consuming and yet, when she had looked into Zoe's eyes, she had decided to fight with every ounce of her being. Eva was no longer the cowering little girl or the terrified teenager who had been brutally tortured for being who she was. She had become an adult who, like a lioness, wanted to protect what was hers.

Eva looked down at Zoe lying beside her and marveled at what God had given her. It was not the first time Eva had thanked God for Zoe's love nor, she suspected, was it going to be the last. She leaned down and kissed Zoe's cheek softly. Zoe's eye had started to bruise before they had gone to bed and now the injury had become a purplish mass. Eva was not in any better shape. Muller's parting gift to her was a split lip and bruised cheek. She carefully felt her swollen lip and sighed again. Eva brushed Zoe's hair back from her face and looked at the damage that had been caused by Rhimes' gun. Zoe's neck was also bruised from where both men had held her tightly.

The police had arrived and arrested Muller and Rhimes, taking them from David so he could take Friedrich to the hospital to have his injured wrist tended. Eva had barely registered all the faces and questions, and had been thankful that Alberta was there to deflect most of the curious and concerned tenants who had congregated in the corridor outside the apartment.

Earl had temporarily given the women a bit of privacy by propping the broken front door up in the frame; he also put a blanket over the hole where he had taken down the remains of the shattered balcony doors, promising to do a proper job once he had the necessary tools and supplies. Afterwards, he had cleaned up the lounge, which resembled a war zone with bits of broken furniture and other detritus scattered about. One wall would have to be repainted as it sported a large bloodstain and a couple of bullet holes. After Earl had told them he was going to stay the night, the two women had made their way to their own bedroom, undressed and dropped their bone-weary bodies into bed.

Eva threw back the light blanket and sat on the edge of the bed for a moment before she got up. She put on her robe and slippers and left the bedroom, padding quietly over to the hole in the wall that used to be their balcony doors. Drawing aside the covering blanket, she gazed out at the rain.

One of the darkest chapters of her life was now closed. Eva ruefully considered that every time she had thought Muller was out of her life, he reappeared. Finally, she was now certain he was going to get his comeuppance. Those he had murdered would also get their justice. It was too late for them and too late for Zoe's mother, but it was going to happen.

Eva was filled with euphoria. She was exhausted and ached all over, but a peace had settled over her that she did not want to end. She felt truly free from Muller's grasp; a huge weight had been lifted off her shoulders and she was a little light-headed because of it. Eva smiled to herself as she ducked through the blanket and went out on the balcony.

Lightning streaked across the night sky, briefly illuminating the clouds and blotting out the star shine. Eva stood and watched the heavy rain cascading down. She smiled, took a step forward, and stuck out her hand to catch the raindrops. She sighed and looked into the heavens.

"It's over, *Mutti*," she said aloud, knowing her mother's spirit would be watching and be proud of her. "It's finally over." Eva smiled and brushed away the tears that fell down her cheeks. "It's finally over," she repeated and shook her head in wonder.

After a while, she came back inside and went into the bathroom to get a towel to dry her wet hair. Peeking out from beneath the towel to see her reflection in the mirror, she smiled and poked her tongue out at herself.

She winced at the deep bluish bruise on her cheek. "Ow," she muttered. Her lip was not any better. Eva shook her head and was about to leave when she glanced in the mirror again and for a moment saw her own teenage face looking back at her. "Getting hit in the head one too many times," Eva said to herself. After a short pause, she smiled and said, "You can come out and play now." She winked at the mirror before turning off the light. As she was about to head back to bed, she stopped at the spare room.

Earl was wide awake; he turned over in bed upon glimpsing Eva's silhouette when she opened the door. "Hey there," he said and patted the side of the bed. "How're you doing, Slugger? Been playing out in the rain?" he asked.

Eva laughed at the new nickname she had acquired. Earl had not been able to believe he had missed seeing Eva take on Muller and win while he had been busy fighting Rhimes.

"I'm great. I was just enjoying the lightning," she replied, chuckling. "You look like you've gone ten rounds with Buster Malone," she added and gently touched Earl's bruised face. "Does that hurt?"

"Nah," Earl replied. "I gotta tell you, though, for an old guy, Rhimes sure can punch."

Eva smiled. "He was a champion boxer in his younger day," she revealed.

"Now she tells me!" Earl grumbled, good-naturedly. "How are you doing?" he repeated, brushing his fingertips across Eva's cheek.

"I've never felt better," Eva honestly replied. "Is your mother really Jewish?" she asked, recalling Earl's comment to Muller.

Earl laughed and shook his blond head. "No, she's Catholic," he said.

"Why did you tell him she was Jewish?"

"To annoy his Nazi arse." Earl grinned, a mischievous light in his eyes.

"You could have gotten yourself killed," Eva admonished him.

Earl sat up a little more in bed and leaned back against the headboard. "I could have but I didn't. It doesn't matter, does it?"

"It matters to me if you get yourself hurt or...ki-killed." Eva's voice caught in spite of her euphoric mood.

"Well, I will try not to get myself killed. You don't have any other rampaging Nazis after you, do you?"

Eva shook her head. "I don't think so," she said. Obeying a sudden impulse, she leaned over and kissed Earl on the cheek. "Thank you, my friend."

"For you, Miss Mull...um, I mean Miss Haralambos," Earl said, "I would do it all over again with one exception."

"What's that?"

"I would duck when Rhimes comes at me with that right cross." Earl grimaced and felt his bruised cheek.

"Did we hear from David about Friedrich?"

"Aye, Freddy has a broken wrist." Earl winced. "He's going to be fine. David is the lucky boy that didn't get a poker in the head. Go to bed and stop playing in the rain."

"Yes, Mother," Eva joked. She gave him a pat on his unbruised cheek before leaving the room.

Eva re-entered her bedroom to find the bedside lamp on and Zoe sitting up in bed with her sketchbook. Eva smiled at the look of concentration on Zoe's face.

"What are you doing up, love?" Eva asked. She took off her robe and went over to the bed and sat beside Zoe to look at the sketch.

Zoe's pencil flew across the page creating an image of the previous night which amazed Eva, as she watched the drawing spring to life. On the paper, the sketched Eva was down on one knee with the poker ready to strike, a determined look on her face and her eyes blazing. Eva's hair was slightly disheveled, giving her a wild look.

Zoe stopped and answered, "Drawing my hero."

Eva smiled in response to the compliment. "That's me?" she asked.

"Oh, that's you," Zoe replied. She put the sketchpad down and turned to Eva. "Oh, Evy, you were magnificent!" she cried, kissing her very tenderly on her injured lips. "Your hair is wet. Did you go and have a bath?"

"No," Eva said. "I was outside watching the rain."

"And why were you standing outside getting wet?"

Eva smiled. "You're going to think it's crazy."

"No, I won't." Zoe scooted over and Eva lay down next to her.

"I love it when it rains," Eva explained. She sighed as Zoe snuggled up against her. "I love the smell."

"I prefer to be in bed rather than outside getting wet," Zoe murmured, causing Eva to laugh.

"I wanted to make sure last night was not a dream," Eva said.

"So you got yourself wet to prove it?"

"No," Eva said. "When I was younger, I would go outside and stand in the rain catching the raindrops in my mouth. I was just remembering a time when all I worried about was whether Fritz would be pulling my pigtails again." Eva reminisced about the carefree youngster she used to be.

There had been a time in her life when she had not been afraid to go to her stepfather and sit on his lap. A time she had not been afraid to hear her name spoken by the man whom she adored as her father. That was a long time ago. Her love for the man had turned to absolute fear when he became more violent as she grew older. Eva had not been sure for a long time if his changed behavior was her fault, or if the man truly had his own demons to contend with.

Zoe gazed at her. "You felt like a kid?"

"Something like that," Eva murmured. "Something special happened last night, Zoe." Eva held the other woman close to her and shut her eyes. "I don't have the words to tell you how I feel."

"I think I know," Zoe replied. She took Eva's hand and kissed it. "I've always wanted to hit that bastard in the balls and, what was sweeter, you did it."

"I did, didn't I?"

"Oh, my God, you were an avenging angel," Zoe gushed. She wriggled out of the covers and knelt on the bed. "The look on your face!" she exclaimed. She got up on one knee and held an imaginary poker in her hand. "Whap! Whap! Whap!" she cried, striking the air with her imaginary poker while jumping on the bed, making Eva bounce.

Eva laughed at Zoe's antics. "I didn't go 'whap', love."

"I know but I've been dreaming that you have and it was so good. Oh, Evy, the look on *his* face when you punched him!" Zoe clapped her hands together, causing Eva to start at the sound. "Straight into his balls!" The young woman laughed. "You looked heroic."

"You think so?" Eva snickered, caught up in her partner's excitement. "I don't think it was heroic since I was on my knees."

Zoe shook her head. "I think it's heroic. For years you were terrified of him, Evy. Every time his name was mentioned, you looked so scared even when we thought he was dead. Yesterday, you stood up to the bastard."

"I wasn't facing him alone, Zoe."

"Did that help?"

"More than you will know. You are *my* angel."

Zoe touched Eva's face. "You are truly a gloriously gorgeous woman."

The two women looked at each other and then kissed. "I love you," Eva whispered breathlessly. "You gave me the strength to do that."

"I can't believe we did it," Zoe said. She settled back under the covers and into Eva's arms.

"How's your head?" Eva carefully prodded the back of Zoe's skull.

"A little sore," Zoe admitted. "We do look a little worse for wear, don't we?"

"A little."

Zoe gently felt along Eva's bruised cheek. "Bastard," she said. "I hope they hang him."

"Oh, I'm sure there is a special place in hell reserved for Hans Muller and Erik Rhimes," Eva replied. She pulled Zoe closer to her. "You were very brave last night."

"I make a great punching bag," Zoe joked ruefully.

"No, I'm serious, Zoe. You gave me the courage to stand up to him—"

"I didn't give you that. That's always been inside you and it just came out last night." Zoe smirked. "I loved the look on the pig's face when you said 'no' to him."

"It was the first time in my life I said 'no' to him," Eva revealed, smiling broadly.

"And you avenged my mama's murder," Zoe added. "I'm quite sure God has a very special place for you when it's time to call you home."

"Well, I hope it's not anytime soon," Eva replied. "We did it, love, we actually did it." Eva could not believe it, even though she knew what had happened; the reality was starting to sink in.

"We did it," Zoe echoed Eva's words. "But I can't believe David and Friedrich went to the wrong apartment!"

Eva snickered. "It's not their fault that Mrs. Jenkins let Rhimes and Muller into our real apartment."

"Someone should tell that woman that a Greek accent is very different from a German one. Doesn't she know the difference?"

"I don't know, love. I would think she would," Eva replied. "Well, we did have a hand in confusing her with our sister story. Maybe she thought they were good Germans who were Greek as well."

Zoe frowned. "I'm confused, Evy."

"So is she," Eva said, grinning. "I don't really care at this point why Mrs. Jenkins doesn't know the difference. We might have a problem with our sister story, though. Maybe we should tell people we are friends."

"I have a better idea." Zoe snuggled closer. "I think we should tell them that we are married."

"I wish we could, Zoe, but that's not going to happen."

"I know, but I can dream," Zoe replied. She fell silent for a moment before speaking again. "How's Friedrich?"

Eva winced. "He's got a broken wrist."

"Ouch!"

"Elena is rather sweet on him." Eva smiled at the memory of the young man and woman on the dance floor.

"I think she's into the 'heavy like' stage."

"Oh, well then, there's no hope," Eva quipped, causing Zoe to laugh. "I think they look cute together."

"I hope she finds as much happiness as I have." Zoe tweaked Eva's dimpled chin. "David is also a nice guy."

"Hmm, he's all right."

"Just your type," Zoe teased.

Eva looked down, frowning. Zoe shook her head and smoothed the crease between Eva's brows with her fingertip. Eva said, "My type is in my arms."

"Oh, I know that," Zoe said. "It's just that you seem to befriend tall, blond men."

Eva realized what Zoe meant and laughed. "Do I?"

"Oh yes," Zoe nodded. "Earl is tall and blond, and now David is tall and blond."

"Willy was tall and blond," Eva added thoughtfully, thinking of her childhood friend.

"See what I mean?"

"I guess I do," Eva admitted. "But I like my woman short and red-haired," she said. "There's only one type that matters." Eva leaned down for a kiss that would leave Zoe in no doubt about how she felt.

"Ah, stop!" Zoe cried.

Eva groaned. "Why?"

"Earl's in the next room!" Zoe whispered. "Besides, your lip is bleeding again."

"I know. So?" Eva whispered back then touched her lip.

"We can't make love while he's in the next room. I don't want Earl to hear us."

Eva let out a frustrated sigh. "We must stop having people sleep over."

Zoe reached over, got her sketchpad, and brought it over to rest on Eva's stomach. "Evy," she said as she gazed at the drawing.

"Hmm?"

"I love you." Zoe looked into Eva's eyes and let out a contented sigh.

Eva held her partner tightly and sent a silent prayer of thanks to heaven for the woman in her arms, and for the courage that had been needed to capture Muller and end his threat forever.

Chapter Seventeen

Four weeks later, it was December. Eva put her hand over her mouth as she yawned. The waiting was driving her crazy. Next to her sat Earl. He was leaning back against the wall, his eyes shut, and his long legs stretched out in front of him, catching up on his sleep. His shift had ended less than an hour ago, but even though Eva knew he was tired, Earl had said he was determined to stay awake for this event.

Glebe Public School was the location and inside a classroom sat the hopeful art college students. Eva once again got out of her seat and peeped through the door to see if Zoe had finished her exam. Zoe had her head down and was using her pencil eraser quite industriously.

Eva went back to her seat. She took the newspaper that she had brought with her and turned the pages aimlessly until one article made her pause. "Oh," she said, a little startled at what she had read.

"What's the matter?" Earl asked, not bothering to open his eyes.

"There's an article here about the Nuremburg Trials," Eva replied and showed the article to Earl, who opened his eyes and leaned forward.

"You know this Albert Dredger?" Earl asked.

Eva continued to stare at the newspaper. "I used to go to school with him," she replied in disbelief. "It says he murdered people in the Buchenwald concentration camp."

"I hope they hang the bastard," Earl said and leaned back against the wall.

Eva glanced at her friend and shook her head sadly. "So many lives destroyed."

"Are you feeling sorry for Dredger?" Earl asked. "Don't feel sorry for him. He made his choice."

"I'm not, Earl. I feel sorry for what we all lost," Eva replied. "I was just surprised to see his name."

"You've been saying that for weeks now," Earl replied.

Eva folded the newspaper and set it aside. "I know," Eva replied. She had been reading the daily newspapers in disbelief at some of the names that were mentioned in connection with the trials. "I know when I see Muller's name, it won't be a surprise."

"I'm going to throw a party when he gets executed," Earl opened his red-rimmed eyes again and glanced at Eva. "I'll drink a toast to his demise."

"I might drink to that," Eva mumbled. She got up from her seat and stretched. "These chairs are murder." Eva went over to the examination room door and peeked inside.

"How are they doing?" Earl asked.

"Zoe is erasing something and Elena is scowling," Eva replied. She took another peek into the classroom. Zoe was now writing furiously, which made her smile with affectionate indulgence. "I think Zoe's on a mission."

"Oh, good. Wake me when she's finished," Earl muttered.

Eva glanced back at her friend and her smile broadened. "Why don't you go home to bed? They won't find out the results for a few weeks."

"Nup." Earl shook his head. "I want to be here."

"You know—"

"Zoe and Elena were the first students I have taught for nearly ten years. I want to stick around and see how they do," Earl said, ending in a huge yawn, and promptly closed his eyes once more. "Or rather, how I do." He shifted position and shrugged his wide shoulders against the chair back.

Eva did not pursue the matter. Instead, she went back to sitting and waiting, while mentally reviewing the past few weeks.

Eva opened her eyes when she heard a noise. Friedrich had entered the building and was making his way towards them. He was looking a sight more healthy than he had the night that Eva had fractured his wrist with the poker, though his lower arm was still in a cast.

"Have they finished yet?" Friedrich asked. He took off his coat a bit awkwardly because of the cast, and draped it over an empty chair.

"No, not yet," Eva replied.

"Oh, good. I thought I would miss them." Friedrich sat next to Eva and was silent for a moment. Finally, he spoke again. "Want to hear some good news?"

"Did the Australians win the cricket?" Eva quipped and got a chuckle from Earl, whose eyes were still closed.

"I didn't know you liked cricket," Friedrich said in surprise.

"I don't." Eva shook her head. "Zoe does. I don't know why but she loves the game. I blame Earl for introducing her to it and Vegemite."

"Australia is 5 for 250," Friedrich replied, unbuttoned his suit jacket with his good hand.

Eva said, "I thought there were eleven on the team."

Earl's eyes popped open and he looked at Eva, who grinned at him mischievously. "Was that an attempt to be funny?" he asked.

"Yes."

"Don't give up your day job. Germans don't have a sense of humor. And I must remind you that Zoe was eating Vegemite before you met me."

"I already gave up my day job," Eva said, chuckling. "And yes we do have a sense of humor, but it's too sophisticated for you Aussies. Plus Zoe might have eaten it before, but every time you're over, the two of you just about go through another jar of Vegemite."

"Ha, ha, ha." Earl leaned over and ruffled Eva's hair. "You're just too funny."

"You were saying you had some good news," Eva prompted.

"Oh, yes," Friedrich answered sheepishly. "I got a telegram today about Nuremberg."

"Oh?"

"Muller will be brought before the court in January," Friedrich stated, waiting for Eva's reaction. A tiny smile played on her lips as she leaned against the wall. She was satisfied that finally Muller was going to pay for his many crimes. Eva had been right when she had told Earl that she was not going to be surprised or feel sorry for the man. She felt nothing for Muller except contempt. Eva glanced at the smiling Earl.

"I think we're going to have that party sooner than we thought," Eva told her friend.

"What party?" Friedrich asked.

"Earl is throwing a party for Muller's execution," Eva explained.

"Hope they hang the bastard and then shoot him," Earl remarked, yawning. "I would go over there and volunteer if I could."

"Won't Muller be dead when they hang him? What's the point of shooting him as well?" Friedrich asked. "Not that I'm going to complain."

"Just to make sure he's dead," Eva replied. "He survived an exploding house." She explained to Friedrich about Muller's miraculous escape from the German headquarters in Greece that had allowed him to evade the Greek Resistance as well as the Americans. Eva was still unsure how the entire escapade had happened.

The trio fell silent for a moment before Eva turned to Friedrich. "Friedrich, what are you doing for Christmas?"

"Not having it," Friedrich replied. Earl guffawed and nearly fell out of his chair.

"See, I told you Germans had a sense of humor," Eva laughed.

Friedrich smiled. "Why do you ask?"

"Zoe and I are having our first official Christmas dinner in Australia. We celebrated last year, but we didn't have our own place and ate with the other immigrants in the public housing facilities." Eva could not help grinning in happiness. Christmas was her favorite holiday, and this year was going to be made even more special by having her father, Ally, and her friends join her and Zoe in celebrating the birth of Christ. "We would like to invite you, if you want to come."

Friedrich looked down and sighed. "I'm not a Christian."

"I know that," Eva replied. "We want to have our friends celebrate with us."

"I am honored. I will come but may I ask one thing of you?"

"What's that?"

"We have a celebration every year called Hanukah. I usually celebrate it on my own but this year it's different," Friedrich said with a shy smile.

"Freddy's got a girlfriend," Earl sang out teasingly. Eva poked Earl in the shoulder; he stopped and rubbed the area, giving her a mock pout. "You're no fun."

"Behave," Eva said, waggling her finger at him. "When is it?"

"Hanukah is held over eight days and tomorrow is the eighth day," Friedrich replied. "Elena and I would like to invite you to attend." He spoke rather stiffly, clearly anticipating a polite refusal. "I don't know if you want to come, but if you don't..."

"We would both be honored to join you," Eva replied.

Friedrich had his head bowed. He seemed to be waiting for a rejection, and when it did not come, he looked up at her in surprise. "Really?"

"Yes." Eva put a friendly hand on his shoulder.

Friedrich leaned forward to address Earl. "Would you like to come, too?"

"If it involves food, drink, and being with my mates, count me in," Earl replied. He got up from his seat and stretched. "I'm going for a smoko; want one?" he asked Eva, who shook her head. He walked down the small corridor and out of the building, leaving Eva and Friedrich alone.

Eva turned to Friedrich. "Did you really think I would say 'no'?"

Friedrich did not answer for a moment, clearly trying to decide if he should tell Eva what he thought. "Yes, I thought you would say 'no'."

"Last December, we celebrated Hanukah with Elena in one of the immigrant housing rooms we had to stay in before finding and affording our own place," Eva revealed. "It was a beautiful ceremony and although we didn't have the menorah, we made do."

"I am so used to prejudice and ignorance, but not used to being the ignorant one myself," Friedrich explained slowly. "I have an apology to make."

"Why?"

"Because I am an idiot."

"I don't think you're an idiot," Eva reassured him.

"Yes, I am." Friedrich nodded. "I let prejudice blind me."

"What do you mean?"

Friedrich leaned back against the hard wooden chair and sighed. "I fully expected you to say 'no' because you were...um..."

"I was a Nazi?" Eva suggested. She was not surprised to find Friedrich thought of her that way. She was used to people judging her, but it stung nevertheless that Friedrich thought of her as a Nazi when he had to have known that she was nothing of the kind.

"No, I know you weren't a Nazi; but you are a Christian."

Eva smiled despite the serious nature of the conversation. "You know, Friedrich, I'm used to being called a Nazi, but I haven't had anyone be upset with me for being a Christian before."

"That sounds even more idiotic when said aloud." Friedrich shook his head. "I can't believe—"

"It's all right. It sounds stupid because it is stupid," Eva said. "As stupid as killing someone because they are Jewish."

"I have done what I accuse others of doing." Friedrich looked over at the classroom door, which remained shut.

"It's easy to do," Eva shrugged. "We all have our prejudices."

"You're letting me off the hook." Friedrich wiggled his finger at her. "I'm sorry. Elena has told me a lot about you and Zoe. She loves you both and..." Friedrich stopped when he realized he was about to reveal more than he wanted.

"You love Elena." Eva grinned.

"Yes, I love Elena." Friedrich couldn't help but smile. "She has been so sweet, helping all these weeks, and she is a beautiful woman."

"Well, that's obvious," Eva said.

"Yes." Friedrich nodded. "Elena loves both of you very much, and if it wasn't for you and Zoe, I wouldn't have met her."

Eva covered her mouth with her hand and snickered, hoping the noise would not disturb the prospective students in the classroom. "Or nearly got your head squashed or your wrist broken."

Friedrich glanced down at his plaster cast and laughed. "Ah yes, that would be a reminder."

"Talk about falling in love," Eva said, which caused both of them to start laughing, heedless of the test-taking students.

"What's so funny?" Earl asked as he came back from smoking his cigarette.

"German joke," Eva replied. The conversation was interrupted when the door to the examination room opened, and the would-be students filed out.

Zoe and Elena were the last to emerge. They were greeted by their friends, with Friedrich giving his girlfriend a very chaste kiss while Earl made gross "kissy" noises.

"Don't mind him, he needs to sleep." Eva shook her head and greeted Zoe with her own chaste kiss on the cheek. The two women fell in step together as they made their way out of the building. "How did it go?" Eva asked.

"Hmm, English is a funny language," Zoe replied, "but I think I did well."

"Really?"

Zoe smiled. "Yeah, we had great teachers," she said a little louder so Earl could hear her.

"Of course you did," Earl said proudly, puffing out his chest.

They exited the building into brilliant sunshine. It was noon and the temperature was already overwhelming. Eva could see heat shimmers rising off the asphalt. She winced when she spied a youngster without shoes running across the courtyard.

"Friedrich invited us to celebrate Hanukah with him tomorrow night," Eva whispered to her partner as they climbed into Earl's car, settling in the back seat together.

Earl opened the door and stuck his head inside. "Hey, Freddy can't start his beast. I'll just go over and see what the matter is," he said before leaving the two women alone.

"Elena mentioned that earlier," Zoe said, referring to Friedrich's invitation. "I saw this beautiful menorah at the store."

"They would like that." Eva brought Zoe's hand to her lips for a quick kiss. "I had a very interesting chat with Friedrich."

"He finally said more than hello?" Zoe grinned. "Elena is definitely in 'heavy like.'"

"He loves her."

"He actually said that?"

"Yep," Eva nodded. "It slipped out."

"He told you that he loves Elena?" Zoe said incredulously. "He can't say more than two words to you without getting all shy."

"I know. That's why it was an interesting chat."

"What else did he say?"

"He asked us to come to Hanukah and when I said we would go, he admitted that he didn't think we would accept his invitation."

"That is very odd," Zoe observed. She snuggled closer to Eva's side. "Did he say why?"

"Because I'm a Christian," Eva said, giggling.

Zoe looked at her, a very puzzled expression on her face. "And that makes you laugh?"

"Yes." Eva sat back, a beaming smile plastered on her face.

"I think the heat is getting to you." Zoe put her hand over Eva's forehead as if testing for a fever.

Eva playfully twisted her head away from Zoe's hand. "Zoe, he thought we wouldn't go because we were Christians."

"Yes, I understood that."

"He didn't say it was because I am a Nazi."

"But you're not a Nazi." Zoe frowned.

"Don't frown." Eva smoothed the wrinkled forehead with her fingers. "For once someone has thought of me as something other than a Nazi."

"Oh." Zoe finally understood but was obviously still puzzled by Eva's behavior. "This is really making you giddy, isn't it?"

"Yes," Eva said and pulled Zoe into her arms for a kiss.

"Well, hooray for prejudice against Christians," Zoe snorted. "You're finally going to start work tomorrow. Looking forward to it?" she asked, changing the subject.

Eva sat back, closed her eyes, and held Zoe in her arms. She had spent the last three weeks in orientation, then being moved from center to center so she could understand how the entire department worked. It was not really grueling work and she had found the new employment very enjoyable. Tomorrow she was going to start work on a more permanent basis at the George Street Immigration Center. "I'm a little scared," Eva admitted.

"Why?"

"New people; I'll have to prove myself again; silly things," Eva replied. "I don't know, I'm just a little apprehensive."

"Want me to come and hold your hand?" Zoe asked, looking into Eva's eyes. Eva tilted her head down and kissed Zoe.

Just at that moment, Earl got into the car and glanced at their reflection in the rear view mirror. "Hey, you two, stop that! My car isn't used to women smooching in the back."

Eva stuck out her tongue at her friend, feeling quite jovial. She took Zoe's hand and held it as the car moved smoothly away with Earl at the wheel.

"You can't stop smiling about that, can you?" Zoe said. She opened the door to their apartment and went inside, followed by Eva.

"No," Eva said and looked at the pile of letters they had brought in with them. "Bill, bill, bill." Eva flicked through the mail and stopped, staring at the envelope in her hand.

"Big bill?" Zoe asked from the sofa.

Eva did not answer but kept staring at the letter. Grumbling about giving up her comfortable spot, Zoe went over to join Eva. "Immigration Department," Zoe read the English words on the envelope carefully. "Are you going to open that, or are you trying to read it with your X-ray vision?"

Eva handed it to her. "You read it," she said nervously and started to pace. She could not bear the thought of the letter denying something she had dreamed about since she had discovered the identity of her real father.

Zoe shook her head and neatly ripped the envelope. Eva sat down on the sofa but was too keyed up to stay put and sprang back to her feet, much to Zoe's amusement. "Evy, they're not throwing you out of the country," she said.

"I know," Eva replied. She started to bite her fingernail. Being thrown out of the country was not what worried her. It was the dreaded "I'm sorry to inform you..." letter arriving. "Read the letter, Zoe," she said aloud.

Zoe took Eva's hand and held it. "Don't bite your fingernails."

Eva said, "Zoe, can you read the thing, please?"

"Dear Miss Muller—"

"I knew it! They didn't give it to me!" Eva threw her hands up and started to pace. "I knew they wouldn't give it to me...I just knew it. I wonder if I took my mutti's maiden name—" Eva rambled.

"Eva!" Zoe yelled. "Will you please sit down? Let me continue."

Eva stopped in her tracks"But..."

Zoe put down the letter. She gently pushed Eva to the sofa and made her sit. "Will you please calm down? I don't believe I'm saying this to you. What's gotten into you?"

"I'm nervous, love. I've never wanted anything so badly before—"

"Never? Not even me?" Zoe teased.

"You were easy to get," Eva joked and smiled through her nervousness.

"Pah." Zoe smiled "All right, where was I?"

"'Dear Miss Muller,'" Eva said.

"What was your mother's maiden name?" Zoe interrupted herself, her curiosity clearly getting the better of her.

"Mitsos," Eva replied.

"Eva Mitsos? That doesn't sound right."

"Zoe! Read the damn letter!"

"Dear Miss Muller, I am writing to inform you that your application to have your surname changed from Muller to Haralambos has..." Zoe stopped for effect, which only made Eva growl. "I love it when you do that." Zoe grinned and moved away when Eva made an impatient lunge for the letter. "Hey, you asked me to read it!" Zoe said.

"Zoe, you're torturing me," Eva said plaintively. "Please read it."

"...has been approved," Zoe quickly finished and covered her ears as Eva bolted up from the sofa, screaming in delight.

Ecstatic, she engulfed Zoe in her arms and kissed her soundly.

"Well hello, Miss Haralambos!" Zoe laughed. "I do like the sound of that."

"Thank you, Miss Lambros." Eva held her partner and sighed contentedly.

"Evy?"

"Yes?"

"Let's hope the neighbors don't think we have more Nazis in here and come storming in," Zoe said, giggling. Then her tone changed, becoming so solemn that Eva's good mood sobered as well. "I have something to say to you," Zoe said.

"Oh?" Eva pulled away a little and looked down at the other woman. "Is something wrong?"

"No, but I've been thinking. You know the story we keep telling people about us being sisters?"

"Yes, the one we keep mixing up," Eva said wryly.

"Yes, well, they wouldn't ask why we are so different if they didn't have to."

"Right," Eva replied, a little perplexed at where the conversation was going.

"Well, I've been thinking."

"You said that already," Eva reminded her. "Zoe, you're torturing me again."

"I want to change my name to Haralambos, too," Zoe stated very quietly, watching Eva in a clear attempt to gauge her reaction.

"Are you serious?" Eva asked. She had a feeling that what Zoe was proposing was something much more than just a change of name.

"I'm very serious. I know how much it means to you to be known as Haralambos instead of Muller, and we did get married."

"I despised the name Muller, Zoe, but you don't hate your name," Eva reasoned.

"Yes, that's true," Zoe agreed.

"I want you to think about this."

"I have thought about it," Zoe replied.

"No, I *really* want you to think about this, Zoe. I would love for you to have the same name, but I don't want you to give up your family." Eva took her partner's hand and led her to the sofa where they both sat down. "I didn't know your parents, Zoe, but they raised you and they must have been some very special people."

"They were special people," Zoe said. "They would have loved you."

"Well, why do you want to change your name? Nikolas and Helena Lambros raised a daughter whom I love more than anything in this world. You should honor them," Eva reasoned.

"I just wanted to share the same surname with you."

Eva's frown was replaced with a beaming smile. It was not what Zoe had said but the sentiment behind the words that made Eva's heart melt. "You own my heart, Zoe." Eva's voice broke a little and she swallowed as she held Zoe's hand against her bosom. "I would love to have you change your name, but you are a Lambros and the Lambros name stands for courage and love. I don't want you to reject who you are."

"I won't be rejecting my family, more like joining with you. If you were a man, I'd be expected to take your name."

"If I had never found my real father and taken his name, I would have changed mine to Lambros," Eva revealed, much to Zoe's visible surprise. "Don't change your name, love. Please."

Eva watched intently as Zoe bowed her head, obviously considering Eva's words. Zoe finally looked up and nodded in agreement. Without another word, Zoe rested her head on Eva's shoulder and put her arm around Eva's belly, making her sigh.

Chapter Eighteen

The sound of crashing came from the bedroom and Eva popped her head out of the kitchen. More crashes were followed by a screech and then a loud thump. She listened intently, not at all worried about the strange noises.

For the last couple of weeks, Zoe had been able to laze about while she was on her annual holiday. Zoe was not a morning person. She had had most of the past month to enjoy being at leisure, and now it was difficult to convince her to get up early. Eva had tried to get her partner out of bed as soon as the bell on the clock started to ring that morning. Zoe stubbornly refused to budge, except to grab the annoying alarm clock and toss it out of the open bedroom window. They would have to buy another clock, since things had a tendency to stop working when Zoe reacted violently to their insistence that she rise on time.

Eva smiled, watching Zoe hop out of the bedroom on one foot, seemingly unable to find her other shoe. Zoe's bangs fell across her eyes as she turned to peer at the wall clock, then she fell on the floor, grunting her displeasure.

Morning in the Haralambos/Lambros household was anything but serene. *Yesterday had been a red-letter day for us but today was proving to be somewhat more of a challenge,* Eva thought. Aloud she asked, "Zoe, are you all right in there?"

"Argh! I'm going to be late!" Zoe exclaimed. "Found it!" she said, spying the missing shoe under the coffee table.

"You know if you had gotten out of bed when the alarm clock went off, you wouldn't be rushing." Eva stated the obvious as she held an inviting mug of tea in her hand.

Zoe looked up at Eva, giving her a sheepish grin. "It's not my fault we went to bed so late."

They had spent the previous night at Earl's home playing poker, which had gone really well until Eva started to lose. She had to recoup the matchsticks she had lost to Earl. Elena had got out of the game early. The rest of their friends had watched the remaining two players, their game as serious as if they had had real money at stake. The contest had gone on until midnight when Zoe had dragged a reluctant Eva away after promising Earl another game.

"He took all my matchsticks!" Eva objected.

"Oh, yeah, we were going to go bankrupt," Zoe said. She tied her shoelaces, got up and gave the smirking Eva a quick kiss before heading into the kitchen.

"You're late," Eva warned, putting the tea mug on the counter.

"I know," Zoe said as she grabbed a piece of toast and began munching.

There was a knock on the door. Eva answered it. Elena stood outside, wearing a harried expression on her face as she tried to juggle her breakfast as well as her handbag.

"Morning, Elena," Eva welcomed the young woman, ushering her inside. "Come in. The tortoise isn't ready yet."

Elena smiled. She hurried over to the sofa and dropped her handbag on the floor. "Phew, I couldn't wake up this morning," she said, flopping down on the cushions and beginning to devour the piece of toast she had brought with her.

Zoe came out of the kitchen with a piece of toast in one hand and her cup of tea in the other. "Hey, El," she said through a mouthful of crumbs.

"Hi, Zoe. Aren't you ready yet?"

"Nope. I'm just having breakfast." Zoe swallowed. "Want some?"

"I have mine." Elena held up her toast. "I think someone was late getting up today," she teased.

Zoe hastily finished her piece of toast, washing it down with tea. "I didn't see you banging on my door to get me up. Were you out with Freddy last night after the game broke up?"

"In a manner of speaking," Elena said quietly, a blush tingeing her cheeks pink. "Come on, we're going to be late!"

"Okay, okay. The restaurant isn't going anywhere!" Zoe mumbled. She was about to go and put the mug in the kitchen, but she was blocked from going into the kitchen by Eva, who had been listening to the conversation between Zoe and Elena with a great deal of amusement.

"I love you, gotta go. I can't wait to hear about your first day," Zoe said, rapid fire, trying to give Eva a quick kiss, but Eva held her in place for a moment, then smirked again and kissed her more thoroughly. Upon being released, Zoe picked up her handbag and rushed out of the door, banging into Alberta, who stood in the corridor bemused by the manic rush.

"Sorry, sorry. Gotta go," Zoe said. She gave Alberta a kiss on the cheek and bolted down the stairs with Elena in tow. Eva shook her head at her partner's behavior and went into the bedroom to make her own preparations for work, first waving hello to Alberta as the older woman came into the apartment.

"Eva, are you ready?" Alberta called out.

"In a minute," Eva called back from the bedroom. Judging from the sounds coming from the lounge, Alberta was tidying up the messy lounge. Eva came out of the bedroom, pulling on her sweater.

"Eva, this is such a beautiful drawing," Alberta said as her gaze fell on a drawing of a young woman reading, the trailing edge of the curtain lightly draped over her shoulder as if a breeze had blown it on her.

Eva greeted the older woman more properly with a kiss on the cheek. "Morning, Ally. Yes, Zoe's getting really good," she said, indicating the artwork with a nod. "She's very talented."

"Hmm. How long did you sit for it?"

"A couple of days," Eva replied. She picked up her lunch and put it in her bag. During the posing session, she had enjoyed just sitting there reading and occasionally looking up at Zoe as the budding artist attempted to capture her image on the paper. She had loved watching Zoe draw, sometimes seeing a furrowed brow and the tip of her tongue sticking out while she concentrated on a difficult area. Bringing her thoughts back to the present, Eva asked Alberta, "How's Father doing this morning?"

"Oh, he's looking forward to meeting some of the congregation. He was quite excited." Alberta smiled. "I think we'd better hurry, or we'll miss our bus."

Having finished getting ready, Eva closed the door to the apartment behind her, and the two women made their way down the steps and into bright sunshine.

"I've been thinking of testing for my driver's license," Alberta said while they stood watching the traffic lights, waiting to cross the road.

"I didn't know you could drive."

"Oh, yes. I used to drive the tractor on my brother's farm before the war. I got my license just before signing up. Do you know how to drive?"

"No, never learned how. I guess it would be easier to get a car. Zoe would like to learn, but I'm not sure if Sydney is ready for Zoe on wheels," Eva said. Her partner would enjoy the freedom of having a car; she already loved to tinker with Earl's vehicle. Now that the money from the new job is coming in, they may be able to afford the payments. She would have to talk to Zoe about it.

As the bus made its way through the rush hour traffic, Eva looked out the window at the scenery blurring past. She and Alberta had managed to find seats next to one another just before the bus became "standing room only". Eva sighed as she recalled the many days of riding standing, her feet tired and sore. She watched her fellow passengers and played a game that Zoe had invented, trying to match the person to a job. Sometimes Zoe had come up with the strangest occupations, which had amused Eva and, of course, had taken her mind off her sore feet.

"I think a car would be good right about now," Alberta muttered. She was being struck in the shoulder by a woman's handbag.

Eva grinned, leaned over her stepmother, and poked the bag out of the way. The owner of the handbag gave her a pointed look and made a rude noise before moving herself further down the bus.

Alberta burst out laughing, shaking her head.

Eva went back to staring out of the window. The bus went down City Road and past the entrance of Sydney University. She wondered how Zoe would enjoy going to college. It was going to be very different for her partner, who had never experienced anything like university life. Eva still remembered her time at the Berlin campus. She had had a great time once she had got over her jitters. She had met so many different people and learned so much.

Eva's thoughts naturally turned to Greta Strauss. She had met Greta at the university and in so doing, had finally realized that there was a reason she did not like boys. Eva smiled to herself. She had not thought about Greta in a long time and felt a little guilty that she had not been faithful to the memory of her first love. Eva daydreamed, remembering those carefree days before the war.

She had registered at the office and spent the rest of the day taking a slow tour of the campus where she would spend the next few years. Mutti was so proud of her and had taken photographs just before she left. Her stepfather had been silent and only grunted his assent to the pictures, but she knew he was proud of her in his own way. Eva was overawed as she walked out around the university grounds. She had a grin plastered on her face all day.

Tired from walking around, she noticed that some of the other students were sitting on the grass. Eva followed their example. She took off her sweater, put it on the grass, and sat down on it to protect her dress from stains. She turned her face to the sun, enjoying the beautiful spring day, but frowned as a shadow fell over her. She opened her eyes and looked up.

"Hello," Eva said to the figure silhouetted against the sun. The figure moved and plopped down beside her.

"Hello. You must be new; you have the new, fresh look about you," a young woman said, offering her hand. "I'm Greta Strauss."

"Eva Muller," Eva replied. "You don't look as though you're new."

"Oh, no. I'm an old hand at this. I just came here today to lend a hand at the registration office. You know, answering questions and that sort of thing," Greta replied, smiling.

"Oh." Eva smiled back, suddenly not as tired anymore.

Greta was a tall young woman. Her auburn hair flew about uncontrollably, and she had apparently lost the fight to keep it in any semblance of order. Greta had an easy smile and laughing eyes that made Eva feel quite relaxed in her presence.

This was a pleasant memory compared to what had happened later. Eva had been so young; she had truly been a different person back then. If Greta had been present now, Eva was sure she would be most surprised at the woman Eva had become. Greta had been five years older than her and much more worldly-wise than the naïve teenager. It was sad for

Eva to realize that she could never be that innocent girl again, but the changes she had undergone were not bad, simply necessary.

Eva was drawn out of her trip down memory lane when Alberta tapped her on the shoulder. The bus was nearing their stop. The driver smiled pleasantly at them and the two women got off the bus, heading into the John Curtin Memorial Building that housed the translation section of the Immigration Department.

When Eva had found out where she was going to be working, Zoe had insisted they discover what the building looked like. To that end, they had taken a bus into town, going over the route, and then done a little window shopping, much against Eva's inclinations. Now she followed Alberta into the lobby of the building, trying to get herself ready to begin her new job.

The elevator doors opened and a young woman in a blue and white uniform popped her head out. "Going up!" she announced. A few people entered the elevator along with Eva and Alberta.

As the doors closed, Alberta turned to Eva, who was frowning and biting her lower lip. "Are you all right?" Alberta asked.

"Oh, yeah. I'm just a little nervous," Eva mumbled.

Alberta smiled and squeezed Eva's hand. The elevator stopped on the ninth floor, and the doors slid open, admitting a buzz of voices. The pair got out and were greeted by the sight of an overcrowded waiting area. Eva's eyebrows rose when she looked around at the refugees sitting huddled together and talking, and she smiled. The people were speaking in a dozen different languages. *It's like the Tower of Babel*, she thought to herself.

Eva followed Alberta to the reception counter where a harried young woman was answering telephones. They stood waiting patiently until the receptionist finished with her current call.

"I hope you understand English," the receptionist muttered. "May I help you?" she asked more clearly, looking at Eva and Alberta.

"We're here to see Adam Eden," Alberta told her.

Eva resisting the urge to grin at the name. She had had a good laugh at home when they had received the letter from him informing them of the date and time to report for work.

The receptionist looked relieved. "Thank God! You're the new interpreters?"

Eva and Alberta nodded and received a huge grin from the young woman. "My name is Debbie," she said. "As you can see, I'm the receptionist. What language area will you be in?"

"This is Eva Haralambos and I'm Alberta Haralambos. I'm in the Greek section," Alberta replied

"German and Italian," Eva said, smiling at Debbie.

"Excellent! I need to learn how to ask our clients to sit down, so when you have a free moment and when I can get unchained from these telephones, will you teach me a few phrases?" Debbie asked, getting up and coming around her desk.

Alberta and Eva agreed, then followed Debbie down a corridor which housed several offices. Debbie tapped lightly at the door of the end office and opened it. "Be seeing you around, ladies," she said, excusing herself.

They looked at each other and then stared at the unoccupied desk. Were they supposed to wait? Who were they waiting for? Before Eva could decide what to do next, a middle-aged woman entered the office and sat down, staring at them expectantly. They introduced themselves and got a wide smile in return.

"If everyone appears to be happy to see you two, it's because we are!" The woman motioned for Alberta and Eva to sit down in chairs that stood in front of her desk. "My name is Edith Andrews; I'm Mr. Eden's secretary. We are severely short-staffed and as you can see outside, our clients are getting rather restless."

"It's always nice to be needed," Alberta stated, and Edith chuckled.

"We need you desperately," Edith said. She stood up again and knocked on a nearby door. "Adam, Alberta Haralambos and Eva Haralambos are here." She showed them into the man's office and gave them another smile as she shut the door.

A man in his fifties sporting short salt-and-pepper hair, with more salt than pepper Eva noted, politely came around his desk and extended his hand. "Welcome, ladies. My name is Adam Eden. Welcome to the Translating Department. Please, have a seat."

He waited until Alberta and Eva sat down, then circled back around his desk and took his own seat. "So, I gather you came through our waiting area? It's a jungle out there. Now, Alberta, you will be in the Greek section; we have plenty of work there today. And Eva..." He stopped and began to laugh. "I'm sorry, Eva. All we need now is someone called 'serpent' to join our little group and it would be complete."

Eva gave Adam a grin. She liked the man. He was easygoing and did not seem to have the self-important airs and artifices that managers usually acquired; or at least, that was her experience of managers at the biscuit factory.

"I know that's a bad joke, but once you've heard *all* the bad jokes, you tend to create new ones." He smiled. "Now, getting back to where you will be working. Our German area needs about ten more interpreters than we currently have. I understand you grew up in Germany?"

"Yes. I grew up around Hamburg and then Berlin," Eva explained. "I have a letter here about my name." Eva took out the letter from the Immigration Department and handed it to him. "It came yesterday and I didn't have time to send it in to Personnel."

Eden took the letter and read it through. "I don't see this as a problem. We will make a note and send a copy to the Personnel Department."

"Thank you." Eva smiled at her new boss.

"Ah, so, Berlin; beautiful town. I was there before the war. I guess it's in ruins now. What a shame." Adam sighed. "Okay, now where were we before I took a mental holiday? Ah, yes, most of the clients are Jewish; you don't have a problem with that?"

Eva was taken aback, but bit back an instinctive retort. "No, I don't have a problem with Jewish people."

"That's good. Two of our previous translators had problems with Jewish clients. I won't tolerate racism here. We are here to help people, and since the majority of our clients are refugees, I think we need to show a little patience and a great deal of tolerance." He looked at Eva and Alberta and gave them a sheepish grin. "I'm sorry. I do tend to get carried away. Your workload is going to be rather heavy over the next few days, not because we want to see how good you are, but because the *Patris* docked yesterday. We have to process everyone so they can start their new lives. Hopefully, we will get some slow days soon. Have I scared you enough?"

The women shook their heads. "Very good," he said, glancing down at his files. "Your immediate supervisor is Richard Farmer but he is away today. You'll get to meet him tomorrow. He's in charge of the section where both of you will be working. Edith will show you the staff cafeteria, which has some very interesting meals, and give you the slow tour of the place. I guess after that you may want to familiarize yourselves with the various government departments that handle refugee matters, even though I know you just completed the three weeks of training as a government employee. As much as I would love to get you two working, I think you need some time to get to know how we do things before I throw you into the deep end."

He escorted the women to the outer office and Edith led them outside once again.

It was a whirlwind of a morning as Edith patiently explained some basic procedures and showed them where they should go. Alberta and Eva each had their own little office where they could meet with clients and assess the various problems and needs that would be presented daily.

Some time later, a bemused Eva sat in her office, looked at the volumes of information in front of her and smiled happily. To her amazement, the tiny office also had a radio, not a standard item in a government office. Eva was delighted when she saw it. She was told it was given to the interpreter who occupied the office previously. He had left it behind when he had moved on to another position. This was going to be a lot more interesting than packing biscuit boxes every day. It would be a challenge, but she did enjoy challenges. She could not wait to tell Zoe about her day when she got home.

Sydney Art College was a short bus trip away from the restaurant, so Zoe had decided that she wanted to go and see it. Convincing Elena to go with her was not difficult and, at the end of their shift, the two young women boarded the bus and headed towards the College. It proved to be a large institution, and Zoe was mesmerized by the sight of it.

"So do we stand here or do we go in?" Elena asked after they had got off the bus and were standing on the College grounds.

"Are we allowed?" Zoe asked, a little uncertain as to how a college actually worked. "Is it like a normal school?"

"I don't know, Zoe. I guess if we get stopped, we can say we are just looking."

"That's what we are doing, isn't it?"

"Yes," Elena said. "Come on, let's go." She tugged on Zoe's sleeve to get her to move. After a short hesitation, Zoe followed her friend through the gates. She looked around at the students sitting on the grass, talking in couples or small groups. Elena pulled on her arm again, regaining Zoe's attention. "Does this intimidate you a bit?" Elena asked.

"Yeah," Zoe mumbled as they wandered into a reception office and walked up to a desk where a severe looking older woman sat, scribbling on a collection of papers. From her deep frown, she seemed very unhappy. Zoe looked at Elena, who shrugged. "Is this where students register?" Zoe asked the woman.

"Yes, it does say Registration Desk," the woman replied tartly, pointing to the sign in front of the desk. "Are you here to register?"

"Yes, sort of, but not today," Zoe stammered, which only earned her a disapproving look.

"You sound Greek," the woman said, sneering. "*Are* you Greek?" She made it sound as if Zoe's nationality was a disease.

"Yes," Zoe replied. She had been intimidated by the woman at first, but now she was getting annoyed by her tone. "Do you have a problem with me being Greek?"

Elena rolled her eyes. "Not now, Zoe," she whispered.

"Got too many Greeks here," the woman muttered, opening a large ledger. "What's your name?"

"My name isn't down in the book yet," Zoe replied. She was startled when the woman closed the book with a loud thump.

"Well, stop wasting my time then!" The woman sniffed and returned to her work, ignoring the younger women.

"Racist cow," Zoe muttered as they walked away. She glanced back and shook her head in disgust at the woman's behavior.

"Zoe, you're not going to make life easier for yourself if you get annoyed at everyone who is racist," Elena pointed out.

"No, I guess not."

They walked several minutes before deciding to claim a patch of grass that was not already occupied. "I can get used to this." Zoe smiled, forgetting the minor annoyance at the registration table. "Oh, this is nice. So, El, what's with you and Friedrich?"

Elena fidgeted with the information sheets she had picked up while in the office. "I like him a lot, Zoe. He's funny and smart."

"Friedrich is funny?" Zoe asked.

"He is. He's funny and he makes me feel comfortable. He is so sweet and gentle. He lost his family in Germany, too, and we've been talking a lot."

"So has he kissed you yet?" Zoe asked and looked away. She did not want to make her friend uncomfortable by staring at her.

"Yes," Elena admitted with a sweet, shy smile.

Zoe grinned at her. "About time, I'd say. Then what happened?"

"You are nosy, aren't you?"

"Hey, you asked me about Eva."

"Yeah, and I got way too much information!" Elena laughed. "I also seem to remember that you were showing me how much you loved Eva."

"I showed you?"

"See what a little bit of the demon drink does to you, Zoe?" Elena teased her. "Remember the night of the dance?"

"Oh!" Zoe blushed a little and then smiled at the memory of her lover trying valiantly to control Zoe's groping hands.

"You love her a lot, don't you?" Elena asked, bringing Zoe's pleasant recollections to an end and reclaiming her wandering attention.

"Yes!" Zoe replied with conviction.

"I think I could love Friedrich that way, but I may have a problem." She looked at her friend shyly and revealed, "I'm not a virgin."

"You're not a virgin?" Zoe's eyes popped open in amazement.

"Didn't I just say that?"

"Oh, I heard you but what does that have to do with kissing Friedrich? You know, El, kissing someone doesn't mean..."

Elena clearly wondered if Zoe was teasing her, but she was quite serious. Elena shook her head. "Sometimes, Zoe, you are such a surprise."

"Why? What did I do now?"

"Um, would you like to walk with me? I would feel more comfortable talking about it in a less public place."

"Sure," Zoe replied. She picked up her handbag and followed Elena down the jacaranda-lined path; the clusters of purple blossoms on the trees gave the walkway a serene look. The young women walked silently together for a few moments.

"You know I was in Bergen-Belson during the war?" Elena asked.

Zoe nodded. Elena had told them about the concentration camp when they had first met, but she had barely mentioned it since. Zoe had not wanted to pry and unintentionally cause her friend any anguish by bringing up bad memories.

"My mother was there, too, for a short time." Elena went quiet, and Zoe just walked next to her, taking the other woman's hand and giving it a tiny squeeze in a subtle show of support. Elena smiled. "You know, Zoe, you are my best friend, and I've wanted to tell you this for a long time, but I didn't have the courage."

"You know you can tell me anything, El."

"I know, but can I ask a favor?"

Zoe nodded.

"Can you please not tell Eva? I know you two discuss everything together but, well...I would feel more comfortable if you didn't tell her."

"Okay."

"It's not that I don't like Eva, I do but—"

"Elena, I give you my word I won't tell Eva," Zoe promised. "Not until you want me to. I can keep confidences."

"All right." Elena took a deep breath, visibly trying to collect her thoughts. They walked a little further in silence. Elena's head was bowed. It was obvious that she was trying to pluck up the courage to continue her story. Zoe stopped near a bench and sat, pulling Elena down beside her. The trees gave them some privacy.

"When I was fifteen...um..." Elena stopped. She bit her lip and waited until she was ready to go on. Zoe waited, holding Elena's hand and projecting patient support. "On my fifteenth birthday, one of the guards came into the barracks and took me outside. He said the commandant wanted to see me, since it was my birthday. He took me to the commandant's office, and then he left."

Zoe had an idea of where this was going, and the idea horrified her.

Elena looked up at Zoe, then back down to where their hands were entwined. "He...um...he raped me," she said quietly. Zoe did not say a word as she wrapped her arms around her friend and hugged her. "He told me that was my birthday present," Elena added. Silent tears ran down her face. Zoe held Elena as her own tears spilled over.

"I'm so sorry, El," Zoe whispered. They embraced for a few minutes. Zoe tenderly wiped the tears from Elena's face with a handkerchief.

"You're my best friend, Zoe, and I wanted to tell you but—"

"You can tell me anything, El. You know that. I will never betray your trust."

"Do you think Friedrich will still want me?"

"He would be a total fool if he didn't. You are a gentle and loving woman, Elena. It wasn't your fault that you were raped. You are not to blame," Zoe said, kissing Elena on the cheek. "Are you going to tell him?"

"Well, he's going to know when we...you know, get married. I have to tell him."

"You're going to get married! When did this happen? When did he propose?"

"Whoa, stop!" Elena pulled her hand out of Zoe's grasp and held it up to halt the flow of questions. "He hasn't asked me to marry him yet."

"Why not?"

"Oh, I don't know, Zoe, but he hasn't. I know we haven't been together long, but it feels like I've known him all my life," Elena said.

"If he asks, will you say 'yes'?"

"I know I've fallen in love with him. And I want to."

"Wow, I haven't been to a wedding in such a long time," Zoe said smiling and then stopped as a thought occurred to her. "I am invited, aren't I?"

Elena put her arm around Zoe. "Yes, you are invited, but he hasn't asked me yet."

"He will."

"How can you be so sure?"

"I have a feeling about it," Zoe replied. "He would be an absolute fool if he didn't want you."

"But with what happened..."

"Did you want that to happen?"

"No!" Elena shook her head, her eyes wide in shock at Zoe's unexpected question.

"Then it's not your fault. How can it be?"

"I don't know, maybe he'll see me as..."

"El, Friedrich would be the biggest idiot on the planet if he didn't want to marry you because of that," Zoe reassured her friend. "Anyway, I want to be a bridesmaid and I would be very annoyed if that doesn't happen."

"I promise, if I get married, you will be my bridesmaid."

Eva opened the door to the apartment and put her handbag down. She was tired, but it was a different kind of tired from the one that she had grown used to while working at the biscuit factory. Where the factory made her ache all over, she found that now she was not physically tired, but that her new employment left her a little drained mentally.

Eva was about to call out but paused when she saw Zoe asleep on the sofa, several books scattered around her and stacked on the floor. She knelt beside the sofa and brushed away Zoe's bangs. "Zoe," she whispered, kissing the other woman softly on the mouth.

"Oh, hi there," Zoe mumbled. She opened sleepy green eyes and smiled. "What a nice way to wake up."

Instead of replying verbally, Eva kissed her again. Zoe made room for her on the sofa and they snuggled up together.

Zoe said, "I had a headache, so I thought I would grab a few minutes snooze time."

"All gone?" Eva caressed Zoe's head, and she nodded.

"So tell me, what was your first day like?" Zoe asked. "If you tell me your day, I'll tell you mine."

"Well, it was different. Very busy." Eva took Zoe's hand and began stroking her thumb across the knuckles. "I helped a few people today," she quietly related with a touch of pride in her voice. "It felt good."

"You look happy." Zoe reached out and brushed a strand of Eva's hair out of her eyes.

Eva smiled down at the woman in her arms and nodded. "I am," she said, tilting her head to steal a quick kiss. "Want to go to dinner and a movie, Miss Zoe?"

Zoe grinned. "Wow, you mean, go on a date?"

"Yep."

"With who?" Zoe teased.

"Only me."

"Hmm." Zoe considered for a moment. "Well if it's the best that I can do," she teased back, her fingers seeking out the ticklish spots on Eva's ribs. Eva batted her hand away, and Zoe asked, "So what's at the cinema anyway?"

"*Casablanca*, with Humphrey Bogart and Ingrid Bergman."

"Sounds great. Why don't you go and get changed, and I'll tidy up in here."

"It's a date," Eva replied. She gave Zoe a quick kiss before walking into the bedroom to change. For the first time in a long time, Eva felt her life was not going to come crashing down around her. Muller had been captured, her real father was back in her life and all seemed right. Life in Sydney was taking a turn for the better. Eva whistled happily as she unbuttoned her shirt, getting ready to go on a date with her beloved partner.

A full moon illuminated the walkway as Eva and Zoe moved quietly up the path. Zoe bumped into the taller Eva, causing them both to giggle. The two women continued on their way into the building's foyer, where the landlady was taking out her cat.

Mrs. Jenkins nodded as Zoe and Eva paused. "Hello, girls, did you have a nice evening?" she asked, smiling at them fondly.

"It was wonderful, Mrs. Jenkins," Eva replied.

"Good, good. You young people need to get out and enjoy life. Good night, girls," Mrs. Jenkins said and went into her apartment, closing the door behind her.

"She knows," Eva leaned in and whispered.

"Knows what?" Zoe whispered back.

"About us," Eva continued to whisper and smiled at Zoe's alarmed look. "Yesterday when we were doing our laundry...remember?"

"We didn't do anything," Zoe said, frowning.

"Remember the duel with the wet towel?" Eva reminded her and Zoe nodded. "Well, Mrs. Jenkins was in the stairwell," Eva continued.

"Oh."

"When you left she came over and we talked about this and that," Eva recounted as they stood in the foyer. "She then asked me if we were really sisters."

"Took her long enough," Zoe said, giggling at the landlady's obliviousness.

"Well, I couldn't lie to her outright so I told her."

"Oh, I guess she didn't die on the spot since she just spoke to us," Zoe said. She sobered. "When do we move out of the apartment?"

"We don't," Eva reassured her. "She *was* a little upset that we lied to her."

"She's upset that we lied, but not that we're lesbians?" Zoe asked, not quite believing what she had been told. "It's not like we can declare our love to everyone."

"I know, love. She said that she has a sister who is a lesbian and she understands."

"She understands about what?"

Eva looked as though she would rather not impart the next piece of information. Zoe crossed her arms over her chest.

Eva took a deep breath and said, "Mrs. Jenkins understands we have an illness and can't help acting on our unnatural desires."

"A what? An illness?" Zoe stopped walking and stood stock-still, certain that Eva could see the scowl on her face in the semi-darkness. It was a minor miracle Zoe had not screamed in outrage. "You have got to be kidding."

"Zoe, she doesn't know anything about us, doesn't know how much we love each other, and she's at least trying to understand in her own way. Mrs. Jenkins believes what a lot of other people believe, what doctors say is wrong with lesbians and homosexuals like Earl," Eva tried to reason with Zoe. "Isn't it better for her to think we are sick than for us to be abused because we are different?"

"I don't know what's worse," Zoe replied. "We aren't sick. We just love each other. You would think we were murderers or something." She let out an exasperated sigh.

"I know that, love, but isn't it better for us?" Eva asked.

"It is," Zoe nodded in agreement. "At least we won't have to deal with her hatred, just her pity."

"She's not going to stop trying to set us up on dates, either." Eva smiled and looked down at Zoe, who smiled back.

"All we need is a good boy to show us what we are missing and then we will be cured, right?" Zoe asked, only partly joking. In truth, she did not have a lot of patience for ignorant people like Mrs. Jenkins, but she had a lot less for outright bigots, so she would live with the landlady's misconceptions and be grudgingly grateful the situation was not worse. They could have been looking for a new apartment.

"Something like that, I'm sure," Eva replied and held the door from the lobby for Zoe to pass. They walked up the stairs in silence. Zoe waited patiently for Eva to open the door. Eva was about to escort her into the apartment when they both spotted Elena walking up the stairs with her young man.

"So where have you been, Miss Elena?" Eva asked loudly.

Elena and Friedrich reached Elena's apartment, hand in hand. They stopped at Eva's call. "We went and saw *Casablanca*," she said. She threaded her arm through Friedrich's, and he gave her a shy smile in return.

"That's where we were!" Zoe remarked, and the two friends shared a laugh. "Where were you? We didn't see you."

"Um, we were at the back," Elena said quietly.

"Did you see any of the movie?" Eva asked. Elena's face turned a bright shade of pink.

"So you missed the bit where Rick kissed Ilsa on the tarmac, and then they flew away like Superman, high into the sky," Zoe teased.

Elena stuck her tongue out rudely, which only made Zoe laugh harder.

"How's the wrist, Friedrich?" Eva asked her friend, seeing the plaster cast had been removed.

"Good as new," Friedrich replied and joined in the chuckles. "Good thing I wasn't hit in the head, eh?"

"I hear kissing helps in the healing," Zoe teased.

"Well, I guess we will leave you two lovebirds alone; it's been a long night," Eva said, waving goodbye and preceding Zoe into their apartment.

As Eva closed the door, Zoe wrapped herself around the taller woman and looked up into the blue eyes that reminded her of the Aegean Sea. "I hear kissing increases brain power," she said, waggling her eyebrows. She stood on the tips of her toes and kissed Eva.

"Then we should both be geniuses by now." Eva snorted, and they laughed. "Did you like the movie?" Eva asked. Zoe followed her into the lounge and sat down on the sofa next to her, cuddling close.

"Oh, yeah, it was so romantic!" Zoe enthused.

Eva gave Zoe a quizzical look. "Did we see the same movie?"

Exasperated at her partner's obtuseness, Zoe swatted her on the arm, which earned her a hug. "Sing it to me again?" Zoe pleaded. Eva had sung her the song *As Time Goes By* as they walked home from the cinema. The warmth of the evening, with the sounds of the cicadas in the trees, added to the wonder of the night.

"Why, I can't remember it, Miss Zoe. I'm a little rusty on it," Eva replied, quoting a line from the film and grinning.

"I'll hum it for you," Zoe said, remembering the lines uttered by Ingrid Bergman in the film. She began humming the song a little off-key. Eva's grin turned lopsided. Zoe broke off her humming and demanded, "Sing it, my sweet Eva."

Eva caressed Zoe's cheek and sang a few lines of *As Time Goes By*, then bent down and kissed Zoe tenderly. Eva's eyes shone as brilliantly as stars as she gazed lovingly at Zoe, who sighed and fell back into her partner's embrace.

Eva sang the rest of the song; her voice was sweet, the sentiment conjured by the lyrics even sweeter. When Eva finished and looked deeply into Zoe's eyes. Zoe could see the depth of the love that was reflected back at her, and she shivered at the intensity of emotion that washed over her.

"I love you," Zoe softly whispered. Eva gathered her close, cradling Zoe in her arms, and suddenly stood up.

"Eva! Your back!" Zoe protested.

"What back?" Eva replied, her eyes twinkling. Zoe snuggled against her, reveling in her partner's strength. "I bet Rick wanted to do this to Ilsa," Eva whispered in Zoe's ear. Carrying Zoe, she walked to the bedroom and closed the door with her foot.

Chapter Nineteen

"This is nice," Zoe mumbled. Her head was propped on Eva's chest, and her voice sounded hollow to her own ears.

Both women had awakened before dawn and stayed in bed cuddling, neither of them wanting to get up. The window was open; a light breeze ruffled the curtains as the sounds of a typical early morning in the city drifted in. The milk truck could be heard as it made its usual stops along the street, soon squeaking to a halt and idling outside their building. A moment later the tinkling and clanking of glass bottles began as the milkman started his deliveries, moving from apartment to apartment. Very soon, the bakery van would bring its load of fresh breads and pastries, and the early morning rituals would be blended into the new day. The streetlights were still on in the predawn darkness, a flickering dimly glimpsed through the moving curtains.

"Did you like the campus?" Eva asked, playing with Zoe's hair.

"Apart from the racist woman? Yeah. It's big, though. Elena and I got lost a couple of times." Zoe smiled, while Eva formed a mental picture of Zoe trying to find her way around the huge campus and getting lost. She had teased Zoe many times about her inability to follow a map as well as her appalling lack of any sense of direction. The baited trap snapped as she heard a deep rumble as Eva tried to hold back her laughter.

"Stop that," Zoe mildly rebuked, slapping Eva's belly, which only caused Eva to laugh harder. Zoe went on, "It really wasn't my fault this time. Elena took a left turn when she should have taken a right."

"Zoe, you could lose your way in Larissa," Eva teased. Zoe gave her a mischievous grin and proceeded to tickle her. Eva squealed and fought off Zoe's hands. "Okay, okay! Stop! I'll stop teasing you," she promised. Zoe gave her a triumphant smile and put her head back down on Eva's chest.

"Don't mess with Zoe Lambros, or else," Eva said, kissing the top of Zoe's head.

"Tell me more about yesterday?" Zoe asked.

Eva thought back to her first day of work at the Translation Department. "Ally and I walked into one of the busiest places I've ever been in. People everywhere. It was nice, though. You remember the story of the Tower of Babel?"

"Oh yeah, where everyone used to speak the same language, and then God didn't like that Nimrod guy and made people speak different languages?"

"Yes, well, this place sounds like it. The *Patris* docked yesterday and it was incredibly busy — far busier than I expected. There's a ton of information to remember, but I think it's going to be really good. The people are nice, very friendly."

"I hope you don't have to deal with any Stalks like at the factory," Zoe grumbled. "You know, Jack Stalk would have made a great Nazi." Zoe traced the tiny scar on Eva's shoulder.

"I don't think there are any Stalks there, but there is a Debbie. She's the receptionist and a really nice person. She does all the heavy lifting."

Zoe looked puzzled. "Heavy lifting in an office?"

"Yeah, all those files she carries!" Eva said. Zoe groaned at her bad joke.

"You know your jokes are getting worse than Earl's!" Zoe complained. She directed a mock scowl at Eva as she laughed. "I don't care if she has to lift things, as long as *you* don't have to. I don't want you to hurt your back again."

Eva grinned. "Nah, I don't think so. I think the heaviest thing I'm going to be lifting in that office is my cup of tea," she said.

"Do you know the only thing I will miss about you not working at the factory?"

"No, what?" Eva asked. Zoe did not answer immediately; she had become engrossed in blowing a piece of fluff across Eva's chest. "Zoe," Eva said, slightly impatiently.

"Oh." Her attention recaptured, Zoe looked at Eva with a smile. "I'm going to miss not being able to escort you home."

Even though Zoe hated getting up in the morning, she would do so whenever Eva worked the nightshift. She would take the bus to the biscuit factory and wait for Eva to finish her shift. Then after riding the bus home together, the women would stop off at the bakery and pick up raspberry tarts for breakfast. It was moments like these that both Eva and Zoe cherished.

Eva sighed, suddenly realizing that she would miss Zoe's presence at the end of the day, too. "You can escort me home if you like. The college is only ten minutes away. I can always wait to carry your books."

"That's if I get in," Zoe reminded her.

"You'll be accepted," Eva said reassuringly. "I know you will."

"I hope so," Zoe sighed. "If I had a car I could come and pick you up," she said. "Earl can give me lessons. That's if I had a car. And if I had a license to drive this imaginary car."

"You want to drive?"

"Yes."

"I don't see why you can't."

Zoe beamed. "You mean I can get a car? Wow. What color would you like?"

"The color of your eyes," Eva whispered, and took a sweet kiss from Zoe's lips before continuing in a teasing tone, "Do you think the world is ready for you and a car?"

"Ah, Miss Eva, the world will never be ready for me," Zoe replied and nuzzled Eva's neck. "Hmm, smells like cookies here, need to investigate."

Eva wrapped Zoe in her arms, and they both started laughing.

Zoe sat in the kitchen eating breakfast and reading *The Woman's Weekly*, a magazine she had found one day while she was waiting for Eva's shift to finish. English was a hard language for Zoe to learn and she found that reading magazines helped her. One of the side effects of reading was that she was soon addicted to the serialized story that appeared every week. A Greek/English dictionary nearby, Zoe would look up any word that she could not decipher or she would ask Eva for an explanation.

"Oh, no!" Zoe's anguished cry rang out. Just coming in the front door, Eva dropped her handbag and rushed into the kitchen, fearing that Zoe may have hurt herself. Zoe paid her partner no real attention, absorbed as she was in the magazine.

"What's the matter?" Eva asked, a trifle breathless.

Zoe wailed, "Derek is leaving her!"

Eva rolled her eyes. She sat on the stool next to Zoe and looked at the magazine over her shoulder. "Who's Derek?"

Zoe looked up and frowned. "Don't you remember? Derek is Maggie's boyfriend, and now he's gone back to Jane, but he can't decide if he wants Maggie or if he wants Jane," she explained with exaggerated patience.

"So hasn't he left already?" Eva asked, getting up to make herself a cup of tea.

Zoe and Eva had had an ongoing discussion about the serial story ever since Zoe had told her about it. Their animated conversations had caused a smile or two on the bus, especially from the conductor, who often joined in since the day he had remarked that his wife read the serial every week as well.

"Derek did, but he came back and then he went again," Zoe said, flapping the pages at Eva for emphasis.

"And now he's gone for good?"

"Yeah," Zoe said and went back to reading. "Sort of. He can't decide who he wants."

Eva left the kitchen to answer a knocking at the door, while Zoe remained behind, still perched on her stool. She looked through the open door into the lounge as a grinning Earl came into the apartment; he was carrying a box under his arm. "G'day, my favorite interpreter!" he greeted Eva, giving her a kiss.

"You're in a cheery mood!" Eva remarked as she directed him into the kitchen.

"Hey, Wiggy." Zoe greeted Earl with a wave, and returned her attention to the magazine.

Earl grimaced. "Don't tell me she's still glued to that story," he said to Eva.

"Yes. Derek left Maggie to be with Jane, but Derek loves both Maggie and Jane," Eva said.

"I reckon Jane should dump that low life. Oh, hell, now you're getting me involved!" Earl protested, and Eva chuckled.

"To what do we owe the pleasure of your company this morning? Not that I'm not happy to see you," Eva said, sipping her tea.

"You are in the presence of the newest factory supervisor!" Earl proudly proclaimed, which got him a whoop from Zoe and a hug from Eva. "I found out last night. I think Jack is going to have kittens when he finds out. I bring you gifts!" He opened the box to reveal seven large mangoes. Zoe grinned. He knew Eva loved them and he must have stopped by the fruit market and picked some up in celebration.

"Mangoes!" Eva said, picking up one of the ripe reddish-yellow fruits and sniffing it, her ecstasy obvious.

Zoe looked at her partner's enraptured face and teased, "She is so easy. Give her a little fruit, and she's yours for life."

Eva stuck her tongue out and went to the sink to peel the fruit. "Congratulations, Earl. You've worked hard. Which section are you going to be in?"

"Cookies."

"Ah, my favorite." Zoe looked up and waggled her eyebrows at Eva, which earned her a puzzled look from Earl. She did not give him a chance to comment. "Hey, Earl, how's The Beast?"

"Good, why?" he asked, clearly bewildered by the sudden shift in topic.

"I'm going to get a car!" Zoe said brightly. A look of mock fear crossed Earl's face.

"Oh, no! I'll inform the traffic authority to remove all the light poles," he said.

Zoe snorted. "Cut that out! Can you teach me?"

"Me? Teach you how to drive?"

"Yes, you know, I get behind the wheel and you teach me to drive."

Earl met Eva's eyes over the top of Zoe's head, and he grinned. "Sure, Stretch, I'll teach you, but you must promise not to hit any old ladies or small animals or anything like that."

"Promise. Thanks, Wiggy!" Zoe jumped off the stool, abandoning the magazine. She put her arms around his neck and gave him a kiss on the cheek, delighted by his agreement.

"Hey, now that I'm here, I'll give you a ride in to work, check out your new job, if you want me to?" Earl suggested. He looked expectantly at Eva.

"I would love to show you around," Eva said, handing him a cup of tea.

"Can you drop me off at work?" Zoe asked. She heard another knock on the door and went to answer it.

"Sure," Earl agreed.

Zoe went to the door and let Elena into the apartment.

After Earl and Eva finished their tea, Alberta arrived and everyone headed out. Elena and Zoe were dropped off at the restaurant, while Eva and Alberta traveled to the Immigration Department with Earl. He filled them in on the latest news from the factory, making Eva laugh when they stopped at a traffic light and he took advantage of the moment to do an excellent imitation of Jack Stalk falling over a pallet of cookies.

"You should drop by more often," the female elevator operator said as she stopped the elevator on Eva's floor. It was clear that she was speaking solely to Earl since he and Eva were the only ones on the elevator. Alberta had stayed in the lobby talking to someone she had met yesterday.

"Oh, I'll be around, since my girl is working here," Earl said. He put his arm around Eva's waist, not noticing the crestfallen look on the operator's face.

Eva poked Earl in the side as they got off the elevator and the door closed behind them. She shook her head at his shenanigans, taking his hand and leading him to the busy waiting area.

"Wow," Earl exclaimed, looking around him. All the chairs were taken and more people were sitting on the floor or standing. Little children were running around and playing noisy games. "Is it this busy all the time?" he asked, raising his voice to be heard.

"Nah, they tell me this is the quiet period," Eva replied, laughing at the horrified expression on Earl's face. "Yeah, it's the busy season. The *Patris* came in, and this is the latest batch of immigrants."

Eva showed him to Debbie's desk. There was no sign of the receptionist at first, then Debbie's head popped up from behind a filing cabinet.

"Debbie, this is my good friend Earl Wiggins," Eva said. "Earl, this is Debbie, our overworked receptionist."

Debbie gave Earl a huge grin of welcome. "Hi there, Earl."

"Hi. You're not working my girl too hard, are you?" Earl smiled in return, his arm still around Eva's waist.

"You must be Eva's boyfriend," Debbie said.

"Guilty on all charges," Earl replied and doffed his hat at her.

Debbie smiled. "Oh, no, she had an easy day yesterday. Today the fun begins," she said, her eyes twinkling.

"Can't wait," Eva replied. "I'll just show Earl around, then I'll come and pick up the files." They walked down the corridor together, Earl slipping his arm around Eva's shoulders.

"Hey, nice office!" Earl said. He plunked himself down on the client's chair that sat in front of her desk. "It needs some posters and stuff. I'll get you a couple. And you need a photo, too."

Her arms folded across her chest, Eva grinned at him.

"What?" Earl asked.

"You know Debbie is going to spread the word that you're my boyfriend."

"Of course," he said smugly.

"You are incredible." Eva bent over and kissed him lightly on the mouth.

"I am, aren't I?" Earl replied, puffing out his chest. "So many kisses from you and Zoe today; I think I could get used to this."

"Hey, thanks for volunteering to teach Zoe to drive," Eva told him. She took off her sweater and sat down in her chair.

"As long as she doesn't kill me or run over any animals, it's going to be great."

They both laughed.

"I miss you at work." Earl glanced at Eva. "Stalk is driving me crazy."

"Stalk has been driving you crazy for years," Eva reminded him, still grinning.

Eva kissed Earl goodbye at the elevator. She stood watching as he gave her a wink before the doors closed. She turned to find a grinning Debbie waiting behind her with a stack of files in her arms. "The fun begins!" Debbie repeated the statement from earlier. Shaking her head and smiling, Eva walked down the corridor and into her office.

She spent the morning interviewing clients, each one with their own concerns. She found she was enjoying the job even more than she had thought she would. After the fifth client had left, there was a subdued rap on the door and Debbie stuck her head in.

"Oh, so there you are. We thought maybe we lost you between Mrs. Rosenthal and Mr. Hermann," Debbie said. "Morning tea is at ten o'clock and we didn't see you come out, so I thought I would come in and rescue you." Debbie entered the office with a cup of tea and placed it in front of Eva.

"Oh no, I'm still here," Eva replied. Giving Debbie a sidelong glance, she picked up the teacup and took a sip. "Thank you, that's nice. Did you want to ask me something?"

"Well...yes and no. I'm on my tea break, so I thought I would come in and see how you were getting along, you know."

"I see," Eva said. She continued working, marking the file with her notes about the client and the actions she had taken to get them accommodation.

After a moment, Debbie said, "I think Mr. Hermann was quite taken with you. He wanted to know if you are married, and could he send flowers."

Eva smiled. Mr. Hermann had been her fifth client of the day. He was Jewish, a concentration camp survivor, and quite charming and gracious. She had enjoyed talking to him. They had spent a bit of time talking about Berlin University, where he had lectured in History before Hitler forbade Jews to teach.

Debbie sat down in the chair opposite her desk, gazing at Eva with an expectant look on her face.

"So, I guess you drew the short straw?" Eva asked, knowing the whole office wanted to find out all about the new girl. She had been expecting it. When she had started working at the biscuit factory, one of the girls had cornered her and asked her personal questions. Eva had not been forthcoming with her answers, and soon developed a reputation for being aloof and cold. It was not until the incident in the store room, when she and Earl became a "couple", that she had become aware of the interrogation that all new staffers were subjected to as a matter of course.

"Yeah, and since I'm a natural born busybody, it was a good choice," Debbie said with a smile. "Mr. Hermann really does want to send you flowers. He told me you should expect some later today."

Eva laughed. She liked Debbie and her easy-going manner. "What would you like to know about me?"

"Oh good, you're going to play the game! I've had to play question and answer games with all the new people. You're easy."

"Didn't say I'll answer them," Eva responded. She laughed at Debbie's crestfallen look.

Debbie groaned in frustration. "Why can't things be simpler? Oh, all right. Let's start with the easy bits. What's your full name?"

"This sounds like an interrogation!" Eva said with a mock frown.

She got a snort in reply. "Ve haf vays of makink you talk," Debbie said in a very bad German accent, which only made Eva laugh even more. She put down her pen and folded her hands on the desk, giving Debbie her full attention.

"So much for my interrogation skills," Debbie said. "So are you going to answer?"

"What was the question?" Eva asked, although she knew full well what Debbie had asked.

Debbie rolled her eyes. "We know your first name; do you have a middle name?"

"Oh, *that's* the question," Eva responded. She sat back and said smugly, "Eva Theresa."

"Hmm, nice names."

"I think so," Eva said.

"Moving right along, Eva Theresa. Okay, how old are you, what's your date of birth, and where were you born?"

"I'm twenty-seven. I was born on the 20th of July, 1920, in Vienna, Austria."

"Vienna, what a beautiful city!"

"Yes, it is."

"Siblings?"

Eva smiled. She and Zoe had discussed not giving people the sister story. "None."

"So tell me, Miss Haralambos...by the way, that is a very difficult name to get my tongue around. That doesn't sound German. That's Greek, isn't it?"

Eva nodded.

"And are you going to tell me how you got the name?"

"My father gave it to me," Eva said drolly and watched as Debbie rolled her eyes again.

"So where does the Muller name fit into this? Everyone is really curious to find out."

"Everyone?" Eva asked, a little perplexed why anyone would be interested.

"We're all a bunch of busybodies," Debbie replied and smiled broadly. "You'll get used to that."

"Muller was my stepfather," Eva answered, honestly.

Debbie seemed about to ask another question when she paused. "There was something on the wireless about a Nazi that was caught here in Sydney whose surname was Muller..."

Eva sighed. "That was my stepfather," Eva was not surprised that Debbie would remember since it was such big news.

Debbie's eyes went wide at the news. "Wow. So did you help in capturing him?"

"Yes."

"Do you want to go into another question?" Debbie asked. "I'm sorry to make you uncomfortable about your stepfather."

"Moving on would be a good idea," Eva replied, grateful she did not have to talk about Muller or the circumstances of the capture.

"How tall are you?" Debbie asked. Eva visibly relaxed as the questioning moved away from her name and her stepfather's activities. Debbie continued, "Please tell me you're over six feet because I've got a pound riding on the answer."

"You bet a pound on how tall I am?" Eva was astonished.

Debbie laughed. "Eva, most Aussies will bet on which of two flies on a wall will get up the wall quicker! So naturally we took an office betting pool to find out how tall you are! Deirdre thinks you are five feet ten. Alexander thinks you're five feet eleven. Edith thinks you're five feet nine. We didn't have time to poll everyone else."

Eva laughed. "And you?"

"I think you're six feet because my brother is about your height."

"Close. I'm six feet two inches."

"Wow. That's tall. Yes! I win that round!" Debbie exclaimed. "Moving right along here, so are you and Earl engaged?"

Eva grinned. "He hasn't proposed yet."

"Well, if I know my men, I would say the guy is head over heels in love with you."

Eva smiled and leaded back in her chair. "You think so?"

"Oh yeah. He had the 'she's my woman' look about him."

"Earl is a sweetheart."

Debbie sighed. "Yes, he looks the part. Does he have a brother?"

"A sister," Eva replied.

Debbie took a sip from her own teacup. "That's too bad. Next question. You like jazz music?"

"How do you know that?"

"You have the radio on when you don't have a client."

"Oh."

"It's not loud but I can hear it when it's quiet outside and the music travels. I love jazz myself so it's nice."

"I love jazz and opera."

"Great taste in music. So do you live with family or by yourself?"

Eva was not sure how to answer that question or whether to leave it alone. She liked Debbie, and she was sure Zoe was going to come into the office later in the week. She and Zoe now introduced each other as apartment mates, which satisfied most people's inquisitive natures and made concealing their true relationship somewhat easier than having to pretend to be sisters.

"No, I live with Zoe," Eva told Debbie. "She's my apartment mate. You'll probably see her up here at some point. She's about five feet five with short red hair and green eyes."

"I look forward to meeting her." Debbie stood and went to the door. "Thanks, Eva, you're a good sport. I think that's enough interrogating for today."

Eva watched the door close and shook her head slowly before taking the next file off the pile. It perplexed her why people were interested in her. While it was true there was always an element of getting to know someone new in the workplace, Eva found it a little unsettling. She was also somewhat bemused by all the questions. She opened the file, picked up her pen, and went back to work.

"Eva, can you please take Mrs. Marangos?" Debbie asked, sticking her head through Eva's open office door. "Sorry about this. We're trying to get her seen quickly, and Alexander has a difficult couple."

"Sure, Debbie. Have you got her file?"

Debbie grimaced. "We sent it down to Filing and they've misplaced it."

Eva blinked. She was so used to Debbie being on top of everything, even in the two days she had been there, that she found this mix-up disconcerting, but she pushed it to the back of her mind and nodded. Getting up from her chair, Eva followed Debbie to the front desk where an old woman stood waiting patiently. Her back was hunched, and she supported herself with a cane. Eva introduced herself and escorted Mrs. Marangos to her office and into her client chair. "How are you today, Mrs. Marangos?" Eva asked in Greek.

"Ah, not so good, my child," the old woman responded in the same language, shaking her head. Eva smiled despite what Mrs. Marangos had said, trying to be reassuring. "My little red box is missing," Mrs. Marangos went on.

"Little red box?"

"Yes, my little red box. It was outside my house, and now it's gone, and I don't know where it's gone to!" the old woman wailed.

Eva was at a loss as to what this little red box could be. She went around her desk, and knelt down beside the chair and held her as she started to sob. "Don't worry, Mrs. Marangos, we'll find your little red box," she said. "Can you tell me a little about it?"

"It's red," the old woman said through her weeping.

Eva was stumped. "Was it round or square?"

"It was red and it was long."

"Red and long," Eva repeated, having no idea what the old woman was referring to.

"Yes."

"Was it in your garden?"

"No. It was outside my house."

"Outside your house and it was red and long," Eva said once more, trying to think of something that was red, long, and stayed outside. She had no clue.

"My little red box is missing, and it's so important I find it!"

Eva was completely baffled and could only kneel there, feeling lost. Mrs. Marangos glanced at her and began to wail again.

Eva needed to speak to Debbie; surely she would know about this since she had a file somewhere. As if in answer to her thoughts, there was a soft rap on the door and Debbie entered quietly, sliding the correct file on Eva's desk.

Going back to her desk, Eva tried to look through the woman's file as discreetly as she could, searching for any reference to red boxes. She was not having any luck, and the woman was staring at her in clear disappointment.

"You're not interested in helping me?" Mrs. Marangaos asked, wiping her face with a handkerchief.

Eva looked up guiltily, certain she appeared like a child caught with her hand in the cookie jar. "I am, Mrs. Marangos," she said. "I just need some more details." Eva closed the file and smiled at the woman before getting up from her chair. "I'm going to go outside and get you something to drink, okay?"

"Yes, thank you, my child."

Eva closed the door and scratched her head. She was trying to think of what this little red box could be as she walked up to the reception area. Lost in thought, she only looked up when she got there. Half the interpreters were there, doubled over, laughing out loud.

"Oh, gosh, Eva, you should have seen your face as you came out of your office!" Debbie exclaimed.

Eva glanced around at the grinning faces and realized she had been the victim of a prank. "I was set up, wasn't I?" she asked, not quite believing she had been so handily fooled. She had not expected anything like this to occur. She felt like an idiot, but realized that the frustrating situation with Mrs. Marangos was actually quite funny. "You set me up!" Eva repeated.

"Yes!" Debbie burst out laughing.

Eva shook her head, although she joined in the hilarity. At last, she held up a hand to quiet her colleagues, remembering that Mrs. Marangos was sitting in her office. "Uh, I have Mrs. Marangos in my office, I need some water, and what is this little red box?"

The question got another round of chuckles from the assembled group before Debbie put a glass of water in her hand and explained, "It's the mail box. The post office does that sometimes. Usually they leave it outside her house, but they must have moved it again. Mrs. Marangos is a little senile, so we try and help her when we can."

Eva nodded. "Red, long box...I guess that's my initiation here, right?"

Debbie grinned and nodded.

"I get it now. So what do I tell her?"

"Tell her that the little red box will be put back in a week or so, but there is another red box just up the street and she can put her letters in there."

"All right," Eva muttered in German as she walked away back into her office amidst the laughter of her coworkers.

"You can't be serious!" Elena exclaimed.

Zoe grinned and nodded. "It..." Zoe stopped and held up the cat for a quick inspection under its tail. "*She* is so cute!"

"Zoe, she is a cat," Elena said with some distaste. Zoe knew that her friend disliked cats. There was something about the way they looked at her that made Elena uneasy, or so she had informed Zoe.

"Well, she's not a dog." Zoe cuddled the animal to her chest. The cat immediately began to purr, much to Zoe's delight. The emaciated animal had been on top of the rubbish bin when Zoe had come out to add a garbage bag to the others from the restaurant in the alley. "I'm going to take her home," Zoe said.

"That cat's got fleas," Elena said, continuing her best to dissuade Zoe from taking the cat home.

Zoe glanced back at her friend. They were standing outside the restaurant, and the smell of garbage from the alley was rather unpleasant. "El, she looks so sick."

"That's because she's a wild cat."

"Doesn't look wild to me." Zoe smiled at the cat and was met by a blue gaze. "I love her eyes."

Elena snorted.

Zoe smirked. "Her eyes remind me of Eva's."

"I hope you don't tell Eva, because I don't think I would find it romantic if someone told me my eyes looked like a cat's."

"They're the same color, El." Zoe looked into the cat's face and said, "I think I'm going to take you home, Ourania."

"Ourania? What does that mean?"

Zoe smiled. "It means sky in Greek. Her eyes are as blue as the sky."

"You are hopeless," Elena said. "I bet Eva takes one look at the flea bag and tells you to take it away."

"Why would she do that?"

"Don't you have to ask her if you can keep it?"

Zoe held the cat protectively against her chest. "No, Eva's not my mother, you know."

"But don't you have to clear it with her first?"

"What?" Zoe frowned, not quite understanding what Elena was getting at.

"You know, Zoe, you know how she is supposed to be your head..."

Zoe could not help giggling. "My head? My head is on my shoulders, although I do love the head on *her* shoulders."

Elena rolled her eyes. "That's not what I meant. The man is the head of the house."

"All right, but what does that have to do with this cat?"

"Well, when you take her home, what will Eva do?"

Zoe smiled. "That's easy. Eva will fall in love with her."

"How do you know?"

"Oh, I know she will." Zoe tapped the side of her head with her free hand. "Eva is soft-hearted."

"You are so sappy," Elena shook her head.

"Wait until you have gone from 'heavy like' to 'love' and then tell me about being sappy," Zoe said. "It will be 'Freddy said this' and 'Freddy said that' all the time."

"No, it won't," Elena said confidently.

Zoe merely laughed and held the cat to her chest. "Come on, let's get our coats and take Ourania home."

"Little red boxes," Eva muttered to herself, opening the door to the apartment. Her initiation into the Interpreter Division had been memorable if only for the fact that she had thought she was going to go mad trying to figure out what Mrs. Marangos had been talking about. She smiled to herself. "Well, it sure beats lifting boxes of biscuits," she said aloud. Eva was about to call out to Zoe when a black and white cat padded up to her and lay down at her feet.

"Oh!" Eva looked down at the cat lying on top of her feet. "Where did you come from?" Eva went down on her haunches and picked up the cat, who did not object but started to purr, making Eva smile.

"I knew it."

Eva looked up and saw Zoe leaning against the bedroom door frame, grinning. Zoe pushed away from the doorway and came up to Eva. "Well, hello." Zoe stood on her toes and kissed Eva's lips. "I told Elena you would fall in love with her. This is our newest family member."

"What's her name?" Eva held up the cat and gazed into its eyes. "She has blue eyes."

"Yes, I noticed that," Zoe smiled "Her name is Ourania. Ourania meet your second mama, Eva."

"I like the name."

"So can we keep her?"

"Of course we can. Why wouldn't we?" Eva asked, a little confused by Zoe's request.

Zoe merely giggled. "So tell me, Miss Eva, about your day."

"Not as exciting as Ourania's day," Eva said and led her partner into the lounge carrying Ourania in one hand, and her handbag under her arm.

Chapter Twenty

Sunlight streamed through the open bedroom curtains on yet another summer's day. It was Christmas Eve in Sydney, and instead of the snow and roasted apples that a European like Eva was used to, Christmas here meant hot, humid weather and ice cubes in her drinks in an effort to stay cool.

Eva groaned and shifted under the comforter. She was not a happy woman. Instead of sleeping in, and later snuggling up to her partner, she was alone in bed. *Well, not quite alone,* Eva amended. She scowled as she heard a gentle thump and knew instantly without looking what had caused it. A soft "meow" moments later told her she was spot on.

Eva raised her head and saw the new addition to their family — Ourania, their black and white "tuxedo" kitty. Zoe's penchant for naming everything from cars to cats would not be denied. They had adopted the stray cat, only having to deal with some reservations from their landlady. Ourania was now perched on the edge of the bed staring at Eva with great interest.

"You're not the beauty I wanted to wake up to," Eva growled at the cat. Ourania yawned in indifference. "Yes, well if you feel that way..."

Eva lay back down and stretched, trying to get the kinks out of her back, which was a little stiff. She listened to the sounds of the city, to the noises of many people up and about, getting on with a new day.

She chuckled when she felt the cat slowly walk up her legs and make its way up her chest where she looked down at her imperiously. Eva stroked behind the cat's ears, getting a contented purr from the animal. She started to laugh when Ourania decided she was going to make Eva her mattress and began to fluff Eva's chest with her paws before settling down.

Letting out a sigh, Eva let her thoughts drift to her partner. Zoe was somewhere in the apartment and she was not sure why the other woman was not in bed with her. If Zoe had been sick, Eva would have known about it, but that was not the case. In fact, Zoe had been acting strangely for a few days now. Eva frowned. Zoe was being secretive, which was not at all like her. Eva often joked that Zoe could not keep a secret to save her life; she could tell instantly when something was wrong with the woman that held her heart, which made Zoe's current behavior all the more puzzling.

"It's a secret, isn't it, Ourania?" Eva asked the cat.

The cat glanced up at the sound of her name and meowed.

"No offense, but I wish Zoe was here instead of you, kitty," Eva stated as she stroked the silky fur of the cat's back. "Okay, enough of this." She lifted the indignant animal off her chest. Ourania gave her an annoyed look, struggled out of Eva's grasp and scampered away.

"Yeah, right, go warn her, traitor." Eva put on her robe and slippers before stopping at the window and pulling the curtains back completely. Blue sky stretched as far as she could see. Despite it being December, there was a lazy summer feeling in the air; it was a day that required nothing more than sitting outside and lazing about. Eva walked through the apartment, frowning at the unnatural quiet. Normally, a record would be playing on the gramophone or the radio would be on.

Ourania passed her and promptly lay down in front of the spare bedroom, clearly waiting for her favorite caress. It had not taken long for the cat to figure out that Eva would indulge her whenever she lay down.

"You are almost as bad as Zoe," Eva quipped but she went down on her haunches and scratched the kitty's temptingly presented belly. "Not that I mind," she added, giving the cat a last friendly pat as she straightened up.

Eva opened the door to the spare bedroom to find Zoe sitting serenely at the art table that stood beneath the window. Zoe leaned forward and rested her forearms on the table. "Hi, there," Eva greeted her partner, and leaned a hip against the door jamb.

"Hi."

"What are you doing?"

"Stuff," Zoe replied, her innocent expression belied by the twinkle in her eyes.

Eva, not at all fooled, repeated, "Stuff?"

"Yeah, Christmassy stuff."

"Ah." Eva nibbled on her lip in thought. She was not exactly worried, but she was a little perplexed by Zoe's uncharacteristic behavior and curious to find out what Zoe was up to. "I woke up to an empty bed."

"Hmm." Zoe nodded. "I wanted to get up early."

"To do the stuff?"

"Yep."

"I wanted to cuddle," Eva pouted. "Instead of a cuddle, Ourania sat on me."

"Really?"

"Yes, really. I want a cuddle." Eva opened her arms in invitation.

Zoe laughed at the invitation. Leaving the art table, she melted into Eva's embrace. "You know that pout always works," Zoe said.

"Yeah, I know," Eva replied with a smile. She leaned down and captured her lover's lips with her own. Tasting Zoe, the unique and delicious flavor drove her desire to new heights. The kisses became more insistent, more passionate. A soft moan escaped Zoe as Eva nuzzled her neck. Eva got a shock when Zoe pulled away. "Stay," Eva implored. Instead of obeying that desperate command, Zoe slipped out of her arms and returned to the art table, leaving Eva unsure of what had just happened.

"Zoe," Eva beseeched. She tried to take hold of Zoe but the other woman evaded her grasp and walked out of the room, pausing on the other side of the door.

"I'm going to have a bath and get ready to go shopping with Elena," Zoe said, smiling.

Eva growled in frustration. "Zoe."

"Yes, Evy?"

"What are you up to?"

"Can you stay like that while I get the camera? You are so cute," Zoe teased.

"No, I can't. What are you up to?"

"Me?" Zoe pointed to herself. "I'm just going to get ready." She escaped the room before Eva had a chance to reply.

The rest of Eva's morning was spent alone, since Zoe kept her secret and departed with Elena in tow. Left on her own, Eva decided she had better go finish her Christmas shopping and pick up supplies for the Christmas party that she and Zoe were holding Christmas Day.

The department store was utter chaos. Eva detested shopping but she could not avoid this duty. She had left her gift buying to the last minute and it was her own fault, she knew that. This was her punishment — a store full of frustrated, angry people and frolicking, noisy children getting in her way. The din was unbelievable, as was the crush of shoppers.

Eva sighed when she was hit from behind by a child who was racing through the crowd. She shook her head as she tried to get out of the way of yet another careless youngster.

"You obviously don't have children," a woman said tersely to her before chasing after the errant child.

"Merry Christmas to you as well," Eva muttered. She decided she had had enough of the claustrophobic environment. She exited the department store and stopped on the pavement. A gust of hot wind blew against her, which caused her to close her eyes in exhaustion. "Next year I'm doing my Christmas shopping in July," she muttered to herself.

"What's the fun in that?"

The voice startled her. Eva turned to find Santa Claus in his full regalia of a red woolen suit, black boots, and hat. She could not believe that someone would willingly torture themselves that way in the heat. Combined with the humid weather, today's blazing hot temperature made the tar on the roads nearly sizzle. Eva looked down at her light cotton pants and white shirt, then her gaze traveled back to the poor Santa Claus.

Eva hated summer; she detested it, in fact. A wave of nostalgia swept over her as she wiped away the perspiration that was running down her neck. She missed baking gingerbread with her mother and grandmother, watching the snow fall and writing to the *Christkind*, who was a winged figure dressed in white robes and a golden crown. Her grandmother had told her stories about the *Christkind*, who delivered gifts to all the children. Eva had always looked forward to seeing what presents he had left for her. She smiled to herself. He had always left books and always the ones she wanted the most.

"Have you been a good little girl?" Santa asked, putting his arm around Eva, who was taken aback by Santa's familiarity.

"Uh," Eva managed to say before Santa smiled and pulled down his beard to reveal a familiar young and handsome face. "Earl, what in God's name are you doing?" Eva exclaimed. She pulled him out of the sun and under a canopy where there was some shade.

"Oh, God, next time I agree to be Santa, kill me," Earl moaned, fanning himself. "They want me to wear this until I get home. I'm going to die before then. Do you think the kiddies will mind if Santa drinks a beer?"

"Santa isn't supposed to drink beer," Eva reminded him.

"All that rubbish about milk and biscuits; they should leave beer and peanuts," Earl muttered.

"At least stay out of the sun." Eva wiped the sweat from Earl's brow with a clean handkerchief from her handbag. "Here," she said, handing Earl the water-beaded bottle of Coca-Cola she had bought before leaving the store.

Earl did not bother to thank her. He simply gulped down the cold drink, and when he had finished, rubbed the empty bottle again his overheated face. "Ah, that is so good."

Eva grinned at the sight of her friend in raptures over a Coca-Cola. "You're welcome."

"Where's Zoe?"

Eva lost her smile and scowled in annoyance at the mention of her wayward partner. She was still puzzled over Zoe's uncharacteristic behavior over the course of the last few days. She was not sure what the problem was and at some point Eva had thought Zoe might be trying to surprise her with a Christmas gift. She had even gone to Elena to try and get the information out of her. Elena had not known, which only increased Eva's frustration.

"I don't know," Eva replied tightly.

Earl seemed surprised. "You don't know where Zoe is? You live with her and you don't know?"

Eva sighed and pursed her lips before replying, "She's up to something."

"How do you know?"

Eva gave him a look that spoke volumes. "I know when Zoe is up to something."

"What is she up to?"

"I don't know."

Earl laughed, causing his cushion-created belly to bob up and down. A child walked by and laughed as well upon seeing Santa's jolly good humor. "Ho, ho, ho!" Earl cried out as the girl and her mother walked away. Still chuckling, Earl said to Eva, "I think it's payback time."

Eva grinned. She would love to go home and find Zoe wrapped like a present under her Christmas tree. That reminded her of the surprise she had given Zoe on their first Christmas in Australia, a few months after they had first arrived in Sydney. The event was still fresh in Eva's mind, and she let her thoughts wander to a much more pleasurable time.

Eva looked out the door with anticipation and grinned devilishly. Everything was going as planned. She had managed to get a Christmas tree; it looked a bit scraggly but it was unmistakably a traditional evergreen. She had decorated it with bright streamers and the few lights that she had been able to find at the shops. She turned around and surveyed the room. The immigrant housing wasn't much to look at, but they were in the process of finding a new apartment to move into after the first of the year. Satisfied that all was perfect, she lit the few candles she had bought and placed them around the room. Zoe loved candles so Eva had bought as many as they could afford.

The sound of Zoe and Elena in the hallway alerted her to their arrival. Eva scrambled away from the door and bolted behind the privacy screen she had set up. She knew Zoe was going to be awfully confused when she entered their apartment. Earlier, Eva had suggested that Zoe take some time out to go shopping and relax. She had not been surprised when Zoe had accepted the suggestion, not noticing Eva's mischievous smile.

"Well, love, I hope you're going to enjoy your Christmas present," Eva murmured, grinning. She removed her robe and inspected herself carefully. Dressed only in lace panties — the kind she knew Zoe would absolutely love — and a red ribbon strategically tied across her breasts, Eva hid her discarded robe behind a chair. She giggled like a schoolgirl when the ribbon kept slipping. She managed to tie the bow again and then positioned herself underneath the Christmas tree, her body surrounded by the few presents they were able to afford and waited for Zoe to enter.

"Eva, I'm home..." Zoe entered their apartment alone, and stopped mid-sentence. Eva imagined the confused expression on Zoe's face when she spotted the screens. "What's this?" Zoe called.

"If you're alone, come around the screen," Eva called back. She waited breathlessly for Zoe to appear.

Zoe came around the screens with her few packages, walking gingerly. Eva arched her back and held her provocative pose, her body illuminated by the glow of the Christmas tree and the candles. She watched Zoe's eyes bulge with excitement and her lips begin to tremble. The packages tumbled out of her grasp and onto the floor.

"Breathe, love," Eva suggested and ginned when Zoe closed her eyes and opened them again, as though in disbelief at the sight before her.

"Oh." Zoe managed to say at last. She tried to fan herself with her hand. A huge grin spread across her face and she licked her lips in obvious anticipation.

"Happy Christmas, love." Eva crooked her finger at the stunned young woman. "Come over and open your present."

"Oh yeah!" Zoe walked over quickly and straddled Eva. "Oh my, hello there." She leaned down and captured Eva's lips, tasting her, the kisses becoming more insistent, more passionate. A soft moan escaped from between Eva's lips as Zoe nuzzled her neck, tangling her hand in Eva's hair.

"Oh God, Evy, you are so gorgeous," Zoe mumbled as she kissed Eva again, her hands softly cradling the ribbon-covered breasts.

"No," Eva pushed Zoe's hands away and got a very startled look.

"Huh?"

"You have to untie it," Eva said with a naughty grin, "without using your fingers." She laughed when Zoe lowered herself down and with her teeth tried to untie the ribbon. She managed to make the knot even tighter, and the young woman groaned in frustration.

"Are you sure I can't..."

"Nope," Eva shook her head.

"Hmm, this could be a problem," Zoe muttered. She suddenly grinned broadly. "Don't move."

"I'm not going anywhere," Eva said. Zoe's reluctance was clear when she got off her and raced to the kitchen. Eva chuckled when she heard the loud noises coming from the kitchen; it seemed as if Zoe was impatiently throwing things on the floor in her search. A triumphant cry preceded Zoe's return from the kitchen, brandishing a pair of scissors.

"Oh, I don't know—" Eva was cut short when Zoe touched her lips.

"I'm not using my fingers," she said, wiggling her fingers and grinning. Zoe carefully slid the scissors between the ribbon and Eva's flesh. Eva flinched; the metal was cold, but she trusted Zoe. With a snip, the severed ends of the red ribbon fell away. "Gosh, I love unwrapping presents," Zoe said.

Eva laughed as Zoe's hands traveled down her body and stopped short at the black lace panties. Stuck in the waistband was a tiny card which Zoe retrieved using her teeth. "Thee, no hanths," Zoe mumbled and then took the card out of her mouth.

Zoe read the card and looked up, clearly touched by the beautiful words Eva had written. She whispered, reading the lines aloud, "For all Eternity, my love, my body, my soul. Merry Christmas, Love Eva."

"I'm yours." Eva took her partner's hands and kissed them. "Forever and ever."

"And ever," Zoe said. Eva open her arms. Zoe did not need a second invitation and molded her body against Eva's. Eva started to kiss her tenderly, their bodies intertwined, until Zoe put her hand over Eva's heart.

"Evy, as much as I'd love to start a new Christmas tradition and make love to you under the Christmas tree, do you think we can go to bed now?"

Eva smiled. "Absolutely." She stood up and extended her hand to help Zoe. Zoe looked at her, a goofy grin wreathing her face. "Are you getting up?" Eva asked her dumb-struck partner.

"Just admiring the view." Zoe scrambled into Eva's arms. "Come on, Miss Eva, I want to go climbing." Zoe took her hand and led her into the bedroom.

"Yes ma'am," Eva chuckled and shut the bedroom door.

"Hey, no daydreaming here. It could be dangerous." Earl snapped his fingers in front of Eva's face to get her attention, and she wrenched her thoughts back to the present.

"I was thinking." Eva smiled wickedly at the still vivid memories.

"I know, I could tell."

Eva leaned in and whispered into Earl's ear. "Oh, Santa, I was a *very* good girl last Christmas."

Earl was horrified and drew back in shock. "You're not supposed to say that to Santa! Now go on your way before anything bad happens."

Eva grinned and kissed him on the cheek before walking off down the street with her packages. Zoe's gift this year was not going to surpass last Christmas, so she had bought some gifts that she knew Zoe would like. She also made a reservation for the weekend to the Blue Mountains Hydro Majestic Hotel. A trip to the mountains to cool off would be a wonderful treat for both of them.

"So, did Eva show up?" Zoe asked Elena as they made their way back into the apartment carrying their parcels.

"She sure did, like you said she would. But she didn't show up until yesterday, so she took a little longer to break her patience than you first thought."

Zoe laughed. Her partner was predictable and she knew that her strange behavior had aroused Eva's curiosity. Zoe had not wanted to make it easy for Eva to figure out what she had planned.

"It's driving her crazy." Zoe laughed. "I love it."

"Have you got everything?"

"Oh, yeah." Zoe grinned "She is going to be so surprised. Let's get started."

Eva returned to the apartment and hesitated when she saw Elena standing outside her door, her hands clasped behind her back as though she was on sentry duty. "Everything all right, Elena?" Eva asked.

"Fine." Elena lightly knocked on the door a couple of times.

"What are you doing standing in front of the door?" Suspicious, Eva narrowed her eyes.

"Waiting for you."

"Why?"

Elena held up a blindfold. "Zoe would like you to cover your eyes with this."

"What?"

"Zoe wants me to blindfold you."

"Zoe wants you to blindfold me?" she repeated slowly.

"Are you going deaf, Eva?" Elena waved the blindfold at her.

"I thought you said yesterday you didn't know what was going on with Zoe," Eva accused.

"That isn't what I said." Elena crossed her arms over her chest, the blindfold dangling from one hand. "You asked me if I thought Zoe was acting weird. She wasn't. Zoe was being Zoe." The dark-haired woman smiled at her. "You didn't ask me the right question."

"My apologies," Eva grumbled, much to Elena's apparent delight. Zoe had no doubt told her that Eva would not be easy to convince, and it was true. Both Zoe and Eva were stubborn, but it seemed that Elena thought she was up to the challenge.

"So, we can stand out here and debate this, or you could play along so I can get home," Elena told her and brandished the blindfold again.

Eva eyed the cloth with some trepidation. "Zoe told you to do this?" she repeated, still unsure.

"No, someone paid me a ridiculous amount of money to have a debate with you," Elena responded sarcastically, but her smile took any sting out of the words.

"I'll take that as a yes."

"Yes, and if you don't hurry up Zoe is going to be mad."

Eva sighed. She trusted Zoe and that was that. She turned around and waited for Elena to tie the blindfold in place. She smiled to herself when the shorter Elena found it difficult to reach her head.

Finally, Elena tapped Eva on the shoulder. "Bend your knees, I'm a shorty." Eva bent down enough to allow Elena to slip the blindfold on her. "You can't see anything, right?" Elena asked.

"Only my eyeballs," Eva replied feeling a little tense but trying to stay calm by joking about the situation.

"You two are going to drive me crazy," Elena muttered. She took Eva's hand, opened the door, and entered the apartment, towing Eva behind her. "Zoe, I've got her," she called.

"About time," Zoe replied. "Okay, you can go now."

Eva felt a light material brush against her when someone whom she assumed was Zoe moved past. Eva hated being in the dark and fought against the panic she could feel rising even though she knew that she was not in any real danger. Zoe had arranged all of this, whatever all of this was. She needed to remain calm. Eva took a deep breath and let it out slowly, determined not to spoil Zoe's surprise.

"Thank you, mistress. Anything else I could do for you?" Elena asked good-naturedly, helping Eva to a chair.

"You can take out the garbage while you're here," Eva said. She laughed when Elena made a rude noise in reply. The sound of the apartment door closing told Eva that Elena had likely left the apartment. "Or maybe not," Eva muttered. Raising her voice, she asked, "Are we alone?" She was not sure where Zoe might be. She could smell flowers nearby and next to her was what she thought was a candle by the odor of burning wax.

"Oh, yeah," Zoe whispered into her ear, making Eva jump a little. She reached up and removed the blindfold, blinking in amazement at the sight that greeted her eyes. The lounge had been decorated to resemble a Bedouin tent, something that she and Zoe had seen while in Egypt. It was gorgeous. The Christmas tree was a little out of place for a true Bedouin tent, but it made a fabulous display, decorated as it was with lights and assorted ornaments. The windows were covered in colorful cloth. Eva's astonished gaze moved around the room, taking in everything. There were cushions thrown around the room and real sand on their floorboards, which she found quite interesting.

"I've got plastic underneath to protect the floor," Zoe said. She continued to stand behind Eva, concealing herself from direct view.

Eva grinned but did not look back, not wanting to spoil the rest of the surprise. Her partner had gone to a whole lot of trouble to create this wonderful scene.

"Zoe, this is beautiful, where—" Eva was prevented from turning around by Zoe's hands on her head.

"Not yet. Close your eyes," Zoe whispered into Eva's ear. "Trust me."

Eva closed her eyes. She heard a rustling sound.

"You can open them now," Zoe said.

Eva slowly opened her eyes. Standing before her was Zoe, dressed in a belly dancer's outfit that had undergone major alterations. The bottom part was made out of a deep green translucent material that had been covered in glittering emerald beads. Her top consisted of thin multi-colored scarves draped over a very brief bow that just barely covered her breasts. The color of the bow and the bottom part of the costume was the same as her eyes.

"Oh," Eva managed to say when she could finally breathe and close her gaping mouth. Zoe was gorgeous, and she had made an all-out effort to surprise her.

"Surprised?" Zoe asked.

Eva nodded.

"Good, because there's more." Zoe led Eva to a pile of cushions and helped her sit down. Then Zoe went over to the gramophone and wound it up. Cranking the handle caused some interesting shimmies under her costume that made Eva's eyes bulge. The music began and Eva's heart rate increased exponentially as her lover began to move in one of the most sensual dances Eva had ever seen.

It was part belly dance and part vertical sex — that was how she would later describe it. The gyrations her lover was making caused Eva to blink and then grin. Zoe began to dance in her lap and shake her hips in a provocative way that made Eva feel a little warm. She tried to put her arms around the swaying woman, but her hands were brushed away each time.

"Not yet," was all Zoe said before leaning down and giving the startled Eva a feather light kiss. "Patience."

Eva laughed, knowing her partner lacked patience and made an art form of not waiting for anything. She found was that it was rather frustrating being on the receiving end of this seduction. Eva watched as Zoe removed her scarves one by one, draping each around

Eva's neck and giving her soft kisses whenever a scarf slithered away from Zoe's torso. "How many of these things do you have on?" Eva asked impatiently.

Zoe laughed but gave no other answer as she continued to dance. The final scarf was removed and draped over Eva's shoulders. "Merry Christmas, Evy," Zoe said straddling her.

Eva could hardly wait. "Oh, can I open it now?"

"Oh yeah." Zoe giggled but grabbed hold of Eva's hands when they twitched towards the bow tied around her breasts. "Not with your hands."

"Oh." Eva grinned in response and nuzzled Zoe's neck, kissing her until she got to the bow. "Um, this is going to be tight."

"I have faith in you," Zoe said. Blue eyes met green for a long, sizzling moment before Eva went about trying to untie the bow with her teeth. After a few growls and more laughter from Zoe, she finally managed to untie it.

"Oh, nice," Eva said with glee. "Can I use these?" she asked, holding up her hands. Zoe grinned and shook her head. "This is going to be interesting," Eva said.

"Want to go into our room?" Zoe said, licking her lower lip. Eva found the shine momentarily fascinating. "I've got a few more things in there that will make it more interesting," Zoe continued, giving Eva a significant look as well as a little shimmy.

"Tough choice, love," Eva said with a giggle. The giggle turned into a gasp of appreciative lust when Zoe hopped off her lap, causing the entire outfit to fall apart. "Oh nice," Eva murmured as she was led into the bedroom. Just before they left the lounge, Eva glanced up to find some mistletoe hanging above the doorway. "Wait," she said and brought Zoe into her arms. "Merry Christmas, love."

"Merry Christmas, Evy," Zoe replied, and arched up on her toes for a passionate kiss. "Now let's get mushy inside the bedroom," she said, leading Eva inside their room for a few hours of delightful, early afternoon surprises.

Eva leaned forward in her chair on the balcony, watching Zoe pacing below on the front lawn. Her partner had been outside for the past hour waiting for the postman. The hour gave her a bit of time to clean up the lounge area from Zoe's surprise gift. Zoe has wanted to help, but Eva had to kick her out since Zoe was nervously getting in the way and not being much help. It had been quite a Christmas Eve so far and Eva hoped that the letter Zoe was expecting would be the bonus to a wonderful, if slightly traumatic year.

Eva spotted the portly postman coming up the street long before Zoe caught sight of him. When Zoe saw him, she did not wait but ran to meet him. Eva watched as her partner literally tore the envelope from the man's hands and raced back up the street.

"Why doesn't she just open it?" Eva said aloud as she observed Zoe disappear into the building. A few moments later, she heard the front door open and slam shut with a bang.

"Did we get any mail?" Eva asked, glancing over her shoulder.

Zoe just gazed at the envelope.

"Are you going to open it or just stare at it?" Eva teased.

"You open it," Zoe gave the letter to Eva and leaned back against the railing, trying and failing to adopt a casual attitude.

Eva shook her head. "No, it's addressed to you."

Zoe dropped the act, took the envelope and tore it open. "Oh, Evy, you read it," she said plaintively.

Eva smiled and took the letter from Zoe's hand, realizing for the first time that the other woman's hand was shaking. Leaving the letter aside for a moment, Eva got up and pulled Zoe away from the balcony, taking her inside the lounge.

"It's going to be all right."

"Evy?"

"Yes?"

"Read the letter. It's driving me crazy!" Zoe sighed and began to pace. Eva retrieved the letter and skimmed through it before she read it out loud. A broad smile lit up Eva's face when she found what she wanted. Zoe had her back to her and missed seeing the proud look that Eva cast her way.

"All right, are you ready?" Eva asked Zoe, who merely waved at her to continue.

"*Dear Miss Lambros, it is with great pleasure—*" Eva did not get a chance to finish as Zoe started yelling and jumping up and down at the first words, which clearly meant she had passed the Art College examination. Zoe danced around the lounge then literally threw herself into Eva's arms, causing both women to fall over onto the sofa with Zoe lying on top of Eva.

"I passed," Zoe said in amazement. "I really passed."

"I said you would." Eva laughed.

"I'm going to Sydney Art College." The young woman's voice rose in her excitement.

"Yes, I heard," Eva smiled at the look of absolute joy on Zoe's face.

Zoe sighed contentedly. "Evy, this is a dream. This is my dream — no, this is *our* dream. I'm actually going to art college." Zoe could not quite contain her excitement. Eva recognized the moment when it dawned on her that Elena was going to get her results. "Elena!" Zoe exclaimed. She quickly got off the couch and raced out of the front door, leaving it wide open in her haste.

Eva sat up and started to laugh. She was still laughing when Elena and Zoe both started to scream in delight; she could hear the excited babble of voices coming from the corridor. Both women came back into the apartment and danced around the lounge together while Eva watched, her own spirits high.

The excitement caused Panayiotis and Alberta to come by and see what the commotion was about. That in turn brought Mrs. Jenkins, who came to investigate the screaming, no doubt fearing a repeat of the violence that had resulted in Muller's capture. The apartment was filled with laugher and a little mayhem. Eva sat back on the sofa, soaking up the atmosphere. After a very shaky start, what with having a difficult time of finding employment and then rampaging Nazis, 1947 was finishing off on a very high note indeed — having her father and Alberta in her life, herself finding enjoyable work, and Zoe getting into Art College.

Chapter Twenty-One

"This is so wrong, absolutely so wrong," Eva muttered to herself. She stood on the balcony wearing a white cotton shirt, long tan shorts, and was barefoot. She had a bottle of beer in one hand and cigarette in the other. "I'll never get used to this," she muttered and took a sip of her beer.

Eva knew she would never get used to the searing heat in the middle of December. Their first Christmas in Australia was drizzly, a little cool, and was spent in the refugee housing. They didn't have much materially but they did have each other. They also had Elena — their first friend.

Eva turned to see the preparations for their Christmas lunch was well underway. Zoe had cooked a turkey with baked potatoes, avoiding the ham in deference to Elena and Friedrich. The table was beautifully set and Eva smiled on seeing the menorah at the center of the table. It was a clash of beliefs, but as Zoe put it, Jesus was a Jew so the menorah was appropriate.

Eva wasn't so sure but she wasn't going to argue. It reminded her of a few nights previous when they celebrated Hanukah with Friedrich and Elena. During the evening, Friedrich started talking to her about the war and politics. Eva wasn't sure how it happened, because they were so engrossed in their discussion, but she and Friedrich had reverted to speaking in German until Elena reminded them that Zoe and Earl were not German and couldn't follow the conversation. Eva looked around in apology to Earl then over to Zoe. The look that Eva got from Zoe wasn't what Eva was expecting — not one of reproof but a joyous look that spoke volumes. Eva's shyness had evaporated and both Friedrich and Elena were seeing a side to her that she kept hidden. It might have been the wine that relaxed her, but it was quite a nice evening.

"Alright, lunch is ready," Zoe said, bringing Eva out of her daydream.

Eva stubbed out her cigarette in the ashtray on the table outside and smiled. Zoe had originally put the ashtray there to stop Earl from flicking them on the ground. Eva came inside where it was marginally cooler and sat down at the head of the table. She wasn't sure why she was placed there, but Zoe had a plan and she wasn't about to breach it.

After saying a prayer, they dove into the meal. Eva sat back and took a deep breath. Apart from the weather, the scene before her reminded her of home; a time when things were less complicated. She missed those days and, she had to admit to herself, she missed her stepfather — at least the loving stepfather of her youth. Earlier in her life, he would be so gentle and kind with her that it was usually easy to forget the hard military man that lurked just below the surface. She especially missed her mother and grandparents. She missed her family more than she cared to admit to Zoe.

"Hello, anyone home?"

Fingers snapped in front of her which brought her out of her second daydream of the day. She glanced at Zoe across the table who was giving her a worried look. "Sorry, I was just thinking of home."

"It's hot in Germany this time of year?" Earl inquired.

Eva shook her head. "No. It's usually freezing cold. There was a roaring fire in the fireplace and the smell of chestnuts..." Eva stopped and looked across at Zoe. *You're worrying her,* Eva thought to herself. She said aloud, "And it's not that time anymore. Time for some new traditions."

"Usually what we do after a big Christmas lunch is go down to the beach and enjoy the surf," Earl chimed in again.

"Well, that's certainly a different tradition."

"I've never had Hanukah where the temperature reached one hundred and five degrees before." Elena chuckled. "Our first Hanukah here was very cool. It was wet and windy."

"That was right after you arrived?" Earl asked.

"We were in the refugee camp and were in a dormitory with other women. We weren't sure how to celebrate Hanukah because we didn't have a menorah or candles, but Zoe and Eva wanted to make it special for me."

"So how did you do it?"

The three friends looked at each other and smiled. It was a memory Eva treasured. She didn't know anything about Jewish beliefs, but Elena had told them the story of why the Jews celebrated Hanukah and explained its importance. Elena's longing to celebrate it was so strong that Eva wanted to make it special.

"Zoe drew a menorah on some paper she found and Eva found some sticks. The paper menorah was cut and the sticks sat glued to the paper. So we lit the sticks and ate the food we had," Elena replied. "It was my first Hanukah in years."

"It was our very first," Zoe replied and smiled across the table at Eva. "Our first Christmas as a family was also quite memorable."

The three friends looked at each other and burst out laughing. "We were sent into the dining area ready for a big Christmas dinner to find a naked Yugoslav man with an apple in his mouth amongst the food," Eva replied and couldn't quite contain the giggles at the memory. "He was lying right across the table stark naked," she continued but had to stop when the memory of the man made her laugh even harder.

"It was quite memorable," Elena added.

"Good thing it wasn't cold..." Zoe stopped and glanced at Eva who was laughing so hard she had tears running down her face. Then she noticed that Friedrich, Earl, and Panayiotis look at each other for a moment before they burst out laughing. "What did I say?"

"I'll tell you later," Eva managed to say and wiped the tears that ran down her face. Eva could still remember the look on Zoe's face at that time they saw the man on the table. Although her partner had grown up with three older brothers, the sight of the naked man made Zoe blush to a deep shade of red before she turned and ran out of the dining area, quickly followed by Elena.

"You know, I can continue this great tradition..." Earl pulled his chair out and began to step away from the table.

"NO!" Everyone cried out in unison and then dissolved into laughter.

Eva wiped the tears from her eyes and met Zoe's gaze for a moment. New traditions, new friends, old friends. Family. The laughter turned into light banter as Eva took a sip of her wine and silently thanked God. She was truly blessed.

A few weeks later, Eva sat at the kitchen table, smiling over her steaming cup of tea as Zoe came into the kitchen for a moment, then left, came back inside a moment later, and turned on her heel, leaving again. Zoe was in a "tizzy", as Earl was fond of saying. Ever since Zoe had received the acceptance letter from Sydney Art College, she had been nervous, excited, and sometimes bordering on the slightly insane in anticipation. She had gone over the route that she and Elena would take to the College in minute detail. Zoe had even traveled there and stood outside the gates just watching the students file inside, her expression wavering between determination, apprehension, and sheer joy.

It had been a nervous wait for them both, after Zoe found out her exam results, to see if she would also get the grant necessary to finance her attendance at the college. The letter guaranteeing the financing had arrived only a few days later, causing another round of celebrations, because Zoe and Elena had both been accepted into the College and both had received the grants to pay their tuition, which meant they could finally quit their jobs at Hatton's By The Sea restaurant.

Both young women had given their notice at the same time. Although their boss had yelled at them more times than he had smiled during the course of their employment, he had been clearly sad to see Elena and Zoe leave.

"Zoe, eat some breakfast," Eva called out, knowing what Zoe's response was going to be. She had made the same suggestion an hour previously.

Zoe came into the kitchen looking quite flustered. Her hair fell across her eyes as she turned to see the wall clock. "I can't eat, Evy."

"You're going to be hungry."

"Did you eat on your first day at university?" Zoe sat down to tie her shoelaces.

Eva's smile broadened. "Yes, a big hearty breakfast that my *Omi* made."

"You're what?"

"My grandmother," Eva translated. "She made the best omelets I have ever tasted."

"Better than mine?" Zoe stopped fidgeting and looked over at her, focusing her full attention on Eva for the first time that morning.

"A touch better," Eva replied honestly.

"Humph." Zoe sniffed.

Eva laughed at Zoe's reaction as she got up from the table, left the kitchen to answer the knock at the front door. Elena stood outside the apartment, wearing a harried expression on her face as she tried to juggle her notebooks and her bag.

"Morning, Elena." Eva welcomed the young woman as she came into the apartment. "Zoe is nearly ready."

Zoe came out of the kitchen and greeted her friend. "Morning, El."

"Hi, Zoe. Aren't you ready yet?"

"Nope. My 'mother' wants me to eat breakfast."

"We don't have time! We're going to be late!" Elena urged.

"Okay, okay. The college isn't going anywhere," Zoe mumbled. She handed Eva the mug of tea she had brought out from the kitchen, picked up her notebooks and her bag from the coffee table, and rushed out the door with Elena on her heels.

Eva shook her head as she closed the front door behind them. "Ah, how quickly they grow up," Eva said aloud as Ourania wandered out of the bedroom.

The cat had spent the morning under the bed and out of Zoe's reach. Ourania had apparently decided it was not safe to be near Zoe's path, after Zoe had accidentally stepped on the cat's luxurious tail. "'Once more unto the breach,'" Eva said to the cat. She picked up her own handbag and prepared to head off to work.

Zoe felt more than a little nervous as they entered the Registration office. The waiting room was filled with students. She and Elena looked at each other and sighed. They each took a seat and waited for their turn.

After what seemed like hours, Zoe and Elena finally found themselves in front of the registration clerk's desk.

"Oh no," Elena groaned softly, nudging Zoe's ribs with her elbow. "It's her."

"'Her' who?" Zoe asked as she looked around the room to see who Elena was talking about.

"You know...when we came to the college before. You irritated her, remember? The racist cow, I think you called her?"

"Oh. Oh! Oh no," Zoe muttered.

"Yes?" the clerk asked, glancing at the two women disdainfully.

"I'm Zoe Lambros and this is my friend Elena Mannheim."

"You're here to register?"

"Yes." Zoe handed over the letter, which outlined the courses she was taking.

The clerk frowned. "Do I know you?"

"Well, you do and you don't," Zoe replied, which only made the clerk's frown deepen until it look like someone had drawn the corners of her mouth down to her chin.

"Is that supposed to be funny?" the woman asked acerbically.

"No, ma'am."

"You look familiar," the clerk repeated. "I'm sure it will come to me, but then you're Greek and all Greeks look the same to me."

"We do?"

The clerk sighed. "Peasants," she said, and looked up Zoe with pronounced annoyance. "All right. Here is the schedule and what you need to know." She handed Zoe a bundle of papers and a book. "If you have any problems or questions, you will find a list of people in there that you can ask for help. Don't ask me. It's not my job."

"Thanks," Zoe said shortly, reining in her own annoyance. She waited with barely concealed impatience while Elena gave her name and received the same information, as well as the same attitude, from the clerk. It seemed the woman was not overly fond of Jews, either. Having completed their registration, the two friends walked out of the office and back into the sunlight.

"Same racist cow all right," Zoe said under her breath, biting off each word. Elena shook her head and led her onto the grass.

Jacaranda trees provided a little shade against the hot sweltering sun. Elena sat cross-legged on the ground, munching on a sandwich she had brought from home. It was clear that the hours of waiting had made her hungry. Meanwhile, Zoe tried to figure out where their classes were going to be. She lay sprawled on the grass with a map of the college in front of her, tracing routes with a fingertip.

"Eva reckons I can't read a map," Zoe said, frowning in concentration.

"You can't," Elena's muffled reply came as she took another bite from her sandwich.

"Elena, you are not a comedienne."

"I can read maps, though," her friend replied with a smug grin.

"Be quiet," Zoe grumbled good-naturedly as she went back to her perusal of the map. "Hey, you want to go to the beach later?"

Elena sat silent, ignoring Zoe until Zoe flashed her an annoyed look and Elena finally replied, "Am I allowed to talk now?"

"Since when do you do what I ask? Do you want to go to the beach afterwards?"

"Sure. Can I bring Friedrich?"

"I don't see why not. Earl said he had the whole week off, so we can go in his car. You bring Friedrich, Eva will be home by five thirty, and we can grab Father H and Ally—"

"Um, excuse me, are you Zoe Lambros?"

Zoe looked up at the owner of the voice and found herself staring at a pair of legs. She looked up further, squinting. The sun was behind the woman, and she could not see her face. "Yes, that's me," Zoe replied.

"Oh, finally I found you! My name is Kiriakoula Evagenlopoulos, and I belong to the Hellas Club." After introducing herself, Kiriakoula sat down next to Zoe on the grass, folding her legs beneath her in an elegant, lady-like manner.

"I would never have guessed that," Zoe said. She got a nudge from Elena to remind her to watch her manners. "What's the Hellas Club?"

"Yeah, I know my name does tend to give it away, doesn't it? Well, it's a club where all the Greek students get together and we help each other. Would you like to join us?"

"How did you find me?"

"Well, there's a list in the Registration Office of all new students and I looked for all the Greek names."

"What do I have to do to get in?" Zoe asked. The girl had black eyes and the blackest hair Zoe had ever seen. Her skin was pale, which combined with her otherwise dark coloration made her look like a creature from a scary film. Zoe decided she was going to be tactful for once and was not going to let *that* impression slip out. "This is Elena," she said, introducing her friend.

"Are you Greek?" Kiriakoula asked Elena, who shook her head.

"I'm German. Elena Mannheim, pleased to meet you." Elena's outstretched hand was ignored and Kiriakoula gave her an odd look.

"Oh," was all the young woman said before turning her attention back to Zoe. "We only allow Greeks into our club."

"Elena is an honorary Greek," Zoe replied, giving Elena a grin.

"We don't fraternize with the enemy...or Jews," Kiriakoula replied, scowling her disapproval.

Zoe's smile vanished as she regarded the young woman in front of her with dislike. Zoe found it disturbing to meet this hostility directed at her dear friend, but she did not find it all that surprising. Zoe had been this woman before she had met Eva; full of hatred and bitterness at someone who was not Greek and therefore had to be the enemy.

"I don't consider Elena the enemy," Zoe said. "She's my best friend."

"Well, she's German," Kiriakoula said as though that was sufficient reason for her prejudice.

"Yes, that's quite obvious. And you think all Germans are the enemy?"

"With all my heart," Kiriakoula responded in Greek and got up from the grass. "If you lie down with the enemy, you are not a real Greek," she told Zoe, her disdain clear.

Zoe's acceptance and understanding of the woman suddenly evaporated. It was replaced with anger at the woman's words. "Go to hell," Zoe returned in Greek. "Bitch," she quickly added, which only caused the other woman to spit in her direction, narrowly missing her.

Zoe was furious. It was only Elena's tackle that kept her on the ground and prevented Zoe from taking a swing at the sneering Greek woman. Zoe fell face down onto the grass while Elena sat on her and prevented her from getting up.

"No! Stay put," Elena urged Zoe. The fracas was attracting attention as various students paused to watch.

"I'm going to twist her big ugly face into a pretzel. Racist bitch," Zoe yelled, unable to move since Elena had apparently decided she was going to sit on her until her anger had dissipated.

"What did she say to get you all ready to twist her into a pretzel? She's bigger than you, Zoe, and I think she would twist *you* into a pretzel."

"Get off me, El," Zoe ordered. Elena remained where she was, which only angered Zoe further.

Elena said, "No. Not until you cool off."

"I've cooled off," Zoe replied, but her fury was still evident in her constricted tone.

"Yeah, I believe that," Elena replied. "Zoe, you can't fight racism by twisting faces into pretzels. Although it might be fun trying, it doesn't solve the problem."

"It's going to make *me* feel good," Zoe insisted. She spied the bigoted Greek woman who was responsible for her tirade talking to another student. Both students looked back and laughed, their mockery sending a renewed surge of anger through Zoe. "Ooh, I wish I could twist that head of hers!" she raged.

"Zoe! You could get expelled and that wouldn't look good for your first day. Anyway, she has probably had bad experiences with Germans. If I let you up, do you promise to behave?"

"No," Zoe replied, pouting.

"Come on, Zoe, please? If you go after that girl and get caught, you *will* get tossed out and you *will* lose your grant. Is that what you want?"

Zoe continued to pout. "No," she said grudgingly after a moment. She did not think she could bear Eva's disappointment anyway, and getting into a fight with a bigot was not worth the trouble it would cause. "All right, I won't go after her."

"Promise?"

"Yes, now get off me."

Elena got off Zoe slowly and watched her sit back up. Zoe still scowled and looked in the direction where Kiriakoula had disappeared with the other student.

"What did she say?" Elena asked.

Zoe remained silent for a long moment. She did not want to hurt Elena's feelings, even though her own were now simmering rather than incandescent. She knew how much it hurt Eva when racist barbs were directed at her because of her German accent; she had seen the frustration and hurt in her partner's eyes. Zoe also knew how racist taunts felt since she had been the recipient of such on many occasions.

"Zoe?" Elena prodded.

"She said that she believed in her heart that Germans were the enemy, and that if I didn't believe that then I wouldn't be a true Greek," Zoe replied.

"You know that's not true, Zoe."

"I know it's not true, El, but that's not the point."

"You can't jump to my defense every time I'm called a nasty name," Elena said and put her arm around her. "You wouldn't have time for your studies if you did that. Forget her. What did you tell her?"

"I told her to go to hell and called her a bitch."

"Did it make you feel better?"

"No. If I'd twisted her face like a pretzel, *that* would have made me feel better," Zoe said insistently as she got up off the grass and helped Elena to rise so they could both go on to their first class. "You know, I could have done it, too, despite her size."

"Uh huh," Elena replied and started to laugh when Zoe gave her a disgusted look. "Zoe, she was bigger than you. She would have stomped you flat."

"You forget Eva is a big girl and I can handle her."

"Eva *lets* you handle her," Elena said with a chuckle.

Zoe glanced at her friend. "You're a funny woman."

"Thank you," Elena replied and they laughed as they went arm-in-arm down the jacaranda-lined walkway.

The two women wandered through several corridors before coming to the right classroom. Elena obviously felt somewhat vindicated since she was the one who found the room after Zoe was forced to admit that she was lost.

"Don't say a word," Zoe grumbled to Elena as they entered. Zoe took a seat in the front of the class. The room filled up quickly as other students filed in and took their seats.

Zoe watched a casually dressed young woman walk to the front of the class and lean on a table that held books and drawings. She tried to catch a glimpse of the artworks but could not make out anything clearly. Zoe glanced around the room, hoping she was not going to have the racist Kiriakoula in the same class, and was relieved when she did not see the Greek woman. The lecturer held up her hands to quiet them down. She was not a tall woman; she had dark brown hair and blue eyes, which Zoe found fascinating since they were the same shade as Eva's.

"Welcome to my class. My name is Lucia de Nobrega; you can call me Lucia. I see we are going to have a big group this time around. If you joined this class to learn to create what is in your mind's eye, then you are in the right place. If you came to look at naked bodies, I believe the biology class is in the Carslaw Building." Lucia smiled.

The students chuckled at the small joke. Zoe and Elena looked at each other and grinned. It certainly seemed as though they were going to have fun in this class.

"In a moment, I will go around the room and get each of you to introduce yourself and tell us why you chose this class. Now before we do that little exercise, let me give you my philosophy about art and artists. Whether drawing, painting, or writing, an artist gives of him or herself fully. Giving of yourself is usually done most comfortably with loved ones, but here you will learn to express yourself through your art. How do you do this? You have to lose all kinds of prejudice. You cannot have a prejudice and be a great artist. You don't come here to learn how to be a bad artist; you want to reach inside yourself and become the best that you can be. Being prejudiced will blur your vision — it won't allow you to look beyond what you think you know and how you view it," Lucia said, her gaze intent as she looked at the students.

"Secondly, I want you to lose your inhibitions," Lucia continued. "I'm not saying you have to run around naked across the campus..."

The room burst out laughing. Elena poked Zoe in the ribs. "If I dared you, would you do it?"

Zoe glanced at her friend and whispered, "How much?" and then turned back to the teacher. Elena did not answer.

"That's a nice little visual, isn't it?" Lucia asked. "Now I want you to be free about yourself and what you look like. Look at yourself in the mirror and create some funny faces, dance in your own home while singing. You can sing off key as long as the neighbors don't call the police!" Lucia got another chuckle from her class and continued, "If you allow yourself to look silly and act silly, you will find that your inhibitions will be lost. Everything you are feeling will be expressed in your art. You have to *give* a little part of yourself to your artwork. Okay, that was a mouthful, wasn't it? Now while I take a break, you can each tell me about yourself and why you are here."

Zoe listened carefully as her classmates introduced themselves. Elena had her turn, and then it came to Zoe. She got up and looked around the room.

"Boy, I'm glad this is not a class for public speaking," Zoe said self-consciously, and got a laugh from the class. "My name is Zoe Lambros. I've been in Australia for a little over a year, and I'm living out my dream of learning how to draw and be an artist," she finished quietly, and sat down with a slight blush warming her cheeks.

"Eva!" Mrs. Jenkins waved at Eva and Alberta as the two women walked up the sidewalk towards the apartment. She was coming down to them as quickly as she could, and Eva had to stop herself from laughing when the stout Mrs. Jenkins tried to run but went back to walking when she could not muster up the energy.

"I wonder what she wants," Alberta whispered. "I hope it's not another date for you."

"She knows about me and Zoe."

Alberta did not have time to respond as Mrs. Jenkins came to a halt in front of them. The woman was a little out of breath.

"Good afternoon, Mrs. Jenkins," Eva said.

Alberta asked, "How are you, Nelly?"

"I'm fine, thank you," Mrs. Jenkins replied. "Eva, you may have a problem."

Eva was surprised. "Oh?"

"Your pet is screaming its head off in your apartment!" she said. She took a handkerchief from her pocket and dabbed the sweat off her face. "It's so hot today."

"Ourania?" Eva was really surprised now. "She's pretty quiet."

"I'm not sure what it is, but it's screeching, and it scared Mrs. Deakin in number seven."

Eva looked at Alberta and shrugged, nonplused by Ourania's supposed behavior. She hoped Zoe had not brought home any more pets. At that moment, Earl's car pulled up and distracted her for a few seconds before she turned her attention back to the waiting landlady. "I'm sorry, Mrs. Jenkins, but I'm not sure what the noise is. I'll go and have a look."

Mrs. Jenkins said, "Yes, please do that. Mrs. Deakin's ticker isn't all that strong."

Eva was sure she had a bemused expression. Having delivered her message, Mrs. Jenkins walked away. Eva wasn't sure what was going on, but she was going to find out soon enough.

"Hey, Earl," Eva greeted Earl as he walked with her and Alberta to the apartment. As soon as the three of them entered the foyer, they heard screeching and what sounded like very bad singing.

They arrived at Eva and Zoe's apartment door and Eva unlocked it, feeling a little trepidation. The volume of the noise trebled, spilling out into the corridor. Eva stood stock-still in the doorway, watching in absolute fascination as Zoe, clad in shorts and Eva's blue shirt, which was too big for her, waltzed around the lounge, singing (or doing what passed for singing) at the top of her voice with Elena, who was also clad in shorts and a shirt.

"Is this some new form of therapy?" Earl yelled, trying to be heard over the din.

Eva went over to the gramophone and shut it off.

"Hey, Eva!" Zoe bounded up and kissed her. "We were inhibiting."

"Uninhibiting," Elena corrected her.

"You were scaring Mrs. Deakin in number seven!" Eva replied as Alberta and Earl came inside.

"Mrs. Deakin can't hear a single thing! We weren't that loud," Zoe said scornfully.

Eva raised an eyebrow. "Well, Mrs. Jenkins heard you and so did we, from the foyer downstairs."

"Oh," Zoe said. She sat down on the sofa, her exuberance a bit deflated.

"What was that about?" Alberta asked Zoe.

"Our art teacher told us in order to be great artists, we have to lose our inhibitions and be silly. So, in order to do our homework, we first have to sing and dance."

"And scare old ladies," Earl added. He got a slap on the leg from Zoe. "Ow, stop that, Stretch, or I'll dunk you in the deep end!"

Eva and Alberta laughed when Earl and Zoe got into a tussle. Zoe was hauled up and carried into the bedroom and the screams of "Save me, Eva" were drowned out by peals of laugher and "Oh, uncle, uncle."

Eva went inside the bedroom to rescue Zoe from Earl's teasing clutches, still laughing.

Chapter Twenty-Two

Eva spent the morning at the Immigration Department trying to help a Greek couple get settled in their new apartment. Even though Eva wasn't hired to work with the Greeks, she helped out when, at times like this, the other translators were overwhelmed. She was rewarded a few hours later by the gooiest Greek *baklava* she had ever tasted, delivered to the office as a gift from the grateful couple. Her colleagues were eating it when the doors opened and Mr. Hermann came in with a bunch of flowers and a huge grin on his face.

"Ah, *Fräulein*," the old man greeted her.

Eva didn't want to have Mr. Hermann feel obligated so she attempted to cut him off easily. "Mr. Hermann, the flowers you sent over before the holiday was more than enough thanks. Don't feel like you need to spend your money on flowers. I'm only doing my job."

Eva's eyebrows shot nearly into her hairline when the old man went down on bended knee. "Oy, I'm not as young as I used to be," he grumbled and then looked into Eva's eyes. "Thank you for all you've done. No amount of flowers could thank you for how much better my life has been with your help. You have been most sweet," Mr. Hermann told her, smiling. "And if I was twenty years younger, I would ask you to go out with me," he teased before Eva helped him up rise to his feet.

The day seemed all the more special because of the appreciation expressed by her two clients, Eva mused to herself as she worked at her desk. She glanced up when there was a knock on the door; it opened and Debbie stuck her head inside.

"You're going to starve, and I'll have Earl berating me for not looking after you!" the receptionist said. She came into the office and around Eva's desk. "Come on, go to lunch!" Debbie said, flapping her hands like a farmer's wife shooing chickens.

"Uh..."

"Don't 'uh' me. The clients will be here when you get back." Debbie pulled Eva out of the chair and gently shoved her out the door, much to Eva's amusement.

"Okay, I'm going, I'm going." Eva walked down the corridor and noticed Alberta standing at the reception desk. "You sent Debbie after me, didn't you?" she accused.

"Oh no, not me," Alberta replied. "She came to my office and bullied me out."

"Will the two of you go to lunch, already!" Debbie exclaimed, giving both women a mock glare. Her grin broadened when Eva and Alberta shrugged at each other and walked away.

An hour later, Eva and Alberta returned to a very quiet waiting area. A few clients sat on wooden chairs waiting for their appointments, but the usual noisy din had been replaced by the much quieter whirring of the ceiling fan.

"Anything exciting happen while we've been gone?" Eva asked Debbie, who for once was not attached to the phone or trying to do ten things at the same time.

"It's pretty quiet. Doesn't happen often, so savor the moment," Debbie said happily. She looked down at her ever-present appointment book. "Eva, you have a Mrs. Wagner coming in soon and after that..."

"After that?"

"Nothing. You're free for the afternoon!" Debbie exclaimed, showing a shocked Eva the book. "The clients over there are for Ally and Deirdre."

"Lucky me," Alberta said with a grin, picking up the files and giving the other women a tiny wave as she returned to her own office.

Eva picked up Mrs. Wagner's file and walked down to her own office. She spent a few minutes looking over the notes Debbie had made about the reason Mrs. Wagner had an appointment. Putting the file aside, Eva went to her bookcase and took out a book on family law. Sitting down at her desk, she opened the book and began reading. She did not realize the time until there was a knock on the door and Debbie came in. "Mrs. Wagner is here," she announced, ushering the woman inside then closing the door.

Eva stood to welcome her client, looked up and blinked. It had been so many years. Could this woman be...? But no, Greta was dead. Wasn't she? This woman had the same long auburn hair, the same hazel eyes as her former lover, the same regal bearing, the same fine features. She was thinner and older but...

Eva fell back down on her chair in shock. She could not begin to believe that the woman standing in her office was Greta Strauss, her first lover. It could not be Greta. That was impossible! Nevertheless...

"Greta?" Eva breathed.

"Eva? Eva Muller?" the woman whispered. "It can't be my Eva."

Greta came around the desk. Eva remained where she was sitting, frozen and made mute by disbelief.

"My dear God, it is you!" Greta cried. She knelt in front of Eva and embraced her. "Oh, dear God. I don't believe this," Greta muttered as she took hold of Eva's hands. "You don't believe this, do you?"

Eva shook her head, which caused Greta to laugh through the tears that were streaming down her face. "You're supposed to be dead!" Eva said when she found her voice.

"Dead? Why would you think I was dead?" Greta asked. She got up, pulled the other chair around and sat down next to Eva.

Eva said, "Reinhardt told me that he told Father that you were my lover—"

"Reinhardt? Jurgen Reinhardt? That fool?"

"B-b-because he found out about us and he had you shipped off—"

"Good grief, he lied to you, Eva. That man couldn't tell the truth if his life depended on it!" Greta cried.

"You're alive," Eva said in wonder "Where did you go?"

"Where did I go?" Greta repeated, clearly not understanding the query.

"After we burnt the synagogue," Eva said quietly. "On *Kristallnacht*."

"Oh! After Jurgen and the boys decided they were going to continue without us and then you took off; is that what you mean?"

Eva nodded.

"Well, I followed them and got up to all sorts of mischief. It was quite a night. You missed out on all the fun. Then I went home to meet John and plan our wedding. You forgot about that?" Greta asked.

Eva shook her head. "I remember about John."

"Oh, come now, you're still not holding a grudge against me for that?"

"No, I knew you had to marry John," Eva said. She was unsettled by Greta's description of *Kristallnacht* as "fun".

"I missed you at the wedding." Greta brought Eva's hand up for a kiss. "I didn't think you would miss it altogether."

"I...uh..."

"I asked after you," Greta said. "I was a little hurt you didn't come to my wedding."

"You went to my...father?"

"Yes, and he told me you were unwell and he'd sent you to Austria to recuperate."

Eva sighed. "It's a long story."

Greta leaned over and wiped away Eva's tears. "Eva, I can't believe it's you. You've cut your beautiful long hair," she said, stroking the shortened locks. "You have to tell me why you did that. I think we need to sit down and have a good heart to heart. Would you have dinner with me tonight?"

Eva tried to gather her scattered thoughts together. "Um...I can't tonight."

"I know. You need to get yourself together. How about tomorrow night? I can come over to your place and we can get reacquainted?"

"That would be fine," Eva stated, still somewhat shocked at the woman's unexpected resurrection and unable to think clearly. "I'm married," she blurted.

"Really? Well, this is going to be interesting," Greta said. "Excellent, we can catch up on old times." She rubbed her thumb across Eva's cheek; the caress was possessive rather than tender. "I've always said I have perfect timing."

By the time Greta left the office, Eva felt as if her world had turned upside down and she was not sure how the situation was going to work out. The shock of seeing Greta in her office ebbed away, to be replaced by the realization that all these years she had wrongly believed she was responsible for the woman's death. The unwelcome revelation made Eva sick to her stomach as well as dizzy, with a tension headache sawing through her skull.

She remained in a daze for the rest of the afternoon. It was a good thing her stepmother had gone to meet her father in the city. Eva didn't want to talk to anyone except Zoe.

For over eight years she had believed that her father had sent Greta to her death because she had been Eva's lover. All the abuse and humiliation Eva had suffered at his and her uncle's hands, the abject loneliness she had felt at being viewed as a deviant, and the constant threat of more violence came crashing back into her mind, a maelstrom of unwanted memories. She felt as though she had been punched in the head. Emotionally, she was a wreck. When it was time to leave, she mechanically signed off and said her goodbyes to Debbie.

"Hey, are you okay?" Debbie asked in obvious concern.

"Yeah, just tired," Eva responded. She walked out of the building, too caught up in her internal anguish to even notice how she caught the bus home. Eva walked the few meters home from the bus stop, but never afterward remembered the journey. She climbed the stairs up to the apartment and opened the door, dropping her briefcase to the floor and calling, "Zoe? Are you home?" There was no reply.

Eva sat on the sofa, numb with exhaustion. "Oh, God," she exclaimed. She desperately wished that Zoe would return. She needed her partner so much that her chest ached. Eva fell back and let her head rest against the cushions. Her time with Greta seemed as though it had happened a lifetime ago. She cast her mind back, getting past the lingering guilt and letting old memories come surging to the fore.

Autumn winds blew Eva's long black hair across her face as she walked quickly to a small teahouse just a few blocks away from the university. It was much frequented by students and the crowd usually overflowed onto tables set out on the pavement.

She smiled when she caught sight of her lover, Greta, sitting just inside the teahouse. The sight of her lover always brought a smile to Eva's face. Greta was older and always looked so sophisticated, causing Eva to wonder why Greta had fallen in love with an eighteen-year-old girl when she could have got anyone to fall for her charms. At that moment, Eva did not care. She greeted Greta with a chaste kiss on the cheek, mindful that the true nature of their relationship had to be concealed.

"I'm so happy to see you," Eva exclaimed.

"How was your day?" Greta asked.

"It was all right. Frau Mazzili is getting more insane as the days go on." Eva laughed lightly. Her Italian professor was a little eccentric.

"Let's take a walk," Greta suggested.

"In this weather?"

"It will add a rosy hue to your cheeks," Greta said, chuckling. "I have something important to tell you."

"All right," Eva acquiesced and followed Greta out of the teahouse. They walked quietly for some minutes before Greta repeated, "Eva, I need to tell you something."

"Have you decided to come to the camp next week?" Eva asked, hoping Greta had changed her mind about attending a youth camp with her.

"No, sweetheart," Greta said. "I think I'm a little too old for that camp."

"What's this about then?"

"Well..." Greta took off the glove on her left hand and showed Eva a diamond engagement ring on her third finger. "Do you like it?"

"It's nice," Eva replied, confused.

"Just nice?" Greta raised a brow.

Eva faltered. "I'm not sure what to say."

"Well, how would you like to be my bridesmaid?"

Eva stared open-mouthed, not caring who might be watching them. She was absolutely incredulous that Greta would even ask her. "You're getting married?"

"Yes," Greta said matter-of-factly. "That's what usually happens when a woman gets an engagement ring from a man."

"But you're a lesbian!" Eva made no attempt to modulate her voice.

Greta laughed and put her fingers over Eva's lips, pressing firmly. "Shh, sweetheart, I don't think everyone is supposed to know that."

"But how can you get married? You're in love with me, aren't you?" Eva asked, desperate to hear an explanation that she could accept. The situation seemed like a nightmare. Greta loved her, not some man!

"Come on, Eva, you really didn't think this was forever, did you?" Greta asked. "Your naivety is very sweet," she said, caressing Eva's cheek. "I suppose that comes of being so young."

"I thought you loved me," Eva said, shattered. Greta was the first woman she had ever fallen in love with; she had thought their special bond would last beyond eternity. "You said we would go away after I finish university and be together always."

"Oh, my innocent Eva," the older woman said and kissed her lightly on the lips. "It's just that I'm getting married and things have changed, they are different now."

"What's different now?"

"Eva, darling, I do love you, but you have to understand; what we had was special but it has to end. Can't you see that?"

"But I love you," Eva cried.

Greta smiled. Once, that expression had warmed Eva to the core; now it sent a chill through her. "And I love you," Greta repeated slowly, as if to a not very intelligent child, "but now, I'm getting married."

"I thought you said you didn't like..." Eva blushed. "You know...with men."

"I don't," Greta sighed. "Still, I have to look after my future."

A ray of hope shone through her despair. "So you don't love him?" Eva asked, perhaps too eagerly, but she was not concerned with appearing sophisticated at the moment.

"Heavens, no," Greta replied. "He's old enough to be my father, but he's a good Party member and, well," she shrugged, "it pays to be on the right side of our Führer."

Eva tried not to cry but was losing the battle, her tears silently rolling down her face. Her belly was a howling wasteland. She thought she was going to be sick.

Greta tenderly tipped her chin up. Even now, Eva felt a thrill at the touch of her lover's hand. "Oh my little Eva, you always had a gentle heart. I do love you, yes, but you have to let go and move on with your life."

"But..." Eva was aware that she was blubbering though she did not care. Greta removed a handkerchief from her pocket and wiped Eva's wet face.

"Eva, you have to move on," Greta said. "One day you will find that you will also have to marry a man whom you don't love and never will love. That's what we all have to do. It's the only way a woman can survive in this world, my dear. We earn our living on our backs, one way or the other. Better you should learn the lesson now, eh?"

"No, I won't," Eva shook her head, her heart rejecting Greta's cynical view. "I won't ever marry anyone if I don't love them."

Greta sighed. "One day you will, trust me, you will. What we had together was nice and I will always treasure the memories."

Eva made a last, desperate bid to sway her lover from this madness. "But it doesn't have to end."

"Do you want me to cheat on my husband?" Greta asked, her manner teasing.

"No." That had not been her intention. Eva did not know herself what she had meant, only that she wanted Greta to tell her it was all a very poor joke, that they would remain together no matter what happened. Looking into Greta's cool grey eyes, Eva understood at last that it was over. She caught her breath as pain lanced through her breast, the ache of a heart broken into pieces.

"Well then, I can't just come out and tell John that I don't want to marry him because I'm a lesbian, now can I?" Greta said, arching an eyebrow.

"No," Eva replied miserably.

"Are you sure you don't want to be my bridesmaid?"

"No." Eva shook her head, feeling even sicker than before. "No, I'm sure."

"Well, I would like you to but if you don't want to, I understand. I'm going to invite you anyway."

Eva could scarcely believe the other woman's thoughtlessness. Had Greta always been this careless of her feelings? Eva tried to think but it was too difficult. The two women walked down the street in silence until they came to Eva's home.

"You will be at the Hitler Youth meeting tonight, won't you?" Greta asked when a group of Brown Shirts passed by and smiled at them.

"I can't..."

"Eva, you promised me," Greta wagged a finger at her. "You promised you were going to be there. Believe me, it's going to be quite a night."

"My Mutti..."

"Eva, this will be our last night together. You don't want our last moments to be painful ones, do you?" Greta asked, causing Eva more heartache with her apparent unconcern for Eva's wounded feelings. "Please come with me tonight." Her voice dropped into a purr that Eva found difficult to resist.

Eva sighed. At the moment, she wanted to get away and lick her wounds in private. "All right," she said. At least she would be able to see Greta one last time. Perhaps she could persuade Greta to return the engagement ring and give up her marriage plans. It might happen.

"I promise it will be a night you will never forget." Greta laughed and gave Eva a very chaste goodbye kiss on the cheek. Eva watched her leave. "I love you," she whispered, knowing Greta could not hear but felt compelled to say the words anyway.

Eva curled up on the sofa and let out a heart-rending cry that no one was around to hear. "Oh, Zoe, where are you?" she wept, letting the emotional agony overwhelm her.

"You know I really hate that game," Elena said.

Zoe looked back at her friend and shook her head. "You just don't understand it. It's like chess."

"I'm sure, but chess is quicker," Elena said as they climbed the stairs of the apartment building.

Zoe had decided to go for the women's cricket team trials at the college and did not think she would be picked, but to her surprise and despite not having played the game before, she was. Zoe had seen the notice and decided she wanted to learn how to play. It was late when she and Elena left the college grounds and slowly made their way home by bus.

The two women parted to go to their respective apartments. Zoe opened the door and entered a darkened lounge. "Hmm, how odd," she muttered to herself. Normally, the lights would be on. She took a few steps into the room; Ourania rubbed up her leg and meowed loudly.

"Where's Eva, Raney?" she asked the cat and picked her up to stroke her. "Maybe she had to stay late at work." Ourania purred in response.

Zoe put the cat down and peeled off her shirt to take to the laundry basket. On her way back, she passed the sofa and noticed Eva's handbag lying haphazardly on its side with half the contents spilled on the floor. She scooped up the fallen items, picked up the bag and went into the bedroom to put it away, wondering a little at her partner's uncharacteristic sloppiness.

Lying on top of the bedspread was Eva, still in her work clothes. The dark-haired woman had not even removed her shoes. Zoe stared in surprise for a long moment. Very quietly, so as not to wake her sleeping partner, Zoe went over to the wardrobe and pulled out a blanket, placing it gently over Eva's body.

"What happened, Evy?" Zoe whispered looking down at Eva's tear stained face. The explanation was going to have to wait until Eva woke, she decided. Zoe left the bedroom and closed the door behind her, trying to be as quiet as possible. She went into the kitchen and noticed the dinner she had cooked that morning had been taken out of the icebox and left on the counter. Zoe lifted the lid of the dish and was surprised to find that Eva had not eaten a bite. She had apparently come home, left her bag on the floor, gone into the kitchen, taken the food out and then left it when she went into the bedroom to fall asleep. Was she ill? Zoe was getting more worried with each new revelation.

"Damn it to hell," she muttered and put the food back in the refrigerator. "I'm going to kill whoever hurt her." She left the kitchen in a very black mood.

Zoe was still deep in thought as she went to the bathroom. She had just filled the tub for a bath when she heard Eva's pained cry coming from the bedroom. She dropped the bath salts into the tub in her haste to get to the other woman. Zoe ran into the bedroom to find a sweat-drenched Eva looking extremely pale, doubled up as if in pain, and breathing in shallow gasps.

"It's all right, love. I've got you." Zoe held her as Eva sobbed. "I've got you," she repeated in reassurance. Zoe was also shaking, her concern skyrocketing. "What's the matter, Evy, are you sick?" Eva continued to shake and did not respond to Zoe's question, which only made Zoe more anxious to find out the cause of such distress. "Is Father H all right? Is he hurt? What is it?"

"Hold me," Eva begged as Zoe got into bed with her and held her shaking partner. She kissed Eva and tried to soothe her, rocking the weeping woman in her arms. Eva's sobs tore at Zoe's heart. She had thought after Muller was captured that all of this would end but there had been only a brief respite. She decided that the bath could wait until the morning, as could further inquiries into the cause of Eva's agony.

Zoe woke with a start and a very uneasy feeling in the pit of her stomach. She turned over to look for Eva, but her partner was not in bed. She got up, put on her slippers, and walked out of the bedroom. Zoe could see Eva sitting on the sofa, her strong profile outlined in the light from the open curtain although the rest of the room was dark. Ourania was being held by Eva in her lap, the cat curled up and purring as Eva's fingers stroked through her fur. Zoe sighed. She padded over to the sofa, her footsteps muffled by the rug.

Eva looked up and gave her a tired smile. "Did I wake you?"

Zoe knelt beside the sofa and took Eva's hand. "No, I just woke up and you were gone."

"I couldn't sleep."

"So I see." Zoe took the cat out of Eva's arms to make a little room for herself. After she joined Eva on the sofa, the other woman leaned into Zoe's embrace and let out a heavy sigh. "Want to tell me what happened yesterday?" Zoe asked.

"I can't." Eva swallowed thickly.

Zoe's heart clenched at the sight of the unshed tears swimming in Eva's eyes. "Did someone hurt you?" she asked.

Eva shook her head. "No," she rasped. "Not...not yesterday."

"Evy, I love you and I can't stand to watch you hurt so much. Please tell me."

"Would you still love me if I had died back in Greece?" Eva asked, her voice a bare whisper.

"Did you have that nightmare again?" Zoe asked. "I will love you till I die," she said. "You know that." Back in Greece, she had thought about life without Eva and pondered that very question when Eva was lying in the American medical tent hospital back in Larissa, recovering from her wounds. Zoe had lost her family and many of her friends, and the idea of losing Eva made her feel physically ill.

Instead of answering her question, Eva asked one of her own. "What if I told you that I didn't want to be with you?"

Zoe blinked in the semi-gloom and wondered what was going on in Eva's mind. "I don't...if you told me that, it would shatter me into a thousand pieces," she answered honestly. "Evy, you're scaring me. What's the matter? Talk to me!"

Eva took a deep breath. "Do you remember I told you about Greta Strauss?"

Zoe nodded. "Greta was the first woman you fell in love with."

"She told me she didn't want to be with me anymore," Eva continued. "Came right out and told me, like our love was nothing to her."

"Then this Greta person was the biggest idiot on the planet," Zoe replied, fierce in her partner's defense. "I wouldn't give you up no matter what."

Eva smiled for the first time since Zoe had found her on the bed a few hours ago. "What if you were going to marry some man?"

"I would probably say that I had rocks in my head." Zoe stopped talking when she realized that Eva's question about dying in Greece and Greta's abandonment in Germany were connected. She cleared her throat. "Were you thinking of Greta? It's not your fault, love. It's not your fault she was killed."

"She's not dead," Eva whispered. "She walked into my office yesterday."

Zoe was stunned. It was obvious that Eva was shell-shocked as well. Zoe did not know how she would react if she were in that position — not that she had a former girlfriend or boyfriend from her past. Eva was her first lover and her last. There would be no others as far as Zoe was concerned. Nevertheless, she could empathize with Eva's feelings.

"Wow," Zoe said when she had found her voice again. It was not a surprise that Eva was so unsettled. She now understood why Eva had had the nightmare. Even though she had never met the woman, she disliked Greta Strauss intensely for what she was putting Eva through.

"You know Zoe, as she walked into the office, I was about to introduce myself," Eva went on. "I froze. I stood there like I had been punched. What's that cricketing term Earl uses all the time?"

"Hit for a six."

"Yes, I was hit for a six. I didn't know what to do. She hadn't been sent to a concentration camp. Reinhardt lied to me. She had gone to her uncle's place in Hamburg..." Eva stopped. After clearing her throat, she continued, "I was thinking of how I was going to tell you, and I couldn't stop crying. I love you, Zoe. I love you so much! You own my heart, my body, and my soul, and I don't think I could ever go on without you."

"I'm not going anywhere, love. I'm staying put," Zoe replied, brushing away Eva's tears with the flat of her hand. "I made a promise to you on the ship that I would love you and care for you. I vowed before God that you are my partner for life."

"Partners for life," Eva whispered. "I never told you; on *Kristallnacht* Greta told me we couldn't be together anymore because she was going to get married."

"I'm confused. She was going to get married?"

"Yes." Eva sniffed back her tears. "She said that I shouldn't have thought it was forever."

"What was forever?"

Eva glanced at Zoe and sighed. "My love for her. Her love for me."

What a callous, cold-hearted bitch, Zoe thought to herself. Aloud, she said, "Greta was right, you know."

"She was?"

"Yes." Zoe smiled and held Eva's hands. "She made a horrible mistake letting you go, but I'm glad she was an idiot, because you belong to me now. I would never do that. She must be so stupid. I want to spend the rest of my life waking up to you, loving you, and being there for you." Zoe tangled her fingers in Eva's hair, brought her head down, and kissed her passionately. They parted and gazed into each other's eyes. Eva returned Zoe's kiss and held her tighter.

"I wasn't expecting it, Zoe, for her to speak to me that way. I thought we would be together, and then after that night, everything changed. And not for the better," Eva said. "After all that time, after so much has happened, Greta was the last person I expected to come through the office door. It was just...it was as if someone had hit me."

"I'll bet she was surprised, too."

"I'm not sure. I was so shocked that I don't even remember what I said to her," Eva admitted. "Last time I saw her, I was so upset she was leaving me, and then we burned down the synagogue and I got scared."

"Is that why you left your friends and went home?" Zoe's question was one she had wanted to ask ever since she had found out about Eva's part on that fateful night.

"No, it made me sick to see the rabbi being beaten," Eva replied quietly. "I did nothing to stop Reinhardt. Greta was urging him on and I couldn't believe what was happening. We were so wrong, Zoe. So wrong!"

"You were essentially my age," Zoe said, brushing a lock of Eva's hair out of her eyes.

"But you're smarter than me, Zoe. You have a backbone," Eva said and looked away, her shame apparent.

Zoe sighed. She had often wondered where the root of Eva's insecurities lay and thought that the cruelties she had endured in Austria at the hands of her uncle were the cause but not necessarily the beginning. Now she knew — it had started with that Greta woman and gone downhill from there. Zoe was not surprised that Eva's confidence in herself had taken such a mauling.

She gently turned Eva's face towards her and whispered, "You didn't go through a war and have your family killed and see your friends die. You were innocent. You didn't know anything about life other than going to school and being in the Hitler Youth. You were brainwashed into believing that the Jews weren't human."

"Don't try and excuse my inaction, Zoe—"

"I'm not trying to, Evy. I'm just telling you what happened. If you didn't have a backbone, you would have participated in urging Reinhardt to kill that rabbi, just like Greta was doing. You have a heart. Greta didn't."

"She promised that she was going to whisk me away and we would live in the mountains," Eva ruefully said. "Back then, I believed what she told me."

"What else did she promise you?"

Eva wiped her wet face with a handkerchief. "She promised to love me forever. I wanted so desperately to hear that and I believed it. Oh, how I believed!"

"Evy, why did this upset you so much? I know having her show up like that without any warning was a bombshell, but why did it hurt you so much?"

Eva sat still for a moment before she answered, "I thought I was responsible for her death. For years I thought it was my fault. That's been pressing on me for a long time, Zoe."

"Oh." Zoe finally understood. "Isn't it time to let go of the guilt?" she asked. "Evy, you've been through enough without carrying that with you."

"I know," Eva responded and fell silent.

"What is it that scares you, Evy?"

Eva gazed into Zoe's eyes for a such a long time, Zoe thought she may never answer that question. Eva finally spoke up but her voice sounded strained, she finally revealed her fear. "I fear that you will stop loving me."

Zoe wanted to slap herself. It was Eva's biggest fear; she had known that but having Eva say the words made it all the more frightening. Not only had Greta turned Eva's world upside down but Eva's biggest fear was exposed. Zoe could see the unshed tears that threatened to spill but Eva held back. "Do you remember what I said to you back in Larissa, in the Church?" Zoe asked knowing Eva wouldn't forget that night. It was the night Eva kissed her and the world came into focus for the first time in years.

Eva nodded and a tiny smile appeared making her eyes crinkle. "You're not alone."

"That's right and you've never been alone since then, so I'm not about to let you go now."

"I know, love, but..."

Zoe inwardly groaned. She should have seen this coming; Eva told her what Greta promised her and then cruelly had taken her heart and crushed it. Zoe took Eva's hands and held them tightly. "I want you to listen to me. You've had this fear that I'm going to leave you since Egypt..."

"Larissa," Eva admitted.

"You have to let go of this fear, Evy. I'm not leaving. I told you that I'm not, but you seem to want to hang on to it like a life preserver."

"I don't want to hang on to it."

"Yes you do. You see if in the future I decide to leave, you can say to yourself that you always knew it would happen. That you don't deserve to be happy. That you don't deserve to be loved."

Zoe watched Eva's face closely. She knew what she said was exactly what Eva was feeling and thinking, and it was confirmed when Eva gazed down at her hands; it was confirmation that Zoe was right. Zoe gently tipped Eva's chin up and gazed into her eyes. "I will never leave you. I will never hurt you. I swear to God that I will never ever let you go unless you want to go."

"I will never leave you," Eva replied hoarsely, her voice heavy with emotion.

"I will never leave you either, so we are stuck with each other," Zoe said and leaned in for a kiss. They parted and smiled at each other before Zoe voiced her opinion on Eva's former lover. "I don't like this Greta woman."

"You've never met her."

"I don't need to meet her, I know she's a bitch," Zoe replied vehemently.

"At the spa, I wondered if this was God's punishment for me. I thought it was my fault Greta was sent to a concentration camp and murdered. I was a bad person and this was my punishment."

Zoe swallowed hard and tried to control the rage building inside. Rage — not against Eva, but rage against those who had taken an innocent teenager and tried to destroy her soul. "The spa" was Eva's euphemistic way of referring to the horror of the town of Aiden, where her father had sent her to be with his brother, Dr. Dieter Muller. After Eva was beaten by her stepfather, it was the place she was taken to heal. It also was supposed to have rehabilitated Eva, cured her "deviancy", and changed a fundamental part of who she was, or so her tormentors had thought.

Eva seldom talked about her time in Aiden. It was obviously too painful to discuss and, yet, little bits of information would come out when they talked, giving Zoe an idea of the horrendous, inhuman treatment meted out to a teenage girl whose only crime had been to love another woman.

"It was not God's punishment," Zoe stated flatly, her words made bitter by the knowledge she possessed.

"At the time I thought that it was, Zoe. That He was punishing me for being a lesbian," Eva's voice broke. "I thought that if I hadn't fallen in love with Greta, she would still be alive. That's what has haunted me all this time."

"How can a God of love make you suffer, Evy? He wouldn't. It wasn't God that caused your pain," Zoe tried to reason. She knew Eva understood the truth in her heart, but she was now dealing with the guilt and pain of an eighteen-year-old and not the mind of a twenty-seven-year-old.

"There was a priest who would come to me every so often." Eva shut her eyes and swallowed. "Sometimes he would be so kind and try to help me."

"And other times?" Zoe asked, although she had a feeling that she already knew what Eva was going to say.

"He would tell me I was going to burn in hell." Eva shook her head. "I told him once I wasn't going to hell, because I was already there and it couldn't be any worse."

Zoe let her own tears silently spill down her face, glad she was partially concealed by the darkness. "What did he say to that?" she asked when she thought her voice would not betray the gut-wrenching ache that had started to sear through her body in sympathy for the monstrous treatment her partner had endured in the past.

"He told me that it was worse, and if I wanted to survive, I would tell them what they wanted to hear." Eva let out a ragged breath. "He saved my life."

Zoe blinked, surprised. "How?"

"I gave them what they wanted," Eva replied. "I showed them that their experiment worked."

Zoe took Eva into her arms and held her. They sat in silence for a long time. "You did the right thing," Zoe finally concluded.

"I know," Eva replied. "It led me to you."

Zoe smiled. "And I thank God for you."

"Life is a circle," Eva said softly.

"And it started with Greta?"

"No. It started when Greta wanted me to be at the Youth rally instead of at home."

"*Kristallnacht*," Zoe said, getting the connection. "Why did you go?"

"I gave my word." The smile vanished, and Eva answered the question in a tired, resigned tone. "I also hoped to persuade her not to get married. I loved her that much. I would have done anything for her. If I hadn't gone..."

"You would be dead," Zoe finished her lover's sentence. "Evy, you wouldn't have been able to stop them from killing your mother. They were a frenzied mob."

"Zoe, I find it hard to believe they would mistake my mother for a Jewess."

"Maybe Reinhardt was correct in that your stepfather ordered her dead. But after we know that he lied about Greta, is there anything we can believe? Why do you think the mob wouldn't have made a mistake with your mother?"

"She wore a big gold cross around her neck; she never took it off," Eva replied, scrubbing at her red-rimmed eyes with the back of her hand. "I just can't..."

"Evy, please stop beating yourself up over something you can't change," Zoe pleaded, knowing that it would take more than words to alter Eva's thinking. Nevertheless, she had to try. "You have to stop hurting yourself."

"I'm not—"

"Yes, you are. You are letting those bastards hurt you again," Zoe answered. She gentled her tone when Eva flinched. "Muller is gone; he's in Nuremburg and will rot in hell soon. Your uncle will get his turn. I can't bear to see you in pain. Greta is not dead, like you've thought all this time, but your mother is gone. None of what happened in the past was your fault."

"I know, Zoe, and I try not to think about the past, but seeing Greta today just caught me so off guard."

"What did she want?"

"I think she wants to resume our relationship."

"In her dreams," Zoe snorted. "You're mine."

"She wants to have dinner and talk."

"Okay," Zoe said, trying to recall everything that she had to do later in the day. "When is she coming for dinner?"

"I can't remember," Eva replied a little sheepishly. "I was so stunned, all I could do was agree to invite her to dinner."

"Is she coming back to the office?"

"Yes," Eva nodded. "I think I made an appointment for her."

"Well, I'm going to come over to your office in the afternoon. Do you want me to do that?"

"Yes," Eva answered eagerly.

"Well, that's settled then," Zoe declared, giving Eva a kiss. "You think a warm bath would be nice?"

Eva nodded.

Zoe got off Eva's lap and helped her partner up. Putting her arms around Eva and hugging the taller woman, she said, "I'm sorry I wasn't here yesterday when you came home. Together, we will work this out." Unbuttoning Eva's sleep-wrinkled shirt, Zoe let it drop to the floor, then put her arms around the slender waist and looked up into the woman's tired face. "Greta is a stupid bitch for giving you up, but her loss is my gain," Zoe said smiling, and led Eva into the bathroom to give her some much-needed comfort and care.

Chapter Twenty-Three

David Harrison was a happy man. His meeting with his boss at the Immigration Department had gone very well. He was given a commendation for the capture of Muller and Rhimes, which he had been asked to pass on to Friedrich Jacobs as well. In addition, two more suspected war criminals had been arrested. The last few months had proven to be quite fruitful for the federal agent and his partner.

David entered his office carrying additional files on new German immigrants which he needed to cross-check with the wanted list. As he put down the files, he got smacked in the face by a crumpled ball of paper.

"Good aim, Freddy. I think the bin is over there," he said and pointed to the empty wastebasket near the desk. Around the wicker container were a dozen crumpled balls of paper. "Oh no, you're not attempting yet another love letter are you?"

"Shut up," Friedrich muttered, going back to his writing.

"Wouldn't it be quicker to just tell the girl?"

"I can't," Friedrich replied, his frustration clear.

David sighed and sat down in the chair opposite his friend's desk. "Mate, this is one time I can't help you. Just tell her you love her."

"What if she doesn't love me back?"

"Oh, bloody hell," David said beneath his breath as he shook his head. "Do you think she's interested in you?" he asked aloud.

"Uh, yes."

"Where is the problem?"

"Unlike certain people, who shall remain nameless, I am trying to find a woman to marry and have a family with. And I think I have."

"Yeah? I don't see the problem, Freddy."

"For life."

"Sounds like a death sentence." David snickered. He stopped when he saw the chagrined expression on Friedrich's face. "Sorry, mate. Elena is a nice girl."

"I know." Friedrich crumpled another sheet of paper and threw it. It landed next to the other discarded balls on the floor near the bin.

"Here." David placed a list and a stack of files in front of Friedrich. "This should take your mind off love letters for a while."

"What's that?"

"The latest immigration list. The boss man wants us to cross-check them with the wanted list."

Friedrich rolled his eyes. "As if they would put their real names down!"

"You know some of them are that stupid. Pete found three last week. Same first name, surname, and age. No wonder they lost the war. You take half, and I'll take half. We can go through them to see which boofhead used his real name."

Friedrich looked at the long list of names and sighed. "Then what?" he asked.

David grinned. "Then, Freddy, we get to see happy snapshots. Just imagine thousands of photographs just waiting for us to examine."

Friedrich made a face, but took the first sheet with the names on it and began to read down the list, pausing now and then to make a check mark with his pen.

"I'm going to come by your office after my morning classes, all right?" Zoe put her arms around her partner's waist and glanced up, noting Eva's smile. Zoe also noted that some tiredness remained etched into Eva's face, and she wanted more than anything to make Greta disappear. Her long chat with Eva in the early hours of the morning had exposed Eva's anxiety over Greta's reappearance in her life. Eva had felt better once she was able to express her shock and put things into perspective. They had talked while Zoe helped her with her bath, although Eva could manage quite well on her own. The shared gesture of affection and caring had helped them both to recover a little from the emotionally fraught situation.

"Only if you don't have classes this afternoon," Eva reminded her, and lightly kissed Zoe on the lips.

"I don't have any afternoon classes today," Zoe said. "My last class is at eleven o'clock. Earl has some books he wants to give me. He's working night shift this week so I won't hassle him too much," Zoe said. "I'll be by around noon." Both women turned when they heard Elena call out Zoe's name from the corridor.

"You're going to be late." Eva tapped Zoe on the nose with her forefinger.

"Are you feeling better?"

"Much better," Eva said, her smile widening.

Zoe was not sure if Eva was just trying to reassure her, or if that was indeed how she felt. Eva was very good at shielding her feelings sometimes. Zoe gave Eva a quick kiss before she left the apartment.

"Come on, Zoe!" Elena yelled again. She was checking her watch and looked quite agitated by the time Zoe came bounding down the stairs.

"I'm coming," Zoe muttered as she stopped at the last step. She had an idea and pursed her lips in thought. "Hey, El, one more minute okay?"

Elena scowled at her. "Okay, but hurry, will you? I hate standing up in the bus!"

Zoe went further down the corridor and knocked on the door of Father H and Ally. "Good morning," Zoe greeted Panayiotis when he opened the door. "Can I speak to you for a minute?"

"Absolutely! You want to come in?" the man asked, holding the door open although his body blocked Zoe's view of the interior of the apartment.

"Um, no thank you, Elena is waiting for me. I think Eva needs you this morning."

"She does? Is something wrong?" he asked, frowning.

Zoe grimaced. "Yes."

"Are you two fighting?"

"No! No, I mean...I think it's best if Eva tells you about it."

Panayiotis' frown deepened. "You're acting a little strange, Zoe. Are you sure you don't want to come in?"

"No, it's not me that needs you, it's Eva."

"All right, I'll go and see her now."

"Thanks," Zoe said, giving him a kiss on his cheek, with the newly growing beard present, before running back down the corridor and out of the front door with Elena in tow. He was the perfect person to speak to Eva; she needed her father and his calming influence at such a turbulent time.

Zoe had tried to give her partner some comfort, but Eva's father had helped many people in his role as village priest. Zoe was glad she thought of asking him and was thankful he was here in her life to help Eva.

"What was that about, Pany?" Alberta asked, coming up to stand by her husband as he closed the door.

"I don't know. Zoe was acting very strangely. She said Eva needed me."

"How very odd. What do you think it is?"

Panayiotis shrugged. "I'll find out in a few moments, I guess. Are you going to work with Eva today?"

"No, I need to go to the Circular Quay office today; they are short staffed down there. I'm taking the train." She looked down at her watch. "Actually, I'm going to be late if I don't leave right now."

"Okay," he said. Alberta kissed him, picked up her handbag, and walked out of the apartment. *It is going to be a busy day*, he thought. He went into the bedroom and picked up his Bible. Panayiotis left his apartment, walked up the stairs to Eva's apartment and rapped on her door.

Eva opened the door and smiled, clearly pleased by his unexpected visit. "Good morning, Father. Come in." She ushered him inside. "Want a cup of tea?"

"Oh, I just had one. Eva, you look like you've had a very rough night. Are you all right?"

Eva's smile faltered. "Did Zoe come to you?" she asked.

"My child, if Zoe hadn't come and I had seen your face today, I think I would have guessed there was something wrong," Panayiotis said as he put his arm around her shoulders. Eva melted into his embrace, resting her head on his shoulder. "Want to tell me about what's bothering you and what's got Zoe acting strangely?" he asked. They walked to the sofa and sat down. He took Eva's hands and held them, watching her intently.

"It's a long story, Father, and you have to go to church," Eva said.

Panayiotis smiled. "I love long stories and you are my daughter. In any event, you belong to the congregation and therefore I'm already in church. Why don't you tell me this long story."

Eva sighed. "In 1938, I had a friend...well, she was someone whom I absolutely loved with all my heart."

"A lover," Panayiotis said matter-of-factly, earning a startled smile from his daughter.

"Well...um, yes." Eva was unused to being so open about her sexuality, especially with her father. Panayiotis had a way of just stating the obvious, and he would continue to do so even though it somewhat embarrassed Eva.

"Did this friend have a name?" he asked.

"Greta Strauss."

Panayiotis stroked his beard in thought. "Is this the same Greta Strauss who made Muller so demented?"

"Yes, the same Greta," Eva continued. "Well, she was the first person...uh..."

"You had sex with," Panayiotis furnished, heedless of Eva's blushes.

"Father, do you have to be so blunt?" Eva protested.

"Why? You mean you didn't have sex with her?" Panayiotis asked with mock surprise.

Pink crept over Eva's cheeks and tinged her ears. "Um, yes, I did."

"Well what do you want to call it then?" Panayiotis gave his daughter a gentle poke, causing her to let out an embarrassed giggle.

"Well, she was my first lover," Eva said, not looking him in the eye. "I thought she had died because Reinhardt went to Muller and told him about us."

Panayiotis nodded. He had spent many years as a priest listening to the members of his congregation when they came to him with their troubles, looking to him to help them find a solution. It was not an easy task. Many times in the past, he found himself worrying and lying awake at night, seeking solutions to ease his people's burdens. He thought that if he applied what God said in the Bible, most problems would be overcome. What he could not solve by applying God's word, he prayed about to find other ways of helping. However, this was one of those situations not covered by his usual process; dealing with his daughter's lesbian lover was not covered in the Bible or in his seminary classes.

"You blamed yourself for her death?" Panayiotis asked.

Eva nodded. "For many years I thought that if I hadn't fallen in love with her, she wouldn't have died, mother wouldn't have died and..." Eva stopped and closed her eyes, visibly composing herself.

"Oh, my sweet Eva, you don't know what would have happened if you had chosen not to do the things you did. We all have doubts about our actions. What if I hadn't gone on the train? What if I had escaped, like you and Thanasi wanted me to? What would have happened? I would have been safe, but I wouldn't have met Alberta. My life would have been quite different."

It would have been very *different*, Panayiotis thought to himself. Eva and Zoe had tried to persuade him not to go on the transport train to Thessaloniki because the Greek Resistance was going to bomb the line. They had tried everything they could think of to stop him, but he had gone on the train anyway and the line had been bombed as predicted. He regretted nothing except the grief his supposed death had caused.

Eva nodded, acknowledging his statements and train of thought.

"You cannot blame yourself for something you couldn't control," Panayiotis continued.

"Father, Greta turned up yesterday in my office."

Panayiotis' bushy eyebrows shot up. He had not been expecting *that* revelation. "Well, she's not dead then," he said, glad to hear some good news.

"She said that Reinhardt lied to me. She hadn't died. She had gone to her uncle's place or something like that. My mind was numb, so I only half remember what she said," Eva recalled. "I was so shocked. She wants to pick up where we left off, though she's married now, I think. At the office, she gave her last name as Wagner."

Panayiotis bent a penetrating look at his daughter and asked, "Do you still have feelings for her?"

"Zoe wanted to ask me that question all night but she resisted." Eva smiled sadly. "I know what this is going to do to Zoe."

"Does Zoe have a reason to be worried about Greta turning up?" he asked, watching Eva's face closely for any sign of dissembling.

"No!" Eva pulled away from him and shook her head violently. "Absolutely not."

"Did you tell Zoe that?"

"Not in so many words, but..."

"Hmm." Panayiotis stroked his beard again, happy to feel like he's starting to look like a real priest once more, and grinned inwardly at the annoyed look on his daughter's face, put there by his non-committal hum. "You might want to tell her."

"Father, Zoe knows how much I love her," Eva said.

"So why did you get upset when you met this woman again? Why not surprise or happiness that she was alive?" Panayiotis asked. "What happened when you came home? Did you two talk about it?"

Eva sat in silence for a moment with her head bowed, playing with the ring on her finger. "Zoe wasn't here; she hadn't come home yet and I sat by myself." Eva sighed. "I was upset and I wanted her to be here very badly."

"I would be unsettled if someone whom I thought was dead was standing in front of me," Panayiotis stated. "You and Greta were lovers in the past, so I can understand that her reappearance made for a distressing situation."

"I don't know why it just unsettled me so."

"Do you still have feelings for this woman?"

Eva looked up. "No."

"She was your lover and you don't have feelings for her?" Panayiotis asked, deliberately sounding doubtful. "Not even a little?"

"Father, I don't love Greta," Eva answered. She paused. "I know I don't."

"Is she like Zoe?"

Eva laughed out loud. "No," she said. "They are two very different personalities."

"How so?" he asked and watched the expected transformation take place. Panayiotis always enjoyed asking Eva questions about Zoe because his daughter's face would light up, glowing with love. No matter how she was feeling at the time, the mention of Zoe would lift her spirits. He had recognized that in Larissa and more so for the brief time he had been living close to them in Sydney.

Eva sat back on the sofa and smiled. "Zoe is passionate about what she believes and doesn't give up on anything. She has this unconquerable spirit that I love so much."

Panayiotis was surprised by Eva's declaration. He had been fully expecting Eva to tell him how beautiful Zoe was and how much she loved her because of that physical beauty. "This love you have for Zoe is much more than how beautiful she is?"

Eva nodded. "Zoe is the most beautiful woman I have ever met, but it's not her outer beauty that is so special. It's what's inside of her. She cares deeply and she loves with her whole soul. I love her so much," Eva said quietly, her wonderment clear as she considered the woman who held the prominent place in her heart. "Greta can't have what she wants to get from me."

"What's that?"

"My heart. And my soul. They both belong to Zoe." Eva looked down and sighed. "I loved Greta once, very deeply, but I can't compare it to what I have with Zoe. Greta is not in Zoe's league. Never was and never will be."

Panayiotis was quite moved by Eva's declaration. It was a profession of love that, in all his years as a priest, he had never heard a husband or a wife declare so vehemently for their partner. He knew the two women loved each other, but it was the first time he truly understood how deeply Eva's feelings ran for Zoe. He had no doubt that Zoe felt the same way about Eva. Panayiotis put his arms around his daughter and gave Eva a hug and a kiss on the top of her head. "Thank you for sharing that with me," he said.

Eva smiled. "Talking about Zoe is one of my favorite pastimes."

"So I gather," Panayiotis said. "Now, what are you going to do?"

"Greta wants to have dinner and talk."

"Alone?"

"I don't think she wants to have dinner with me and everyone else in the building," she quipped, getting a mock glare from him.

"Is that what you want?" he asked.

Eva shook her head. "No, I want Zoe to be there with me. Greta is coming over to the office in the afternoon and I've asked Zoe to be there."

"And then she will come here?" he asked. Eva nodded. "Hmm, well I have to meet this Greta." Panayiotis kissed the top of his daughter's dark head a second time. "I'll be here if you want to talk to me."

"Thank you, Father," Eva replied, kissing him on the cheek. "Are you happy?"

"I am more than happy, Eva. I have two beautiful daughters, a wife who loves me, a God I trust. What more could a man ask for? I'm blessed." He gave her a smile and cupped her cheek with his hand. "I want you to be happy, too, and to live your life with love and happiness. You love Zoe and she loves you. Nothing else matters as long as you love each other, okay?"

Eva nodded, not meeting his eyes. "You have always supported me and Zoe being together, even though the church says otherwise."

"Love conquers all things, no matter what we go through," Panayiotis said, tilting her face up to meet his level gaze. "If you have love for each other, there is nothing that can destroy what you have with Zoe."

"I love you, Father," Eva whispered as she hugged him tightly.

"I love you too, Eva. Put your trust in God and He will help you. Take this matter up in prayer with Zoe before you meet Greta for dinner. Ask Him for His guidance. Before I go, would you like to pray with me?"

Eva nodded. He led her to where the crucifix hung on the wall. They knelt down together and prayed to the God who had been so good to them both.

The lift doors opened and Eva exited into the unusually quiet waiting room of the Translating Department. Only three people were seated, waiting for their appointments. Eva was feeling more emotionally settled after her father's chat; talking to Zoe about Greta had also eased the awful tension that had hurt so much.

At the reception desk, Debbie was on the phone, but waved at Eva to get her attention. Eva stood nearby and waited patiently until Debbie had finished the call.

"Good morning, Debbie," Eva said.

"Ah, good morning, Eva. Are you feeling better today?" Debbie asked a little shyly. "I was concerned about you yesterday. You are normally a very retiring person, but yesterday I thought you looked upset. Was it a client who upset you? Is something wrong? Can I help at all?"

"I'm sorry I was rather quiet in the afternoon," Eva apologized, feeling a little self-conscious at being the center of Debbie's focus.

"Hey, we all have bad days. Usually mine strikes before I get my you-know-what and I am quiet as a mouse when I'm not yelling!" They both laughed, and Debbie gave Eva a chocolate bar. "I usually find chocolate makes my day ever so much nicer."

"Chocolate!" Eva gleefully said as she popped a bit of the candy bar in her mouth. "Mmmm."

"Hey, another chocolate lover! I'll remember that in the future. Do your cravings strike when you-know-who turns up?"

Eva was puzzled for a moment and gave Debbie a blank look.

"You know...*that* time of the month," Debbie said, keeping her voice low.

It finally dawned on her what Debbie was talking about. "Ah, no," Eva shook her head. "I love chocolate all the time."

"Well, we should feed that addiction."

"Oh, no. I will put on weight if that happens." Eva patted her flat stomach. "Around lunch time, my apartment mate, Zoe, will be coming around, so when you see her, can you please send her to my office?" she asked.

"Sure thing. Does she have a chocolate addiction, too?"

Eva laughed lightly. "Yes, much more than me, but she never gains weight."

"Lucky girl! I have to meet this Zoe and find out the secret."

"Ask her," Eva replied, knowing Zoe's response would be that fat did not like her and therefore stayed away.

"Will do. I've got Mrs. Susman coming in at nine thirty, and then you have Mr. Lieberman at ten thirty," Debbie read off the appointment book. "You don't have any appointments for the afternoon, but Alexander called in sick and he has two appointments. Would you mind covering for him?"

"No, I don't mind. What language?"

"Italian."

"I'll need to brush up on my Italian then," Eva said. She took another bite of the chocolate bar and waved at Debbie before she went down the corridor to her office.

"Are you sure you don't want these?" Zoe asked.

Earl leaned against the door and nodded. "You can have them," he said, yawning. His night shift at the factory had ended several hours previously and he had patiently waited for Zoe to arrive before he went to bed. "So, how's Eva?" he asked.

"Good," Zoe nodded. She flipped through the pages of some magazines that were stacked on a side-table. "Do you have any more of these?"

"I think so." Earl pushed off the door and left the lounge, closely followed by a curious Zoe. He went into a garage that was filled with boxes. An old rusty car, also filled with boxes, was sitting in the center of the space. Earl leaned across it to get a box labeled "Magazines", disturbing a nearby tarpaulin which fell away to reveal a motorcycle.

The motorcycle's grey paint was dull and faded with a little rust visible wherever the paint had flaked off. The sidecar's leather upholstery was torn in places and the metal covering the sidecar was marred by scratch marks. Zoe raced over, excitement bubbling inside her at the sight of the battered vehicle.

"That's an Indian!" she exclaimed, marveling at the machine.

"You know about motorcycles?" Earl asked incredulously.

Zoe laughed and straddled the seat, taking hold of the handlebars. "Father H had one of these back home in Larissa. We used to work on it all the time!"

Earl leaned against the brick wall of the garage. Zoe's excitement flared higher when he asked, "Do you know how to ride?"

"Do I?" Zoe looked over her shoulder at him. "I used to ride Kaliope all over the place when she wasn't breaking down."

"Kaliope?"

"Yes, that was her name, Father H's motorcycle." Zoe rubbed the fuel tank, frowning at the flaking paint. "We painted Kaliope bright red with yellow stripes. Beautiful. Indians are just great motorbikes."

Earl smiled. "If you say so."

"What are you going to do with it?"

"Well, I've been working on it to sell it."

"No!" Zoe jumped off the bike and stood in front of him, her hands on her hips. "You can't do that!"

"Why not?"

"I want it."

Earl smiled. "Zoe, you can't ride the Indian. It's too big for you."

"No, it's not," Zoe went over to the bike and sat on it again. Her imagination conjured the scene of an open country road, the vibration of the engine humming in her bones, the wind in her hair, and Eva in the sidecar hanging on for dear life. She looked down at the sidecar and smiled. *Maybe I would be in the sidecar instead,* she thought and shook her head. Zoe had loved Kaliope and would often race the motorcycle so fast on the outskirts of the village that Father H would yell for her to slow down. "Can I buy it off you?" she asked Earl.

"Well..." Earl drawled, drawing out Zoe's impatient anticipation deliberately. "You really know how to ride?"

"Absolutely!"

"All right." Earl shrugged. "Do you still want to learn to drive a car?"

"No," Zoe replied, running possessive hands over the bike. "Can I buy her off you?"

"You can have her for nothing," Earl replied. "You really love that old piece of scrap metal, don't you?"

"Yes, I do. Can I have it, really?" Zoe asked, hopping off the bike.

"Really."

Zoe screamed in delight and put her arms around Earl. "I love you!"

Earl laughed and Zoe returned to the Indian. "Can I start her up?" she asked.

"Sure," he said. He seemed surprised when the bike spluttered to life and Zoe revved the engine. The sound was almost unbearably loud in the confines of the garage.

"Can I take her for a ride?" Zoe cried over the noise.

Earl smiled and nodded. "I'm coming with you," he quickly added. Zoe shrugged, knowing that if she got into an accident, Eva would have his head on a platter.

"Sure, hop into the sidecar!" she said, motioning in case he could not hear her. She could barely hear herself.

Earl glanced at the sidecar and then at Zoe for a moment before he squeezed his big frame into the sidecar's peeling leather seat, doubling up his legs until his knees hovered perilously near his chin.

With a loud "Yah!" Zoe maneuvered the bike out of the garage and down the driveway. "Hold on Earl!" she hollered. She revved the engine again and took the motorcycle down the quiet suburban street. Curtains twitched in windows all along the way as neighbors peered out to find the author of the noise, and pedestrians turned their heads to stare at them, but Zoe did not care.

She was flying free at last.

Zoe came out of the elevator and glanced around at what was obviously a waiting room. Several people sat on chairs, talking in different languages. Spotting a desk with a receptionist behind it, Zoe approached the woman.

"May I help you?" the receptionist asked.

"Yes, I'm looking for Eva Haralambos. Is she here?" Zoe asked.

"Do you have an appointment?"

"No, I'm her apartment mate," Zoe replied.

"You must be Zoe Lambros," the receptionist said with a smile.

"Yes. How did you know my name?"

"Eva told me to keep an eye out for you. I'm Debbie, by the way."

"You're Debbie? Pleased to meet you!" Zoe had heard about the hard-working but friendly woman from Eva, who liked her.

"Eva is expecting you," Debbie said. "Just go down the corridor to room number seven."

"Thanks. I'm bringing her some lunch," Zoe stated holding up a small picnic basket.

Debbie hesitated for a moment, then crooked her finger and motioned for Zoe to come closer. Zoe did so, leaning over the desk and setting her basket on the corner. "I don't know you at all but you do live with her so I thought I would ask. Eva has been acting a little...I don't know, she's not her usual self. Is she all right?"

"Yes, Eva is fine. She's a very quiet person normally, so it doesn't take much to cause her to appear quieter. That's why I thought I'd bring a lunch today," Zoe whispered, not wanting to talk about Eva especially about Greta showing up.

"Oh, I was just a little worried about her."

"It's good she has a friend here. I've heard a lot about you from Eva. Is it true you run the ship around here?" Zoe whispered to her as she looked around.

"Shhh! They are not supposed to know that," Debbie replied in a loud whisper. "Also, I think Eva has a lot of friends here..." Debbie stopped to answer the ringing phone. She introduced herself and then cupped the phone receiver with her hand. "Thanks, Zoe. It was a pleasure meeting you."

Zoe waved at the receptionist who was now engrossed on the phone as she gathered up her bag and picnic basket, and walked down the corridor. She found the door to Eva's office and knocked lightly. She smiled when she heard "enter."

"Zoe's Meals at your service," she announced as she put the picnic basket down. Eva was sitting behind a desk and her whole demeanor changed in an instant. Zoe walked around the desk and sat on Eva's lap. "Hello there."

"Hello."

Zoe gazed into Eva's eyes and they told her everything was not all right with her wife. *No wonder Debbie was worried.* Those normally sparkling eyes looked quite haunted; not as much as they were during the early hours of the morning, but there was no mistaking the effect this was having on Eva. "How are you feeling?"

"If I say I was all right, would you believe me?"

"Well," Zoe got comfortable and put her arm around Eva's neck. "If you said that to someone who didn't know you, it might be believable. Since it's me, I'm going to say no." Zoe looked intently into Eva's eyes before leaning in and kissing Eva lightly on the lips.

"That was nice."

"I should kiss you more often."

"I hear it increases your brain power," Eva said quietly before she closed her eyes and let her head rest on Zoe's shoulder. Zoe pulled Eva closer to her and kissed the top of the dark head.

"It's going to be all right, Evy, I know it will."

"I'm tired, Zoe."

Zoe's heart nearly broke by those three words. It wasn't the words but the way her wife's voice sounded. "I know, Evy, but we're going to get over this as well."

Eva lifted her head and gazed at Zoe with a look that did break Zoe's heart. "I don't know how much more of this I can take, Zoe."

"You're right you can't take much more of this, Evy. Back in Berlin you were alone, in Aiden you were alone..." Zoe took Eva's hand and held it tightly. "You're not alone here."

"I know."

"Can I ask you a question?"

"Yes but I think I know what the question is."

"Really?" Zoe smiled. "I didn't know you could read minds."

"Only yours."

"What was I going to ask you?"

"Do you have feelings for her?" Eva replied quietly. She looked up to see Zoe gazing at her expectantly.

"Do you have any feelings for her now? See it's a different question," Zoe gently teased.

"I've never loved her, Zoe. I was in 'heavy like' but it wasn't love. I thought it was love, believed for a long time it was love but it wasn't. I've been thinking about this since I got into work..."

"And you've made yourself sick over it," Zoe concluded. "Eva, this Greta woman is going to go away."

"I don't think so, love. You don't know what kind of trouble she is, Zoe."

Zoe sighed dramatically. "What kind of trouble is this bitch?"

"She knows what she wants and won't stop until she gets it."

"In other words, she has you in her crosshairs and is going to go after you?"

"Something like that," Eva nodded.

"Well she will have some resistance to her master plan and I don't give up on what's mine..." Zoe stopped mid-sentence when Eva bent her head and passionately kissed her, pulling her closer. They parted and smiled at each other. "Oh...mine for sure."

"What's that?" Eva brushed Zoe's errant bangs out of her eyes. "You are wonderful."

"Well, of course I am," Zoe joked, getting a laugh. She reluctantly got up from Eva's lap, picked up the basket and took out two plates and a container. "Okay, Miss Eva, we have: yimesta as I promised, a little feta cheese, some olives, and I squeezed some orange juice for you."

"Did Earl bring you over with this basket of food?"

"Nope. Mabel did." Zoe grinned as she put the food on the desk, knowing she was piquing Eva's curiosity.

As predicted, Eva took the bait. "Who's Mabel?"

"Well..." Zoe took a forkful of stuffed peppers and offered it to Eva, who quickly ate it off the fork. "I went over to Earl's so he could drive me over, but then I saw Mabel and I fell in love with her right then and there."

"You fell in love with her?" Eva's brow rose in question and Zoe had to laugh.

"I have wheels! I saw this old motorcycle with a sidecar in Earl's garage and I fell in love with it. Earl sold it to me for nothing."

"My friend Willy used to have one of those, a very fancy vehicle," Eva reminisced. "What type is it?" she asked.

Zoe's eyes lit up. She was having a great day with the discovery of the motorcycle and racing down the street with Earl in the sidecar. The freedom it gave her made her nearly giddy with delight. "It's a 1912 Indian."

Eva smiled. "I used to ride Willy's Indian motorcycle," she revealed, eliciting a squeal of delight from Zoe.

"Oh, I loved those motorbikes. I remember Kiria Despina's son, Klimi, had one of those. He was a policeman. What color was Willy's Indian?" Zoe asked.

"Bright red. But I didn't know you rode a motorcycle."

"Didn't you ever see the old bike at the back of the church?" Zoe asked and offered Eva bite of stuffed tomatoes. Eva chewed for a moment and shook her head. Zoe continued, "We would work on it forever. It used to break down all the time."

"My father owned a motorcycle?"

Zoe nodded. "He would use it to go to the villages when I wasn't riding it around, giving him nightmares that I would end up crashing and flying off Athena's Bluff."

"Hmm." It was apparent that Eva could not quite picture her father on a motorcycle. After a moment, she shrugged. "Isn't it a bit big for you?" Eva asked, picking up her orange juice and taking a sip while watching Zoe over the rim of the glass.

"Yeah, it is a little, but it's okay. With the sidecar, it's perfect. And of course, with your long legs," Zoe ran her hand up Eva's thigh, "it's even more perfect." She waggled her eyebrows and grinned. "Okay we've had lunch, here comes the dessert."

Eva wasn't sure what that meant, but she helped put the containers back in the basket and was perched on the edge of her desk watching Zoe. Zoe took the basket and set it down. She then went over to Eva and looked up.

"Dessert time," Zoe gently pushed Eva onto the desk until she was sitting on it, Zoe stood in between Eva's long legs. "I'm going to have my way with you."

"Oh..."

"Shh," Zoe whispered and leaned in for the kiss, this one intense, longer, and much more passionate. As she kissed the dark-haired woman, her hands began running over Eva's bare legs and up her thighs. Zoe traced a path with her soft lips across the proud chin, pausing to tease the dimple she loved so well, and finally down along Eva's neck.

Eva drew in a sharp breath and held it as Zoe's fingers were taking a tour of their own under her skirt. She released the breath with an audible exclamation when she felt Zoe's fingers at last press against the sensitive flesh. "Oh Zoe..." Eva moaned.

Zoe resumed her kisses, nipping at the sensitive skin of Eva's neck. The tall woman's hands ran down the length of her wife's back, ending up squeezing the flesh of a firm backside. That move earned a groan from the smaller woman, Zoe feeling her control slipping a bit.

Zoe let one hand slide down to caress a muscular thigh, Eva's legs unconsciously quivered once they felt her lover's fingertips gliding along the skin, goose flesh erupting wherever those fingertips wandered. The taller woman fought unsuccessfully to control the shiver that ran the length of her body.

"Zo," Eva husked out, entwining her fingers in the red hair once again as Zoe captured Eva's mouth and didn't allow her to utter another word.

Neither woman realized the door had opened until they heard a loud cough. A very loud cough.

"Oh!" Debbie stammered. "I...um..."

Zoe looked up into Eva's face and found her wife looking very flushed. She didn't want to turn around, but she had to. Very slowly she turned to find a shocked Debbie standing just inside the office with her hand on the doorknob.

"Oh," Zoe muttered and reluctantly let go of Eva's body. "I should have locked the door," she said in Greek.

"Come in, Debbie." Eva invited the clearly bewildered woman into her office. Eva straightened her shirt and pushed herself off the desk and nearly fell to the floor. Her legs felt quite rubbery from Zoe's dessert, but she quickly sobered up now that she had to face Debbie.

Debbie shut the door and sat down in the visitor's chair closest to her.

"Um...I wanted to tell you that Mrs. Wagner is here." She stared first at Eva, then at Zoe.

Eva sighed. "Zoe isn't just my apartment mate."

"Hmm, I figured that out already," Debbie said a touch acerbically.

"Yes, um..." Eva stammered. "It was good while it lasted," she whispered to Zoe in Greek. In English, she continued, "Zoe and I..."

"Are lovers," Zoe interjected boldly.

Debbie inhaled sharply and let the breath out on a sigh. "You're lesbians?"

"Yes." Eva took Zoe's hand and stared at Debbie defiantly.

"You don't look like deviants to me..." Debbie stopped and tried again, faltering in the face of Zoe's glare. "I mean...um...you know, the priest warns us in church...and I like you...oh, dear. Well, since I made a hash of that...well, it's quite a bombshell, isn't it?" Debbie looked concerned. "Does Earl know about you two?"

Eva nodded. "Earl is one of my best friends, and he does know," she told Debbie, who seemed relieved.

"Oh, good, he is such a nice man," Debbie said.

"He is, and he has a heart of gold," Eva agreed.

"Does that mean he is available?" Debbie asked hopefully.

Zoe bit her lip to stop herself from blurting out that Debbie was not Earl's type, since he preferred men.

"No, he is involved with someone," Eva replied before Zoe could speak.

"Oh, what a shame."

"Debbie, can I ask you not to tell anyone?" Eva asked.

Debbie looked at Eva and Zoe. She appeared to have recovered from her embarrassment at find them kissing. "Tell them about what?" she said, shrugging. "Your apartment mate bringing you lunch? I don't think that's even worth a mention on the grapevine."

"Thank you." Eva smiled.

"Eva, I like you a great deal. Your secret is safe with me." Debbie got up and opened the door. "I wish I had an apartment mate who could cook like you do." She gave Zoe a wink and closed the door.

"Bet she doesn't have one that kisses like you," Zoe quipped. "I like her." She turned to Eva and put her arms around her waist. "So are Mrs. Wagner and Greta the same person?"

"Yes." Eva paled.

"Well then, let's meet this Mrs. Wagner," Zoe said fearlessly. Eva was somewhat in better shape than when Zoe first came in which was exactly what Zoe wanted. Whatever happened, they would tackle this Greta problem together. She put away the picnic basket and took her seat to wait for Greta to arrive.

Chapter Twenty-Four

Once Eva had gone to the reception area to fetch Greta, Zoe sat in the empty office and stared up at the ceiling. She could hear voices coming towards the office and wondered how she was going to handle coming face to face with Eva's first lover. It was not something she had thought would ever happen. Yes, Eva had had a lover before her and she sometimes wondered what type of person Eva would be physically attracted to, but she never expected to meet her.

"I bet she's blonde and has legs that go on forever," Zoe muttered to herself. She reached into her bag and took out her sketchbook, trying to find something useful to do with her hands while she waited.

Zoe glanced towards the door when a tall brunette entered the office. "Hmm, I was wrong," Zoe said under her breath. It was obvious that Greta had totally failed to see her.

Eva entered and met Zoe's gaze, giving her a tiny smile before closing the door. Zoe remained seated. She was quite amazed at how the woman was so absorbed in watching Eva that she had not even bothered to look in Zoe's direction.

"Take a seat." Eva offered the chair next to Zoe to Greta. "Before we continue..."

"Eva, I thought this was going to be a private conversation. I'm sure we don't need your secretary to sit in on this." Greta spared a quick dismissive glance at Zoe and proceeded to take off her gloves.

Zoe could not believe the woman's attitude. While it was true she was not Eva's secretary, she found the lack of notice as well as the arrogance rather annoying to say the least. This Greta woman was not making a good first impression, but Zoe had not wanted to like her. She already disliked Greta for what she had done to Eva so many years ago.

Eva sat behind her desk and looked squarely at Zoe before she turned her attention back to her former lover. "This is Zoe," Eva said by way of an introduction.

Greta did not even glance in Zoe's direction again. When she spoke, her tone was clipped. "Yes, I'm charmed to meet you, Zoe. May we please be left alone? The *Fräulein* and I have personal business to discuss."

"I don't think that's necessary," Eva replied. "I have the information you wanted..."

"Eva, I can get that information from anywhere, but I came to see you. Alone." This was said with a slight inclination of Greta's head towards Zoe. "As I said to you before, we have a great deal to talk about."

Zoe watched the woman closely and decided that not only did she not like her, but she found her incredibly rude and her manner far too aggressive and assumptive. She did not like the way Greta refused to listen to Eva at all; she also did not like the fact that the woman was trying to dominate Eva by insisting that Zoe be sent out. Greta's whole superior attitude irked her no end, and she bit her tongue to keep from speaking, remembering her promise to behave.

"We can talk," Eva insisted.

"I thought we were having dinner together? You gave me your word." Greta showed her teeth in a grin. The predatory expression raised Zoe's hackles.

"If Eva gave you her word, then you are invited to dinner." Zoe had had enough and she finally spoke up, getting the surprised look she anticipated.

"I thought secretaries were supposed to stay quiet and take dictation." Greta looked Zoe over, her gaze moving insultingly slowly. Zoe did not show any sign of offense; instead, she let herself smile, although the expression did not reach her eyes.

Greta scowled and looked back at Eva. "I don't understand."

"Greta, I told you yesterday that I was married."

"Yes, yes, I remember but we won't tell your husband." Greta leaned across the desk and took Eva's hands, much to Zoe's annoyance but she kept quiet just as Eva had asked her to. "I hope Zoe knows how to keep secrets," Greta said.

Eva removed her hands from Greta's grasp and sat back in her chair. "I *am* married, and *Zoe* is my wife," she said.

Greta was stunned for a moment and gaped at Eva. She started to laugh but her hilarity petered out when Eva did not join her. "Are you serious?" she said.

"Very serious." Eva nodded at Zoe who did not need any further encouragement. She put her sketchbook down and joined Eva, standing protectively behind her. Zoe placed a hand on Eva's shoulder and squeezed, lending silent support.

"Well, you did say you wouldn't marry anyone you didn't love," Greta said, still looking at Zoe. "Robbing the cradle, aren't we?" she added.

Eva prevented Zoe from doing anything physical by reaching up and holding the hand on her shoulder tightly, but she sensed that Zoe was about to launch a verbal assault. Eva answered the gibe before Zoe could do more than draw breath. "I don't think I'm robbing the cradle."

"I thought you preferred older women." Greta chuckled; it was not a pleasant sound. "Older...wiser...taller..." Her gaze flickered up and down Zoe's petite figure and she sneered.

Zoe merely smiled. She had heard every kind of short joke at least a million times in her life, and once more was not going let words ruffle her feathers. She knew Greta's methods; she had experienced such rude practices back in Larissa with the occupying Germans.

Greta watched Zoe for a long moment and smiled sweetly.

"You find the fact that I'm shorter than Eva to be amusing?" Zoe asked at last.

"No." Greta stifled a laugh behind her hastily raised hand. "I'm sorry; it's just the shock of seeing my treasure with someone like you. I'm sure you can understand what kind of shock it is."

"Oh, I know what kind of shock it was," Zoe said, nodding. She tried to keep the annoyance out of her voice, not wanting to let the woman sense how much her contemptuous attitude stung. Zoe found it hard to believe that Eva had fallen in love with Greta. The Eva she knew and loved was not the submissive type nor was she overly aggressive, but Greta's pompous personality was overpowering and put her teeth on edge.

"Why don't we start anew? Is the invitation still open for tonight?" Greta asked, clearly making an effort to be as nice as possible under the circumstances.

Eva wrote down the address on a piece of paper and handed it over the desk.

"Excellent." Greta got up from her seat, quickly followed by Eva. Eva walked around the desk and went towards the door. "I'll be seeing you tonight," Greta said.

"You can bring your husband if you like," Zoe quipped, sitting down in Eva's chair. She could not help the trace of resentment in her tone.

Greta looked back. "I don't think he would enjoy the company," she said and turned to Eva. "'*Dass Liebe, die aus Trümmern auferstand, Reicher als einst an Größe ist und Kraft*'!" she said before giving Eva a hug and exiting the office, pulling on her gloves.

"What did she say?" Zoe asked, not knowing enough German to translate.

"'And ruin'd love, when it is built anew, grows fairer than at first, more strong, far greater,'" Eva replied and shook her head. "She was always one to believe she could get anything she wanted."

Zoe got up, moved around the desk, and put her arms around Eva's slim waist. "I'll quote you something now."

Eva smiled down at her. "What would that be?"

"'All's fair in love and war,'" Zoe looked up, grinning. "Mrs. Wagner can quote whoever she was quoting..."

"Shakespeare," Eva said.

"Well, she can quote Shakespeare till hell freezes over; she still won't get what she wants," Zoe said, tightening her hold on Eva until the other woman laughed breathlessly.

"I'm sorry she has to come to our home," Eva said as she held Zoe. "I did promise, but I wasn't in my right mind."

"I know." Zoe nodded. "I'm sure I'll want to use my cricket bat over her head, but I will restrain myself," she added, causing Eva to laugh. Zoe was determined to do everything in her power to prevent Greta from getting to her, but it was not going to be easy. *No, it won't be easy at all.*

After knocking on the door, Earl walked into the office to find Eva tidying up her desk. "Greetings, ma'am, your chauffeur awaits. Are we ready to depart?" Earl put on a very bad posh British accent and doffed his hat.

Eva grinned. "You are crazy, you know that?"

"What gave it away?" Earl said, sitting down on one of the visitors' chairs.

Eva looked up from clearing her desk and putting books away. "Hey, thank you for giving me a ride home."

"No worries. When Zoe asks, Earl obeys," Earl joked. "So are you enjoying it? The new job, I mean."

"Yes; there's a word I can't translate into English..." Eva scrunched up her face as she thought of the German word for what she had in mind. "What's the word for when something is just so right?"

"Bonzer," Earl replied, smirking.

"Bonzer? Okay, it's bonzer." Eva grinned more broadly. "By the way, Debbie knows about me and Zoe."

"Oh, boy. That doesn't sound too bonzer to me. How?"

Eva felt her face flush. "Zoe was...um...giving me dessert."

"Giving you dessert?"

"Zoe brought me lunch, and then she also supplied the dessert." Eva smiled, thinking about how much she enjoyed the dessert.

"Zoe supplied..." Earl stopped mid-sentence when he finally clued into what Eva was saying. "Oh!"

"It was a really nice dessert."

Earl shook his head. "I don't want to know."

"Speaking of my dessert loving wife, before we go home can we stop at a florist? I want to buy her some flowers."

"Flowers? Sure," Earl said. "That kid just amazes me sometimes. Okay, so Debbie knows. Is she going to cause trouble?"

"I hope she doesn't or else I'm in trouble. But, no, she said she wasn't going to. After only knowing her a few days, I think I can trust her."

"That's good. Otherwise, it could get a little on the tricky side."

Earl got up and opened the door for Eva, then closed it behind them. They said good night to Debbie, who was speaking on the telephone, and were about to leave when Earl stopped and turned back to Debbie's desk. "Thanks," he whispered in Debbie's ear, and gave her a kiss on the cheek. Debbie's mouth dropped open and she stared as Earl walked over to the elevator with Eva.

In the car on the way home, conversation between the two friends lulled and Eva's thoughts turned to Greta. She was not as nervous as she had thought she was going to be. She was sure it had a lot to do with talking to Zoe both in the morning and over lunch, as well as talking to her father, which had put everything in its proper light. The slight personality duel between Greta and Zoe at the office also did not upset her unduly. She knew

Greta had pulled back from totally insulting Zoe. Zoe had also pulled back and Eva knew that, when the time was right, Zoe could match any verbal assault Greta threw her way. Eva felt a little thrill at knowing two women wanted her, but that excitement was quickly tempered by the fact she also knew Greta only wanted her to prove a point.

When Greta wanted something, Greta would get it no matter who or what was in the way. What her former lover did not know was that it was Zoe who stood in the way. Zoe was tenacious and willing to withstand a great deal to protect what she considered hers. Zoe's strength under pressure was something Eva admired. A great many people underestimated Zoe's abilities and that was how her partner liked it. She wanted people to underestimate her; it gave her an advantage. Eva herself had made that same mistake in Larissa when her father had suggested she take Zoe as her maid in order to help with the identity papers that Eva was forging. Eva had soon learned that Zoe was not a timid village girl but a courageous woman. Greta was going to learn the same lesson if she continued this course. Eva smiled to herself and smelled the flowers she had bought.

The car halted at a stoplight. Eva turned to Earl, who had a faraway look on his face. "So do I thank you or kill you?" Eva asked.

"Huh?" Earl turned to her, obviously unsure of what Eva was talking about.

"Mabel," Eva stated tersely with a mock scowl.

"Not my fault!" Earl said, throwing up his hands in a gesture of surrender that seemed only partially insincere.

"No, it never is. You encouraged her, Earl."

"I didn't, honest. After she came over, we were just talking."

"And how did she find the bike?"

"The tarp fell off. Really it did. I had even forgotten it was there! She took one look at the old rust bucket and she fell in love!" Earl laughed. "When she trains those green eyes on you, you're gone. You know it!"

Eva laughed. "I can't resist her, but I thought you might be able to!" She wagged her finger at the unrepentant man.

Earl shook his head. "No, unfortunately Zoe is my kryptonite as well," he quipped, and the two friends laughed.

"She's been *my* kryptonite, but I think she's the best thing to happen to me, too," Eva said, remembering those cold mornings when she got off her shift at the biscuit factory. Some days when she could not bear one more racist comment or another moment of Jack Stalk's crude behavior, she would find Zoe outside, waiting patiently for her. It had brightened her down-trodden spirits to see her partner there. Even though she had not asked Zoe to come, the young woman had done it anyway, as a gesture of love. The few times Zoe was not outside the factory, Zoe was out of bed and waiting on the balcony when Eva returned to their apartment — a beacon of love welcoming her home.

The light turned green. Earl accelerated the car, saying, "Back to your gorgeous and totally insane wife. Tell me how am I supposed to stop Cyclone Zoe when her eyes go super bright, when she sees the bike, and she's jumping up and down?"

"Kissing her helps," Eva said, chuckling. She knew firsthand that once an exuberant Zoe had made up her mind about something, no one could stop her, no matter what methods one employed.

"Well, that might work for you, but not for me. She fell in love with..."

"Mabel."

"Mabel," Earl scoffed. "What kind of name is that for a bike?"

"She calls our icebox Percy, so I guess Mabel is better than that," Eva said.

Earl turned into Eva's street and stopped at the curb near the building. Mabel was parked outside, and Panayiotis was working on her, removing the old paint and rust. Earl turned to Eva.

"She just fell in love with it," he said. "She wouldn't even give me the time to take the bike out and brush off the cobwebs. She started it up and was off down the street. I was just able to get into the sidecar before she left." Earl stopped speaking and looked pensive, his gaze traveling to Panayiotis. "You're lucky, my friend, very lucky to have a father who understands about your relationship with Zoe. And he's a priest, to boot!"

Eva followed Earl's gaze and smiled when she saw her father scraping paint off the Indian. "Some luck had to come my way, Wiggy; it was just a matter of time. It will happen for you. Have faith."

"Yeah, right, hell will freeze over and pigs will fly."

"Um," Eva hesitated. "I have something to tell you. I forgot with all the excitement over the last few days."

"What did you want to tell me?"

"Mrs. Jenkins knows about me and Zoe," Eva said, earning a shocked look from her friend. "She was hiding when we were acting more than sisterly in the laundry."

"Not a smart thing to do," Earl said. "Is she going to evict you?"

"No, she said she has a sister who is a *homosexual*," Eva mimicked the landlady's over-emphasis on the word. "She said we are sick, but we can get better."

"Another one," Earl rolled his eyes. "Let me guess, she wants to save you?"

"Yes, I guess that's her mission from God or something. She said that I should tell you I'm a lesbian. You would understand and help me see the error of what I was doing."

Earl's smile broadened. "So, Eva, you're a lesbian? I'm shocked. A pretty girl like you and you don't like boys? It's not your fault. It's that short redhead's fault. I knew she was trouble the minute I saw her."

Eva shook her head. "You are very right. It's her fault. She looks at me and I melt," she said, chuckling. "I'm addicted to that woman."

"No cure, eh?"

Eva glanced at him. "Absolutely no cure, in my experience," she said. *The doctors at the spa tried, and no matter the "therapy", it didn't work.* Aloud she said, "So how's the cure of *your* sickness going?"

"Well, I've got major bad luck with my love life," Earl said.

"I told you Joey was only after one thing," Eva quipped. She started to laugh when Earl waggled his eyebrows and gave her a lusty leer. "You bring the beer," Eva told him, "and we can drown your sorrows. But you're still in the dog house about Mabel."

"Awww, come on. Not my fault. Have you ever tried saying 'no' to Zoe?" he asked.

Eva shook her head, knowing he was fully aware that she could not, and would not, say no to Zoe, no matter what. "No," she said. "Why would I deny her anything?"

"So tell me, Miss Eva," Earl teased, "in that case how could I?"

"You're not married to her," Eva replied, her lips quirking up in a cheeky grin.

"This is true, but if I was married to her, I would give her everything she wanted. You have a gold mine there, mate."

Eva had to speak around the sudden lump in her throat. Zoe was such a gift to her. Just thinking about her partner made Eva's heart swell with affection. "I know."

"So is it going to be a tough decision to choose between Greta and Zoe?" Earl quipped, resuming their earlier conversation when they first got into the car, although he watched Eva closely.

Eva was not unaware of his searching gaze. "No contest," she said, shrugging.

"Wish I could be there; I love a good fight." Earl smiled. Eva gave him a peck on the cheek and got out of the vehicle.

She turned and walked towards her father, who was still working on the old motorcycle. "So, you've met Mabel," she said to her father as he industriously scraped the remaining paint from the Indian's body.

"I used to have a bike like this," Panayiotis enthused. "Brings back memories!"

"I used to ride one with Willy," Eva said and gazed at the motorcycle.

"Willy?"

"Old childhood friend," Eva explained. "Zoe told me you rode one."

"Oh, yes. Just after the Great War ended, I would zip around Larissa in one. Had the sidecar too." He smiled, his teeth flashing white against the color of his beard. "I would take your mother up to Thessaloniki in it and we would spend the day together. Ah, the memories!"

"You took *Mutti* in that thing?" Eva's eyebrows jumped on her forehead in surprise.

Panayiotis just laughed. "Oh yes, she was a skinny thing; but she was tall, like you, so she scraped her knees a bit when she got in."

Eva shook her head and patted her father on the back. "I see Zoe has won you over."

"Won me over? Eva, this is a classic motorcycle! Wait until I clean off the rust and repaint it. Zoe wanted it hot pink and black, but I've convinced her to restore it to its original color."

"Thanks for that much, Father." Eva shook her head and left him to tinker with the machine. She walked up the flight of stairs and entered their apartment to find the table had been set beautifully, with two candles on either side. "Zoe, I'm home!" she called.

"In here." Zoe's voice came from the bedroom. She came out wearing a black jacket, white shirt, and black pants. The outfit made Zoe look more mature than her nineteen years; it was the combination of the jacket with the pants and the severe color, since Zoe normally wore bright colors and rarely wore black.

Eva handed her the bouquet of flowers. "Thank you for today. You made it so special for me," Eva told her as she tilted Zoe's face up and kissed her.

Zoe smiled. "Do you like what I'm wearing?"

"You look beautiful."

Zoe blushed pink at the heartfelt compliment. "Thank you for the flowers; they are beautiful," Zoe said, wrapping her arms around Eva's neck and bringing her down for another quick kiss.

"You didn't have to get dressed up, love," Eva told her.

"I know," she said as Eva held her. "I wanted to."

Eva looked down at the woman in her arms and shook her head. "I'd better go and have a bath," she said.

"Need any help?" Zoe volunteered a little too quickly.

"I would love the help, but I don't think I could have a bath and be ready on time if you 'helped' me," Eva said, playfully chucking Zoe under the chin.

"It was worth a shot," Zoe muttered as Eva went into the bathroom.

Chapter Twenty-Five

Zoe swayed to the music in the apartment as she closed the door and went into the bedroom where Eva was finishing getting dressed. She sat on the bed and picked up the cat who was sitting on Eva's discarded shirt. "Cat hair on everything," she murmured and brushed Eva's shirt with her free hand. Louder, she said, "Father H asked if you could go down. Something about an immigration letter he needs to send with you tomorrow?"

"Yes, he told me this morning," Eva replied. "I won't be much longer."

Zoe admired the woman's tall, lithe figure. Eva was wearing a beige shirt with black pants. Zoe's admiration became more open, and Eva smiled.

"You like?"

"I love!" Zoe scampered off the bed and put her arms around Eva. "Mine," she said.

After a quick kiss, they parted. Eva opened the door to leave, startling Elena, who stood there with her hand raised, about to knock. Eva grinned and moved aside to let the younger woman in before she left, waving goodbye to Zoe.

"Hi, El, what's up?" Zoe asked, seeing her friend's perplexed face.

"I got a letter from Friedrich."

"Isn't that supposed to be a good thing?"

"Um, yeah, I guess. I mean, I don't know," Elena stammered. Zoe took the offered letter and looked at both sides. The paper was completely blank.

"Unless Friedrich is playing at being a spy and writing in invisible ink, I can't see anything," Zoe said.

"Me either."

"Do you think he put the wrong piece of paper in the envelope?"

Elena nodded. "Well, he said he was going to send me a letter. I'm not sure if this is what he had in mind. I guess I'll have to ask him." Elena shrugged. "So are you ready for tonight?"

"Well, yeah, sort of. How often do you have dinner with someone who wants to steal your wife?"

"I don't think that would ever happen to me," Elena quipped.

"Well I hope I don't make a complete ass of myself."

"Don't worry, you'll be fine," Elena reassured her.

"So are *you* ready for tonight?" Zoe asked.

"Well, yeah, sort of," Elena replied, mimicking Zoe and causing the two friends to laugh.

Greta felt nervous, which was highly unusual. She did not know why she was nervous; after all, this was just Eva she was going to see, and she was determined to get her back. She held the piece of paper with the address in her hand and looked up at the building, unimpressed with the area. She wondered what had possessed Major Muller to move into a middle class suburb. He had been a man of refined tastes, as she recalled, but perhaps the German defeat had altered his fortunes. It occurred to her that she had not asked Eva about her father. *Well, I had other matters on my mind.*

She had paid the taxicab to stop further up the street so she could compose herself, checking her hair and makeup in her compact mirror and straightening her long white skirt. Greta knew that the strawberry-colored shirt she wore flattered her coloring. She looked forward to preening under Eva's admiration. The taxi drove away, and she saw the driver staring at her in the rear view mirror.

"Probably a Jew," she muttered in German, trying to recall if his facial features had reflected any sign of that degenerate heritage. Dismissing the thought, she fingered her pendant — set with two diamonds and a ruby — and smiled at the memory of the gift Eva had given her all those years ago. Greta knew Eva had worked very hard to earn the money to buy her that gift. She was a passionate young woman and Greta was very proud of herself for having won her over.

Greta sighed. She swallowed the lump in her throat that particular memory had caused. Greta regretted the day she chose to marry John over continuing her love affair with Eva, and she was determined to make amends.

She checked her appearance in the compact mirror again. She then checked her watch and realized she was a half-hour early. She wondered if she should wait, but decided against it. She had waited too many years already. Walking purposefully to the building, Greta looked at her paper to be sure of the correct apartment number. It only took a few moments for her to negotiate the flight of stairs and find Eva's apartment.

The door was opened by a young woman of obviously ethnic origin — more obvious than the taxi driver she had speculated about. Greta blinked. She had not been expecting a Jew to open the door. Maybe she had the wrong apartment number after all. "I'm sorry. I was looking for the Muller residence," Greta said.

The young Jewess seemed surprised to see Greta. Her mouth opened, then her gaze shifted to the pin that Greta wore. It was normally hidden under the lapel of her coat, but Greta had flashed the emblem to let the girl know whom she was dealing with.

The Jewess' mouth closed so tightly that there was a white line around her lips.

"Did you hear me, little girl?" Greta asked impatiently. *Was the woman retarded? The Führer had rightly sent such people to the camps.*

"Hey, El, who's at the door?" Another young girl's voice drifted from somewhere inside the apartment.

"I'm looking for the Muller residence. Do you know where it is?" Greta said very slowly in German. She noticed the numbers tattooed on the woman's inner arm and she scowled. A concentration camp inmate, of course, just as she had speculated. She should have noticed that right away.

A young woman Greta recognized as Zoe came to the door holding a cat. Her smile seemed forced. Zoe turned to the other girl. "Hey, El, are you okay?" she asked, letting the cat jump down to the floor.

"El" nodded and walked past Greta without saying a word. Greta resisted the urge to slap the stupid girl for her rudeness. Zoe's attention had been momentarily distracted by the Jewess; now she turned to Greta. Her smile became even more strained. "Please, come on in."

Greta nodded; at least this young woman was trying to be a gracious hostess. Just as Greta passed her, the cat arched its back and hissed violently at Greta. "*Verdammt noch mal,* a cat!" She grimaced. "Does that thing have to be here?"

"Yes," Zoe said firmly. She picked the cat up; its tail lashed back and forth, a telling sign of its continued agitation. "She's part of our family."

"Vile creature," Greta sniffed.

"She usually is a very friendly kitty, aren't you, Ourania?" Zoe cooed at the kitty.

"Tsk." Greta clucked her tongue in disgust and glanced around the place. She was surprised to find the apartment small and quite plain. She could not see anything of Eva in the décor. No one would guess that an intelligent, educated woman lived there. "Is Eva here?" Greta asked as she walked over to the bookcase and began to peruse the titles.

Zoe seemed about to answer when her gaze fell upon the swastika pin that was still exposed beneath Greta's flipped-over coat lapel. She swallowed and stared a moment before saying in accented German, "Eva has gone down to see her father. Excuse me for a moment." Zoe, not waiting for a reply, exited the apartment.

Greta turned away from the bookcase and stood in the lounge while Zoe went to take care of her errand. She took the opportunity to look at the photographs which lined the mantle over the fireplace. A large drawing of Eva reading a book hung over the mantelpiece. "Hmm, not bad," Greta murmured to herself. The cat stared warily at her.

"You are such a horrible creature," she said. "Oh look, now I'm talking to a cat! Dear God, how low can I get?" Greta shook her head in disbelief. The apartment was devoid of any character. "Oh. Eva you do need rescuing from this place," Greta said aloud.

Zoe rushed to Elena's apartment. The front door was ajar. Zoe went inside and found Elena huddled on the floor, her back to the sofa, crying softly.

"Hey." Zoe held her friend and rubbed her back in soothing circles as Elena wept.

"I'm sorry, Zoe. I lost it."

"It's okay. I understand." Zoe comforted Elena as best she could. She was angry that their visitor had been arrogant enough to where the swastika pin to their apartment, and that Greta had chosen to wear such an emblem in a country that abhorred Nazis. She found she disliked the woman even more, although she marveled at her brazenness. There could be dire consequences for Greta if the wrong person saw that pin. Arrest, certainly, or better yet, the treatment she had heard was given to women who collaborated with the enemy — a public tarring and feathering. Zoe bared her teeth in a savage grin.

"I'm okay. Go see to your guest. She probably thinks we are both retarded," Elena said, sniffing wetly.

Zoe wiped the tears away from her friend's face. "No. She can sit there and stew, for all I care."

"Um, hello," Friedrich said through the open door, clearly uncertain if he should enter.

Zoe grinned. "You have perfect timing, Friedrich." She ushered the man inside and told him why Elena was upset. After the explanation, Zoe went to Elena and gave her a peck on the cheek. "I'll talk to you tomorrow, okay?"

"Okay," Elena said, and held out her hand to Friedrich.

Zoe closed the door to Elena's apartment and exhaled in a long, heartfelt sigh. She decided to walk down to her father-in-law's apartment and let Eva know that Greta had arrived early. Turning, she was greeted by the welcome sight of Eva coming up the stairs. She hurried over and hugged her.

"Hey, I don't mind a hug, but what's the matter?" Eva asked, stroking Zoe's cheek.

"Greta's arrived."

"Oh. Where is she?"

"In the apartment."

"Then why are you out here?"

Zoe sighed. "Elena opened the door and that vile woman had the nerve to wear a swastika pin to our apartment. Elena saw it and lost it. She was crying, Evy."

Eva was aghast. "I can't understand what would possess Greta to wear such a thing, especially in an Allied country. Is Elena all right?"

"Yeah. Friedrich is with her, now."

"I'm sorry, Zoe. I didn't..."

Zoe looked up into her partner's distressed face. "How could you know, love? It was just a little on the shocking side."

"Are *you* okay?" Eva asked, holding her. It was apparent that she did not care that they were in the corridor, in public view of anyone who might come by; her main concern was Zoe.

Zoe nodded. "I was a little shaken, but it's all right."

"I'll ask her to remove the pin. I don't want to see that symbol in our home."

Zoe smiled, feeling a little better already "You know something, Miss Eva? I think I love you. I'll try and behave myself."

Eva responded with a gentle kiss. "Ready?"

Zoe nodded. Eva took Zoe's hand and opened the door to their apartment, following her inside.

Greta stood up as the door opened and Eva walked through, hand-in-hand with her opposition. That gesture of affectionate support made no difference. Greta was determined to show Eva that she would win her heart back, no matter who stood in her way. This time she was not going to give Eva up as foolishly as she had done before.

"Eva!" Greta greeted Eva enthusiastically, crossing to kiss her on the cheek.

Zoe scowled. Eva tightly squeezed the hand she was holding. "Welcome to our home, Greta," Eva said.

"Thank you, my dear," Greta replied, scowling at Zoe. "I must say, Eva, your hired help leaves a lot to be desired."

Eva frowned and looked down at Zoe. "Hired help?"

"Your Jewish maid bolted out from here and left me here sitting like a dolt! All I did was ask her if this was where you lived—"

"Greta, I think we need to tell you—"

"Dearest, you don't have to apologize for the hired help." Greta talked right over Eva, which had the desired effect of irritating Zoe; her face took on a pugnacious expression. Greta continued talking, forcing herself to hide the smirk that was threatening to emerge.

"Greta!" Eva raised her voice, surprising both Greta and Zoe. It was Zoe's turn to smirk, and she did not bother to hide it at all. "Sit down — please," Eva continued in a more reasonable tone. "Zoe doesn't understand German all that well so can we speak English?"

Greta sat down immediately. "Of course," she said in English, giving Zoe an assessing look from beneath her lashes.

She had not been expecting the once shy and reserved Eva to raise her voice in what was almost a reprimand. This was something new. She could see a change in her former lover that she found rather unsettling. Before anyone could say anything further, there was a knock on the door. Zoe rolled her eyes and went to answer it. A bearded man stood there in grey overalls — *some kind of laborer*, Greta assumed.

"Oh...I'm sorry I interrupted you," he apologized, his gaze lingering on Greta.

"No, Father, perfect timing," Eva said. She took the man by his hand and tugged him inside. Zoe continued to smirk in the background. Greta drew herself up, biting her lip in confusion. "Greta, this is my father, Panayiotis Haralambos. Father, this is Greta Wagner," Eva said.

Greta understood the words but they made no real sense to her.

Panayiotis smiled and offered his hand. "I'm pleased to meet you, Miss Wagner."

Greta looked at the extended hand with distaste and a considerable amount of bewilderment. She looked between Eva and the man. "I thought Hans Muller was your father," she said, wanting an explanation for this bizarre turn of events.

"I think I'll leave you ladies in peace. Good evening, Miss Wagner. It was a pleasure to meet you," Panayiotis said, handing the keys of the motorcycle to Zoe, who grimaced at him as he left.

"I don't understand, chipmunk, what's going on?" Greta asked Eva.

A slight blush spread across Eva's cheeks and she glanced down as if shyly pleased. "I haven't heard that in many years."

"What does that mean?" Zoe asked.

Greta laughed and decided to toy with Zoe. "We were enjoying each other's company when a chipmunk raced down the tree and terrified my Eva."

Zoe apparently found the story amusing until the word "my" came out of Greta's mouth. The gauntlet had been thrown and they both knew it. Greta watched for Zoe's reaction, letting an enigmatic smile cross her face as she waited for the inevitable explosion. She had only met Zoe once, but that had been enough to inform her of the other woman's combustible temperament.

"Oh, Miss Eva, you have some tales to tell me later," Zoe joked at last, causing Greta to frown. She had not expected Zoe to back away from the barb.

Greta switched gears. "So Eva, where did you pick Zoe up from?" she asked, making her tone as insinuating and nasty as possible. She would make this girl — this *child* — look like a fool. The veil would be lifted from Eva's eyes.

Her plan backfired, she realized a moment later. Greta recognized the closed-off expression on Eva's face and realized that the situation was not as straightforward as she would have liked it to be.

"She didn't pick me up from anywhere. I picked her up," Zoe responded, eliciting a raised eyebrow from Eva. "Well, I did. It was my master plan to get close, then whammo!" Zoe said, sliding onto Eva's lap and planting a kiss on her mouth. "Got what I wanted, thank you very much."

"Yes, indeed," Greta said dryly, pursing her lips at the unwelcome reminder of Eva's romantic attachment to Zoe. "This get-together has been full of surprises."

"What did you think the evening would be like?" Zoe asked. She moved off Eva's lap and brought a chair over, sitting down next to her.

"I thought I would spend some time getting reacquainted with my lover," Greta said with a smile, deliberately needling.

"Ex-lover," Zoe growled.

Greta made a decision to see how far she could push the child and where it would lead. She needed to salvage the situation. She was the adult here, *and* Eva's lover, and if someone was going to be with Eva, it would be her. What the thick-headed Zoe apparently did not know was that she was declaring war and the victor won the ultimate prize — the right to claim Eva as her own. Greta's smile widened; it was not a pleasant expression. "Afraid of the competition?" she asked, trying to irk Zoe further.

"I'm sorry. I wasn't under the impression I was in competition for my wife's affections," Zoe replied, then smiled sweetly at her.

Greta smiled, refusing to be antagonized. This was only the opening salvo of the battle. "Of course not." She turned to Eva, who had a bemused look on her face. "So, Eva, tell me what is going on, apart from you being married to Chloe."

"My name is Zoe."

"Pardon my mistake. I'm sorry, Zoe. I used to have a maid called Chloe," Greta apologized insincerely. "How long have you been together?"

"Over three years," Eva replied. "We met in Greece when my stepfather was stationed in Larissa."

"Hans Muller is your *stepfather*?"

Eva nodded. "I found out the night my mother died," she added quietly.

"Oh, I'm so sorry, Eva. I had no idea. When did that happen?"

"The day you told me you were getting married." The quiet tone turned iron-hard.

"Oh," Greta said. She realized that she would have to work hard to earn back Eva's trust. The woman before her was not a naïve teenager anymore; that was quite evident. "So you were in Greece during the war?"

"Yes. Larissa."

"Never heard of it," Greta replied. She had traveled to Greece before the war. She was an amateur archaeologist and, of course, had had to visit Athens and the Acropolis. "Was it a little backwater village?"

Zoe kept her mouth shut, but her eyes gleamed with suppressed annoyance.

"Actually it was quite an important village. It's situated between Athens and Thessaloniki, so it was a vital supply line during the war. That's where I found out my father was the local priest," Eva said with studied casualness.

Greta's eyes went round in shock. "Your father is a *priest*?"

"He found love and now he's married to Alberta and they live downstairs," Zoe added quite seriously.

"This is getting stranger by the moment. So how did you two get together?"

"I wanted to kill her," Zoe said with a grin. Greta gave her a horrified look. "Didn't work out," Zoe continued.

"Why? I mean I can see it didn't, but what happened?" Despite her dislike of Zoe, Greta found herself genuinely interested.

"I thought she was a cold-blooded Nazi and I was a member of the Greek Resistance," Zoe explained, her expression and tone betraying nothing except the utmost sincerity.

Unconsciously, Greta's fingers strayed to the swastika pin she wore. "Oh."

"I found out she wasn't a cold-blooded Nazi, which was really good since I fell for her," Zoe said, glowing when she glanced at Eva. "So where were you during the war?"

Greta gave the young woman a predatory smile. "I was a cold-blooded Nazi," she said. "At least you had the good sense to get involved with a Christian," Greta added to Eva, noticing the gold crucifix around Zoe's neck.

The smile pasted on Zoe's face remained intact. "Well, it's a good thing you weren't in Larissa instead of Eva."

"You would have killed me?" Greta asked, not believing that this child would have been able to do anything of the sort.

"In a heartbeat," Zoe replied, just as seriously as before.

"I think we are all getting a little too serious," Eva interjected, putting her arm around Zoe's waist. "Why don't we have dinner?"

The three women left the lounge and went to the dining table. Zoe went into the kitchen and brought out the meal, while Eva uncorked a bottle of wine and poured Greta a glass. Greta watched the two women over the rim of her wine glass. The evening had not started as she had hoped. Eva was a more confident woman than she remembered, and then there was Zoe to contend with. She needed a new plan to deal with Eva's very possessive lover, and with the changed Eva herself.

Chapter Twenty-Six

Greta sipped her wine and continued to study the two women. They were seated side by side. Occasionally Zoe would push her vegetables to the side and Eva would push them back. She found this behavior very odd. "I take it you don't like vegetables?" Greta asked Zoe with a hint of a smirk.

"No, not much," Zoe said. She looked sideways at Eva, who was grinning.

Greta turned to Eva. "So tell me, Eva, whatever happened to your stepfather?"

"He was arrested for war crimes," Eva replied evenly, wiping her mouth with her napkin.

"What? Why?"

"Because he killed innocent people," Zoe said.

Greta snorted. "Were they really innocent? No one gets killed because they are innocent."

"Is that right?" Zoe asked, cocking her head to one side.

"Of course. People choose which side to support. Only babies are innocent. They don't have the ability to decide. You wanted to kill Germans, didn't you?"

"Yes, but—"

"Of course you did. That's why Resistance groups sprang up like mushrooms. No one is an innocent during war. Do you consider Churchill a war hero?" Greta asked, illustrating her point.

"Not in the true sense of the word. He rallied his people, and that makes him a hero to them," Zoe replied, sipping her tea.

"I think Churchill is a war criminal rather than a hero. He killed those innocents you referred to in Dresden. I was there, and I saw with my own eyes the death and destruction. Where is he now? He is venerated and worshipped by the masses because of his heroic deeds. The victor writes the history of the war, Zoe."

"It's amazing how you are so blind," Zoe said in an astonished tone. "Hitler bombed London, also killing non-combatants, women and children. Is he a hero to you?"

"Zoe, you don't understand. Adolph Hitler was the best thing to happen to Germany. He had the solution to Germany's problems."

"The solution was to start a war that killed millions," Zoe muttered.

"Hitler didn't kill millions. That's nonsense," Greta scoffed. "He gave Germany its pride back, gave men their jobs back. He was what Germany needed."

"What about the millions of Jews who died?" Eva asked, taking Greta by surprise. She was certainly not expecting her former lover to care anything about Jews.

"Millions? Hardly. Concentration camps were set up so the undesirables could work for the Fatherland. They were treated humanely," Greta said, wondering if Eva really believed the lying propaganda published by the Jews and their allies.

Zoe seemed dumbfounded. "Do you honestly believe that no Jews died in the concentration camps? No Poles or communists, no retarded people...none?"

"Oh, don't be silly, of course they died. The old and sick die every day, and it happened in the camps too."

"So millions of old and sick people died a natural death in those camps?" Eva asked.

"Millions? Where did you get that figure from?"

"It's the truth, Greta. It's a little hard for millions to just disappear."

"Oh, please." Greta flapped a dismissive hand. "Eva, you of all people should be aware of your history. As I said, the victor writes the history books. The facts have little to do with what is written, and in years to come, the truth of what happened in those camps will come to light."

"It already has. The Nazis murdered millions of people, innocent people, because of their race or just because they wanted to." Zoe was now angry. "Haven't you been following the Nuremburg Trials? Don't you read the newspapers? The list of former guards and commandants who've been executed for war crimes is as long as your arm."

Greta snorted and shook her head. "Zoe, you are so ill-informed. There is no proof that millions of Jews died. The trials are lies and the victors set the agenda. Please, this is ridiculous. How can any intelligent person swallow such obvious falsities?"

All the talk about millions dying made Greta wonder if both of these women knew the reality of what was going on. They were being fed lies. She would have to do something about that, if only to free Eva from the messy situation she had put herself into.

Eva put a calming hand on Zoe's shoulder "Why don't we get some dessert?" she whispered to Zoe. Zoe nodded then got up and went into the kitchen. Eva watched her go then turned back to Greta who had an ugly smirk on her face.

"Greta, I don't think spouting Nazi propaganda at Zoe is going to make this dinner enjoyable for either of us," Eva said, angry with the woman who was clearly amused by Zoe's upset. "Zoe's entire family was killed during the war. I'm not sure what you are trying to do, but stop it. Excuse me for a moment." Eva walked into the kitchen.

Zoe stood near the sink with her head bowed. A cheesecake sat forgotten on the counter. Eva put her arms around her partner and kissed the top of her head, knowing Zoe was frustrated at Greta's resolute delusions.

"Are you okay?" Eva asked.

Zoe shook her head. "She can't believe those lies, can she?" Zoe looked up, tears tracking down her face. Eva brushed them away and kissed her. "I'm sorry, Evy, I tried," Zoe said.

"I know you did, love. Thank you for making the effort."

"Go back outside. It's rude to keep our guest waiting," Zoe said, wiping away her remaining tears with the heel of her hand.

Eva held her tighter. "Not until I know you're okay."

"I'm okay. Can we talk about this later?"

Eva nodded and gave Zoe another quick kiss before taking the cheesecake out with her. She placed it on the table. Eva gave Greta a warning look while Zoe brought out the plates.

"I'm sorry I upset you, Zoe," Greta said as Zoe sat down. She sounded sincere. "I think I should have listened to what my father said many years ago. He told me never to discuss politics or religion at the dinner table."

"Good advice," Zoe mumbled, still appearing somewhat subdued.

"I see some beautiful prints," Greta said, motioning to the framed photographs sitting on the mantelpiece. "Are they yours?" Greta asked Eva, making a clear effort to steer the conversation in another direction.

"Yes, it's a relaxing hobby," Eva said, grinning at Zoe. "But Zoe is a very talented artist."

"So, you did that piece?" Greta asked, pointing at the portrait of Eva reading a book.

Zoe replied, "Yes. Eva sat patiently for me."

"That's a very nice portrait."

"Thank you," Zoe said quietly. "Drawing relaxes me."

"Hmm, much like music. I do enjoy a good opera," Greta said, smiling pleasantly. "Oh, Eva, do you remember when we went and saw *Romeo and Juliet*?"

"Remember it? I think I won't ever forget it!" Eva laughed. She turned to Zoe, who was looking at her, puzzled. "It was so bad, half the audience left and the other half stayed to see how bad it would get!" Eva said to her.

"Which half were you in?" Zoe asked.

"We stayed!" Eva said. "Romeo couldn't remember his lines, Juliet fell off her balcony, and it got worse!"

Greta continued laughing. Involuntary tears threatened to destroy her carefully made-up face; she cautiously wiped them away with the point of her napkin. "We had to stay. We spent good money for it!"

"Oh, God, don't remind me!" Eva said.

"Do you like opera, Zoe?" Greta asked once the hilarity had died down. From her expression and the tone of her voice, it was obvious that she was being condescending again.

"I love opera," Zoe said with a smile. "My favorite is *L'Africaine*."

"*You* love opera?" Greta sounded incredulous.

Zoe grinned. "One of the many things I've come to love through Eva."

"I didn't think you would be an opera fan, Zoe. I thought you would be more interested in be-bop and jazz," Greta said.

"I didn't think I would be an opera fan either, but life has a way of just giving you what you least expect," Zoe quipped. "Who would have thought I would have fallen in love with the most beautiful woman on the planet? You can't buck Fate, so I married her."

Eva gave her a smirk, but did not want to interrupt her. She knew that when Zoe got passionate about a topic, she put everything into it. She was not going to remind Zoe that it was Eva who had done the proposing.

"Eva introduced me to opera and I loved it," Zoe concluded.

Eva smiled. "I love jazz."

"*You*? You hated jazz!" Greta said.

"I didn't hear the right people performing it," Eva replied. She squeezed Zoe's hand under the table. "Zoe introduced me to it and, of course, to Greek music."

"That's amazing. You used to think jazz was for peasants, and Greek music? You had no regard for it. Now I am amazed."

"My tastes have changed," Eva said, glancing at Zoe.

Greta looked at her watch and sighed. "I would love to continue chatting with you, but John — my husband — is waiting for me. Thank you for the wonderful dinner. Perhaps we can do this again some time."

They walked to the door. Zoe handed Greta her coat.

"I think maybe next time we avoid politics at dinner," Greta suggested. She ruffled Zoe's hair as though the other woman was a young child. Zoe brushed her hair back into place and her annoyed scowl at being treated in such a patronizing manner became a weak smile when Eva bent a warning glance at her.

"It was good seeing you again, Eva." Greta kissed Eva on the cheek. "I've missed you."

They said their goodbyes and Eva closed the door, then turned.

"Come here," she said. Zoe fell into her embrace. "I love you and thank you," Eva whispered to her partner, getting a hug in return.

Zoe exhaled. She was sitting on the sofa with Eva. The verbal altercation with Greta had worn her out. She had prepared herself for an onslaught, but the German woman was just the most frustrating person she had ever met.

"I don't like her," Zoe mumbled. "I thought she was a bitch before I met her, and now I think she's the devil's own spawn."

"I know, love."

"Was she always like this?"

Eva sighed. "Yes. She was very determined when she wanted something."

"Or someone?"

"Or someone." Eva took Zoe's hand and held it. "Back then, she wasn't so aggravating. I think the war has changed us all."

"How did you change?"

"Oh, gosh," Eva sighed. "I was so naïve. I trusted what people told me nearly all the time. I had dreams of traveling and being a photographer." She smiled sadly. "I believed Greta when she told me that we would travel the world together. Do you remember when you asked me about my dreams for after the war?"

"Yes," Zoe replied. They had been sitting in Eva's office in Larissa. Zoe, believing Eva was a Nazi, was surprised to find the woman was working for the Resistance. Zoe had wondered then what motivated Eva. "I remember," she said.

"I had no dreams. I doubted very much whether I was going to see the end of the war. If I did survive the war, who would want me?" Eva replied. She sounded devoid of any self-pity; it was clear that she voiced what she had truly believed. "And other stuff."

"Other stuff?"

Eva sighed again. "I sometimes wonder what kind of mother I would have made. Muller wanted me to marry and have perfect Aryan babies." Eva stopped speaking, and Zoe understood she was unwilling to talk about what might have been had they not met and fallen in love with one another.

Zoe looked up and met Eva's eyes, wishing she could take away the shadows there. "You deserve better." She reached up, caressing Eva's cheek.

Eva smiled, leaned into Zoe, and kissed her. "I didn't know what I was going to do. Then you walked into my life and, for the first time in five years, I had some hope. I wasn't sure how we would survive, but I had someone to walk with me."

"I've always said I have good timing," Zoe said, trying to lighten the mood.

"You have excellent timing. Do you know when I noticed you?"

"You noticed me?"

"I tend to notice people that hit me with stones, and I definitely noticed you," Eva teased.

Zoe laughed. Back in Larissa, she had been outside Eva's house watching the Major Muller getting out of a large black car when she heard footsteps, noticing Eva walking by with two guards protecting her. To this day, Zoe was not sure what had possessed her, but she had scooped up a rock and had thrown it at Eva, hitting the taller woman in the back of the head.

"I didn't hurt you, did I?" Zoe asked solicitously, patting Eva on the arm.

"Well, you did a bit," Eva replied with a mock pout.

Zoe grinned and kissed the arm she was patting. "You didn't let your shadows come after me; I've always wondered about that."

"No. Want to know why?"

"You felt sorry for the peasant?" Zoe asked, snuggling closer.

"Don't be silly," Eva gently scolded. "You are not a peasant. I don't want you talking that way."

"Well, I am, Evy," Zoe persisted.

"I don't like you to describe yourself that way; you're a gifted artist and my best friend."

Zoe smiled. "All right, I'm not a peasant. Now tell me when you noticed me!"

"I was in Father's office when you came into the church the day he asked you about coming to work for me. He had already told me you were feisty and that you wouldn't be too friendly. I didn't see you, but I heard you. I fully expected you to turn him down. Later, when you threw that rock and I saw you, I finally realized who you were."

"Turn down the opportunity of working for the most gorgeous woman in Larissa? No way I was turning that down," Zoe joked. "I'm a friendly sort of girl! Hey, I didn't speak that day, so how did you know it was me?"

"Yeah, very friendly; I had the bruise to prove it!" Eva said with a smile, clutching her head as though the blow still pained her. "How many feisty, unfriendly, green-eyed young women were there in Larissa?"

"I don't know. Did you go in search of green-eyed, feisty women?"

"Didn't have to, you came to me." Eva shook her head and joined in Zoe's giggles over their first meeting.

"Come on, I think I've had enough of memory lane. Let's go to bed."

"What about the washing up?"

"Tomorrow," Eva said. Taking Zoe's hand and pulling her off the sofa, she turned off the lights, and the two of them went into the bedroom.

Brushing away her tears, Elena put her head on Friedrich's shoulder. She felt so safe in his arms. At first, Friedrich had been shocked by her story about her time in the concentration camp, but the more she told him, the more apparent it became that he loved her and was determined to be supportive.

"I love you, Elena, and I'll be here for you," Friedrich said. "Um...I'm not good with words, but..."

Elena hugged him. "Words are overrated."

Friedrich grinned and kissed the top of her head. "You know, you are the first woman who has ever said that to me."

"How many have you talked to?" Elena teased.

"I've had dates before. David would set them up. Great disasters," he said, shaking his head. "I spent so much time trying to write that letter to you. You did get that, didn't you?"

Elena smiled. "I got a letter from you, but the paper inside the envelope was blank."

Friedrich seemed genuinely confused. "Huh? I'm sure I put that letter in the right envelope...oh, God!"

"What?"

"Oh, God! El, I'm going to die tomorrow."

"Why? Where did you send it?"

"I made some notes for David. Oh, damn, I must have left the letter I wrote you on his desk!"

Elena could not help herself. She began to laugh hysterically. Finally, her mirth subsided and she hiccupped. "I'm sorry; that's so funny," she gasped.

"Are you sure the letter you got didn't have anything on it?" Friedrich asked, a hopeful expression on his face.

She hated to dash that hope, but she had to be honest. "Quite sure. It was a blank piece of paper."

"David might not go back to the office tonight, and I'll have time to get it off his desk," Friedrich said as he looked at his watch. "I have to get going, Elena. It's late."

Elena hesitated for a moment, then put her arms around his neck and pulled him down and kissed him. "I think I love you, Friedrich."

Friedrich blinked. "You do?" he asked. "Really?"

"Yes, really."

"Oh," Friedrich said quietly and then after a moment, his face creased into a huge smile. "I don't think we need the letter," he said. "I love you too, Elena."

Eva stirred and opened sleepy eyes. Looking at the clock, she saw it was only two o'clock in the morning. She grimaced, put her head down on her pillow again and then she heard the banging. It stopped but started up again after a moment. Zoe was fast asleep, cuddled up next to her. Not wanting to wake her, Eva slid out of bed quietly, put on her robe and slippers, and turned on the lights in the lounge.

She looked through the spy hole in the door and did not see anyone, but she knew someone was out there. The banging started again, then stopped, and she went back into the spare bedroom. Feeling apprehensive, she picked up Zoe's cricket bat, hefted it in a two-handed grip, and made a couple of practice swings.

After a quick look to see that Zoe was still asleep, she closed the door to the bedroom and walked purposefully to the front door. Taking a deep breath, she swung the door open, raising the bat at the same time, ready to strike. Eva was shocked to see a crumpled figure lying on the floor against the wall on the opposite side of the hallway, his long legs stuck out and taking up a good portion of the corridor.

"Matey! Evvaaaaaa! Come and hava...uh...drink!" Earl said, giving her a sloppy grin.

Eva laid the cricket bat aside. Earl was sprawled on the carpet, and he seemed very drunk. Three empty bottles rolled on the floor and she realized where the banging had come from. Earl had been throwing the bottles against the door and then thumping on the door with his feet. She went to Earl and knelt beside him. Eva could smell the reek of alcohol and grimaced. "You're as drunk as a skunk."

"I stink, huh?"

"Yeah, you do. Come on, let's get you inside." Eva tried to get him up, but Earl was unmovable.

"Nah, leave me here. I like it here," Earl slurred, curling up on the carpet as if he planned to sleep there all night.

Eva tried to move him, but she felt a twinge of pain in her back and had to stop her efforts before she hurt herself. "That was smart, Eva," she said beneath her breath. She straightened and put her hands on her aching back. "You are a big boy, Earl. I need some help." Eva walked into the apartment intending to elicit Zoe's help in getting the big man inside. She did not want to wake her father because of the old injury that still troubled his knee. Eva did not want to wake her Zoe, either, but she could not shift Earl alone and she knew that if she tried again, she was sure to aggravate her troublesome back even more.

Kneeling beside the bed, Eva caressed Zoe's cheek. "Zoe," she whispered.

"Huh?" Zoe grunted. Instead of waking, she snuggled closer to the pillow.

"Zoe, I need you, love."

"What for?" Zoe mumbled.

"Earl is outside. He's drunk, and we need to move him out of the hallway," Eva said as she shook the other woman a little.

Sleepy green eyes opened and Zoe frowned. "Did you say Earl is drunk?"

Eva nodded. "Come on, help me get him in."

"You didn't try to move him, did you?" Zoe asked, obviously struggling to shake off sleepiness. When Eva did not reply, Zoe focused on her, now seeming much more aware. "Eva! He weighs a ton. Did you hurt yourself?"

"I wasn't thinking. I tried to move him and felt a twinge. I think I'm going to need your loving touch later," Eva said.

Zoe shook her head. "What am I going to do with you? Does it hurt?"

"I felt just a tiny twinge. I promise that you can do anything you want later," Eva said as she gave Zoe a conciliatory kiss. "Come on, let's get the drunk inside."

"Remind me about the 'anything you want' bit after," Zoe said. She rolled out of bed, put on her robe and slippers, and gave Eva a slap on the behind as she followed her into the corridor. Zoe's eyes widened when she saw Earl asleep on the carpet.

"Hey, Wiggy, wake up." Zoe shook the big man, who stirred and opened his eyes. He smiled blearily up at Zoe. "Matey, Zo...Zo...Zoeee."

Zoe wrinkled her nose and waved a hand in front of her face. "Phew, you stink, old boy."

"That's what Eeevvvaaa said."

"Come on, let's get inside."

"Why?"

"Because I said so!" Zoe growled in his ear. "Move it!"

"Okay," Earl replied. He managed to get to his feet, although it was clear that his legs were rubbery and refused to cooperate without an effort. Eva's eyebrows rose.

Zoe took one of Earl's arms and Eva took the other. Between them, the two women had a hard time trying to keep the teetering man upright. "Let me take most of his weight," Zoe said, tugging on Earl to get him to lean against her. "You okay, love?" she asked as they struggled inside.

"Yes, but I'm going to suggest he lose some weight," Eva grumbled.

Earl belched. His breath smelled like a brewery. "Hey, Evaaaa...you look...um...nice."

Eva rolled her eyes. With Zoe's help, she managed to maneuver Earl to the sofa, where he collapsed and promptly fell asleep. She and Zoe stood watching him for a few moments. Eva felt a certain tenderness towards the man. With his face relaxed in sleep, the years fell away and he looked like a boy, reminding Eva once again of Willy.

"Leave him here. I doubt we can get him in to the spare bed," Eva said. She went into the spare bedroom, picked up a blanket, put it over Earl, and tucked it in around him.

"What do you think happened?" Zoe asked, a slight frown marring her smooth forehead.

"I don't know. I guess we'll find out in the morning," Eva said wryly.

"Poor Wiggy," Zoe responded, kneeling by the sofa. She gave him a kiss on the cheek. "I'll go to his place tomorrow and get him a change of clothing." Zoe stood and turned to Eva, scowling. "Now, missy, what were you thinking, trying to move him by yourself?"

"I wasn't thinking, Zoe."

"You can say that again. How are you feeling?"

Eva rubbed her back. The pain had subsided somewhat. "I think it was just a twinge. I'm okay."

"You sure?"

"Yep. Come on, let's go to bed," Eva suggested, taking Zoe's hand.

Zoe put her arm around Eva's waist. "When are you going to learn to take care of yourself?"

"Zoe, don't yell at me. It's okay. At the time all I could think about was the fact that I didn't want to wake you."

Zoe looked at her, frowning. "I think we need to have a chat later."

"Yes, *Mutti*," Eva said meekly as she followed the other woman to bed.

The clatter of the early morning milk truck and the sound of a distant train's whistle echoing in the semi-darkness woke Eva. She stirred, trying to remember what day it was. A moment's thought and she realized that it was Friday. Eva really wanted to stay in bed and just snuggle up to Zoe, but she knew she had to get up and see to Earl, who would be nursing a hangover, before heading into work. She reluctantly let go of Zoe, put her robe on and quietly closed the bedroom door behind her.

Earl was sitting up on the sofa, clutching his head in both hands. Eva watched him for a moment before going over to sit down on the sofa next to him. She put an arm over his broad shoulders and asked, "Do you want something for the headache?"

"Yeah, a gun," he grunted.

"Don't have one of those, but I have some aspirin."

"Did I cause a fuss last night?"

"You don't remember?"

Earl's bloodshot eyes rolled in her direction and he winced. "Uh...no."

"Well, you went dancing down the corridor stark naked." Eva grinned, but stopped teasing her friend when she saw the look of total horror on his face. "Nah, I'm kidding."

"Oh God, Eva, you have one twisted sense of humor." Eva went into the kitchen and poured him a glass of water, then got a couple of the painkillers and handed them to him.

"You make quite a drunk, Earl. You threw some empty bottles against the door to get our attention, then you fell asleep in the corridor."

"Argh. So how did I end up here on the sofa?"

"Well..."

"Oh damn, Eva, don't tell me you tried to move me? Please don't tell me that, because if you did I'm going to get an earful from Zoe..."

"Yes, I did."

"I'm a dead man," he moaned.

"Nah, I got a tongue lashing instead."

"Are you okay?"

"From Zoe? My behind is a little scorched, but my back is fine. Now, why did you get drunk?"

"Oh, I went out drinking with my mates and I went back to my place with Joey and we drank some more."

"That's not so bad, except for the drinking."

"It gets worse."

"What did you do?"

"I had a visitor." Earl grimaced. "My sister came over and was very surprised to see me and Joey. You know, together. It was pretty obvious what we were doing."

Eva blinked. "Oh."

"She disowned me." Earl sighed. "Told me never to speak to her again until I've come to my senses. Joey got upset and left so I decided to drown my sorrows again and went back to the pub."

"Oh, no."

"Oh, yes." Earl nodded. "I can't remember what happened after that."

"Why didn't you come here straight away?"

"You had your visitor. How would it have looked if I'd turned up?"

"It would have saved us from Greta's racist taunts and kept Zoe from getting upset."

"That sounds like it was a fun night."

"Oh yeah, the event of the year," Eva deadpanned.

The bedroom door opened and a very sleepy Zoe shuffled out, dressed only in a short nightshirt and underpants. Her eyes were still half-closed as she stumbled towards the bathroom, clearly oblivious to the presence of their guest.

Eva grinned as Earl covered his eyes with a hastily upraised hand. "Zoe," she called.

Zoe glanced up, focused on Earl and yelped. She yanked the hem of her nightshirt down over her panties, ran back into the bedroom and slammed the door shut.

"Not so loud, Stretch!" Earl yelled after her, then seemed to regret his outburst. "Ow." He held his head. "Somebody stop that earthquake," he muttered. After a long moment, he scrubbed a hand through his hair and said, "Hey, she's cute when she's just woken up."

Eva smiled. "Yes, she is, and she's going to be mortified you saw her like that."

A few moments later, the bedroom door opened again and Zoe came out wearing trousers and a red spotted white shirt that she had tied at the waist. "I forgot you were here," she said. A slight blush pinked her cheeks. Zoe went over and sat by Earl's side. "So, big guy, you got a little sloshed last night."

"Sloshed is a good word."

"Yeah, so is stinky," Zoe said as she sniffed ostentatiously around him. Earl stuck out his tongue. Zoe ignored the rude gesture. "Where're your keys?" she asked.

"You're not driving The Beast!" he exclaimed, flinching at the volume of his own voice.

"I have wheels!" Zoe shot back.

"Oh, I forgot about Mabel." Contrite, Earl searched his pockets until he found his keys. "Where are you going?"

"To your place to pick you up a change of clothes."

"Oh. All right, then." He handed the keys to Zoe, who got up and patted him on the shoulder. Eva held the door open for her.

"Drive safely," she admonished Zoe, who rewarded her concern with a quick kiss.

Chapter Twenty-Seven

The hot weather brought Eva and Debbie out of the office and into Hyde Park, which was only a few minutes walk away from the Immigration Department. With its beautiful walkways and a fountain in the center, the park was truly an oasis in the middle of the central business district of Sydney. Eva stopped and gazed at the stone fountain for a moment as the sparkling water showered down; she enjoyed the haze of cooling mist that she could feel on her skin. The beautiful day brought out many office workers, and they were sprawled all over the grass, eating their lunches and talking in small groups or more intimate couples.

Eva had not been aware of the park until today when Debbie stuck her head in the door and dragged her out of the office into the bright sunlight. The park was introduced to Eva as one of Debbie's favorite spots, mainly when the usually busy lunchtime people traffic had subsided. Eva had been very surprised to see the metaphorically chained-to-the-desk receptionist go out for lunch until Debbie revealed that between noon and one o'clock, the entire office usually closed for lunch.

Eva sat with her back against a tree and perched her lunchbox on her lap. The smell of cut grass reminded Eva of her childhood home; it was a smell she associated with carefree summers.

"So, what do you think?" Debbie asked as she took a bite of her lunch. Tearing off a crust, she tossed it away; the bit of bread was devoured by pigeons that came flapping from the trees, squabbling amongst themselves for the treat.

"It's really nice," Eva said. "I didn't know it was here."

"Yeah, it's a well kept secret." Debbie laughed at her own joke; the park was of considerable size and a feature of the downtown area.

Eva grinned. "Zoe and I went to the Botanical Gardens a few weeks ago. Beautiful place."

"Yeah, I enjoy it there myself. Hey, I've been meaning to ask you; those photos in your office, did you take them?"

"Yes, they're mine," Eva replied. She opened her lunch box to reveal a huge piece of mousaka, which was one of her favorite dishes.

"What's that?" Debbie pointed at the lunch box.

"Mousaka. It's Greek. It has eggplant, potato, minced meat, and pasta."

"Looks very rich."

"Yes, Greek food is very rich," Eva said, remembering the smells and sights of the dinner table in Larissa.

"I hope you don't mind me asking, but how do you stay so slim?"

"I walk most mornings when I have the time, and on weekends Zoe and I rent bicycles and ride around Centennial Park," Eva replied as she took a bite of her lunch. She and Zoe had come across that park quite by accident one Sunday. Zoe had watched people passing by on bicycles and wondered where they could rent a couple themselves. The women were given directions, rented bicycles, and spent a relaxing time cycling around the park, which was one of the most serene places in the city.

"Oh," Debbie said, and went back to her lunch. After a moment, she asked, "Have you been a photographer long?"

"A few years."

"Does Zoe take photos?"

"No, Zoe is an artist. She paints. She occasionally takes a photo of something she wants to paint later, but her painting and drawing is her true talent. I have a nice photo of her painting me taking a photo of her," Eva said as she smiled at the memory. It had been a rainy day, and the two of them had spent that Sunday indoors. Eva had wanted to take photographs of Zoe painting. It was not until later that Zoe had showed her what she was working on.

Debbie laughed, the sound scaring away some of the pigeons. "How old is Zoe?"

Eva gave her a smirk. "Is this another interrogation?"

"I'm sorry, Eva, that was out of line," Debbie apologized. "I'm sorry if I'm asking so many questions; it's just that I find you so interesting and of course with what happened yesterday...I've never met any lesbians before."

"We're not Medusa's children," Eva quipped and took a bite.

"I didn't mean that...um...Zoe was all over you...um..." Debbie stammered and then stopped.

"Zoe is nineteen years old and she's Greek."

"Wow, she's so young." Eva raised an eyebrow at Debbie's comment which only made her blush. "I didn't mean..."

"It's alright. She is younger than me."

"Does she drive?" Debbie steered the conversation away from yesterday's events to something safer.

Eva laughed at the expression on the receptionist's face before answering. "No, she rides a motorcycle called Mabel."

"Mabel?" Debbie said. She looked down at her watch and tapped it for Eva to see. "I think we'd better be heading back."

They picked up their rubbish, made a final check to see that they had not left anything behind, and walked away until Eva stopped.

"What's the matter, did we forget something?" Debbie asked and looked over at the space where they had been sitting.

Eva remained silent, feeling very unsettled. Someone was watching her. She glanced around at the other people in the park; they were not paying any attention to her. Nevertheless, she could feel that she was being stared at, just like the time when she and Zoe had been together on the hilltop above the harbor — except these watchful eyes were hostile. The hairs on the back of her neck prickled.

"Are you all right, Eva?" Debbie pressed, sounding a trifle anxious.

"Yes, I'm fine," Eva reassured her and began the slow walk back to the office. The feeling was still present as she exited the park, and lasted until she and Debbie entered the building.

Friedrich was hot and frustrated. He took off his jacket and rolled up the sleeves of his white shirt as he worked on trying to find the right numbers for the combination. The large grey safe was old; the paint was peeling off, and the exposed iron surfaces were turning rusty. It had been in the office for a very long time and was seldom used. Friedrich wanted to ask David why they had never used it before, and frowned at the lock that refused to open, no matter how many times he attempted a different combination of numbers from the sheet of paper that he held. He let out a frustrated sigh as David walked through the open door with two cold bottles of Coca-Cola.

"You won't ever make a good burglar, Freddy," David said.

Friedrich scowled at him and he went back to his contemplation of the safe. "And you can't copy numbers correctly."

"I'm a lover, not an accountant," David replied, earning another scowl from Friedrich.

"I won't even try and understand that joke," he said.

"I know; I'm a true comic genius. George and Gracie get their material from me."

Friedrich snorted when yet another combination was tried and failed to open the lock. "What's in this safe?"

"Nothing at the moment."

Friedrich sighed and scrunched the paper in his hand, throwing it in the bin. "Well, the numbers you gave me don't work."

"Really?" David teased and patted him on the back. "Here have a cola, it will cool you down."

"Did you have a chance to go over that list I gave you this morning?" Friedrich asked, taking a long swig of the soda. The cold liquid felt wonderful going down.

"Yeah, I did. I've requested passport photos from the Immigration Department, and they should arrive some time on Monday. Then we can try and match them with the photographs we have."

"And where are we going to store them?"

"In the safe," David said, trying without success to hide a grin.

Friedrich rolled his eyes. "You are a funny man."

"I told you, I'm a comic genius. Come on, Freddy, smile. You'll have the weekend to court the lovely Elena. I'll have to get another safe, but until then you can take the photos home with you, and I'll take the list."

"I'll order the new safe," Friedrich muttered. He went to his desk and picked up the telephone receiver.

"Don't forget to keep the numbers in a safe place, Freddy," David said then yelped in mock injury when he got hit in the head by a folded newspaper thrown by Friedrich, who had had enough.

Zoe maneuvered her motorcycle into the office building's basement car park and looked around for a suitable spot in the crowded facility. She found a small space in a corner and turned off the ignition just as a large Ford was parking, its owner giving Zoe a dirty look when he was forced to accept the space next to hers. Zoe pulled off her soft leather helmet and gloves and put them in the sidecar, grinning at the driver. She patted the bike fondly then strolled the short distance to the steps leading up to Eva's workplace.

"Hi, Zoe," Debbie said.

"Hello, Debbie! Wow, it's hot in here!" Zoe picked up a magazine that was lying on one of the low tables and fanned herself.

"The Federal Government Sauna. We're open for business," Debbie joked.

"Is Eva still seeing clients?"

"No, she's gone down to the file room, and if you think it's hot up here, you should be subjected to our filing room. We call it hell."

"Hell?"

"Boiling hot all the time, even in winter," Debbie explained. She went on to tell Zoe that their filing room was situated below the basement car park. It had no ventilation, and it was stuffed with all the old files from the various departments in the building. As a receptionist, Debbie had the misfortune of spending a considerable amount of time down there filing away the old, closed records. She hated the cockroaches that survived in the heat, and she hated the mice that scurried around and left their calling cards in between filing bays. She always gratefully accepted any offer by the interpreters to take files down there themselves.

"Eva hates the heat," Zoe said. Her partner suffered a great deal in the summer, and cold baths were always a treat. Beyond that, Zoe had found a unique way to cool Eva down during the very warm nights by taking a towel and wetting it, then placing it over Eva's feet. It made it easier for her to sleep. They had tried sleeping out on the balcony, but mosquitoes had made a meal out of them, so it was either a cold bath or a wet towel. Zoe loved the heat; being a child of the Mediterranean, high temperatures did not bother her as much.

"Does she really?" Debbie asked.

"Oh, yeah. She's a winter bunny that one. Give her a cold day and she's happy," Zoe replied. "So how long do you think she'll be?"

"I'm not sure. She was going to pick up some files for herself, and she said she would get a few that I needed. All depends if she can find the others before passing out from the heat."

Zoe frowned. She was not sure if Debbie had been kidding about the lack of ventilation. "Is she okay down there?"

Debbie glanced up and met Zoe's concerned look. "Oh, I'm sorry, Zoe. It's a joke around here about hell. It's not that bad."

"Oh, okay. I wouldn't want to find that Eva had passed out or anything," Zoe muttered, not fully understanding the Australian sense of humor. "I'll just wait here." She thumbed through the magazine that she had been fanning herself with, not really interested in the articles. She would look up occasionally to check if Eva had returned. Zoe finally found an interesting article but stopped reading when she heard the door open. She put the magazine down, thinking that Eva had returned. Getting up to greet her partner, Zoe got a nasty shock when she saw Greta walk into the reception area.

Wow, Zoe thought. Greta was dressed impeccably. She wore a cream-colored silk shirt with a burgundy-colored tight skirt and matching shoes that gave her an extra two inches of height. Her auburn hair was restrained in a Psyche knot at the nape of her neck. *She's gorgeous*, Zoe thought, suddenly self-conscious. She ran a hand over her short cropped hair and glanced down at the casual shirt and pants she was wearing.

Greta walked up to the reception desk and stood there looking very impatient, waiting for Debbie to end her telephone call.

"I want to see Miss Muller, hmm, sorry, Miss Haralambos," Greta demanded in heavily German-accented English. "My name is Greta Wagner."

"Have you got an appointment?" Debbie asked.

"No," Greta said flatly. "Is she free? I won't be long."

"I'm sorry, Mrs. Wagner, Miss Haralambos isn't in the office at the moment. Would you like to leave a message for her?" Debbie asked.

"Oh?" Greta's brows drew together in a frown.

Zoe looked back at the entrance, praying that Eva would not come through the lift door. She turned her attention back to Greta, who seemed far from happy.

"Give her my telephone number." Greta pushed a piece of paper at Debbie and turned on her heel to leave. She caught sight of Zoe and paused. With a smile on her face, she went over to Zoe and extended her hand, which Zoe took politely.

"We meet again. Hello, Chloe," Greta said.

Zoe refrained from making a nasty remark and smiled, although the expression felt stiff on her face. "My name is Zoe."

"Of course. I'm sorry, Zoe, I get very forgetful with names. The older one gets, the more one forgets."

"I wouldn't know about that," Zoe muttered.

"No, of course not. You're still a teenager," Greta stated. "Are you waiting for Eva?"

Zoe nodded.

"How sweet and considerate of you. I'll wager Eva loves that," Greta said, drawing her gloves back on.

Zoe wondered why anyone would wear gloves just for the sake of fashion when the day was so hot. "What are you doing here?"

"I was hoping to speak to Eva," Greta answered.

"Why?"

Greta cocked her head to one side and regarded Zoe with an artificial smile. "My, you are the jealous type, aren't you? What are you worried about, Zoe? Are you worried I'm going to steal her away from you?"

"I'm just curious as to why you are here. I'm not worried about my wife being stolen away."

"Of course you're not. Although I know if an old lover turned up, I would be very worried. You know, comparing notes and all of that. I'm sure you have nothing to worry about." Greta regarded Zoe steadily. It was clear that the woman enjoyed taunting her, and Zoe held on to her control, reminding herself that if she showed Greta how much she was angered by her insults, the German woman would win the skirmish.

"I want to thank you," Greta said.

"For what?" Zoe asked, a little suspicious of this sudden show of gratitude.

"For making sure Eva got out of Greece. It was an ingenious method to get away, don't you agree? I didn't think Eva was so cunning, to pretend to work with the Greek Resistance, you know. I'm sure it was just part of her plan."

The implication that Zoe herself had been used as the means for Eva's escape — and nothing more — was obvious. "Is that right?" Zoe asked, trying and failing to keep the brittle tone out of her voice.

"Oh, yes. In any event, she escaped and that's the important thing. Well, I'm happy for you," Greta continued. "You are fortunate to be married to Eva. She is a very sexy woman."

"She is."

"And you're a child. Is it difficult..."

"I don't think you know Eva as well as you *think* you do," Zoe replied.

"Zoe, dear girl, I was Eva's first lover, so I know all there is to know about her, including how she looks after she's satisfied. She knows how to pleasure me, and I know how to satisfy her. I'm sure you are doing your best." Greta sighed in an exaggerated fashion and glanced at her watch. "I would love to continue chatting with you, but I have to go. Give my regards to Eva, won't you? Thank you, my child." She patted Zoe's cheek, then spun around and walked off, leaving a humiliated young woman in her wake.

After the lift doors closed on Greta, Zoe let out a frustrated cry. She sank down into the nearest chair and put her head in her hands, rocking back and forth. *Oh, gee whiz, Zoe, that was the dumbest thing you have ever done!* she scolded herself. *How to make yourself look more stupid in one easy lesson.*

Debbie approached Zoe and put her hand on her shoulder, apparently drawn by Zoe's distress. She looked concerned. "Zoe, are you all right?"

Zoe brushed away her tears and took a deep breath, trying to banish the awful feeling of humiliation that clenched in her chest. "Yes, fine," she muttered.

"Do you know Mrs. Wagner?"

"Yes, I do, sort of." Zoe took another deep breath, growing slightly calmer. "Did Mrs. Wagner give you a phone number?"

"She wanted me to give it to Eva."

"Can you destroy that number?" Zoe asked, hoping Debbie would just throw the number in the nearest bin.

"I can't do that, Zoe. I'd get into trouble if Mrs. Wagner made a formal complaint that I didn't give it to Eva."

"Oh. You can give it to me and I'll give it to Eva."

Debbie shook her head and smiled an apology. "Can't do that either."

"Okay, thanks anyway," Zoe said.

"Would you like a cup of cold water or something? You look a little flushed."

"No, I'm fine."

Debbie clearly did not believe Zoe was as fine as she insisted, but it was equally clear that Zoe did not want her to push any further. The receptionist went back to her desk to finish cleaning up, leaving Zoe alone to mop her face with a handkerchief and use the damp cloth to try and calm the hectic color that blazed in her cheeks.

A little while later, the lift door opened and Eva walked into the reception area, carrying several large folders under her arm. Zoe had been absently flipping through a magazine, but she abandoned it when Eva approached her.

"Hey, Zoe, I won't be too long," Eva said. "Just have to drop these off and get my bag. Have you been waiting long?"

"Hi. Um...no, not long," Zoe replied softly. "I'll wait here until you finish."

Eva seemed surprised by this quiet response and turned to Debbie, who was picking up leaflets and brochures from the information roundabout. Debbie crooked her finger for Eva to join her. Despite the fact that they lowered their voices, Zoe could nevertheless overhear the conversation, although she pretended not to eavesdrop.

"What's wrong with Zoe?" Eva asked the receptionist. "Did something happen while I was away?"

"Mrs. Wagner came in looking for you a few minutes ago and I got the impression Zoe knew her," Debbie replied.

"Did they talk?"

"Yeah. I'm not sure what they said because they were speaking in German, but Zoe was upset afterwards."

"Oh. What did Mrs. Wagner want?"

"She asked me to give you this." Debbie leaned over to her desk, picked up the piece of paper with Greta's phone number, and passed it to her.

Eva looked at the paper for a few seconds and stuck it in her pocket. "Thanks, Debbie," she said.

"Is everything all right?"

"I don't know," Eva said, frowning. She disappeared from the reception area and returned a few moments later with her handbag. Passing the desk, she gave Debbie a key. Eva took Zoe's hand and they took the stairs down to the parking area in silence. Unable to wait any longer, Eva stopped at the bottom of the stairs and turned to her. "Zoe, are you all right?"

"I'm fine," Zoe mumbled.

"Everything all right with Earl?"

"Mmm. He said he was going to spend the night at his place in case his father called."

"Do you think he will?" Eva asked, trying to get Zoe to open up to her.

Zoe shrugged and walked over to the motorcycle. She retrieved the helmet and gloves, climbing into the sidecar to allow Eva to drive.

Zoe sighed and settled into the sidecar. Greta was everything she wasn't and it played on her own insecurities. The war was not over. She had lost this battle, and the knowledge of her loss was very bitter, indeed.

The apartment was quiet. Eva walked out of the bathroom with one towel tucked around her body and another towel wrapped around her wet hair. The cool bath had relaxed her a great deal and she felt invigorated. Wandering into the kitchen, she found it empty. She padded back out and looked at the balcony, which was also empty.

"Zoe?" Eva called out and a faint, "Here," came from the bedroom. Eva strode to the bedroom and opened the door. Zoe was curled up on the bed. "Are you feeling all right, love?" she asked, concerned.

Zoe nodded, which did nothing to alleviate Eva's anxiety.

Eva laid down on the bed beside Zoe then gently turned Zoe towards her. She was very surprised to find the young woman had been crying. Eva was perplexed. "What's wrong, Zoe? Why were you crying? Was it something I said?"

"No. D-d-did Debbie tell you about Greta coming to see you?"

Eva nodded. "Debbie mentioned that Greta came by. She also said you talked with her, and you looked upset. Did Greta do anything to upset you?"

Zoe nodded and sniffed.

"Do you want to talk about it?" Eva asked.

"You're going to think it's stupid."

"No, I won't. Would I be wrong if I said you don't want me to see Greta?"

"You can see her; I can't stop you," Zoe said defensively, sounding miserable at the same time.

"If I wanted to see her again, it would be up to me, right?"

"Yes, of course. I wouldn't mind," Zoe replied.

Eva stayed silent, just staring at her partner. "Can I tell you something?" she finally asked, believing she understood the reason behind Zoe's upset.

"Yes."

"You don't lie to me very well," Eva said. "What you are really thinking is that you want Greta to go back to Germany and to disappear."

"Not really," Zoe replied. "I want her to disappear, but going back to Germany is not an option," she said with a forlorn smile. "Evy, I can't stop you from seeing anyone you want to."

"But you don't like it?" Eva continued her questioning. Since the moment Greta had come back into her life, she had known that she needed to have this conversation with Zoe at some point. She also needed to find out what Greta had said to Zoe earlier at the office that cause her so much distress.

"No, I don't like it. But...I know you want to see her because she's a friend of yours, and I don't think I have the right to tell you not to see her."

"Yes, she was a friend of mine, but that doesn't mean I'm not going to take your feelings into consideration." She kissed the top of Zoe's head, scooping her closer and curling her body around the smaller woman. "What are you worried about?"

"I'm not worried," Zoe said.

"Zoe, don't lie to me," Eva gently scolded, lifting Zoe's chin and looking into her eyes. "We have always been honest with each other. Greta bothers you; you can tell me that. I'm sure if I were in your shoes, she would bother me as well."

Zoe looked sheepish. "I don't like her."

"I know," Eva said "What did she say to you?"

Zoe took a deep breath. "That she knows how to satisfy you, among other things."

Eva was taken aback. "You satisfy me in every way, Zoe."

"Do I?" Zoe asked hesitantly. "Do I make you happy? You know..."

"Oh, Zoe!" Eva exclaimed. Zoe's insecurities had been laid bare, and all Eva wanted was to reassure her. "You make me deliriously happy."

"What if she wanted to win you back?"

Eva frowned. Greta was playing cruel games and she hated the way Zoe was being abused. "Your touch is the only one I want. I want to wake up with you, go to sleep with you, share my bed and my life with you." Eva caressed Zoe's cheek and brushed away the tears that had begun to spill silently from the other woman's eyes. "She can't win me back. You are the only one who owns my heart. Do you believe me?"

Zoe nodded, closed her eyes, and snuggled against Eva.

"Zoe, when we made our vows before God, I truly believed in what I was promising. I didn't say those words because they sounded nice. I've committed myself to you and that's the end of that. Do you remember what I said to you about eighteen months ago?"

"That there are three people in our marriage; you, me, and God, and that makes us stronger," Zoe replied.

"And with God in our marriage, nothing on earth can break us apart. God is still in our marriage, love. Just because a woman I knew so many years ago wants to steal my heart, doesn't mean she's going to. I can't give it away; you have it."

"I'm sorry, Evy. It's just that Greta makes me feel like a kid, out of my depth."

"Out of your depth? I don't understand."

"She's more sophisticated, a woman of the world, and I'm a peasant from some insignificant Greek village."

Eva shook her head as she took Zoe's hand and placed it on her chest near her heart. "Zoe, you own my heart, my body, my soul, and, you aren't a peasant from some insignificant Greek village. I don't ever want to hear you say that again. You are a beautiful Greek woman with all the qualities I love. You are kind, gentle, loving, talented, and you make me feel like the luckiest woman alive. I look forward to each day because I know I'm going to be with you. Don't you know that? Every night I thank God you are with me."

Eva very slowly leaned down, pressing her lips to Zoe's. With her kiss, she wanted to leave the other woman no doubts about her love. She deepened the kiss and was rewarded with a quiet moan. She slipped her hands under Zoe's cotton shirt, running them over her back, reveling in the feel of Zoe's smooth skin.

"Oh, God. Stop," Zoe managed to say.

"Stop? Why? For once, we're alone."

"Yeah. I want to apologize and ask you something. I don't think I can do that if I'm not able to think straight."

Eva grinned. "Well, we don't want that."

"Eva, I'm sorry. It's just that Greta made me feel so stupid. She said some things that I just couldn't get out of my mind."

"It's all right, love, I understand," Eva replied and kissed her again. "Greta doesn't know what we share. I want you to remember what I said to you, okay?"

Zoe nodded.

"Can I continue where I left off?" Eva asked.

"On one condition."

"Oh?"

"You lose the towel," Zoe replied. She removed the towel from Eva's body and flung it out the bedroom door.

"Now where was I?" Eva leaned in closer and kissed Zoe. Their kiss deepened. Eva knew that making love with Zoe was, and always would be, the closest thing to heaven on Earth she could ever achieve. That was the last coherent thought she had before she set out to erase any doubts Zoe may still have harbored about their relationship and Eva's love for her.

Illumination from the street lamp filtered through the open window, leaving bars of light and shadow in the room. It was another warm evening and the sound of the cicadas reached Eva as she lay in bed, content to stay curled up with Zoe. She looked down at the sleeping woman who was tucked against her, bangs falling over her closed eyes. Eva grinned when she noticed a small hickey on Zoe's neck. She was sure it would be noticed and joked about. Zoe was an outgoing person in general, but tended to be rather shy when it came to sex.

She found the contradiction in her partner's personality quite endearing. Where Zoe was outgoing, chatty, and quietly aggressive outside the bedroom, inside she let Eva take the lead. However, over the last couple of months, Eva had been pleasantly surprised to find Zoe's naturally boisterous personality was coming through in their lovemaking.

"Ah, Zoe, my love, you are one of a kind," Eva whispered to the sleeping woman, who mumbled something unintelligible and burrowed even closer to her. She lifted Zoe's hand and looked down at the ring on her finger. Zoe always wore the ring, a cheap tin-plated thing that Eva had found in one of the ports in which the ship had docked. She could still picture the look of total surprise on Zoe's face when she had blurted out, *"Will you be with me? I want to spend the rest of my life with you."*

Eva sighed contently. A year and a half had passed since that moment. The two of them had settled into a new country and gained a greater understanding of each other and their little quirks; each delightful discovery made her love Zoe all the more.

Zoe snuggled closer and let out a sigh. Her slim, bare arm was draped across Eva's flat belly, drawing Eva's attention back to her lover. She smiled as her eyes drifting closed as she followed Zoe into sleep.

Chapter Twenty-Eight

Friedrich smiled, putting the flowers next to the chocolates. He sat down to write a note to Elena, wanting it to be just right. Putting the tip of his pen in his mouth as an aid to thinking, he smiled as he scrawled some of his thoughts in the card.

The door opened and David walked in with files under his arm, stopping when he saw the flowers. "Oh, Freddy, are the flowers for me? I'm touched." David planted a kiss on the top of Friedrich's head, which earned him a slap on the leg. "Hey, that's no way to court me!"

"You are such a heathen. Go away," Friedrich said.

"Why, Freddy, don't you love me anymore?" David planted his elbows on the desk in front of Friedrich, batted his blond eyelashes, and put on a flirtatious smile that was more than a little mocking.

Friedrich groaned. "I wouldn't go out with you if you dressed up in a frock and heels. You'd make an ugly woman."

"You mean I'm not a good looking sheila?"

"You're an ugly sheila, all right."

"Oh, I dunno, Freddy. I made a pretty good Juliet in high school."

"You played Juliet?"

"Sure did. I was told I was the best Juliet ever in our all-boys high school. We didn't include the kissing, but the dying part was fun." David struck a pose as if he was on a balcony and opened his arms in search for Romeo. "'Romeo, Romeo, wherefore art thou, Romeo?'" he called in a falsetto voice.

"Probably ran far away from you, since you're so ugly." Friedrich grinned and flinched as he was cuffed across the head.

"Drama critic!" David huffed.

"What are those files in your hands, Juliet?"

"The Immigration Department sent the passport photos, so it looks like we're working tomorrow," David said happily.

Friedrich realized his weekend off was going to be spoiled once again. "I thought my request was so late in the day that they wouldn't be here until Monday. I was planning on spending the weekend with Elena," he whined. The complaint got a chuckle from his friend.

"I feel for you, my friend. My heart goes out to you." He picked up the box of chocolates. "Hey, chocolates, too. Not bad. You actually listened to all my pep talks. Good boy."

"Yeah, pep talks on how to get a woman to fall for me in one easy lesson. I think I did okay without your help."

"Excuse me? Let me remind you, old boy, that if it wasn't for me, you would still be standing there um-ming and ah-ing all over the place. When you marry the lovely Elena, I want you to name your first-born after me." David shook the chocolate box. Friedrich continued to write but cast a dirty look in his direction. Not at all deterred, David went on, "Naming your first-born after me will ease my pain at losing the future Mrs. Harrison. You remember that gorgeous redhead a few weeks ago?"

Friedrich remembered that particular incident all too well. They had been trying to find a Polish general who had collaborated with the Germans, when the department received word the man was in Sydney. At the time, David had been with his new girlfriend, half-way through their dinner date at the restaurant when Friedrich had called him with the information. The man they found was not the Polish general after all, and by the time David returned to the restaurant, his date had left in disgust. David had taken every opportunity since then to remind Friedrich about that incident's role in losing him the "future Mrs. Harrison".

"How was I to know that Polish guy had the same name as our general?" Friedrich asked, shrugging.

"Let's not get into another debate about it. I could have had my potential wife won over at dinner that night."

Friedrich snorted. "Sure, and I'm a regular Casanova." He accepted the folders, putting them in his briefcase. "I ordered the new safe. They will be bringing it on Monday."

"Hopefully that will keep our secret files secret."

Friedrich sealed the letter and put it in his shirt pocket before putting on his jacket and retrieving his hat from the hat rack.

"So, Casanova, are you going to snuggle and cuddle with Elena?" David asked.

"Why?"

"Well, snuggling and cuddling lead to 'you know', or so they tell me," David said. "I could probably learn a few things from you, eh?" He slapped Friedrich on the back as they left the office.

Friedrich knew his friend was joking. David was a real ladies' man with his boyish good looks and charm. The man was not ready to settle down, but Friedrich was certain he himself had found the right girl in Elena — the "future Mrs. Jacobs".

The full moon lit up the pavement as Friedrich walked towards the block of apartments, muttering to himself. He held the flowers in one hand, his briefcase in the other and the box of chocolates under his arm. He hoped he was not going to drop the chocolates, since they had been banged around enough by David's shenanigans.

Friedrich stopped walking and looking at the heavens for a sign. Naturally, none was forthcoming. "Will you marry me...um...I want to marry you," Friedrich mumbled to himself, trying to find the right words to propose to Elena. He turned when he heard footsteps. Mr. Haralambos was walking slowly towards him on the path. Friedrich sighed and took a good grasp on the bouquet. He was nervous. He probably did not need to be, but he had never asked anyone to marry him before. He was sweating a bit so he tucked the flowers under his arm, took out his handkerchief and dabbed his brow.

"Good evening, Friedrich," Panayiotis greeted him, putting an arm around his shoulders. "How are you tonight? Sit down for a moment."

"Oh, Mr. Haralambos. I-I-I'm...good," Friedrich stammered.

"You don't look good to me. Come over here and have a sit down before you fall down." Panayiotis led him to a small park bench just outside the grounds of the apartment block.

"Ah, thank you."

"Are those for Elena?" the man asked, grinning when Friedrich nodded.

"So..." Friedrich sighed. "Oh, God, I am so terrified."

"What are you talking about?"

"Um...Elena likes you. She told me she talks to you."

"I like Elena. She's a good girl," Panayiotis said. "We have long chats together."

Friedrich knew what those chats were about. Elena had confided in him that she found Panayiotis easy to talk to even though he was not a rabbi but a trained Greek Orthodox priest. The man would listen while Elena told him about her experiences at the Bergen-Belson concentration camp. It was difficult for Elena to tell Friedrich; she tried but would burst into tears, making Friedrich feel helpless at the pain she still suffered, and angry at those who had hurt her in the past. Elena needed someone to help her deal with the horrendous memories. Panayiotis clearly had earned Elena's trust in the short time she had known him and that was good enough for Friedrich.

"Thank you for being there for my Elena," Friedrich nodded. "Mr. Haralambos, I want to ask her to marry me," Friedrich said shyly and looked up over the top of his black-framed glasses, brushing away a mosquito that was buzzing him.

Panayiotis squeezed his shoulder. "That's excellent news."

Friedrich said, "Yeah, but I don't know if she wants to."

"Hmm. So how would you know, if you don't ask her?"

"I wrote a letter, but it got lost."

"You were going to propose marriage to her by letter?" Panayiotis' bushy eyebrows went up; it was apparent that he was resisting the urge to chuckle.

"Yes," Friedrich replied. "But this time, I got her some flowers, chocolates, and I've written what I want to say—"

"Throw it away."

"The card?"

Panayiotis nodded and put his free hand on Friedrich's chest. "Say what's in your heart."

"But—"

"Elena deserves it, my boy. Be yourself. Now go and propose to her." Panayiotis got up, pulled Friedrich up with him, and pushed him towards the apartments.

Friedrich looked towards Elena's building and grinned, then turned back and gave the older man the card from his shirt pocket before he started up the walkway to the entrance.

"Another happy customer," Panayiotis said loud enough for Friedrich to hear.

Friedrich turned and waved at him before he went up the stairs and out of sight.

After arriving at Elena's door, Friedrich stood and closed his eyes, saying a quick prayer before knocking. He waited a few moments until the door opened. He could not stop the smile that spread across his face at the sight of the woman he wanted to marry.

Elena ushered him in and closed the door. "Oh, flowers!" she gushed. "And chocolates! What a treat!"

Friedrich grinned. He made a mental note to himself to thank David for his suggestion. Elena gave him a chaste kiss on the cheek. Friedrich looked around the lounge and noticed candles on the decorated table.

"I'm sorry I was so late...um," Friedrich stammered, realizing it was getting late and he had promised to be here earlier.

"That's okay. I figured you had been delayed," Elena replied. She went to the kitchen, leaving Friedrich alone. He heard water running, and supposed Elena must be putting the flowers in a vase. Sure enough, she returned after a few moments and put a vase full of flowers on the table. Elena tilted her head down and sniffed, clearly admiring the blooms while Friedrich fidgeted.

I should have asked David how to do this! he berated himself, regretting having given the card to Mr. Haralambos. "Elena, I...um...I need to talk to you."

"Is something wrong?" Elena asked as she sat down. She was frowning, which did nothing to reduce Friedrich's apprehension.

He turned his back on her for a moment, thinking furiously. When he finally turned around, he gave her a half-hearted smile and sat down on the sofa.

"Friedrich, what's wrong?" Elena persisted, beginning to look worried.

"Well, you know I sent you a letter, but it turned out to be the wrong piece of paper. It would have said everything I wanted to say. Then I wrote a card, but when I came over here, Mr. Haralambos took it from me and said to say things from my heart, but now I can't find the words to ask whether you want to marry me or not." Friedrich took a breath and continued. "And it would have been nice...umm..."

"Yes," Elena said, smiling broadly.

"It would have been really nice if I did it the old fashioned way, you know, and—"

"Friedrich," Elena interrupted, "I said yes."

"It was so romantic and everything, and now I don't know how to say it—" Friedrich stopped when he realized what Elena had just said. "Huh?"

Elena shook her head at him and grinned. "I said, yes, I'll marry you."

Friedrich's eyes went wide, and he dropped to his knees in front of the young woman who would soon become Mrs. Friedrich Jacobs. "You mean you *want* to marry *me*?"

"I don't see anyone else asking me," Elena joked.

"You sure you mean you want to marry *me*?" Friedrich pointed at himself in total disbelief. *She wants to marry me.* Friedrich hardly believed his ears. He had prayed so hard for this moment to occur, and hoped he would have the right words to convince her that he was the one. Nowhere in his plans did it occur to him that Elena would not *need* convincing.

"*Yes*, I want to marry *you*." Elena pointed at him. Friedrich stood and scooped her up in his arms and whirled around the room.

"Whoo-hoo!" he yelled, twirling the laughing young woman. He put her down and, as Elena watched, he fished around in his pocket. "Um, I hope you like this. It was my mother's..." He smiled as he placed a diamond ring on her finger.

Elena looked down at the single diamond sparkling in the light and put her arms around his neck. "Oh, Friedrich, this is so beautiful!" she cried as she kissed him tenderly.

After a moment, they sat down on the sofa together, Friedrich watching as Elena continued to admire the ring. "I'm sure my mother would be proud to see you wear that ring; a beautiful ring for a beautiful woman," Friedrich said shyly and gave her a quick kiss.

"*Mutti* would be so happy," Elena sniffed back the tears.

"I want you to do something for me," Friedrich got off the sofa and went down on his knees.

"I thought I said yes already?" Elena teased.

"Elena, I want you to finish college."

Elena sat back and gazed at her new fiancé. "You do?"

"Yes, it's important to you and I want you to be happy," Friedrich replied and took Elena's hand. "We can get married, if you want, after you finish. What do you think?"

Elena put her arms around Friedrich's neck and kissed him in answer.

Eva woke with a start. She looked down at Zoe who was sleeping through the storm and marveled at how she could do it. Zoe wore a very happy smile on her face, which made Eva grin in reaction.

Eva snuggled down and scooped her still-sleeping partner closer to her. She could feel Zoe's breath on her chest and it tickled a little. She ran her hand lightly through Zoe's red locks, remembering their lovemaking after her bath and remembering later as they cuddled and talked. *I will have to do something to stop my wife from painting me naked.* Eva smiled. She had threatened revenge, but she did not think Zoe took her seriously since the conversation had descended into a tickle fest.

Talking to Zoe was like a soothing massage: it relaxed her. Eva shook her head at the analogy that she had conjured up, but that was how she felt.

Zoe loved to talk. And she talked about everything from little things like the day's events to quirky, sometimes profound things that came to her mind. She also told terrible jokes, something Greta had never done during their time together. It was just one of the many differences between the two women. There was one thing Zoe did not talk about to her last night and that was what Greta had said to get her upset, so upset that she did not want to discuss their conversation.

Eva considered Greta and frowned. She did not want Greta to upset Zoe, and her former lover had somehow managed to find Zoe's weakness and exploit it. Eva was sure that was the reason Zoe had been quiet and had not wanted to talk about what had happened at the office.

I'm not going to let my wife suffer because of a former lover, Eva thought to herself as she looked down at Zoe, who began to stir and open her sleep-blurred eyes.

"You're frowning. You're going to get worry lines," Zoe gently scolded, tracing the lines on Eva's brow with a fingertip. "What were you thinking about?"

"I've made a decision," Eva said quietly.

"Hmm?"

"I'm not going to see Greta again."

Zoe hitched herself up on an elbow. "Not that I don't like that idea, but why not?"

"She hurt you and I don't like it when you hurt," Eva replied, stroking Zoe's cheek with the back of her hand. "You're too precious to me."

Zoe swallowed as Eva continued to caress her cheek. "I love you," she whispered and let her head rest on Eva's chest. Eva leaned down and kissed her.

Zoe's hand fell across Eva's stomach as they held each other. Eva was certain she had made the right decision. She looked at the rain-splattered window and sighed. "I don't think we can go riding, today."

"Oh, I don't know..." Zoe murmured and rolled on top of Eva, causing Eva to chuckle and then reverse their positions.

"You are insatiable, you know that?" Eva stared into Zoe's mischievous emerald eyes. "You are so addictive."

"I have one addiction, Miss Eva," Zoe replied a little breathlessly as she flipped them over and moved so that she was lying on top of Eva again.

"Oh?"

Zoe nodded. "One very tall, blue-eyed, dark-haired, absolutely captivating, drop dead gorgeous wife."

"Really?" Eva teased.

"Oh, yes. My favorite sport is climbing," Zoe ran her hand down Eva's hip, "over hills and down into valleys," and inside Eva's thigh, which drew a little gasp from her and made Zoe grin. Then she brought her hand up Eva's belly again. She ran her hand over Eva's breast as she continued the tour, "And over peaks." Zoe smiled impishly. "Climbing up your body is one of my favorite sports." She leaned over and blew a raspberry in between Eva's breasts, causing her to giggle.

"Do you plan on going climbing today?" Eva asked.

"Oh, yes!" Zoe repeated enthusiastically. As she was about to launch an assault, they heard a knock on the door, which made Zoe groan loudly and collapse on top of Eva. "I'm going to kill whoever is on the other side of that door," she muttered. "Don't move; I'll be right back."

"I'm not moving a muscle," Eva responded, watching as Zoe grumpily got out of bed and put on a robe.

Zoe admired Eva for a few seconds and waggled her eyebrows at her. "You will remember where we were?"

"Over hills and down into valleys," Eva replied with mock solemnity, earning a wicked chuckle from Zoe as she left the bedroom to answer the summons.

Zoe ran her hands through her hair as she closed the bedroom door and did a little happy skip on her way to the front door. She opened it to find Elena standing in the corridor with what seemed like a mile-wide grin on her face.

"Elena, it's eight o'clock in the morning, and it's Saturday. Please tell me we don't have any classes today!" Zoe ushered her friend inside, hoping she hadn't forgotten any classes or else she was going to be extremely upset.

"Look." Elena stuck her hand under Zoe's nose.

Zoe looked down and saw the ring. They looked at each other and then both young women screamed at the same time, shrill with excitement. Zoe embraced her friend and danced around the room, hollering and yelping. All the hollering brought Eva out to check on the cause of the commotion. She leaned against the bedroom door, watching the two women dancing about.

Zoe caught sight of Eva and ran towards her, stopped and stood on the tips of her toes and kissed her. "Elena is getting married!"

"To whom?" Eva asked, her eyes twinkling.

Elena gave her a grin. "He asked me last night!"

"Why didn't you tell me?" Zoe cried out, then remembered what she had been doing last night and gave Eva a quick glance before turning to her friend.

"Well, it was late, so I didn't think you would be up," Elena said. "He was so cute last night, not at all what I expected."

"You didn't..."

Elena looked blankly at Zoe, who arched a brow at her. It finally registered on Elena what Zoe was trying to ask. "No!" she cried. "We're going to wait until we're married."

"I'm happy for you, Elena." Eva came over and gave her a hug.

Elena seemed very surprised to find the tall woman giving her a hug and awkwardly hugged Eva back.

"I'll just go and put on some clothes," Eva continued, releasing Elena.

Zoe gave Eva a playful slap on the behind as she passed, and blew her a kiss when Eva waggled her eyebrows at her before disappearing into the bedroom, leaving her and Elena alone in the lounge.

"Wow, I wasn't expecting that," Elena whispered. "She gives good hugs."

Zoe nodded. "Oh, yeah, she does," she said. *And Evy's a great kisser and a great lover,* Zoe silently added to herself, but she was not going to tell her friend about her partner's abilities in the bedroom. "So, how did he do it? Was he romantic and everything?" she asked, taking another look at the ring.

"How did Eva propose?" Elena asked.

"Oh, God, Eva is the most romantic woman. Sick with the flu and nearly ready to pass out, she still went down on her knees," Zoe replied, almost swooning with the remembrance.

"Oh, she beats Friedrich in the romance stakes!" Elena said. "Do you remember that letter he sent that wasn't a letter?"

"The blank piece of paper?"

"Well, that was supposed to be his proposal!"

"No! Oh, God, that's funny!"

"Yeah, but last night he brought flowers and chocolates. He was so sweet," Elena sighed. "I want to thank you."

"What for?"

"For agreeing to go the dance with David. Friedrich is so shy that he wouldn't have asked me in a million years. Would you do me a favor?"

"If I can."

"Would you be my Maid of Honor? You're about the only family I have, so..." Elena did not finish because Zoe wrapped her arms around her and gave her a tremendous hug, squeezing the breath out of her.

Friedrich hummed a song under his breath as he walked down the corridor of his office building, a huge smile on his face. He had placed a carnation in his lapel that morning. He paused and sniffed the flower as Joe, the new janitor, stopped his mopping to watch him, shaking his head. Friedrich greeted the man with a nod and continued to hum when he entered his office.

"Good morning, David," Friedrich greeted his partner, who was sitting with his feet propped up on the desk.

"Good morning?" David swung himself around, his feet hitting the floor with a thump. He cast a glance out of the window to the miserable weather, then turned to his friend with a mock scowl. "Okay, who are you and what have you done with Freddy?"

"The Nazis got me and have replaced me with a spy," Friedrich joked as he took off his jacket.

"That's pathetic, Freddy. They would have replaced you with someone who told better jokes. So, you got some 'you know' finally, huh?" David grinned and returned to reading his file.

"Better than that, Mr. Harrison...much, much better."

"Nothing is better than 'you know', Freddy," David muttered. He peeked over the edge of his file, watching while Friedrich took off his hat and with a flourish sent it sailing towards the hat rack. It missed and fell in the rubbish bin. David burst out laughing, shaking his head.

Friedrich shrugged. Nothing could disrupt his good mood. "You're going to a wedding, David."

"Did Edna finally settle on a new date?" David asked, referring to their mail clerk, who had invited them to her wedding only to have it postponed due to the groom's shattered nerves.

"Not that I know of." Friedrich retrieved his hat, then put his hand over David's file. A huge grin stretched the muscles of his face as he delivered the greatest piece of news of his entire life. "She said 'yes'," he told David.

"Who said 'yes'?" David asked with a twinkle in his eyes.

"Miss Elena Mannheim, soon to be Mrs. Friedrich Jacobs — a gorgeous, intelligent woman."

David grinned. He got up and put his arm around Friedrich's shoulders. "So you finally asked her. Good one, old boy!"

"She said yes, do you believe that?"

"No, but then I don't understand women," David replied. He ducked to avoid Friedrich's playful punch. "So when is the big day?"

Friedrich settled in his chair, still smiling. "We haven't discussed it, but I hope it's soon."

"Me, too. You're too happy." David was hit on the head by a balled-up piece of paper thrown by Friedrich. "Are we going to do some work today, or daydream about the lovely Elena?"

"We have to work?"

"Yes, that's what they pay us to do." David shook his head and wondered if his friend was going to accomplish anything today. "Here are the photo files we received last night, remember? You go through this lot and I'll go through these. For your information, we got another shipload yesterday we'll have to start on after we finish this bunch."

David handed him the files and the photographs from the Immigration Department and they settled down to go through the thousands of names, cross-checking them against their wanted lists.

Friedrich stopped for a moment and glanced over at David. He had a question that needed to be answered. "David, would you be my best man?"

"Only if you pay me." David grinned and got another crumpled ball of paper bounced off his head. "Yes, of course I'll be your best man. Who else would organize your bucks' night?"

The two agents settled down to work once again and spent the next couple of hours looking at their respective lists. Friedrich scowled at the photo in his hand and checked it against the photograph that the Immigration Department had given them. The woman looking back at him had lighter hair than the one in the photograph from Immigration, *but that would not be hard to change*, he thought to himself.

"I think I may have something," Friedrich said.

David got up from his desk and stood behind Friedrich, who handed him the information sheet on the woman in the photo. Friedrich read the reports and was sickened. He had read many reports that had made him sick to his stomach, but even he was shocked by what he was reading now.

"She worked at Bergen," David said quietly.

"And Auschwitz...my God," Friedrich whispered as his mind registered that the names of two of the most wanted war criminals were connected with the woman. "Dr. Kurt Gutzeit, Dr. Bruno Weber, and Dr. Josef Mengele...she assisted all of them."

"'The Angel of Death.'" David pulled over a chair and sat down next to Friedrich. His hatred for the man known as the Angel of Death — Dr Josef Mengele — was well known in the department, and especially to Friedrich. David had spent time in Germany searching for the man who, through his hideous genetic experiments, was responsible for the deaths of thousands of Jews sent to Auschwitz. David had spoken to survivors of that horror camp and listened to countless tales about the man who had decided who lived and who died.

Friedrich recalled an interview David had had with one survivor, Hani Schick, a mother of twins who, together with her children, had been subjected to experiments by Mengele. She had told David of Mengele's tortures and how her two children had died agonizing deaths.

Friedrich took a deep breath and put the file down. His earlier good humor had evaporated. "Where is Mengele?"

"Probably halfway to Argentina," David replied, still reading the file. "Weber has been arrested and is awaiting trial." He picked up the photograph and stared at the smiling, happy woman. "These men are animals, but you would think that a woman would have had more compassion," he whispered to himself. "What does the Immigration file say?"

Friedrich picked up the paper, his hand shaking a little at the realization that a member of the "medical team" from Auschwitz — the monsters who had taken the Hippocratic Oath and then butchered thousands — was apparently in Sydney. "According to the transportation papers, her name is Erika Wagner. Her photograph matches that of Greta Inga Strauss, assistant to Drs. Mengele, Gutzeit, and Weber. Mrs. Wagner is married to John Wagner and arrived here 10 January. I don't have any information on him."

David held the two photographs in his hand. "I want to find this bitch, Friedrich."

Friedrich could only agree with all his heart.

Chapter Twenty-Nine

Friedrich sat back in his chair and let out a discontented sigh. It had been a frustrating day, although neither he nor David was at all surprised that the address on the immigration papers had proven to be wrong. He had not thought that Strauss would put down her correct details. Some of the criminals they were seeking had "kangaroos in the top paddock", as David described them, meaning they were not very bright. This woman, though, was very smart, and from the eyewitness accounts, also very dangerous.

He and David had spent the afternoon looking for the address the department had listed for her, which had turned out to be nothing but a hole in the ground at a new building site. Neither man was very happy about their findings, and to add insult to injury, it was still raining. The very warm, muggy weather, the rain, and the wild goose chase had resulted in two cranky investigators.

Back at the office, the whirring overhead fan did nothing to alleviate Friedrich's discomfort as the humidity sapped his energy and his willpower.

"Freddy, go home," David said. He came into the office carrying another stack of files, letting them drop on his already messy desk.

"Do you think she's still here?" Friedrich asked, mopping sweat from his brow with his shirt sleeve.

"I don't know, mate. I hope she is." David sighed. He picked up the photograph of the Strauss woman and put it up on his notice board, then took two steps back to look at it. "If she is, I want to make sure we don't have any cock-ups or spying janitors to fuck things up."

Friedrich looked up sharply at David's swearing, but chose not to say anything about it since they were both tired and irritable. "Why are you putting her picture up if we don't want to alert the grapevine that we know that she's here?"

David looked back at him sheepishly and took the photo down. "I'm getting old, Freddy."

"Aren't we all," Friedrich muttered. He took the photographs from David and put them in the file, which he placed in his briefcase. "I'm going home. I suggest you do, too. Good night, David."

"Night, mate," David replied. "Wish I had a nice lady to go home to," he added, and Friedrich heard the man's wistful statement as the door shut behind him.

Friedrich closed the car door and ran up the path to the block of apartments, putting his briefcase on top of his head as protection against the rain that continued to pelt down. He opened the foyer door and bumped into Panayiotis, nearly knocking the older man over. Friedrich's quick reflexes prevented Panayiotis from hitting the hard ground.

"Oh, I'm sorry, Mr. Haralambos," Friedrich said, holding Panayiotis by the arm and steadying him as the man regained his balance.

"Quite all right, Friedrich," Panayiotis replied.

Friedrich bent over, retrieved Panayiotis's cane, and handed it back to him. "How is Mrs. Haralambos tonight?"

"Oh, she's fine; has a little headache. You know how it is; the older you get the more aches you get."

"Yes, sir," Friedrich agreed. "I mean, I don't know about that, but..."

Panayiotis chuckled and clasped Friedrich's shoulder. "I know what you meant. So, young man, did you propose?"

Friedrich beamed. "Yes, sir. It wasn't all that romantic, but she said yes."

"It's not the delivery that counts; it's what's in your heart." Panayiotis patted Friedrich's chest with a big hand. "Elena is a good girl."

"Yeah, I know."

"Good boy. Now go up and see your fiancée, since I'm sure she is looking forward to seeing you."

"Yes, sir, good night!" Friedrich replied. He picked up his briefcase, then bounded up the stairs.

Friedrich stopped at the landing and tried to smooth his rain-dampened hair with the palms of his hands, then took off his tie and shoved it into his briefcase. He checked himself again before going to Elena's apartment and knocking. He frowned when he did not get a reply.

Zoe's door opened and her head popped out. Spotting Friedrich, she grinned. "Hey, Friedrich, she's over here." She pulled the door open wide and held it for him as he entered the apartment.

As soon as he stepped through the doorway, he was greeted by Eva and Earl, who were seated at the table playing chess. Elena came out of the kitchen with a smile, going over to Friedrich and giving him a hug and a chaste kiss.

"Congratulations, Friedrich!" Eva and Earl both said. Turning his attention back to the board, Earl moved one of his pawns.

"Thank you," Friedrich said shyly. He was even more surprised when Zoe hugged him and gave him a peck on the cheek.

"I'm very happy for both of you," Zoe whispered. She turned away from him to give Elena a hug.

"Are you two free tomorrow for dinner?" Eva asked.

Elena looked at Friedrich, who shrugged. "Yep, we're free. We'll see you tomorrow!"

He and his fiancée bade farewell to their friends and left the apartment hand-in-hand, Friedrich forcing himself not to grin like a fool at the sharp but wonderful feel of the diamond engagement ring that was pressing into his palm.

Zoe closed the door behind them. She went back into the kitchen and brought three cups, giving Earl and Eva a cup of tea before taking hers over to her workspace. She placed both hands on the cup, looked at her work on the art table, and grinned.

"She's not painting you again, is she?" Earl asked as he took a sip of tea, glancing up at the grinning Zoe.

"I hope not," Eva replied. "Zoe, what are you painting?"

"Something for the bedroom," Zoe replied.

"A nice landscape?" Earl asked. He looked at the chessboard, then back up at Eva with a scowl.

"Yeah, a mountain with valleys and peaks," Zoe replied. Eva snorted her tea all over the chessboard, causing Zoe to clap a hand over her mouth.

"Hey, are you all right?" Earl came around the table to pat Eva on the back. She gave a couple of coughs, then rose to get a towel from the kitchen to dry the tea-splattered chessboard and pieces.

"Oh, yeah," Eva said on her way to the kitchen, passing Zoe who was hunched over her artwork. She came back out and, before heading to Earl, she put her arms around Zoe's shoulders. Zoe leaned back into her. Eva pulled Zoe's hair back from her face and whispered in her ear.

Zoe's hands went very still while she listened to what Eva was whispering to her. A bright blush started creeping up Zoe's neck and face. Eva gave her a peck on the cheek before rejoining Earl at the chessboard.

Earl continued to watch Zoe as Eva wiped the spilled tea off the board.

Zoe headed for the balcony door, opened it, and stepped outside into the cool evening air, leaning on the wet railing and letting the light rain fall on her for a few moments.

"Is Zoe okay?" Earl asked. "She looks a bit flushed."

"Yes," Eva replied. She glanced outside at the balcony, giving Zoe a wink. Despite the cool shower she had just subjected herself to, Zoe remained flushed and flustered. And that was all Eva's fault.

Elena closed the door to her apartment and turned to find Friedrich smiling at her. She wrapped her arms around his waist and looked up into his brown eyes.

"I have been floating all day today," Elena said as she hugged him. She leaned up and gave him a kiss, mindful of his glasses. "Did you tell David?"

"Yep, sure did. I asked him to be my best man."

"Oh, that's nice! Eva and Zoe are going to be there for me." Elena took his jacket and briefcase and laid them down on a low table. Taking his hand, she led him to the sofa and they sat down next to each other. "Did you have a good day?"

Friedrich's smile turned rueful. "I'm not sure what a good day is supposed to be like at our office. We lose someone and it's a bad day; we find someone and it's still a bad day."

"Catching them to face justice is good, isn't it?"

Friedrich nodded. "Yes, it's good. But for every one of these people we catch, more escape, and go free."

"Like rats," Elena said quietly.

"Yeah. Today, I think we may have caught one in our net; an assistant to Dr. Josef Mengele."

"Who is Dr. Mengele?"

Friedrich sighed. "I'm so glad you don't know. He performed medical experiments on Jews at Auschwitz. He would decide people's fates as they came in on those trains. I've read one report that said he put up a chalk mark on a bunk and any child not reaching that mark was sent to the gas chambers." He took a deep breath and put his arm around Elena's shoulders, holding her tightly.

Elena put her head on Friedrich's shoulder. She shook her head sadly at yet another brutality against the Jews and shuddered at the thought of children being killed on one man's whim. "Have they caught him?"

"No," Friedrich said, a muscle working in his jaw as he suppressed some powerful emotion. "He's probably off to Argentina or Brazil. That's where a lot of Nazis fled, you know, because those countries are fascist friendly; the nationalistic strong-men who hold high office are sympathetic to the former Third Reich." He sounded bitter.

"Your family died in Auschwitz. You don't think..." Elena did not want to say the words aloud because it pained her to think of Friedrich's family in that butcher's hands.

Friedrich nodded. "My sisters died at Auschwitz. I wish you could have met them, Elena. You would have liked them. They were fun. They were very beautiful girls, dark hair and grey eyes. I got my mother's brown eyes, but they looked like papa. Heidi was a little older than Viveka." Friedrich smiled.

"Heidi and Viveka; they are beautiful names. How old were they?"

"Fifteen," Friedrich said, his voice breaking into the hush that had fallen between them.

Elena gasped at the realization that Friedrich's sisters might have been part of Mengele's experiments. She turned to her fiancé to see silent tears trailing down his cheeks. She brushed them away and said, "I'm so sorry, Friedrich." She kissed him and held on to him. "Do you know where this assistant is? Are you going to catch him?"

"It's a woman; a cold-blooded Nazi butcher," Friedrich said bitterly.

"I'm sure you and David will catch this monster...won't you?"

Friedrich turned to face her. "At lunch time I went down to the synagogue and prayed. I made a promise that I would do everything I can to catch her and send her to Nuremberg."

"I know you'll catch her," Elena said with conviction. She wanted to believe that good people did win out in the end, and that was how things worked. "Do you know where she lives?"

"Nope, she gave a false address. We wasted a couple of hours tracking down an address that ended up being a hole at a construction site. Maybe something will turn up on Monday."

"You never know how these things will turn out, sweetheart."

"Hmm. Do you want to snuggle a bit?" Friedrich asked. He got his answer when Elena put her head back down on his shoulder.

Greta looked out the window and sighed. She felt as though she was a prisoner even though there were no bars on the window. Her dreams of starting a new life had evaporated as soon as she had arrived in Sydney. The promise of freedom was a lie. Australia was on the other side of the world, but even here they were searching for former members of the Nazi party. No matter how far she fled, she could not escape pursuit. Word of her arrival had reached the authorities. How that news got to them was a mystery; one that Greta was determined to uncover.

A few well-placed calls to those who sympathized with the Third Reich's cause allowed Greta to stay one step ahead of the authorities. The best solution would be to find a way out of Sydney but Greta had unfinished business. Eva Muller was here. She was determined to win her former lover back, and then she would leave.

Randolph Wierner was a tall, broad shouldered, young man with blond hair and the bluest eyes she had ever seen. A true Aryan, Greta had thought when she had met him. He had been her contact as soon as she had left the ship and had helped her with the necessary paperwork.

She knew him as Randolph but suspected that was not his real name. Greta really did not care one way or the other, as long as he kept her true identity a secret. The encounter with Eva was a mixed blessing. She was not sure why she had gone to the interpreter service. Randolph had told her it was a stupid move, but she was sure there had been divine intervention at work.

Greta turned to face Randolph, who was standing in the lounge of her new house. "Do they know I'm here?"

"No. I've gone through their files and your name does appear, but it's in the finalized section. They think you're dead."

"I think this is where I say, 'The news of my death is greatly appreciated!'" She laughed at the idiocy of the War Crimes Tribunal's investigator's office. "I thought you said they were thorough."

"They usually are. They caught Muller and Rhimes." Randolph sounded dismissive.

Greta rolled her eyes at the mention of the two men. She had finally been briefed about what had happened and wondered how a man like Rhimes, whom she had thought intelligent, could allow Muller — who must have been out of his mind — to entertain the thought of going after Eva because she was a lesbian. Stupid men!

"Muller was affected by the explosion, although I don't understand why Rhimes agreed to expose themselves by attempting to get Muller's daughter," Greta said.

Randolph shrugged. "I don't know either."

"So what do you know about these agents, Harrison and Jacobs?"

"Nothing, really. They work for the unit. They only capture the idiots who put their real names on their immigration papers and just plod along. Both are insignificant, really."

Greta pursed her lips in thought. She did not like to leave things to chance, but on the basis of what she had heard, it was not likely that the two investigators were going to find anything. She turned back and watched the rain for a moment. "Jacobs...Jewish?" she asked.

"Ja."

Greta let out a frustrated sigh. "They are everywhere, aren't they?"

Randolph snorted. "Just about everywhere you go, there is a Jew."

"It's too bad we didn't have time to finish the *Führer's* Final Solution," Greta said, disappointed. "I met him a couple of times, you know."

"You did?" Randolph seemed impressed. "What was he like?"

Greta grinned. "Oh, he was such a charismatic man, so full of energy and ideas for Germany. His eyes were full of life," she said, thinking back to when Josef Mengele had introduced her to the great man. She had found herself tongue-tied for the first time in her life, which had amused their leader a great deal. Hitler had made a joke to relax her and they had discussed the work that was being done at Auschwitz and what Josef was accomplishing. She sighed as she thought about her mentor — a truly brilliant man whose work was never going to be fully appreciated. She could still remember how the *Führer* had praised the whole team at Auschwitz and how proud she had been to be a part of it.

"A little hero worship?" Randolph commented with a smile.

"A huge case of hero worship. I met him in 1939; he was everything a leader should be. I wish you could have met him, Randolph. He was truly a giant among men. The world owes a great deal to him and men like Dr. Josef Mengele. Speaking of whom, have you had any news of him?"

"Sadly, no, although we believe he may be in Italy."

"I hope he was able to escape those rabid American dogs. What about Bruno?"

"Dr. Weber was arrested and is due to face trial."

"Bruno was also a good doctor, but Josef was truly a marvel to watch. I feel privileged to have worked with him."

"Would you like to go out tonight?" Randolph asked.

Greta gave him a lopsided grin. "I'm a married woman, Randolph."

"Oh, well, I thought..."

"John is a good man — a drunk, but a good man. For now, I play the dutiful wife and leave the talk about divorce until things quiet down. We don't want to alert anyone that I am still alive. I'm sure there are other young women for you to wine and dine?"

Randolph nodded. "I'd best be going."

"Have a nice evening, Randolph, and keep me updated," Greta said as the younger man walked away. She chuckled to herself. Randolph was one of many who admired and wanted her, and if she chose, she could give in to her own desire. But the time was not right for that. She had other business to deal with first.

Friedrich smiled, opened his eyes, and gazed down at the dark head resting on his chest. He sighed contently, holding his fiancée in his arms. *My fiancée*, he thought and wondered if he was dreaming. If he was, he did not want this dream to end. He had found the woman he wanted to spend the rest of his life with. He looked around the room, so different from his own one bedroom apartment. His apartment was very drab and Friedrich mostly used it just to sleep in and seldom ate there, since he had no one to go home to.

Things were going to be very different now that he and Elena were together. Elena's apartment was airy; it had pink lace curtains on the windows. Several stuffed toys that usually sat on the bed had been moved to the dresser. Friedrich loved the bed. It was an antique, steel-framed bed with the most comfortable mattress he had ever felt. He had seen a bed like it in an antique shop; at the time, he had thought it would be great to own and share with someone he loved, but he had put off the purchase.

Grinning, Friedrich stared up at the ceiling. He and Elena had decided not to consummate their love for each other until they got married, but he did enjoy cuddling and lying next to this woman who kissed him with so much love that his heart often felt ready to burst.

"What's the goofy grin for?" Elena asked, gazing up at him. She had been awake for half an hour just lying in Friedrich's embrace, savoring the moments of closeness.

"Good morning." Friedrich kissed the top of her head. Elena cuddled closer. "I was thinking this was a dream and I would wake up any minute."

"Do you want to wake up?" Elena asked.

"No. I want to keep dreaming like this for the rest of my life," Friedrich replied.

"That's so romantic." Elena sighed.

"Does it make up for the proposal?"

"No." Elena gave him a mock glare and then chuckled. "We'll work on your romantic streak."

Friedrich's smile broadened.

"So, fiancé, what are we doing today?" Elena asked

"I have an appointment at nine thirty this morning to see Rabbi Mordecai."

"For the wedding? Isn't that a bit soon?"

"I wish it were for the wedding. Rabbi Mordecai met my father in Auschwitz, and I've been putting off talking to him."

"Why?"

Friedrich sighed. He was not sure if the reason would make any sense to Elena, or to anyone else for that matter. He wanted to believe his family would be back from the concentration camps and continued to hold out hope that, if no one told him that they were indeed dead, then maybe if he wished hard enough they would not be. It was nonsense and illogical and he told himself so, but having someone who was actually there tell him that they were dead would make it real.

He shook his head and answered her, "I believed that if I didn't hear it from someone who saw them at the concentration camp, that somehow it wasn't real. That I would find that it was possible for them to have survived."

Elena closed her eyes and tightened her hold on him, saying nothing.

Friedrich understood her silence; there was not anything she could say, really. He was grateful for the opportunity to continue uninterrupted. "We interviewed the rabbi just after he came to Sydney and one thing led to another, and we talked about my family. I didn't want to hear what he had to say, and told him that I would discuss it another day," he said.

"How long ago was that?"

"Six months," Friedrich replied. "He called me at the office yesterday and said that we really needed to talk."

"Do you want me to come with you?"

Friedrich smiled. "I would love for you to come, but I don't want it to cause you pain."

"It won't cause me any pain. I want to be there for you." Elena stroked his stubbled cheek as Friedrich leaned down and kissed her gently.

"I'd better get up and have a bath," he mumbled although he continued to hold her.

"I've washed the clothes you left behind last week. Do you have a tie?"

"It's in my briefcase."

"Well, Mr. Jacobs, do you want to get up?"

"Hmm, well, Miss Mannheim, I like it here but I do have to get up," Friedrich reluctantly agreed and pulled the covers off. He wore only a pair of boxer shorts. Much to Elena's amusement, they were colored pink. When she saw them she could not stop laughing, and laughed even more when Friedrich explained how he had put his white boxer shorts and a red shirt in the same wash and they had both come out pink.

"Elena, do you have any safety razors?" Friedrich called from the bathroom.

"Top shelf," Elena replied and smirked at the idea that entered her head. She wanted to go in and show him, but she decided against it. She sipped her tea then set the cup on the table and went to where she had Friedrich's clothes neatly stacked. Finding what she was looking for, Elena knocked on the bathroom door to warn him before opening it just enough to put a towel and his clean boxer shorts on the chair next to the door. She closed the door and grinned.

Elena took out the ironing board to iron his trousers from the previous day. Once that was done, she hung them on the hanger and went in search of his briefcase to look for the tie that was probably also wrinkled. The briefcase lay on the floor next to the sofa. She bent down and picked up the case, but lost hold of it. It hit the floor and popped open, spilling files and the tie out onto the carpet. Elena dropped to her knees and was picking things up when she spotted a picture that had slipped from one of the files.

She gasped; it was a photograph of the woman she had seen at Zoe and Eva's apartment, the one who had been wearing a swastika pin. Her name was Greta, Elena recalled. She turned it over but there was nothing on the back to indicate why the German woman's photograph would be in Friedrich's possession. She was somewhat embarrassed by her reaction to the woman. Nevertheless, a sickening feeling settled at the pit of her stomach as she sat back and held the picture in her trembling hand.

Friedrich walked out of the bathroom; he had a towel wrapped around his waist and his chest and shoulders were still beaded with water droplets. He frowned. "Elena, what happened?"

"I dropped the briefcase," Elena said quietly, continuing to stare at the photograph. She tore her eyes away and looked at Friedrich, then blushed and averted her gaze. "I ironed your trousers," she said.

Friedrich took the offered garment and went back into the bathroom. He came back out wearing an undershirt and trousers and walked over to where Elena was kneeling on the floor. He put his hand on her shoulder and went down on his knees to help her collect the files.

"I know that woman," Elena said, her voice barely perceptible to her own ears. The photograph in her hand shook a little as she shivered.

Friedrich seemed shocked. He stopped putting the files back in order and turned to her. "You know this woman?" he asked, indicating the photograph she still held.

Elena nodded.

"From the camp?"

"No, she was here last week."

Friedrich sat down on the carpet, almost falling backwards in his haste. "She was here? In this apartment?"

"No, she was a dinner guest at Eva's and Zoe's — remember the woman who got me so upset that night?"

Friedrich swore vehemently, startling Elena out of her reverie.

She asked, "What's the matter, who is this woman?"

"What do you know about her?" Friedrich asked, sounding urgent.

"Well, Zoe told me that Greta was Eva's first lover and…"

Friedrich groaned. "Elena, please don't tell anyone about this photograph."

"Friedrich, what is going on?" Elena asked as her fiancé sat with a scowl on his face.

"I need to call David," Friedrich said. He got up and went to the telephone.

Elena grimaced and picked up one of the files. Leaning against the sofa, she began to read the papers inside. She let out another gasp, her free hand flying to cover her mouth, as the details in front of her painted Greta as a monster. She could hear Friedrich talking to

David, then looked up as Friedrich knelt beside her once again. He took the file from her hands and put it in the briefcase.

"Did that really happen?" she asked, her mind not wanting to accept what she had read. A part of her did not want this woman to be associated with her friends — with Eva. *If Eva knows about her, that means she really was one of them,* Elena thought to herself. *No, she probably doesn't know. Does she?* It was difficult to reconcile the image of sweet and kind Eva overlooking the atrocities associated with Greta.

Friedrich nodded. "Yes. It happened in other camps, as well, but Auschwitz was where this woman was."

"I don't think Eva knows." Elena thought about her friend who had one of the most gentle of personalities. *I'm sure she doesn't know,* Elena thought, confident in her assessment. Zoe would never stay with a woman who had collaborated with the enemy.

"David is coming over and we're going to question her," Friedrich replied, running his hands through his damp hair.

"Friedrich! I know Eva, and she doesn't know anything." Elena was upset that Friedrich or David would think that Eva condoned this woman's activities, even though she had initially harbored brief doubts herself. "You make it sound like an interrogation!"

"Sweetheart, David and I are just going to ask Eva a few questions. That's all." Friedrich tried to calm her down. Elena was becoming rather angry. He continued, "I hope they are still in."

"They go to church on Sunday morning," Elena muttered. "You really can't believe Eva would know the truth about Greta, do you?"

"I don't know what to believe, Elena. I hope she knows where this woman is staying here in Sydney," Friedrich replied and let out a heartfelt sigh. "I guess I need to reschedule with the rabbi."

Panayiotis and Alberta held hands as they joined Eva and Zoe on the walk home from church. Zoe kept a step ahead of Eva and occasionally looked back at her in-laws. She pursed her lips then shook her head, deciding that she had had enough of not being able to hold hands with Eva in church or outside. She took Eva's hand and squeezed it.

Eva looked down at the joined hands and gave Zoe a grin. "I was wondering how long it would take," she said, winking.

Zoe's response was to stick out her tongue.

"Be careful with that thing." Eva quickly tried to tug Zoe's outstretched tongue with her free hand, and her fingers got caught between Zoe's teeth when Zoe bit down very carefully. The two women's eyes met and they laughed.

Zoe and Eva, flanked by Panayiotis and Alberta, continued amiably on their way home. Each couple then separated to go to their own apartments.

Zoe saw Friedrich and David first and wondered what the two men were doing standing outside their door. Zoe glanced a questioning look at Eva, who shrugged, her own puzzlement made visible by the tilt of her head and the quirk of her eyebrow. After a brief greeting, Eva opened the door and they all went inside.

"So what's up?" Eva asked, folding her arms over her chest and waiting for an answer.

It was clear to Zoe that Eva was feeling uneasy, since David was present.

David began, "Friedrich and I are here on business—"

"I figured that out, David," Eva replied warily.

Zoe turned to Eva, took her by the hand and led her to the sofa where they sat down side-by-side. Zoe's hand went to Eva's knee and gave it a little squeeze. "What's this about? Has Muller escaped or something?" Zoe asked the agent.

"No." David pulled out Greta's photograph. "Do you know this person?"

Eva took the photograph from David. "Yes, that's Greta Strauss." She handed the photograph to Zoe who looked at it, then glanced up in shock at Friedrich, and then looked back at Eva. Eva had a composed look on her face, but Zoe knew there was emotional turmoil going on beneath that placid expression.

"What type of uniform is that?" Zoe asked.

"A nurse," Eva replied, her voice breaking.

Without hesitating Zoe leaned over. "Evy?" she whispered.

Eva closed her eyes for a moment and then opened them. She squeezed Zoe's hand and turned to David, her spine stiffening.

"How do you know Miss Strauss?" David asked, sitting down on the chair facing the sofa.

Eva exhaled loudly. "I knew her in Germany, before the war."

"What was your relationship with her?"

Zoe scowled. "What business is it of yours?"

"Zoe," Eva quietly reproved her, her tone carrying a warning.

Zoe shook her head. "No, Eva. I have had enough of this stupidity. When are they going to learn that you are not a Nazi and never have been? Does every Nazi have to be traced back to you?" Zoe lost her temper completely. Her voice had risen almost to a shout that caused Ourania to flee into the bedroom.

Eva sighed. "Zoe's right. I don't have connections with every Nazi in the world, and it's insulting for you to presume that I do simply because I'm German."

"Look, Eva..." It was apparent that David was attempting to return to the interrogation and not be distracted by the emotions that were running high. "I'm not trying—"

"Of course you are! You are trying to link Eva to whatever this is," Zoe angrily interjected.

"No, I'm not. I'm trying to find out her relationship to the Strauss woman." David sounded patient.

"She was my lover," Eva said. "I lost contact with her back in 1938."

David glanced at Zoe, who was shooting daggers at him. "On what date did you lose contact with Strauss?" he asked Eva.

"Last time I saw Greta was on the 9th of November, 1938," Eva answered.

"You remember so clearly what happened ten years ago?" David asked.

Eva did not look up but kept her head bowed. "I do."

"What the hell does that have to do with everything?" Zoe asked, trying to protect Eva. She knew David was not aware that he was pouring salt into a very raw and open wound, but she blamed him for Eva's distress nonetheless.

"I'm not sure why you are so reluctant to tell me more details. Why did you lose contact?" David asked. He leaned forward, resting his elbows on his knees. "If you have nothing to hide, and I believe you don't, why not tell us?"

Eva gazed at him for a moment. When she spoke, every word was precisely enunciated. "That was the night my mother was murdered and the night my stepfather, Muller, beat me — almost to death. You know the rest of the story. It's probably in your files. Does that answer your question?"

David sat back and ran his hand through his blond hair, clearly frustrated. "*Kristallnacht*," he said. "I'm...sorry...I..."

Zoe snorted in disgust. "You might as well stick a knife in her and twist it, you son of a bitch!" She sneered at the investigator, then took Eva's hand and held it tightly enough to make her own bones begin to ache from the pressure.

"All right, can we all cool down a moment, please?" Friedrich spoke for the first time since they had entered the apartment. "Eva, Greta Strauss is wanted for crimes against humanity under the War Crimes Act. We want to find out everything we can, so we can do our jobs."

Zoe glanced at her partner, who did not seem that shocked by the information but had a resigned look on her face. *What's going on in that head of yours?* Zoe thought.

Eva met her gaze. There was a haunted expression in her eyes which only made Zoe worry more. It was the same look of utter hopelessness that Zoe had seen the first time they had met. She felt a chill shudder up her spine.

Unsettled, Zoe tore her gaze away from Eva, although she continued to cling to the woman's hand. "Why am I not surprised?" she asked, commenting about Greta's war crimes record. "I should have known the woman was no good."

"Greta Strauss was my former lover. I hadn't had contact with her since 1938. I don't know where she is, and I don't know how to contact her now," Eva answered, the strain in every line of her body apparent.

Zoe quickly glanced at Eva, a little surprised at her partner's answer. *Why had Eva not mentioned that they had hosted Greta to dinner in their apartment not that long ago?* Eva appeared totally befuddled and Zoe was certain her partner was not thinking straight at all.

Eva fingered the ring on her finger; Zoe had long ago recognized this as a sign Eva was feeling anxious. Feeling somewhat belligerent on Eva's behalf, Zoe decided to keep her mouth closed and not contribute any information unless the boofhead agents asked for it.

"It isn't my intention to re-open old wounds, Eva." David loosened the knot in his tie. "I really *don't* want to stick the knife in," he said, staring squarely at Zoe. "I want to catch this woman and this is the best lead we've had in ages, so if you can help us, we would really appreciate it. We heard she was in your apartment recently."

Eva took a deep breath, not relaxing one whit. "Greta Strauss, myself, and a few other friends were participating in *Kristallnacht*." She avoided eye contact with Friedrich. "I decided to go home while the others continued and that was the last I saw of Greta."

David sat back. "What happened after that?"

"After what?"

"After Muller beat you."

"That has nothing to do with Greta or your investigation. It's something I prefer not to talk about," Eva replied tersely and stared at David.

Zoe knew her partner was daring him to try and continue that line of questioning. *Don't ask her or I'll thump you,* Zoe thought and glared a warning at David.

David seemed surprised by Eva's reluctance. Nevertheless, his next question made it clear that he would no longer pursue the topic of Muller. "So *Kristallnacht* was the last time you saw her?"

"Yes, until recently, when she came to the interpreter section of the Immigration Department. She was using the name Wagner, her husband's surname."

David and Friedrich looked at each other. "I thought you *said* you last saw her in 1938. Now you *say* she came to your office and saw you?" David asked.

Zoe's rage ratcheted up a notch at the two men but at David in particular. It was plainly obvious to her — and she supposed to everyone else present — that Eva was in shock at the news about her former lover, and therefore confused. "You would be a little unsure of what you were saying if a bombshell was dropped on you," Zoe angrily interjected.

"Yes…no…I mean, I thought you wanted to know when was the last time I saw her in Germany," Eva said, flushing in her embarrassment.

"No, the question was when did you last see Miss Strauss," David explained. "How did she know you worked there if you had lost contact with her?"

"I don't think she knew I was there. I just happened to be the German interpreter on duty at the time."

"A big coincidence."

"I guess so. She seemed as surprised to see me as I was her," Eva sighed.

"Quite. What did she want?"

"Information about family law."

"Why?"

"She wants to divorce her husband, or at least, that's the story she gave me."

"So you invited her to your apartment?"

"No...I mean, yes," Eva faltered over her words again. "I was very shocked when I saw her and I guess I invited her to dinner."

"What happened when she arrived?"

"We ate, we talked, and she left," Zoe said, cutting off whatever Eva was going to say. Zoe barely avoided saying she would have loved to have punched the living daylights out of the woman. Maintaining control was difficult, but she knew that an outburst from her would not help Eva at all, so she bit the inside of her cheek to stay quiet.

"And that was the last time you talked to her?"

"Yes. Zoe saw her at the office later when she came to meet me." Eva smiled at Zoe for the first time since the questioning had started and wrapped an arm around her shoulders. Zoe was tense, but she relaxed slightly in Eva's embrace.

David turned to regard Zoe. "You were alone with Miss Strauss?"

"No. Debbie, the receptionist, was there when Greta came in looking for Eva," Zoe said flatly.

"What did she want?"

"What do you think she was there for?" Zoe asked, ignoring the strangled cough that Eva let out, trying to cover a chuckle. She went on speaking to David. "She was there to see Eva."

David ignored the comment and continued writing in his notebook. "She came to see Eva?"

"Yeeessss," Zoe said, hissing the word in frustration.

"And?"

"And what? Eva wasn't in the office; she had gone down to the filing room."

"Okay, so Eva wasn't there and Miss Strauss saw you."

"Yes."

"You're not being very forthcoming, are you, Zoe?" David asked, his impatience obvious although he was clearly attempting to cover it with a neutral demeanor.

"That's Miss Lambros to you, Mr. Harrison, if you continue to take that tone with me. We're not the enemy. I should think you would have figured that out after Muller."

Friedrich cut in, probably to avoid Zoe and David coming to blows, and asked, "Zoe, did Greta say anything to you?"

Zoe grimaced. "She wanted to speak to Eva. Since she wasn't there, she gave a phone number to the receptionist to get Eva to call her."

"She gave you a phone number?" David interrupted, glaring at Eva.

"Yes, she left a phone number," Zoe said, hoping to deflect the agent's ire.

"Didn't you think a phone number left by your ex-lover would be important?" David asked a very flustered Eva, who merely looked away.

"I forgot," she murmured meekly.

"You *forgot*?" David was incredulous. "We are looking for anything to catch this woman and you have her phone number in your possession and you forgot to tell us. What were you thinking? Do you still have it?"

Zoe inhaled, about to blast the man, but Eva patted her thigh and she deflated, contenting herself with giving David a look of dislike.

"Yes," Eva replied. She went into the bedroom, returning momentarily with a piece of paper that she gave to David. He took it and jotted down the number in his notebook, then indicated the phone with his fountain pen. Eva nodded.

David dialed the number, waited for a few seconds, then hung up. "That's the German Community Club," he said, his frustration apparent.

"I guess I would have had to leave a message for her to contact me," Eva replied. "Can you answer some of my questions? Why are you after Greta? You said something about crimes against humanity. I find that hard to believe."

"Do you know Dr. Kurt Gutzeit?"

Eva froze for a moment; a tendril of fear gripped her heart at the mention of the Schutzstaffel doctor. "Yes," Eva finally said, "I know of Dr. Gutzeit."

"Evy?" Zoe asked, concerned that the other woman was even more pale and looked ready to pass out. Zoe wondered how much more Eva could take with each new question and revelation.

Eva took a deep breath. "I'm all right."

"You don't look all right." Zoe directed her hostile gaze at the two men.

"I know of Dr. Gutzeit," Eva repeated, ignoring Zoe's protective attitude.

"Dr. Gutzeit was at Auschwitz. The woman you know as Miss Greta Strauss was his assistant. She also assisted a Dr. Weber, who did studies on mind controlling drugs, and a Dr. Mengele, now known as the Angel of Death." David handed Eva a sheet of paper and she began to read, scowling as she did so. All of a sudden, the blood drained completely from her face, leaving her white to the lips and shaking. Zoe looked at her with concern. Eva handed her the paper, the tremors in her hand almost making her drop the sheet.

"Oh, God," Zoe whispered as she read about the SS doctors and assistants who had performed so-called medical experiments in Auschwitz. "My God."

"Greta Strauss assisted in those experiments," David repeated.

Eva swallowed, her appearance still sickly. Zoe imagined the woman's heart must be galloping a mile a minute. She leaned in and whispered reassurances to Eva, who merely nodded and kept her downcast eyes on her lap. David cleared his throat; he was obviously embarrassed at interrupting a tender moment between the lovers.

"What do you want from us?" Eva finally asked.

"Help in catching her," David responded. His attitude was suggestive of waiting for an explosion.

The explosion came moments later from an enraged Zoe, who could not hold back another minute. Expletives in Greek peppered the air, surprising Friedrich and David, even though the men had been braced for a tirade. Finally, Zoe continued in English, "You two are insane! Absolutely insane. You're..." Zoe stopped her abuse for a moment, unable to think of the word she wanted in English, which only frustrated her more. "*Arschloch!*" she finally exclaimed. "The last time you wanted Eva's help, you nearly got her killed! You nearly got us all killed! Incompetent *Arschloch!*"

"That wasn't—" David began.

"Shut up! You two *are* Keystone Cops!" Zoe screamed. She got up and walked towards the balcony, her temper still boiling, needing to compose herself somewhat as cursing was getting her nowhere. A moment later she returned, still agitated but no longer quite so close to knocking the men's heads together. "Oh, yes, we know how you are really good at getting in place to capture Nazis," Zoe snorted.

"How were we supposed to know that Mrs. Jenkins told Muller and Rhimes to come up here and then let them in to your real apartment?" Friedrich asked, aggrieved by what he clearly felt was an unfair accusation. "It wasn't our fault we were in the wrong apartment."

"Involving Eva was a stupid idea to begin with!" Zoe said. She and Eva exchanged a meaningful glance.

Eva stood, put her hand on Zoe's shoulder and leaned in. "Zoe, we have to help."

Zoe was not sure who to be angrier with. She was incredulous at Eva's words and furious with David's suggestion that her partner place herself in jeopardy again. She was about to say how foolish the idea was but she caught the look in Eva's eyes and the words remained unsaid, swallowed by resigned acceptance. Eva's previous shell-shocked appearance had changed. She appeared far more in control of herself and her emotions.

Eva turned back to David and said, "We will help you."

"Greta is extremely dangerous," David said. Zoe snorted again, and he shrugged a silent apology at stating the obvious. "Can you call her and get her to come over here?"

"Why not get her to meet me at the office?" Eva asked.

"It's too crowded. I've seen that office. It's packed to the rafters with refugees most of the time." David paused, considering. "Can you tell her you're interested in restarting the relationship?"

"A bit hard to do when I've told her I am married and quite happily at that," Eva said, squeezing Zoe's hand.

David appeared stumped. He turned to Friedrich with a questioning look.

"What if you told her that you changed your mind? Women do that, don't they?" Friedrich asked.

"I'm not the kind of person who changes her mind about the woman I love and have promised to spend the rest of my life with, Friedrich," Eva responded. Zoe liked the young man, and Eva did, too, but he did have a tendency to put his foot in his mouth.

"Greta doesn't know that," Friedrich persisted as he sat down next to Eva on the sofa. "You could say that...that Zoe was cheating on you and you had decided that you want to be with Greta instead. You can invite her to the office, have Zoe there, have a mock argument so she can see you really are fighting—"

"Isn't that rather melodramatic?" Eva asked.

"What about if you invited Greta to your office, allowed her to kiss you and Zoe accidentally walked in?" Friedrich suggested.

"And then I kill her," Zoe piped up, grinning in a bloodthirsty fashion. "I like that plan."

Eva smirked at Zoe's enthusiasm. "I don't think they want her dead, love."

Friedrich persisted, "So, do you think that would work?"

"It could. Then what?"

"You bring her back here and we'll be waiting," David said, tapping his fountain pen on the notebook and blotting the page with ink.

Zoe turned back to David, slightly calmer though still displeased with the man. "You will remember what apartment number it is, won't you?"

David sighed. "We'll be here waiting."

"Okay," Eva agreed. Zoe nodded although she was not entirely convinced of the wisdom of the men's plan.

"We'll come by tomorrow to finalize the plans, and then you can ring Greta and set it up," David said.

They agreed on that arrangement and Eva saw them out. She closed the door quietly and leaned her shoulder against it, letting her head droop down. Zoe's arms wrapped around her partner's waist, her cheek resting against Eva's back.

"If they botch it up, I don't know if we can get out of this one," Zoe whispered. She and Eva had been lucky to escape with their lives when Muller and Rhimes were captured. Zoe was terrified of what would happen, even if they did succeed. The emotional toll it was taking on Eva, even before they put David's oh-so-brilliant plan into action, was making Zoe heartsick.

"They won't," Eva whispered. "I hope to God they don't." Eva turned around in Zoe's embrace, her arms coming up to squeeze Zoe more tightly to her.

Zoe reached up and tenderly stroked Eva's cheek. Her next words were in stark contrast to that caress. "I'm going to kill them if they do. That's a promise."

An unknown period of time of solitude followed. They attempted to strengthen and comfort each other through the hugging that continued long after Zoe's promise.

Eva was disgusted by what she had read about her former lover, a woman she had thought she knew but quite obviously did not. Details of the horrific experiments that Greta had assisted in were making her sick to her stomach, bringing back horrible memories from her own incarceration and brutal treatment from the Schutzstaffel doctors in Aiden intent on "curing" her of her lesbianism.

For both their sakes, Eva tried to clamp down on the rising panic she was feeling. She was not sure how she could pretend to show affection to Greta and not think of what had been done to her and many others by Hitler's Third Reich in general, and the Schutzstaffel in particular. Somehow she needed to focus and not let those memories interfere with what she had to do. She felt Zoe's arms around her and swallowed hard at the flush of emotion that washed over her. Eva turned in Zoe's embrace. "I'm sorry," she said, stroking the younger woman's cheek.

"What for?"

"For what I'm about to do to you," Eva replied and let her tears fall. She did not want to hurt Zoe, but a pretend rift between them appeared to be the only way they could get Greta back to the apartment and spring their trap. "I don't want to do it, but I can't think of another way than to pretend we fight."

Zoe looked into Eva's eyes and put her hand on Eva's chest. "I know I own your heart," she said softly. "Just don't let her kiss you too much."

Zoe tried to joke, but as her voice broke, Eva could tell Zoe was already experiencing pain. "I promise," Eva responded and leaned down. She cupped Zoe's face in her hands and kissed her passionately, causing Zoe to moan as the kiss deepened.

"And not like that," Zoe said a little breathlessly as they parted.

"I reserve those for only you," Eva reassured as she hugged Zoe. It was going to be difficult to fool Greta, and she was not an actress, but she would have to do it. She had to, for all those who had not stood a chance when they were sentenced to their deaths.

Chapter Thirty

"All right..." Zoe said, and paused when she heard an unmistakable sound coming from the bathroom. She quickly ran there, to find Eva on her knees on the tiled floor wiping her mouth. Before Zoe could say anything, Eva retched again and began to heave into the toilet bowl.

Zoe went down on her knees and held her partner as the spasms subsided. She got up and wet a face cloth, then opened the cabinet above the sink and took out a medicine measuring-cup and filled it with water. She brought them back to where Eva was still kneeling on the floor.

"Oh, God." Eva let out a frustrated groan. She took the cup of water; her hands were shaking so much that water slopped over the rim. Zoe steadied it and helped Eva get the cup to her lips. She took a long sip and sighed.

"What's the matter, Evy, are you sick?" Zoe felt Eva's sweaty brow and could not detect the telltale sign of a fever. "You were all right earlier." She tenderly wiped Eva's face with the damp face cloth and looked into her tear-filled eyes.

"It's not that," Eva finally said. She slumped back against the wall, bringing her knees to her chest and letting her head hang down. "I tried, Zoe, I really tried."

"What did you try?"

Eva took a deep breath and sighed again. "I tried not to let what I read in Greta's file get to me."

Zoe finally understood. Without another word needing to be said, Zoe put her arms around Eva and held her. "Evy, it got to me as well and I didn't live through what you went through."

"I tried," Eva repeated in a murmur.

"Would it help to talk about it?"

Eva sighed. "Gutzeit and Weber helped my uncle at the 'spa,'" she said quietly and closed her eyes. Zoe remained silent and held her. Allowing Eva to talk without interrupting was something Zoe knew worked; and, in truth, there was nothing she could say. The only thing she could do was to listen.

"The experiments that I just read about, that Greta helped with, reminded me..." Eva started, and then stopped. She licked her lips and continued. "They wanted to make me stop loving women."

"Bastards," Zoe muttered, unable to stop herself. Zoe closed her own tear-filled eyes and said a silent prayer. "Evy," she whispered and kissed the woman tenderly on her brow. "I've got you." She held her tightly as Eva sobbed. When Eva began to get herself under control, Zoe spoke softly to her, urging her up off the floor, knowing the position was not good for her back. "Come on, love, let's get you up and somewhere a bit more comfortable."

Zoe helped Eva up. They stood for a moment in the middle of the bathroom just holding on to each other for both emotional and physical support. At last, Zoe wiped Eva's face with the hand towel before they left the bathroom and went into the lounge.

"I'm sorry." Eva hiccupped. She scrubbed her wet eyes with the back of her hand.

"You have nothing to be sorry about." Zoe cupped her Eva's face between her palms as the taller woman leaned closer to her, seeking comfort. "You did nothing wrong. The only thing you are guilty of is loving a woman." *The wrong woman.* "We will get that bitch, I swear."

"I made a promise to God not to fall for another woman; I promised Him that I would never ever give my heart to anyone," Eva revealed. She sat on the sofa and pulled an astonished Zoe down with her. "If He would make them stop the pain, I would become a nun if I had to. Celibacy seemed like a small price to pay."

"I think He would have understood that it was a promise you couldn't keep," Zoe smiled. "He knew your heart, Evy."

"Why did He allow them to do that to me?" Eva whispered a thought that had clearly echoed in her mind for years. "How could He forget me when I needed Him the most? Didn't I believe in Him enough?"

Zoe closed her eyes for a moment as her own demons surfaced. "When Mama was murdered, I believed God was to blame and screamed at Him. How could He allow my mother to die; didn't He care?" Zoe opened her eyes and ran her fingers through Eva's thick dark hair, caressing the shining strands as they slipped through her grasp. "Father H came to me and I screamed at him that God was a liar. I refused to let Him help me when I needed Him the most."

"What did Father say?"

Zoe smiled. "He took my hand and said, 'God sent me to hold your hand, and here I am.' God saw you needed Him, Evy, and He sent me to hold your hand. He sent Father H. He sent Earl and Ally."

Eva nodded. She found a handkerchief and blew her nose, giving Zoe a bleary smile. "He gave me a treasure when you came into my life. I'm so lucky to have you."

"He also sent me you, to hold *my* hand," Zoe added. "Together we can withstand everything those bastards can throw at us." She smiled through her own tears. "I want you to know something."

"What's that?"

"You are the most courageous woman I know." Zoe wiped a renewed spate of tears from Eva's face and looked into the woman's bloodshot blue eyes. "You gave me your heart without knowing what I was going to do with it."

Another watery smile curved across Eva's mouth. She said, "I fell in love with you." Eva closed her eyes and leaned against Zoe. "I was so terrified," she added.

"I know," Zoe said. She stroked Eva's back in soothing circles. "You flinched every time I brushed against you when I first came to work for you."

Eva looked at Zoe in amazement. "You noticed that?" she asked. It was obvious that she thought she had disguised her terror enough not to let Zoe know her weakness.

"I would have had to be blind not to, love," Zoe gently replied. "That first day when I helped you with your bath, I touched you and I thought you were going to jump out of your skin."

Eva sniffled. "My heart was racing so much I was afraid it was going to jump out of my chest," she said quietly. "I didn't want you there, Zoe."

"I know; you were trying very hard not to have a bath," Zoe teased. She sobered when she thought back to that day in Larissa. Eva had been terrified. She had tried to appear as if disrobing in front of another woman was commonplace, but Zoe had seen her hands trembling. At the time Zoe had not cared; she had not gone there to care about Eva Muller. Looking back on that time, Zoe understood what had been unclear then.

"I had hoped that Despina would draw my bath and help me." Eva shrugged slightly and sighed. Despina was the Greek housekeeper who had befriended her even though she was the enemy. The Germans had commandeered the use of a large house in the center of Larissa as Muller's residence. Despina had been forced into being their housekeeper, cook, and a maid to Eva until Zoe was hired. For over a year Despina had been the only friendly face Eva could count on amidst the hate emanating from the Greek villagers and the contempt of her stepfather.

"I'm not surprised you were terrified to disrobe," Zoe said.

"I was so ashamed," Eva said. "I thought you would be glad to see the scars."

Zoe was not surprised to find that out. It was true that Zoe had hated Eva with every fiber of her being in those early days, but a fundamental shift had occurred the moment Eva disrobed. Seeing the woman naked and vulnerable, seeing the proof that she had suffered, had defused Zoe's anger. There had been a fragile quality to Eva Muller that still made Zoe feel protective. She had found herself extremely confused by what her heart was telling her even though she had desired vengeance.

"I saw Eva Muller, and not just Hans Muller's daughter that day," Zoe said. "I had so much hate in me, Evy, but seeing you like that, I couldn't hate you anymore."

"You weren't repulsed by my scars?"

Zoe shook her head. When she had glimpsed the large scar that ran across Eva's belly, she had been shocked and pitying. "You looked so scared, Evy. It must have taken so much courage to actually turn your back to me."

Eva swallowed audibly and nodded. "I envisioned you were laughing and enjoying seeing me like that. When you touched me..."

"You tried to move away," Zoe finished Eva's sentence. She could still recall Eva's reaction to her touch. The bathtub had prevented her from going anywhere and the muscles in Eva's back had bunched up tightly as she struggled not to flinch. "I didn't find them repulsive, and I still don't."

"Love is blind." Eva wiped her eyes and smiled tiredly at her partner.

"No, love isn't blind." Zoe shook her head. "To you, your scars are repulsive; to me they are a sign of courage. You withstood everything those bastards did to you and survived. No, I thought you were so beautiful," she said, honestly. "I saw you naked and I knew why I didn't like boys."

Eva smiled. "I...I didn't want a maid, but Muller wanted me to have one and then Father thought it was going to be a good thing."

"The only time those two would ever agree on anything." Zoe smiled. "I fell for you so badly," she said, tipping Eva's face up. "Remember when we cuddled up and I fell asleep in your bed and then Despina caught us?"

Evy nodded.

Zoe knew it was not hard to remember the look of absolute surprise on the older woman's face when she had entered Eva's bedroom to find Zoe lying in Eva's bed next to her, both of them curled up together.

"I remember," Eva said.

"After you fell asleep, I watched you for a bit then I tucked the blanket over you," Zoe confessed. "I touched you and even in your sleep you winced. I knew then that what Muller did to you must have been horrible."

Eva blinked. "I didn't realize..."

"On the ship when you were asleep, I would look at you." Zoe smiled as she recalled the bouts of insomnia on board the *Patris* that had led her to acquire a new hobby. "I would watch you sleep and then very quietly come down from the bunk and kiss you very lightly on the cheek, so as not to wake you. One night you smiled, and I thought you were awake. But when I realized you weren't, your smile told me that you loved and trusted me with all your soul."

"I vowed never to trust anyone again," Eva said, her voice soft, almost shy. "You asked me earlier how I had changed. I trusted more, Zoe. I believed people. I believed Greta when she said she loved me and wanted to show me the world."

"You were in love."

"No, I was naïve and stupid," Eva said, suddenly bitter.

"Remember when you told me to not to put myself down and to stop saying I was a peasant?" Zoe gently admonished. "I think you should do the same thing. You were young but you weren't stupid."

Eva sighed. "I was essentially your age, Zoe."

"So? You were eighteen years old and you were in love, Evy." Zoe took Eva's hand and held it tightly against her chest. "When you give your heart, you give it completely. It's not your fault. It's their fault for betraying your trust."

Eva shook her head. "I seem to have a track record of people betraying my trust. So it must..."

"Stop it." Zoe pressed her fingers to Eva's lips. "I want you to stop beating yourself up because of what those bastards did. Greta, your stepfather, your uncle, and the rest of them are the ones to blame. It's not you."

Eva leaned back against the sofa and closed her eyes. "I loved my uncle Dieter so much. He gave me my first camera and showed me how to use it."

Zoe remained silent and did not give voice to her opinion of Eva's uncle.

"He and Gutzeit were friends," Eva went on in a monotone. There was a far-away look in her eyes that Zoe did not like. When Eva continued to speak, however, more animation returned to her face. "Their goal was to find a cure for homosexuality."

"Bastards."

Eva drew Zoe's hand to her mouth and laid a kiss on it. "I don't want to ever be cured if it means I'll stop loving you."

"How did you convince them that they won?"

Eva looked down at their interlocked hands. "I managed to pass their tests," she said and fell silent. Zoe watched her carefully as the far-away look returned.

"Eva, tell me what you are thinking." Zoe gently tried to coax her partner into talking. Eva's memories were painful and having her bottle them up inside was taking its toll. Zoe's previous thought had been to wait until Eva revealed what she wanted, but it was obvious that this tactic was only prolonging the pain.

The silence stretched on.

"You can't continue like this, Evy; keeping this inside you is eating you up. I'm here to help you. Remember God sent me to hold your hand; why don't you let me?" Zoe finally asked, hoping Eva would break down that mental wall she had built long ago.

"I don't know if can," Eva replied hoarsely and turned to Zoe. "Can I have a glass of water?"

Zoe nodded and got up from the couch. Halfway to the kitchen she glanced back and saw Eva doubled over with her hands over her face. Zoe was not sure how she was going to help Eva, but she was determined to give her partner all the support she could. She entered the kitchen and took down a drinking glass from the cupboard. Zoe looked at the glass for a long moment and then closed her eyes.

Lord, give me the strength to help her; she can't do this on her own," she prayed. *She's the most courageous person I have ever met. I love her so much and seeing her like this makes me want to go and kill every last one of those bastards for what they put her through.* Zoe could not stop the tears from running down her cheeks and did not care that she had sworn in her prayer. God understood what she meant. *She's the best thing that ever happened to me and You sent Father H to hold my hand when I needed You the most. Let me hold her hand, please. Give me the strength.*

Zoe crossed herself and kissed the gold cross that hung around her neck, then filled the glass with water and returned to the lounge.

Eva ran her hands through her hair, took a deep breath and let it out slowly. The humiliation and pain were something she did not want to tell Zoe about. She loved Zoe with all her heart but was terrified of admitting how her own weaknesses — open and raw and so very frail — had been exposed. Eva glanced down at her hand and touched the ring Zoe had given her.

You're a coward, Eva thought to herself. She swallowed and her hand went to her throat where a gold cross hung on its chain around her neck; the cross seemed cool to her touch. Taking hold of it, she bowed her head and prayed.

Father, I don't know what to do. You know how much I love Zoe. If it wasn't for her, I would be dead. You know that. That night at Athena's Bluff, where I stood on the precipice and asked You to forgive me for what I was about to do...and You stopped me, Father. I was ready to end my life and You stopped me. I didn't know why You didn't let me end the pain then, but You had a plan. You sent me this angel. Help me now, Father. Please." Eva kissed the cross. She heard Zoe coming out of the kitchen and steeled herself for the ordeal to come.

"Here you go," Zoe gave her the glass and sat back down next to Eva. Eva could see Zoe looking at her. The other woman's eyes were red-rimmed and she knew what Zoe had been doing in the kitchen. Doubts continued to assail her. Maybe she should not burden Zoe with her memories.

Eva lifted the glass and very slowly drank a mouthful, then held the glass and stared at the colorless liquid. "I...they...uh..." Eva was not sure how to begin the horrible tale. "I've never wanted to talk about this. I thought if I said the words..."

"Words can't hurt you, Evy. No one can hurt you anymore," Zoe said softly. Eva felt herself tremble as Zoe held her in her arms.

"After Muller beat me, I don't remember much of anything. I remember the pain..." Eva stopped for a moment to compose herself. She looked at Zoe. "Tell me if this is too hard for you."

Zoe shook her head. "Go on."

"I can't remember how long the trip took, but it was by car..."

"You were sent in a car? In the condition you were in?" Zoe sounded shocked.

"I was unconscious for most it, but I do remember bits and pieces. I think it's a good thing I can't remember most of it," Eva said, rolling the glass around between her hands. "I was taken to the spa and my injuries were treated. I was a mess. My back, my legs..."

"This was a real hospital?"

"Yes...it was a real spa, but part of it was set off to house its own hospital." Eva sighed. "By the first of the year I was moving about, a little stiffly, but my back was on the mend. Soon after..." Eva stopped and took another deep breath. "They told me that I would have a visitor, and then they blindfolded me."

"Why?" Zoe asked.

"The blindfold was because they wanted my visitor to be a surprise." Eva let out a pained chuckle. The betrayal of that night still hurt. The love and trust in her uncle had been utterly decimated. "I loved my uncle so much."

Zoe held her tighter. Eva leaned in against her partner, needing the closeness.

"He betrayed me, Zoe. I was taken to a room by my nurse and I was told that I would get a visitor and I should wait. I thought, as they had planned, that it was Greta who had come to see me. The woman who came into the room was wearing the same perfume and she spoke like Greta, sounded just like her." Eva closed her eyes, remembering the feeling of joy at the knowledge that her lover had not abandoned her after all. "It wasn't Greta; it was someone that just...they used her to get to me." She hesitated, not wanting to form the words of what was to follow, not wanting to relive it once more. Speaking aloud about it would make the pain she felt at the betrayal even more agonizing, but it had to be done.

Eva braced herself and let the words flow slowly. "The nurse...she laughed at me and called me a deviant. She pushed me to the floor and kicked me." Eva let go of any semblance of control and lay in Zoe's arms, sobbing. She felt Zoe's silent tears join her own. After several minutes, Eva found her voice and continued, "They took me into a room and they beat me. They beat me as though I was an animal. After all that time of healing the wounds my stepfather gave me, they beat me!"

Zoe tightened her hold. Eva appreciated the silent support.

"I never experienced pain like it; it was like someone was shoving hot pokers into my back. I passed out and when I came to..." Eva found her throat dry and constricted. She tried to calm herself by taking deep breaths and drank some more water. "I came to on a bed and I was strapped down to the bed, face up. I could not move; my back was on fire."

Eva felt as though her rapidly beating heart might explode at the retelling. She had not revealed or even hinted at this part to Zoe before; it was a new horror and she thanked God that her partner could never imagine what she had suffered. Since their relationship began, Eva had given Zoe minor insights into her ordeal and then had backed away from the memories. Now that the "spa" was being revealed as the torture house it had been, Eva's vivid recollection made her feel as though she had returned to the place. Nevertheless, she would not allow her building anxiety to overpower her. She reminded herself that the experience was in the past, and the memories could only hurt her if she let them.

"They shoved a cloth-covered stick in my mouth and they put these things on my body," Eva said. "Uh...they sent an electric current through me. I...they shocked me so many times, I didn't think I would live. I remember screaming and screaming; the pain was indescribable. They kept yelling at me that I was a deviant and I was sick."

Zoe's soft kiss was meant to comfort, and it did. "How long did that go on for?" she asked, her voice gentle.

"Months. I had this nurse...she wore the same uniform that Greta has in that photo. I'll never forget her face. It was a cruel face, Zoe. She took pleasure in my pain, laughed at me when I cried. She injected me with drugs that made me sick...and they left me in my..." Eva stopped. She took another deep breath. Even at this moment, the next part was humiliating. "They left me tied to a bed, in my own filth, not caring if I was sick and hurting. They wanted me to become 'normal'. To give up."

Zoe swallowed hard and let Eva rest her head on her shoulder. Eva felt the shudder run through her partner, and understood that Zoe was controlling herself for her sake. She was chilled and grateful for Zoe's warmth.

"I can still feel the needle in my arm." Eva shivered and swallowed audibly. "They...they gave me drugs which made me so sick. I wanted so much to die," she whispered. "They wouldn't let me."

"That's the only good thing they have ever done in their miserable lives," Zoe said and kissed Eva's temple. "I wouldn't have met you and I would have been lost without you. I'm glad they didn't succeed in killing you."

"They nearly did," Eva said. "The doctors sent a local priest thinking he would tell me that I would go to hell and burn forever. I didn't know his name. He was an old man and he became my friend because he was kind to me, in his own way."

"You have a way with priests," Zoe teased and got a small chuckle out of Eva.

"The priest read to me, encouraged me to be strong. He read encouraging scriptures to give me the strength to continue. He told me that God was my protector, He was going to lead me to where I could find refreshment..." Eva remembered the old man, his gentleness and his faith. He had not scolded her or condemned her to hellfire for being a lesbian. She had no doubt that was what her tormentors wanted to happen, to drive her to an even deeper level of despair.

"Your favorite scripture," Zoe said. "Is that why you have Psalm 23 written on the inside cover of your Bible?" she asked.

Eva's Bible was a well-read book. In the margins she kept special notes to herself, a habit that had always fascinated Zoe. The book was a gift from her father and inside the front page was the whole of Psalm 23 in beautiful script.

"I thought it was because it was a scripture of hope," Zoe said.

Eva nodded. "He would recite that to me whenever he visited. He would hold my hand and look into my eyes telling me that God loved me. Then he stopped coming. I didn't know why but they increased...uh...they would leave me for days without any food or water; only that woman would come in, inject me with the drugs and then leave."

"Is that what Greta was working on in Auschwitz? The drugs?"

"That's one of the things listed that Greta was working on. Maybe they thought that the drugs would stop me wanting, I don't know, but they only made me sick." Eva stopped for a few minutes, needing a pause to resume control of her emotions. "I was locked in a tiny room for months; I didn't know whether it was day or night."

"Oh Evy, the cabin on the ship. That was almost a broom closet and we had hardly any room." Zoe bit her lip. "I'm so sorry."

Eva glanced at Zoe, giving her a sheepish look. "That cabin was the same size as the room I was kept in," she admitted. On the ship, Eva had found every excuse not to go to sleep and would delay going to bed till well past midnight on most nights.

Now Zoe knew why; the cabin was a reminder of Eva's windowless prison. "Now I understand why the porthole was open in the mornings when I thought I had shut it the night before," Zoe said.

Ashamed, Eva turned away, but Zoe gently turned her face back towards her. "You have nothing to be embarrassed about, Evy," Zoe said. "If I had been locked up and tortured for months and then found myself in a room that barely had space to breathe, I would be having panic attacks, too." Zoe brushed away the tears that started anew and slid down Eva's cheeks.

"I...I didn't want you to think I was weak," Eva admitted hoarsely.

"I wouldn't think you were weak, then or now. I wish you would have told me so we could have talked with the captain."

"I didn't want that, Zoe, and the ship was so full, we were lucky to have the small cabin to ourselves when so many other people had to share," Eva said.

"So you suffered through it and you didn't complain," Zoe shook her head. "Eva, why on earth did you think I would have thought of you as weak?" she asked.

"What was there to complain about? I was with the woman that I loved and I was free." Eva smiled and wiped her wet eyes with the back of her hand.

Zoe smiled back and kissed her lightly on the lips. "I used to think that the porthole had a faulty latch," she said.

"I know." Eva nodded and looked down at her hands. "I hoped you would just think it was faulty and that was that." Eva's apprehension on the ship had grown when Zoe had repeatedly brought someone from the crew to have a look at the latch.

"Did having the porthole open help?"

"It did," Eva said. "I don't know why but having the window open made me able to bear it a little better."

"And that's why you leave our bedroom window open?" Zoe asked and smiled as Eva nodded. "I didn't know why you insisted on leaving the window open all the time but now I do. I thought it was strange and it must be a German quirk."

"It's an Eva quirk," Eva said. "If I have the window open, it helps me sleep. I can't stand closed-in places, Zoe."

"How long were you a prisoner in that room?"

"I think about six months, and then I was ready to give up. I prayed for God to end my life."

"I'm glad He didn't listen to your prayer, Evy."

Eva looked at Zoe and nodded. "He had a plan for me, Zoe. I didn't know it at the time, but He did. I remember lying in my bed after they had brought me back to the room," she quietly related. Eva fiddled with the last button on her shirt while Zoe watched her closely.

"I was so sick..." Eva said and then hesitated before continuing. "I remember crying out for them to kill me but they didn't. I decided to listen to what the priest told me and give them what they wanted. I had to make them believe that they had changed me to being 'normal', so I did."

"Oh, Evy, did they believe you?"

"Not at first; they thought I was lying so they tested me." Eva took a sip of the water and put it next to her on the coffee table. "They brought in this man who...uh...he...um...raped me. Even though I had been raped before — several times during my 'treatment' — this was the first and only time after I had said I had changed. He raped me to see if I would be excited by a man's touch. I didn't resist him, Zoe."

Zoe clamped a hand over her mouth. "They believed you?" she asked after a moment, her shock and dismay on Eva's behalf obvious.

"They believed that their treatments had worked." Eva's voice faltered. Zoe reached out and took her hand and held it tightly. From somewhere, Eva found the strength to go on. "My uncle made me his prize patient, showing me off to his friends like a trophy. They moved me to a real hospital bed to care for my injuries."

"After moving you to the hospital area, were you in any pain?"

"No, they gave me drugs to numb the pain. I had this nice nurse who took care of me, telling me stories about her family. For the first two months she did everything for me, I was so weak."

"Do you remember her name?"

"Frida. That's all I could remember. She was very gentle and kind."

"You were in the hospital for another two months?"

"Yes, and then Muller came to see me." Eva grimaced at the memory. "He walked into the room and talked about me as if I wasn't there."

"What did he want?"

"I guess he wanted a close-up look that I was 'normal'," Eva replied sarcastically. "After he left, I was drugged again, and this time..." Eva stopped and shook her head.

"It's all right, Evy, I'm right here." Zoe stroked Eva's face, trying to convey her love with her touch. Eva appreciated the gesture.

"I'm sorry, Zoe, I...it's just that..."

"Okay, just take your time," Zoe whispered.

"I woke up and I was hurting so much, I thought they must have found out my ruse and I got so scared."

"What happened?"

Eva squeezed Zoe's hand. "They had operated and sterilized me. I was told that Muller ordered it to be done because he didn't want me to have children in case I relapsed or passed the deviancy on to my offspring, like the insanity that runs in families." Eva closed her eyes; the ache was still strong after all these years. The loss of her fertility made her feel like an incomplete woman. "I know Muller wasn't all that sure that I was cured, but Uncle Dieter must have convinced him that I was."

"Oh, dear sweet Mother of God," Zoe exclaimed and hugged Eva tighter. "I thought you were just so very private about your cycles, or didn't have them very often. I wish I had known earlier, so I could have taken that poker to Muller and not stopped bashing until he was nothing but mush!"

Eva looked at her partner with a sad smile. She had never told Zoe that she had been sterilized; she had been too ashamed to tell anyone. It was another indignity she had had to suffer in silence. For days after the surgery all Eva could think about was how she would never have children, never hear a child calling her *Mutti*. Her ordeal had been made worse by a nurse who talked about her own children, the gossip only increasing the mental anguish Eva had been going through as a result of her loss.

"I remember when I was allowed out on the grounds of the hospital with my nurse, I would see a child and wonder what it would be like." Eva sighed. "When I was growing up, I had so many dolls I treated like they were my babies. I'm an only child and I wanted so desperately to have a brother or sister. I thought when I had my children, I'd have four or five. I guess it wasn't meant to be," she added wistfully.

Zoe said, "It *was* meant to be; it's just that those bastards took that from you."

"My Aunt Adele would carry on about how they would find a nice Aryan man and we would have so many children together." Eva turned her head away and tried not to let the feelings of despair at the memory of her aunt's comments overwhelm her. "She didn't know I couldn't have children and she tried to convince me that getting married was my best option even with my scars and mental illness."

"Who is Aunt Adele?"

"Uncle Dieter's wife. She thought I had injured myself. I don't think Uncle Dieter told her it was Muller who beat me."

"How else would you get beaten like that?"

"My uncle told her that it happened during *Kristallnacht* and that some thugs did it because they mistook me for a Jew."

"You wear a crucifix around your neck, you always have," Zoe said and lightly touched the gold cross that hung around Eva's neck. "Was the woman stupid?"

"I don't know; she believed what Uncle Dieter told her. She also thought I had a mental breakdown because of what happened and the way my mother died. She wasn't all that thrilled with me staying at her home."

"Did she know what happened to you at the spa?"

"I don't know if she knew what was being done," Eva replied. "I went to live with my uncle and aunt after I got out of the hospital."

"How did you cope, Evy?"

"I didn't cope very well in the first few months after leaving the hospital. I was depressed and I still hurt. I was terrified of my uncle realizing I had pulled a ruse. I worked very hard; I thought if I tired myself out, then I wouldn't have nightmares. I re-started my classes at university, taking more classes, even during summer term, to finish up quickly."

"It didn't work, Evy, did it?" Zoe said. "The more you worked, the more tired you got, but it didn't work to block out the memories, did it?"

"No." Eva had revealed the worst but there was one part she did not know if Zoe could understand. But despite her doubts, she would not hold anything back. "I remember one night in Larissa. I had gone out on my own to Athena's Bluff. I remember that it was a clear night." Eva licked her lips. "I looked down at the rocks below and decided to end it all."

"It was a long drop," Zoe said and whistled, surprising Eva.

Eva had not been prepared for what seemed like a matter-of-fact response. "It was," Eva said. "I was praying to God for His forgiveness, because I was going to end it there."

"So *that's* what you were doing on Athena's Bluff," Zoe said. "I wondered why you were there."

"You saw me?" Eva asked in surprise, even more amazed when Zoe nodded.

"I had gone to Thieri's cabin," Zoe said. "I heard a noise and thought that soldiers were going to come in so I crawled out of a window. I hid in the bushes and saw you." Zoe paused; it seemed she was gathering her thoughts. "You were alone and initially I thought your shadows were nearby — you know, the guards that followed you everywhere — but I looked around and I couldn't see anyone. You were so near the edge that I thought it was going to be so easy to push you off."

"You had your chance, Zoe; why didn't you take it?" Eva asked. The cabin was nestled in the woods behind Athena's Bluff. It was indeed a lonely spot and Eva was astonished that Zoe had not taken her revenge that night.

Zoe sighed. "I was about to, but then I heard the guards. They caught up with you and I lost the chance."

Eva smiled. "God had a plan."

"He did," Zoe agreed. They gazed at each other for a long moment. Zoe reached out and lightly stroked Eva's cheek with her fingers. Eva inclined her face, seeking the comfort the contact gave her. "I love you, Eva Haralambos," Zoe said, her voice breaking. She leaned in and kissed Eva again but this time it was a more passionate kiss. They parted and smiled at each other.

"Thank you," Eva whispered and kissed Zoe lightly on the mouth. "Thank you for listening to me."

"Evy, you have gone through so much. We both have. We either curl up into a ball and die, or we manage to hang on," Zoe said. "We need each other."

"For a long time I thought it was my burden alone, Zoe."

"That's where you're wrong. If I had known, don't you think I would have done everything to help you?"

"Yes, but—"

Zoe stopped her by placing her fingers against Eva's lips. "I don't want you to think you can't lean on me, Evy." Zoe brushed Eva's bangs out of her eyes. "If I was hurting, wouldn't you want to help me?"

"Yes."

"Well, then why shouldn't I want to help you?" Zoe said. "You look so tired. I know we asked everyone to come for a barbeque tonight, but we can call it off..."

Eva shook her head. "No, I want to have our friends around."

"Do you want to have a nice warm bath and then cuddle until it's time for the barbeque?"

Eva gave her a weary smile and nodded. "I like the sound of that," she said and let her head rest on Zoe's shoulder, taking comfort from being with her partner.

She was emotionally spent, wrung out from recalling and reliving the past, but having Zoe listen to her, even if she could not do anything to change what had happened, was a true blessing and a catharsis that Eva wished she had not put off so long.

"You're going to do what?" Panayiotis asked incredulously. He was sure he had not heard his daughter correctly. Eva sat on the sofa, her hands folded in her lap, with Zoe nearby looking extremely uncomfortable. He cleared his throat. "All right, tell me again why you are going to help these two try and arrest this Greta person."

"The authorities can't arrest her because they don't know where she is," Eva explained once again. She looked at Alberta and grimaced. Panayiotis noted that Alberta, who was sitting next to him, had a perplexed look on her face.

"I see. So once again you become the bait?" he asked Eva.

"Something like that," Eva muttered.

"I think those two boofheads need their heads read," Earl muttered. "This is a really bad plan if you ask me."

"Uh-huh." Panayiotis scratched his head. "And Zoe is okay with you being the live bait?"

"Hell, no," Zoe muttered. She put a hand over her mouth when she realized she had cursed in the presence of a priest. "Sorry, Father H."

"We don't have a lot of options open to us, Father," Eva responded.

"Really? Why don't they use the resources of the government to track this woman down? Surely the police can find her."

"I don't know."

"Eva, my child, it's not that I don't want you to help them, but—"

"Father, I know, but this is the only way. She has to be caught."

Alberta looked between Panayiotis and Eva, frowning. "What's so important about this Greta person?" she asked.

Eva paused for a moment. "Greta assisted in medical experiments at Auschwitz."

"I don't understand. I ran experiments during the war—"

"On human beings?" Eva asked. Panayiotis felt the corners of his mouth draw down at his daughter's question. She knew her stepmother had only experimented on animals and not on living human beings.

A collective gasp went around the room at the revelation with Earl's "Bloody hell!" and "My God!" coming from Alberta. Panayiotis jerked involuntarily, but his years of experience in the priesthood enabled him to maintain a neutral expression.

"She worked with Dr. Josef Mengele and his...partners, Dr. Kurt Gutzeit and Dr. Bruno Weber," Eva went on, "experimenting on twins and other prisoners. The figures don't really tell the full story and I don't think we will ever know it, but Greta assisted those butchers."

"This woman was your lover?" Earl asked, his disbelief painfully apparent. He shot a quick glance at Zoe, who was scowling.

"Yes," Eva said. There was a great deal of hurt in that single, simple syllable.

"And Harrison and Jacobs want you to bring her to your apartment." Earl repeated what Eva had told them. "This is getting worse and worse. I have a fireplace poker which might come in handy at some point."

Zoe gave him a half-smile at the reference to the last time Eva had taken part in one of David and Friedrich's less-than-stellar plans.

Eva also smiled, but the look in her eyes remained grim. "They want me to ring her and tell her that I'm taking her up on her offer."

"What offer?" Panayiotis broke in.

Eva grimaced "To take me back as her lover because I've decided to leave Zoe."

"This is ridiculous. Who came up with this brilliant idea?" Earl asked. "It's a stupid idea. Any fool with eyes would know that you two are in love."

"Friedrich's idea," Zoe said shortly.

"Friedrich? I was just beginning to like him," Earl grumbled.

"So, what's the plan?" Panayiotis asked, trying to understand the latest upheaval in his daughter's life — *one she could do without*, he thought.

"Well, I call her and give her my spiel, then she meets me at the office. Zoe interrupts...um...when I'm kissing..."

"Jesus wept on the Cross!" Earl raised his voice and got a mortified look from Panayiotis; the swearing was getting a little too much for him. "Sorry, Father H, but that is the most idiotic, absolutely harebrained idea I've ever heard!" Earl's incredulous gaze turned upon Eva. "*You* are going to kiss *her*?"

"Yes," Eva replied.

Earl scowled and got up from his perch on the couch to cross over to Eva. He put his arm around her shoulders. "Eva, my dear friend, you are a lousy liar, and there is no way you are going to convince this killer that you are fair dinkum about her and dumping Zoe."

"You can say that again!" Zoe exclaimed.

Eva gave her a light slap on the thigh. "I don't want to do it, but that's the only solution!" Eva protested. "It's not as if I'm looking forward to kissing another woman, let alone having her hands all over me."

"All right, so we have you trying to convince this killer that you are in love with her." Earl went over the scenario and Eva nodded. "Zoe comes in when you are exchanging chewing gum..."

"Chewing gum?" Panayiotis asked, feeling even more confused.

"Okay, Zoe comes in when you are getting this woman all steamed up about getting back together. What is Zoe going to do?"

"Get my flame thrower and cook her into a crispy critter," Zoe muttered.

"Zoe!" Panayiotis scolded. "As much as we don't like this person, I don't believe that thinking about killing her will make Eva's job any easier."

"I know, but the idea of Eva in Greta's arms makes me sick," Zoe answered, looking into Panayiotis' eyes. "I know she has to do it, but I'm going to wash her mouth out with peppermint mouthwash afterwards."

"So what is Zoe going to do?" Earl persisted, clearly wanting to have the plan laid out for him in detail.

"Zoe is going to come in, see me kissing Greta, then we'll exchange some nasty words, and I'll ask Greta to take me home to pick up some clothes. Greta and I will go home and then David and Friedrich take over," Eva said.

"That's if they can find the right apartment," Earl said. Eva hiked her eyebrow at him and he continued, "Well, I'll be camped in Elena's apartment in case my batting prowess is needed. Where is Zoe going to be?"

Eva looked at Zoe and grimaced. "With you," Eva said.

"No way!" Zoe yelled and shot up from the sofa. "I am not going to leave you."

"Zoe, it's going to be dangerous for you if you are there. I'm not going to let you be put in a dangerous—"

"Let me?" Zoe's eyes narrowed. "*You* won't let me? What about what *I* want?"

"I'm not going to let you," Eva said. It seemed, from the stubborn set of her jaw, that she was determined to stand her ground.

Panayiotis looked at his two daughters. One of them was ready to unleash her full temper, while Eva sat there quietly trying to stay calm. He made a decision. "I think now would be a good time, Earl, for me to show you the kitchen and let these two talk it out privately," Panayiotis said. "Ally, will you join us?"

He got up from his favorite chair and ushered his wife and Earl out of the room.

Zoe turned her back and looked out at the city skyline from the window. She was not going to leave Eva to face the danger by herself. *Not this time.*

"Zoe," Eva whispered in her ear, putting her arm around Zoe's rigid shoulders. "You can't be in our apartment with Greta there, too."

"I don't want you to do this by yourself," Zoe replied, leaning back and closing her eyes. She wanted this whole nightmare to end and wished she had never heard of Greta Strauss or Wagner or whatever the woman wanted to call herself. "Greta isn't as stupid as Muller and Rhimes. We may not be as lucky this time around."

"I know, love, but I don't want you to get hurt."

"What about you?" Zoe turned and faced Eva, putting her arms around her waist. "What about you, Evy? Who is going to protect you?" she asked, looking into her partner's eyes and seeing the resolution there that was just as fierce as her own desire to protect her beloved mate. "Being hurt doesn't always mean physical harm — you know that."

Eva met Zoe's gaze, and Zoe knew her partner understood the truth of the statement she had made. "If you got hurt, Zoe, I don't know what I'd do," Eva said.

"I won't get hurt," Zoe said, thinking she was going to get to be with Eva after all.

"No. You're staying with Earl. I want you with me but I can't have that," Eva explained. "I'm sorry, but that's the way it has to be."

"Arghhh!" Zoe let out a frustrated yell. "You're not going to be safe."
"I'll have David and Friedrich—"
"Oh yes, those two inspire confidence," Zoe said sarcastically.
"Zoe, I'm not going to let you be in that apartment."
"I don't like it."
"I know you don't," Eva sighed. Zoe buried her head in Eva's chest and began to weep. She was terrified that something was going to go wrong and she would lose Eva. Greta Strauss was not Muller, a crippled old man who was out of his mind. Greta was a cunning, evil woman who could easily overpower Eva, and Zoe would not be there to stop her.
"I don't want to see you hurt, love. It would kill me if anything happened to you," Eva said, but Zoe refused to accept her partner's reasoning.

Elena stuck her head around the door, then entered Zoe and Eva's apartment. Zoe had been talking to Eva's father. Zoe turned, spotted Elena and called her over.
"Hi," Elena greeted Zoe and gave her a hug. "I'm sorry."
"Not your fault, El. Where's Friedrich?"
"He doesn't want to come to dinner. He thinks you don't want him—"
"What a load of rubbish," Zoe muttered. She walked out of the apartment with Elena at her heels.
Zoe reached Elena's apartment and knocked just as Elena caught up with her. The door opened to reveal Friedrich with slightly rumpled hair and no glasses, which made him look much younger than he usually did. Zoe simply brushed past him, much to Elena's apparent amusement.
"Okay, what's this about you not wanting to come to dinner?" Zoe asked, folding her arms across her chest and looking quite severe.
"Uh, Zoe, I don't think Eva would want me to be there," Friedrich stammered. "I'm sorry. I don't want anything to hurt Eva or you."
"Friedrich, I don't blame you for wanting to catch Greta. God knows I want to rid her from our lives. I just didn't like the way David was questioning Eva," Zoe said.
"I know and I'm sorry." Friedrich smoothed his hair with his palms and picked up his glasses, which were on a table near the sofa. "I promise we won't let anything happen to Eva."
"You'd better not." Zoe gave him a mock glare, but there was no mistaking that it was meant as a warning. She took him by the arm. "Come on, let's eat!"

A light breeze blew drifts of smoke inside the apartment along with the aroma of grilling sausages and steaks. Zoe pulled Friedrich inside, and Elena followed them. Earl was on the balcony; he stood in front of the barbeque grill wearing one of Zoe's aprons — which was much too small for him — wielding a pair of tongs, and turning the meat. Clad in shorts and a cotton shirt, Eva sat on a wicker chair and grinned at him, her long legs stretched out in front of her.
"Zoe likes hers well done," Eva said.
"I know, burnt sacrifice style," Earl replied and got a chuckle from Eva. "You remember that first time we had a barbeque at Cremorne Point? Zoe came back with her steak, looked me up and down, and said, 'I want to sacrifice this cow to the barbeque gods.'"
Eva laughed. "Oh, I remember that day. I was dead tired from cleaning all day and when you suggested we head to Cremorne, I thought you were mad."
"You enjoyed yourself," Earl reminded her.
"We watched the sun set over the bridge," Zoe said from inside the apartment where she was setting the table. "Very romantic."

Eva glanced back at her lover and winked, then caught Elena's gaze and smiled before she turned away. Eva then spoke softly to Earl so no one else could hear.

Earl turned another sausage and smiled. "I'll be waiting, Eva."

"I know you will, Earl. No matter what happens, keep Zoe away."

Earl said, "I don't think I can guarantee that, my friend. I will try to keep her away, but if Zoe wants to do something, Zoe is going to do it, unless I knock her out."

"Try," Eva replied. She leaned forward, stretched out a long arm and snagged a little piece of the cooked meat from the grill. Popping it in her mouth, Eva chewed vigorously before going on, "Zoe is going to be your only responsibility."

Earl glanced at her. "You are giving me the most important job. What if..."

Eva shook her head. "Do whatever you have to do to keep Zoe safe and away from the apartment. If anything happens to her..." Eva could not continue and glanced away.

Earl set the tongs down and left the grill. He went to Eva's side. "I give you my word: Zoe is going to be safe."

"That's all I ask, Wiggy." Eva smiled up at the burly man.

"Even if I have to lock her in the bathroom," Earl quipped before he went back to his cooking duties. "Did Greta really do that stuff in the file?" he asked.

Eva nodded. "I've read the witness reports and the notes that David and Friedrich had. I don't know this Greta; she isn't the woman I thought I loved."

"People change."

"Not so drastically, Earl. I guess I never took notice before, but she idolized Hitler."

Earl watched her for a moment. "Why didn't you join the party?"

"I didn't believe as fervently in the cause as some of my friends did. Hitler was good for Germany in the beginning, but my mind was made up when I read *Mein Kampf*."

"What does *Mein Kampf* mean?"

"'My Struggle'. It was about his ideals and his beliefs. Did you know he was an artist?" Eva turned her head as Zoe stepped out onto the balcony. She patted her lap and grinned when Zoe accepted the mute invitation and sat down.

Zoe gave her a quick kiss. "Who was an artist?"

"You would hear that bit, wouldn't you?" Eva teased, a lopsided grin on her face. "Adolph Hitler was an artist."

"Oh. He should have stuck to art," Zoe muttered. "So why are you discussing Hitler?"

"I was telling Earl I read *Mein Kampf* and it made me decide that I didn't want to join the Nazi party and be a part of it."

"I would have joined the Communist party if I had been old enough." Zoe took the hot bread roll Earl offered her off the barbeque.

"You? A Communist?" Eva was surprised, since Zoe had never mentioned that she leaned towards socialist policies.

"I loved their colors." Zoe grinned. "It was a change from the blue and white flags, and I found them different."

Earl and Eva laughed as the last of the steaks and sausages were cooked and put onto a large platter. Earl covered the barbeque with the lid and left the two women alone outside for a few moments as he took their dinner inside the apartment.

"Friedrich and Elena are here?" Eva whispered, getting a nod from her partner. "I guess we'd better go inside."

"Hmm," Zoe replied. She snuggled against Eva's chest and showed no signs of wanting to move. "How are you feeling?"

Eva took a deep breath and did a brief mental examination. "A little raw."

"I'll hold your hand." Zoe smiled, then took Eva's hand and kissed it. "I'll always hold your hand."

"In that case, I'm feeling all right," Eva replied. "Come on, love." Eva kissed Zoe one last time. Zoe got up reluctantly and waited while Eva negotiated her taller frame out of the chair. Hands clasped together, the two women walked back inside the apartment to join dinner with their friends.

Friedrich was admiring Zoe's artwork and fidgeting awkwardly. Despite Zoe's reassurance, he was not sure if Eva really wanted him there. He began to study the photographs that were on the wall next to the artwork. One photograph in particular intrigued him, and he went to have a closer look. It showed a river cascading over a steep drop. Friedrich loved waterfalls. They had a magical quality about them that had fascinated him since he was a young boy.

"You like that?" Eva had come up from behind and stood there watching him.

Friedrich jumped when he heard her voice and turned slightly. He gave her a half smile. "Uh, yeah...I like waterfalls," Friedrich said. He was quite intimidated by Eva; she towered over him and always seemed so aloof and quiet. She was standing so close to him that Friedrich could smell her perfume. He did not know anything about fragrances, but it had a hint of jasmine, which he liked. Friedrich met her clear blue gaze, and they both smiled.

"Hmm, so do I," Eva said. "The photo was taken in the Blue Mountains when we went bush walking about a month ago. Very nice spot."

"Y...yes, it is," Friedrich agreed.

"Friedrich, I don't bite."

Zoe came up, putting her arm around Eva's waist and giving the woman a little squeeze. "Are you going to stand here talking, or come to dinner?"

"We're being summoned," Eva responded dryly. She took Zoe's hand as they led Friedrich to where everyone was seated.

Elena had told Friedrich that the large dining table had been Eva's idea. She had enjoyed having dinner parties before the war in the company of her friends. Now Eva's father was seated at the head of the table and Alberta had taken a place next to him. Elena and Friedrich sat down together, while Earl was seated opposite them, and Eva took the seat opposite her father with Zoe next to her. It was a nice arrangement that would make for a light evening.

Panayiotis said a prayer before they started eating, and then matters became a free-for-all as the chatter rose.

"Congratulations are in order for you both I hear." Panayiotis grinned at Friedrich and Elena. "So, have you decided when you will get married?"

"Not yet. Probably later this year," Friedrich replied, taking Elena's hand under the table.

"In my younger days I made wedding gowns, Elena. So if you like, we could sit down and design one for you." Alberta reached over and touched the young woman's hand, giving her a huge smile. Elena returned her smile and looked over at Zoe, who had a huge happy grin on her face. The thought of his upcoming wedding to Elena made Friedrich feel as if he could float on air, although at the moment he was still tethered to the Earth by his continued unease towards Eva.

"Do you need a photographer?" Eva asked.

Surprised, Friedrich looked at Elena for confirmation and finally nodded. "We hadn't thought about photographs."

"I'll let you know if I find a good one for you," Eva teased. That drew chuckles from everyone; Eva's sense of humor caught Friedrich by surprise. "I would love to take your wedding photos."

"Thank you." Friedrich accepted her offer, his nervousness in her presence easing somewhat. "When did you take up photography?"

"Ah, a long, long time ago. Back in Germany, I toyed with the idea of becoming a photographer. It's a relaxing hobby," Eva replied, taking a bite from her salad.

"Do you have a darkroom?" Friedrich asked. Eva nodded, still chewing.

"Are you a photographer, Friedrich?" Zoe leaned over, giving him a friendly smile.

"No. My sisters were. I built a darkroom for them before leaving Germany."

Eva swallowed and said, "We converted the walk-in closet in the spare bedroom to our darkroom, which is good."

"It's great for snuggling and cuddling too," Zoe added, making everyone laugh.

"For that as well," Eva agreed. "Are your sisters here?" she asked Friedrich.

Friedrich put his fork down for a moment and shook his head. "They died at Auschwitz." It was amazing how long grief could linger. He had a wonderful life, with excellent friends and a woman who loved him, but he would always mourn that loss.

"Oh, I'm sorry," Eva said, her gaze focused on her plate.

"And that's why you catch the bad guys, right?" Earl said. "Unless, of course, you get the wrong apartment number!" Everyone laughed again, which broke the tension somewhat.

"Hey, that wasn't my fault, you know." Friedrich pointed his finger at Earl, who was still laughing. "How did we know Mrs. Jenkins would send them up here? I would have rather been with Elena than sitting in a dark room trying to think up ways to kill David for breaking up our date at the dance."

"It didn't help that a certain someone who shall remain nameless got drunk that night," Earl teased. Zoe gave him a lopsided grin. "Who knew you were so amorous when drunk," he continued, batting his eyelashes outrageously at Zoe.

"She doesn't need to be drunk to be amorous," Eva quipped, earning a smack from Zoe.

The evening wore on as they ate and enjoyed themselves. More at ease, Friedrich sat back and relaxed. He knew that the next day they would deal with Greta Strauss and everything else that might come their way, but this night was for fun and the company of good friends.

Chapter Thirty-One

Eva lay awake in bed; the room was dark, the inevitable heat muffling her senses. The sound of the grandfather clock in the lounge could be heard though, as well as the distant grumble of cars drifting through the open window. The rain from the previous day had disappeared, to be replaced by warm and muggy conditions.

Zoe was curled up next to her, her arm draped over Eva's waist. Eva had found the evening they had spent with her parents and friends enjoyable and soothing. However, even with the comfortable feelings she had experienced, Eva was terrified of what was going to happen during the upcoming meeting with Greta. She hoped the meeting was not going to turn into a disaster. Her father had taken both her and Zoe aside and, in his own style, put them at ease, telling them they would have to go through a little more hardship before they could get on with their lives. She marveled at how he always knew the right words to say.

"You're thinking too much," Zoe mumbled.

"I thought you were asleep," Eva replied, brushing aside Zoe's errant bangs and running her fingers through Zoe's hair, scratching the back of her neck a little. Zoe sighed in contentment, and Eva smiled. It occurred to her that if Zoe were a cat like Ourania, she would be purring at the treatment.

"I was asleep," Zoe said, "but your loud thinking woke me up."

"My loud thinking?" Eva asked.

"Hmm. Your body tenses when you are nervous. Do I need to ask what you are thinking about?"

"How am I going to pull this off, Zoe? Greta knows me."

Zoe hitched herself up on her elbow, leaning over Eva and peering at her face in the darkness. "She doesn't know you. You told me that you are not the same person you were back then, so she doesn't really know you anymore."

"Zoe, my personality may have changed, but not how I react when I'm..." Eva found she was a little shy, which was ludicrous since Zoe knew her body intimately.

"Aroused?"

"Uh...yeah."

"I like it when you're aroused," Zoe joked, obviously trying to relax her. "Your eyes go deep blue, and you get a pink flush that travels up your chest." Zoe fanned herself with her hand making Eva shake her head and chuckle. "You are an incredibly sexy woman, Miss H," Zoe whispered, nuzzling Eva's neck.

"Oh, that's nice," Eva responded, letting her hand roam across Zoe's naked back. "Uh, Zoe — that's my problem."

Zoe sighed. "You know making love would take your mind off the other thing we have to do tomorrow. What's the problem?"

"Greta will know I'm not aroused. I mean, she will know," Eva said, embarrassed. She found she could not say anything more explicit to Zoe.

The younger woman put her head down on Eva's shoulder and let her finger trace around Eva's naval. Eva felt Zoe's grin against her skin when she responded to the touch, her hips jolting once involuntarily. Zoe continued the slow teasing motions.

"I think you've had enough time to think about this," Zoe whispered. She rolled on top of Eva's body and stared into her eyes. "I love you, Evy, and I know you are going to have to let yourself go so you can convince the Nazi bitch that you are for real. But for now I want you to make love to me." Zoe leaned down and kissed her passionately, clearly wanting her kiss to erase the thoughts of that woman from Eva's mind. The kiss deepened and they both let out low moans.

"I think you talk too much," Eva said breathlessly as she reversed their positions, her hands roaming over Zoe's body. She looked into Zoe's eyes and let a sexy grin steal across her face. She was about to say something when Zoe put a finger to her lips.

"So, don't talk," Zoe whispered. She reached up and tangled her fingers in Eva's hair.

Eva stretched the length of her body out alongside her lover and ran a strong, yet delicate hand up the span of Zoe's figure, stopping at her face to brush her fingers gently across those soft, full lips. Eva smiled, reaching down once more to capture Zoe's mouth with her own. Zoe moaned at the gentleness of the kiss.

"Is this what you want, my love?" Eva asked. Her lips moved down to Zoe's neck. "Hmm?" she urged an answer, bringing her hand to the underside of a soft breast, brushing her thumb across Zoe's nipple, the flesh hardening under her caress.

"Yes..." Zoe tried to say, but it came out as more of a strangled groan.

Eva continued to tenderly kiss and stroke Zoe's warm flesh. She lowered her body onto Zoe's, her weight resting on her arms. Zoe moaned in pleasure as skin rubbed against skin. Eva covered the inviting mouth with her own. She loved kissing this woman, always feeling as if she would never get enough of it. She reveled in the taste and the different reactions every touch of her own lips produced in the woman she considered her wife.

Softly, Eva whispered, "Remember what I promised you that night you were painting? You had to stand outside in the rain just to cool off from my promise, didn't you?"

Zoe was beyond a verbal answer and simply nodded her head in response.

Eva lowered her voice even more. "You will want for nothing. My tongue, my lips, my voice, everything I have, Zoe...all of it will only ever be for you."

"Please, Evy..." Zoe whispered faintly, arching her back as Eva permitted her fingertips to brush across her taut nipples.

Sliding against Zoe's overheated skin once more, the tall woman slowly enclosed one of the hardened nubs with her mouth and suckled gently. Using her knee, she spread Zoe's legs apart and moved her thigh in to press against the warm wetness she found there. Both women moaned simultaneously, their mutual desire rising higher and higher.

Eva could not help the delighted whimper that escaped from her throat at the feel of her own slickness as she pressed her center harder down onto Zoe's thigh. Eva pressed her leg against Zoe's center, feeling Zoe unconsciously begin to rock her hips against her.

"Please, Evy," Zoe raised her hips slightly, offering herself to Eva's clever caresses. "I can't wait."

Eva smiled at her Zoe's plea. Everything was life and death, and impatience with this woman. That was one of the reasons she loved her. With Zoe, every day was new, every experience was as though she were living it for the first time, no brakes, just flat out. That was what Zoe brought into Eva's life — passion. Once again, Eva was able to experience an enthusiasm for life and all because of the woman who now lay begging underneath her.

Very soon, Zoe cried out Eva's name, her fingers clenching in Eva's hair. The young woman's body convulsed, her back arching with her release.

As Zoe lay basking in the last few shudders of pleasure, Eva moved up, wrapping her arms around the beautiful young woman she loved more than life or breath, and giving her a deep and passionate kiss. Zoe's hands roamed, massaging and caressing Eva's back. Eva reveled in the feel of Zoe's body pressed against her own.

The feel of Zoe's hands on her skin, touching her, caressing her lovingly, drew a soft moan from Eva and she could feel her own need upon her. Making love to Zoe could be so satisfying, but right now, she knew she needed more.

"I want you, my wife," Zoe said with an intensity that surprised Eva. Zoe pressed against Eva's body as Eva rolled them both over. Sliding her hand down the soft skin of Eva's stomach, Zoe swirled her fingers with a teasingly light touch into the tuft of curls that lay between Eva's long, quivering thighs.

"Zoe, I love you so much. I don't ever want to lose you," Eva whispered.

"I'm not going anywhere, love," Zoe responded reassuringly. "*Ever*," she added just before her lips covered Eva's in a fiery kiss.

"Zoe, I need you so much." Eva tore her mouth away. Her legs quickly parted in a silent plea for more touches. Eva gasped and her eyes closed at the pleasurable sensation of Zoe's loving ministrations.

She was sure her exhilaration and enchantment were visible in her face. She arched her back into her lover's touch, making a throaty sound of pure satisfaction. Eva could feel her body being taken to the very precipice by the breathtaking contact with Zoe's body. She surrendered her mouth to Zoe's loving assault, the sensation drawing long moans from her. Zoe's actions drove any logical thought from Eva's brain. She began to moan louder, her hips picking up the pace.

Zoe wrenched her mouth free. "Eva, look at me," she panted.

Eva opened her eyes; her vision was hazed by passion. Finally, she was able to focus on the beautiful young woman above her.

"I want you to see me, Eva. I want you to know who is loving you, know who touches you this way, know who alone can make you feel this way. It's me, my love, only me," Zoe said. She leaned down one last time to capture Eva's lips.

Eva groaned into Zoe's mouth as she felt the climax take away her control, her muscles quivering in irrepressible spasms of delight.

When at last Eva's body stilled, Zoe planted a soft kiss on her sweat-soaked brow and brushed away the short locks of hair plastered against Eva's sweaty face. "I love you, Evy," Zoe whispered.

Eva wrapped her arms around the woman above her, pulling the smaller figure tightly against her body. "I love you too, Zoe. More than you will ever know."

Eva exhaled and glanced at the paper in her hand. She stared at it for quite some time before she rang the number Greta had given Debbie and left a message for the woman to contact her. It did not take long for her former lover to return her call.

At ten o'clock, Eva looked at the ringing phone and took a deep breath before picking up the receiver. She hoped she would not sound nervous and give the game away. She answered the phone in a calm voice, surprising herself.

"Eva, darling, how nice to hear your voice again," Greta said, sounding very cheery. "So when can I see you, or is your wife not going to let me near you?"

Eva could hear the condescension in Greta's laugh. "Eta."

"Oh dear. I haven't heard that nickname in a long time. It must be at least nine years." Greta's voice sounded more bubbly, but still doubtful.

"Things have changed...love," Eva said, rolling her eyes at the endearment and mentally shaking herself to keep her mind on the job.

"How so?" Greta asked.

Eva knew Greta was very much interested in resuming their relationship, but by the sound of her voice, the woman was still playing it cool. "Zoe and I have been having some problems. I mean — ever since you came back, I haven't been able to stop thinking about you. Debbie gave me your telephone number and I've been wanting to call you."

Greta let out another peal of laughter. "Oh, I don't doubt it. That little spitfire must have you firmly under her thumb!"

Eva held out the receiver and looked at it with a shake of her head. Putting it back to her ear, she said, "She is rather..."

"Domineering?" Greta offered. Her chuckling after that reply annoyed Eva even more.

"Bossy is the word I would use. She isn't tall enough to be domineering." Eva cringed at what she had just said and was grateful that Zoe was not around to hear it. "She can get a little violent at times."

"So, what would you like us to do, my love?"

"Can you meet me here? I'm at the office."

"Ah, afraid the little woman would catch us?" Greta asked.

"Well, what she doesn't know won't hurt her. I mean, if you are interested."

"Interested in having a second chance with you? Of course! I want to feel your body under mine and hear your passion. I would be stupid to pass up that opportunity."

Eva grunted. Eva hoped Greta mistook the sound for arousal, not wanting to spoil the ruse.

"Not now, *meine Liebe*, wait until I get there!" Greta continued to chuckle over the line. "I will make you forget that little child."

"Can you come—"

"I can come any time you want me to," Greta interjected and laughed at her own crude joke, much to Eva's silent disgust. "What time do you want me there?"

"Well, how about five o'clock? Zoe has classes at university until six thirty, and she won't be home until late," Eva said, hoping that Greta would take the bait.

"Perfect. It's been a long time, *meine Liebe*, and I am looking forward to getting reacquainted with that gorgeous body of yours."

"I would like that."

Greta sighed. "I'll see you at five. Goodbye, *meine Liebe*."

"Goodbye," Eva whispered, trying to convey a sense of desire. She held the receiver in her hand for a long moment then, with a heavy sigh, put it down in the cradle, ending the call. "God give me strength," she whispered. Eva called Zoe and then David to let them all know the plans were in motion.

Eva spent the rest of the day going through the motions of interviewing clients, and watching the clock. She was sitting at her desk looking at the files in front of her, though not paying much attention, when Friedrich and David showed up.

"Are you sure we can't do it here? It'll be after usual working hours," Eva said hopefully.

"We don't want risk it. Your office workers don't always leave before the cleaning crew arrives. We don't want anyone to get hurt," David replied. "I know you don't want to have her in your apartment, but that's the only place secure enough."

"I know," Eva said, resigned to the fact that she would have to take her former lover to the apartment that she and Zoe called home.

"You take her there, and we will be waiting in the bedroom," Friedrich added.

"Why not arrest her when we get inside?"

"We may lose her if she bolts out the door. You need to block the main door and alert us when you have done so."

"How?"

"Use a word or a phrase and when we hear that, we'll come out."

Eva was not at all sure about the plan. "How about 'I have a wonderful surprise for you'? Would that work?"

Friedrich and David smiled at Eva and nodded. "It's perfect," David said.

"All right, but how will I know you're in place?"

"We plan to be there at five o'clock, before most of your neighbors come home from work. But we can overturn a book on the coffee table and put a flower on top as a signal. Once you see that, you'll know we are there. If you don't see it, do whatever you can to stall Greta until we get there."

After the meeting with David and Friedrich, the day continued to drag, making Eva jump every time the phone rang. She looked in alarm at the door when she heard a light knock. She looked hurriedly at her watch, which read only four o'clock. Her heart in her throat, Eva stood as the door opened. Much to her relief, Zoe's head popped around the door.

"Hello there," Zoe said. Eva opened her arms and Zoe embraced her in a tight hug. "I hoped to see you before *she* gets here."

"Hmm. I'm so glad you did. Is Earl with you?" Eva asked, stroking her partner's cheek.

"Sure is. He's waiting outside, chatting with Debbie and charming her."

"Is there anyone in the waiting room?"

"No, it's quiet, but there must be clients in other offices, though, since I heard some talking."

The two women stood embracing for a few moments, enjoying their closeness. Both were a little startled when the phone rang. Eva leaned out of Zoe's embrace and picked up the receiver. As she listened to the message, her face paled at the news.

"What's wrong?" Zoe whispered.

Eva shook her head. "Um...tell her I'll be ready to see her in a few minutes." She put the receiver down and swore blasphemously in German.

"What's wrong?" Zoe demanded as Eva sighed her frustration loudly.

"Zoe, I think we need to change the way we are going to do this. Greta is early."

"Stupid bloody bitch," Zoe spat.

"Zoe, we need to have an argument. Um, I told her that you...uh...sometimes you got violent."

"What!" Zoe exclaimed. "There is absolutely no way in heaven or on Earth I am going to hit you. I might as well hurt myself. No way!"

"Please, Zoe, this could unravel right this minute! When Greta comes in, I want you to yell at me and slap me, then storm off. Get yourself and Earl back to the apartment and make sure Friedrich and David are in place."

"Stupid bloody bitch, I'm going to kill her." Zoe continued to swear as Eva tried to get control of herself. She heard a soft knock on the door and gave Zoe a quick kiss, feeling as nervous as she imagined an actor might be before the curtain went up.

The door opened and a smiling Greta entered to find Zoe shoving Eva in the chest and yelling in Greek, a language which she did not understand. Nevertheless, it was apparent that Zoe was extremely upset. Greta stood watching them for a moment before clearing her throat to announce herself.

Zoe turned when she heard her and directed her anger at Greta, clear hatred in her eyes. Greta took an involuntary step backwards in surprise. Eva knew that Greta was not used to being intimidated. True to form, the German woman quickly covered up her misstep, a tiny smile playing on her lips, and made a show of removing her gloves.

"Hello, *meine Liebe*," Greta greeted Eva, staring straight at Zoe. Zoe's eyes narrowed at the use of the German endearment. She then addressed Zoe, as if the irate woman was a mere afterthought. "We meet again, little Zoe."

Zoe spat in her direction; Greta narrowly avoided being hit. "Oh my," Greta said, sneering. "You are such a peasant, girl."

Zoe turned to Eva, reverting to German for Greta's benefit. "So you were planning a little rendezvous with the Nazi bitch from hell?"

Eva crossed her arms over her chest and tried valiantly to look indifferent to her partner's abuse. Although she knew it was pretend, each word cut into her like a well-honed razor.

"Hey!" Greta advanced towards Zoe, clearly wanting to stop the tirade against Eva.

"Shut the fuck up!" Zoe turned and screamed at Greta, her face mottled red, her nostrils pinched and white with the force of her fury. "You steal my lover and I'm supposed to sit here and take it?"

"Eva needs a real woman to love her, and you're not it," Greta replied smugly. Her look of triumph was an ugly thing.

Zoe turned back to Eva, who had taken a seat on the edge of her desk; her arms were folded across her chest. Eva was doing her best to seem nonchalant and aloof. She wanted Greta to assume that she had gone through these tirades before, and that she pitied Zoe's lack of control.

"I thought you loved me, but as soon as the Nazi slut comes back, you just have to run off!" Zoe said, her eyes snapping emerald fire.

"Loved you?" Eva said. "Hardly. You were a means to an end." Eva's heart ached as she spoke those words, but she had to go through with the charade.

"Well, little one, I don't think it's much of a contest now, do you?" Greta was obviously enjoying the show. Eva knew that Greta had not seriously believed she would fall for a naïve child, and now Greta's opinion seemed vindicated.

Zoe shouted, "What does that mean, you Nazi whore?" Her body tensed as if she was ready to pounce on the German woman and start swinging.

Greta smirked at Zoe's reddened face. "It means, little Zoe, that I'm going to be making love to her tonight. She will be screaming *my* name, and you're just a little footnote in the life of Eva Muller."

"You Nazi whore." Zoe turned to face Eva. "A means to an end? What the hell are you talking about?"

Eva rose to her full height and went up to Zoe, put her hands on her shoulders and looked into her eyes. "You were my ticket out of Greece, thank you. I needed the Resistance's resources." Eva leaned down, took Zoe's face between her hands and went on, "You know how it is, Zoe, you were in the right place at the right time."

Her heart nearly broke when she recognized the agonized expression on Zoe's face. Neither of them was immune to the ache created by the words they had flung at each other in the past few minutes. Their intellects understood that this charade was not real, but their hearts, so open to each other, wondered otherwise. Silent tears rolled down Zoe's face, and Eva wanted to cry out her denial.

She nearly did cry when Zoe's hand twitched and struck her across the cheek, the sound reverberating around the small office. Zoe staggered back, her shock written on her face. Eva knew Zoe's soul must have been lacerated by that blow. The look in those incandescent green eyes spoke volumes. Without a word, Zoe flung the door open and raced out of the office, disappearing down the corridor.

"Bye, bye, Zoe!" Greta taunted, laughing in triumph.

Eva put a trembling hand against her hot cheek and swallowed her tears.

Earl heard the office door open. He was about to investigate when he caught sight of an enraged Zoe storming down the corridor. Opening his mouth to ask what had happened, he never got the chance since Zoe exited via the stairwell leaving him in her wake. She had not even spared him a single glance.

After a moment's hesitation, Earl followed Zoe down the stairs and into the car park.

"Zoe?" Earl asked with concern. She was doubled over near his car, throwing up. He hurried to her side, placing a gentle hand on her shoulder.

"Earl, take me home, quickly," Zoe said through clenched teeth. She wiped her mouth and stood back up, her jaw clenched so tight Earl feared for her teeth.

Eva's eyes misted over when Zoe stormed out of the office. Her heart ached. The pain she felt was worse than anything that had been done to her — not because of the slap but from having forced Zoe to take part in this charade to convince Greta.

Greta put her arms around Eva from behind, pressing herself against Eva's back. "Are you all right, darling?" she cooed.

Eva nodded and pressed a hand to her burning eyes, hoping Greta would not read too much into the tears that were threatening to spill over.

"Well, you don't look all right." Greta turned Eva to face her. "Sit down and I'll bring you a glass of water," she directed. Eva sat down in the visitor's chair, her mind warring with her emotions, while Greta went to the pitcher of water on the desk and poured her a glass, all solicitousness and grace now that she believed she had won.

Eva took the glass with both hands, fearful of dropping it in her agitation. She was tired and wanted to get this crazy, idiotic plan over and done with. She wanted to go and comfort Zoe, to hold her. *To hell with the Nazis*, she thought, weary to her soul. *To hell with everyone.*

"I want you to come home with me, my love." Greta said.

"Can't," Eva whispered. She cleared her throat. Eva needed to stall to give Zoe and Earl a chance to warn Friedrich and David that she would be bringing Greta to the apartment much earlier than they had planned.

"Why? That she-demon is going to be at your place, and frankly, I don't feel like going another round with her! I think even the Gestapo were gentler."

Eva forced herself to chuckle at Greta's joke about Zoe's temper thinking of some sort of response to get them to the apartment. "I have some papers I need to retrieve before Zoe finds them. Also, I hope she'll still head off to school instead of the apartment."

"Oh, of course," Greta said, getting to her feet. "How about I relax you a bit, then we can go back to your apartment to pick up your papers and clothes. I have a house that we can go to."

"You have a house?"

"Yes, a lovely house; you'll like it." Greta went around behind Eva's chair and began to massage her neck.

Eva groaned slightly as the wire-taut tension in her muscles was released under Greta's expert ministrations. Eva slumped forward, enjoying the massage despite it being at Greta's hands.

Greta smiled at Eva's acceptance. She slipped her hands inside Eva's shirt and began to massage her neck and shoulders more thoroughly. She frowned when she looked down and saw the faint scars. "Eva, did Zoe cause these?"

Eva wondered when Greta would notice and sighed. "No, that's my stepfather's legacy," she said quietly.

"Oh, that brute!" Greta shook her head and put her arms around Eva and unbuttoned her shirt. She lowered Eva's shirt from her shoulders in order to reveal more of her back. "Oh, love, why did he do this?"

"Because I loved you," Eva replied honestly.

"Such barbarity." Greta was obviously angry that Muller had disfigured Eva. "I thought that Zoe hurt you; she has a temper on her."

"Zoe's temper is quite explosive," Eva admitted, which was not a lie.

"Does she hit you?"

"Not often," Eva lied outright, mentally wincing. *In for a penny, in for a pound*, was the Australian saying. She grimaced at what she was going to say next. "She hated touching my back." The truth was that Zoe took every opportunity to touch her back; the scars did not repulse her at all.

"Stupid peasant." Greta kissed the side of Eva's throat

Eva leaned back and closed her eyes, pretending to enjoy the caress as she stopped herself from pulling away from the unwanted touch.

"You are a precious jewel," Greta said. She took Eva's hand, pulled her to her feet, and looked onto her eyes. "I have always loved you, Eva, and I'm sorry I made the decision to marry John. It was a mistake."

"And I didn't realize until you came back that I am still very much in love with you."

Greta smiled. She leaned down and kissed Eva, the tenderness becoming more demanding and passionate as she held Eva's hands behind her back, restraining her. Eva moaned a little, much to Greta's apparent delight. "We have a lot of catching up to do."

"Hmm." Eva let a little sigh escape, as if in anticipation.

"But first, we have to go to your apartment and get this mess over and done with, all right?"

"I'm looking forward to it," Eva replied, and that was the truth. She *was* looking forward to getting this mess over and done with — the sooner the better.

Earl drove at a high speed — narrowly avoiding the attention of police patrol cars — and stopped just around the corner from the block of apartments. He followed Zoe inside the building and up the stairs. Elena opened her door; she had been waiting for them to arrive. She stood open-mouthed as Zoe rushed past her and into the bathroom without a word of greeting.

Earl shrugged at Elena's questioning look and went to Eva's apartment, letting himself in with the spare key. He was pleasantly surprised to find both agents already inside, getting ready for Eva's arrival.

"Greta arrived early, so I would say," Earl paused to glance at his watch, "to expect them here in about half an hour. Eva is going to try and stall her, but I'm not sure how successful she's going to be."

"Okay, we're ready." Friedrich indicated, with a wave of his hand, the five police officers and David, who had gotten up and headed towards the bedroom as planned.

"Okay, if you need my cricket bat, let me know," Earl joked. He closed the door of the apartment and walked down the hall, entering Elena's apartment and closing the door quietly.

"Where's Zoe?" he asked Elena, who pointed to the bathroom.

"What happened?" she asked, concerned.

"I don't know. Greta arrived early and they had to improvise, so I'm not sure what happened, but Zoe was very upset." Earl replied, helplessly shrugging once more.

As soon as she entered Elena's apartment, Zoe rushed to the bathroom and sank to her knees, sick to her stomach. She leaned over, and threw up into the toilet bowl; the taste of bile was acrid and made her even more nauseous. She sat back on her heels on the cool tiles, placing her hands over her face and crying bitterly at what she had been forced to do to the woman that she loved. The look of shock on Eva's face had caused a pain so deep in Zoe's heart that her world had seemed to shatter in an instant, leaving her heart cold and dark, devoid of joy and life.

Earl knocked on the door and entered. He knelt down beside Zoe and held her as she cried on his shoulder. "She's going to be all right, Zoe," he murmured.

"You don't understand."

"Zoe..."

"You don't understand, Earl. I made a promise never to hurt her and I just did." Zoe was heartsick. All she wanted was to hold and love Eva, and apologize for the horrible thing she had done. "She's been abused before by people she thought loved her, and now me. I hit her. I hit my Eva," Zoe cried, dissolving into tears.

Elena came into the bathroom. She looked on helplessly, tears in her eyes for Zoe's pain.

Earl clearly did not know what to do or what to say. He looked to Elena and said that he hoped Friedrich and David would finish the job and let the two women come together again soon, because witnessing Zoe's self-castigation was like watching a slow death.

Zoe ignored them both, and cried until her eyes were as sore as her poor aching heart.

Chapter Thirty-Two

The car turned the corner at Glebe Point Road then came to a stop in front of the block of apartments. Randolph put the vehicle in park and turned off the engine. He looked up at his rear view mirror, watching the occupants of the back seat for a few moments. Greta was all over the other woman. It had been surprising when Greta had informed him that she was going to bring home her former lover. He had thought that he might have a chance with the aristocratic German beauty, but his hopes were dashed as soon as Greta returned with another woman in tow.

To his complete astonishment, Greta had entered the car with one of the most beautiful women he had ever seen. The tall brunette was quite striking, with short dark hair that framed a gorgeous face, but it was her blue eyes that captivated him utterly. He had been about to ask what had happened when Greta had introduced him to Eva — her lover. His mouth had hung open in surprise, causing Greta to laugh at him.

Randolph had been enjoying the ride home, sneaking occasional glances in the mirror to watch Eva snuggling up to his employer. Greta whispered to her as she stroked Eva's face and ran her hands over the lithe body. He nearly lost control of the car when Greta made sucking noises, and he could not help peering into the backseat. Greta caught him looking and cuffed the back of his head, which only got him more interested. He did not think she was too upset, since she made a comment about him joining them later. He was looking forward to that a great deal.

"Stay here, I don't think we will be long," Greta ordered him. She stepped out of the car and held out a hand to Eva. "Are you okay?"

"Yeah. I just hope Zoe isn't there," Eva replied. Randolph looked up at the block of apartments and smiled as he spied a couple on the balcony who were kissing.

"Don't worry, my love, I can handle that little peasant," Greta replied. She took Eva's hand, and the two women walked up the walkway leaving Randolph to watch them with a smile on his face. He was hoping to be called up to the apartment later and to join in the fun.

Elena had been anxiously watching the road from her balcony, hoping to see Eva and Greta. Her best friend Zoe was crying her eyes out, and there was nothing she could do to help her. Elena felt helpless, which brought back memories of her time in the camp when she was powerless to keep her mother from dying. Elena took a deep breath and leaned over the railing, hoping if she wished it hard enough, they would materialize. She smiled grimly as a car stopped outside the building. "Hey, Earl, they're here!" she said.

"About bloody time," Earl muttered as he walked outside to join her on the balcony. He took Elena into his embrace so as not to arouse suspicion. Earlier, they had worked out a plan which enabled them to watch the road while pretending to be a couple, enjoying each other and not the view. Elena and Earl were praying that this whole plan worked out.

"If this doesn't work out, I'm going to take my gun and start shooting," Earl whispered.

Elena was praying, too.

Greta was happy, the happiest she had been since she had left Auschwitz. Her future looked anything but secure, though she was determined to enjoy life. She had never believed in coincidence, so when she had seen Eva again after so many years, she took it as a sign from God. She was a good Lutheran, and this was her reward.

"Are you happy, my love?" Greta asked, leaning towards Eva as they walked up the stairs. She would be very glad when Eva left this awful building and came home with her.

"I am now," Eva responded, giving Greta a smile.

Greta grinned back at her, her imagination roaming ahead to the night of ecstasy they would share. Since Auschwitz, there had been many disappointments but at last, it seemed as if God was answering her prayers.

They passed Elena's apartment, and Eva gave the door a quick look before stopping in front of her own. She prayed that Earl and Zoe got back quickly enough to let Friedrich and David know about the change in plans. She certainly didn't want another miscue like the one they had experienced with Muller.

She opened the door and let Greta inside, glancing around to see if Friedrich had left the sign that they were indeed ready. She smiled when she saw the overturned book on the low table, a single rose resting on top.

Greta spun Eva around and pinned her against the door, holding both her hands over her head. "You know, I know what you are up to," Greta whispered. She began to nibble on Eva's ear, causing Eva to tremble slightly. Greta apparently took that as a sign she was getting her lover where she wanted her. She insinuated a knee between Eva's thighs and pressed herself more tightly against Eva's body.

Eva took a deep breath to calm herself, and gave Greta what she hoped was a sexy grin. "You do?"

"Oh yes, indeed. You haven't had someone make love to you the way you deserve. That child probably didn't know how to please you or what excites you. I know what you need. My mere presence excites you, doesn't it, my love?" Greta's lips curved in a predatory grin.

Eva grinned back as Greta pulled her shirt out of the waistband of her skirt and began to run her hands over Eva's sides possessively, pulling her closer and nuzzling her neck.

"Hmm," Eva agreed, not trusting her voice at this point, nauseated by Greta's attempts to excite her. She closed her eyes as Greta partially unbuttoned her shirt, pulling it slightly off her left shoulder. Greta kissed the exposed flesh and returned her attention to Eva's neck. Eva felt the sharp sting of teeth, and quelled the reflex to shove Greta away.

Eva wanted this gut-churning scenario over and done with. She hoped David and Friedrich were waiting in the next room as the overturned book had indicated. "What about we go into the bedroom and continue this game?" Eva whispered seductively, slipping out of Greta's grasp and taking Greta's hands in hers.

"You don't have any squirrels in there, do you?" Greta smiled. Her eagerness to continue their love-play was transparently obvious.

"Oh, much better than that, my love, much, much better," Eva said, relaxing back against the door again. Greta took this as a cue to continue her advances and pushed her body against Eva's. Out of the corner of her eye, Eva saw the bedroom door open slightly, giving her only a sliver of a view of David's serious expression. Eva's pulse began to race.

Eva decided to end this charade and took Greta's hand on the pretence of kissing it. An instant later, Greta's arm was yanked behind her back, and the women's positions were reversed. Greta was now pinned against the front door, Eva's knee pressing hard into the small of her back. Eva put her weight into restraining the other woman, not really caring much if Greta was hurt. "And now, I have a wonderful surprise for you," Eva crooned, raising her voice a bit.

"Ohhh, Eva, you like it a little rough, eh?" Greta muttered, the side of her face meeting the smooth wood of the door.

Eva leaned in and whispered into her ear, "After what you put my Zoe through, I could kill you." She turned her head towards David, who had already advanced into the lounge, his gun drawn and a dark scowl on his face. Eva released Greta's hands and stepped back. "She's all yours," Eva spat out, moving out of David's way.

"Hey!" Greta yelled as David took over from Eva. He pulled Greta's other arm behind her back and kicked her legs out from under her, dropping her to the floor.

For a few seconds, Eva watched the prone woman yell expletives. Friedrich had come out of the bedroom on David's heels, followed by a number of police agents. Some of the men glanced at her sidelong. Blushing furiously, Eva realized she was still exposed. *How much had they seen?* She buttoned her shirt and ran her hand across her mouth. She was about to run out of the apartment, but stopped and turned back. She went to the bathroom and let the cold water run before picking up a bar of soap to wash her face and neck. Her cheeks were flaming hot; she imagined that she heard a faint sizzle when she splashed the cool water on her face.

She held the towel in her hands and patted herself dry. They had done it again. Eva could not believe that they actually had caught the woman, but at what cost? Zoe had been hurt and for that, she would never forgive Greta — or herself for agitating Zoe to the point where the Greek woman had raised her hand against her. Eva brought up her own hand and touched her cheek where she had been slapped. She would make it up to her partner, hoping it was going to be enough to rid Zoe of any lasting effects.

Eva sighed as she put the towel back on the metal rack, hanging it neatly. Passing through the commotion in the lounge where expletives from Greta were still ringing out, she left the apartment, closing the door behind her, and nearly ran down the corridor to Elena's apartment.

Just as she was about to knock, the door opened and a very concerned Earl stood at the threshold with a cricket bat in his hand. A smile spread across his stubbled face. He dropped the bat and yelled at the top of his voice, "Eureka! You little bloody beauty!" He hoisted Eva in a bear hug, taking her inside and twirling her around the room. He gave her a kiss on the cheek as he put her down.

"Earl, you're crushing me!" Eva cried out, hitting the man across his broad shoulders.

"I am so glad to see you," Earl shouted. He put Eva back on her feet. "When that bitch showed up early, I had visions of this whole thing—"

"Earl, where is Zoe?" Eva interrupted him, her voice strained.

"Zoe's in the bathroom and she needs you, my friend..." Earl did not get to finish. Eva left him and Elena standing there. Her pulse racing, she ran into the bathroom to find Zoe doubled over on the floor, crying.

"Zoe, love," Eva whispered as her heart broke into a thousand pieces at the sight. She dropped to the floor next to her partner.

Zoe looked up at the sound of Eva's voice. Eva saw tears running down Zoe's face and immediately opened her arms in mute invitation. Zoe hiccoughed and fell forward, melting into Eva's embrace. Eva sat back against the tub as she scooped Zoe into her lap. This tender intimacy caused Zoe to weep anew.

Eva held onto Zoe, rocking her back and forth. "I'm so sorry, my precious one," Eva whispered. "I'm so sorry." Eva kissed the top of Zoe's head and caressed her wet cheek.

"I-I-I...hurt you," Zoe stammered in between hiccoughs.

"No, you didn't. You could never hurt me, love."

"I did," Zoe repeated and looked up. She gently placed her hand over the cheek that she had slapped less than an hour ago. "I hurt you."

Eva closed her eyes and shook her head. "No, you didn't. I love you so much, Zoe. I want you to listen to me, all right? You didn't hurt me. I should never have asked you to slap me." She brushed away Zoe's tears with the back of her fingers. Lifting Zoe's face, she leaned down and gently kissed the weeping woman. The kiss deepened as Zoe put her arms around Eva's neck, tangling her fingers in Eva's hair.

"I promised you I would never hurt you, Evy, never," Zoe murmured. "I don't ever want to hurt you."

"I know, love, I know." Eva let her own tears fall unhindered while she held Zoe in a fierce embrace. As they sat there on the floor, Eva whispered to Zoe, reassuring her of her love. "We did it, sweetheart. We did it!"

"Did she hurt you?" Zoe asked.

"I let her kiss and grope me, which made me sick." Eva sighed. "I washed myself before I came here."

"Is that why you smell all nice?" Zoe asked. She relaxed in Eva's embrace causing Eva to relax for the first time in what seemed like days.

"I didn't want to have even a trace of her scent on me," Eva said.

They sat on the floor holding each other until the door opened slightly to reveal the very worried face of Earl, who was sticking his head around the corner. "David said they are ready to leave. Do you want to say anything to the bitch?"

Eva looked down at Zoe, who nodded. "We'll be there in a few minutes," Eva told him.

"No worries," Earl replied.

"Earl?" Eva said.

"Yeah, mate?" Earl replied. He had started to shut the door, but opened it again.

"Thank you," Eva said. Zoe looked up as well, giving Earl a tiny smile.

Earl smiled back. "Anything for you two."

The door closed. Eva stroked Zoe's cheek. "Are you feeling up to it, love?"

Zoe resolutely said, "No, but I'm not going to let her think she's beaten me."

"That's my Zoe," Eva whispered, giving her lover a kiss. "Come on; let's go and stick it up her." Zoe got off her lap, and Eva rose to her feet. "I love you, Zoe," Eva repeated.

Zoe closed her eyes, put her arms around Eva's slim waist and began to cry again.

"Hey, I didn't mean for you to cry. Come on, love, it's okay." Eva held her shivering partner. "I won't let her hurt you again."

Zoe sniffed back tears. "It hurts, Evy."

"I know, love, but the sooner we do this, the sooner we can put it all behind us, okay?"

Zoe nodded. Eva opened the bathroom door, leading Zoe out to where Elena and Earl were waiting. Elena stepped forward and embraced both of them.

"Thank you," Elena said quietly. "I know it hurt both of you to do this, and I want to thank you for getting her here. I think all those that she helped kill would thank you, if they could."

Zoe's tears started anew at Elena's heartfelt words. Eva brushed away her own tears and held Zoe closer. She led Zoe outside where policemen were milling around in the corridor. Eva rolled her eyes when she caught sight of Mrs. Jenkins talking to her father. She hoped he would handle their landlady. She was in no mood to explain this new situation to her.

David spotted them immediately, but finished speaking to an officer before walking towards them. "Thank you," he said earnestly, offering his hand.

Eva took his hand and shook it. "I don't mean to be rude, David, but I hope I never see you again," Eva said as she held Zoe closer to her. "At least, not officially."

David nodded. "I want to apologize for my behavior. I, um...I've been trying to trace this woman and Mengele since the war ended. I made a promise to a young woman and..."

"There's no need to explain. I understand," Eva said, catching sight of Friedrich leading a disheveled looking Greta towards them.

"You betrayed me," Greta said hoarsely. "How could you betray me? You loved me. I know you did!"

Eva stepped forward and looked at Greta in disgust. "Betraying you was the easiest thing I've ever done in my life," she said and held Zoe's hand, giving it a gentle squeeze.

"You used to be so loyal. I could have given you so much. Why?"

"You're a hypocrite. How could you help those who wanted to kill your own kind?"

"My kind? What? It wasn't like that, Eva; you have to believe me."

Eva leaned closer. It was hard to believe that she had once loved this woman with all her heart. "How many died because of you? How many innocent men, women, and children died? How many people died for loving someone of their own gender, which Hitler didn't approve of?"

"But Eva..."

"No, Greta," Eva steeled her voice, determined not to break down in front of those around Greta. "You nearly sentenced me to death with the research you helped with."

Greta looked at Eva with a new understanding, one that was too late in coming. "Good God, I was just doing my job! I was following orders. I didn't know..."

"Everyone was following orders," Eva said bitterly. "They killed innocent people and were following orders. Where was your heart, Greta? What happened to your soul? You condemned innocent people to their deaths," Eva said viciously and stepped forward. Her pent up anger and humiliation at her torture, and the torture suffered by millions of others, was firmly directed at her former lover. "You condemned me, and all I ever did was love you." Eva looked into her former lover's eyes and leaned closer. "You betrayed *me*," Eva said and took a step back, taking Zoe's hand.

"Eva, darling, I didn't know..." Greta stopped and looked at Eva, then her gaze traveled to Zoe, who was smirking at her. "It's her fault," Greta angrily said. "That peasant. It's her fault; she's poisoned your heart."

Zoe rolled her eyes. "Not only are you a Nazi whore, you are deluded!" Zoe put her arm around Eva's waist and squeezed. "I didn't poison her heart. She gave it to me willingly."

Greta snorted.

"Zoe is the best thing to happen to me. She is my life, and all I will ever need," Eva said to the German woman. "You never owned my heart. Not really. I deceived myself then, when I was too naïve to know better. Zoe owns my heart and always will."

"You are the deluded one, Eva darling. This peasant has—"

Zoe's anger finally got the better of her. She let go of Eva and swung with all her might. Zoe's fist connected with the taller woman's nose, sending her reeling back into Friedrich's arms. Eva winced in reflex on seeing Greta's broken nose and the blood that gushed through her hands as she tried to stop the tide. Her mouth trembled, but she lifted her head, a proud expression on her face.

"A peasant that packs a wallop," Friedrich said, leading the woman off before Zoe took another shot at her. He seemed tempted to get in a lick of his own, but Eva watched him control himself with an effort. He did sigh at the bloodstains that marred his once pristine white shirt.

Zoe turned to a mildly amused Eva. "Ow," she cried, holding onto her injured hand.

Eva took it and kissed the sore knuckles. "Come on, love. I think we've had enough excitement for the day," she said. Eva was about to lead Zoe back to their apartment when she spotted her father coming towards them. "Father."

Panayiotis hugged his two daughters "Are you all right?"

"A little fragile at the moment," Eva said quietly. "But we're going to be all right."

"I'm proud of both of you." Panayiotis leaned over and gave Eva a kiss, then did the same with Zoe, who hugged him back. "Go, I'll deal with everything out here."

"Thank you, Father," Eva said. She led Zoe inside and firmly closed the door to their apartment.

Chapter Thirty-Three

Eva and Zoe were alone, standing in the middle of the lounge holding each other, not saying anything for there were no words that could convey what they both were feeling. Eva tried to say what was in her heart, but stopped, closing her mouth. She wanted to tell Zoe how much she meant to her, but the words were inadequate to express her deep feelings. She had to try and convey her thoughts to the woman she loved.

"Zoe...I..." Eva paused once again. She went on, "I love you so much."

Zoe glanced up and cupped Eva's cheek in her palm — the same cheek she had struck earlier. She left her hand there for a long moment. Eva finally took the hand and kissed Zoe's palm. She held it for a while, then led Zoe to the sofa where they both fell onto the cushions, the adrenaline having finally worn off, leaving them tired and shaky.

"We need a quieter life," Eva quipped. They both smiled. "You were really great back there."

"That stupid bitch just thought she could come back and win you like you were some trophy or something," Zoe said, scowling fiercely.

"Well, she was wrong," Eva replied and kissed Zoe's hand.

"What's going to happen to her?" Zoe asked. She put her head on Eva's chest and sighed contently.

"If she is found guilty, a death sentence or life in prison," Eva replied as she looked down at the other woman's head thoughtfully. She had said some hurtful things in the office. "Zoe, um...what I said in the office..."

"Evy, I know you didn't mean it." Zoe looked up into Eva's face.

"God, I love you," Eva whispered. She scooped Zoe into her arms. "The only good thing to come from this war has been you."

Zoe stroked Eva's face, using the tip of her finger to trace the pronounced dimple in Eva's chin. "I would go through everything again if it meant I would fall in love with you." Zoe put her arms around Eva's neck and laid her head on her shoulder. Zoe suddenly froze, and so did Eva, wondering what was wrong.

"What's that?" Zoe asked, pressing against a mildly painful spot on Eva's neck.

Eva felt around the bruise and sighed. "Greta got quite...amorous...in the car as we were driven here."

Zoe twisted around to get a better look at the mark and gently pushed Eva backwards. "Oh, that bitch," Zoe muttered. "Evy, do you think we can stop with the Nazis making our life hell for a change?"

Despite the seriousness of the question, Eva found it funny and started to laugh. She was quickly joined by Zoe and they both collapsed in a heap on the cushions, curled up together, relief making the two women giddy.

Elena leaned over the balcony, watching the police and the crowd that had gathered outside the building. Somehow, the local media had been alerted; newspaper men with cameras prowled around. *Like vultures*, she thought to herself. She watched with satisfaction as Greta was taken away in a police car that also held the man who had driven Greta and Eva to the apartment. Several other vehicles followed in procession.

"May you burn in hell," Elena cursed the woman and took great satisfaction in watching the disappearing taillights of the car carrying Greta Wagner *née* Strauss.

"Hello."

Elena turned to find Friedrich smiling at her, his hat slightly askew, his shirt bloodied, but otherwise looking like a very happy man.

"You were wonderful," Elena gushed as she unbuttoned his shirt. She frowned when she realized his undershirt was also stained. Friedrich looked down and gave her a crooked grin. "Who's blood is that?" Elena asked.

"Not mine," Friedrich said. "Zoe hit Strauss and broke her nose!"

"You're kidding!"

"No, Strauss said something that made her mad and Zoe hit her with a right hook that would have made Buster Malone proud," Friedrich replied. "Remind me never to get Zoe angry with me," he joked.

"Can you stay, or do you need to go with David?" Elena asked shyly.

"Can't go without my shirt, can I?" Friedrich said, removing both shirts and handing them over. Elena admired his bare chest with a grin before going inside to soak the garments in cold water before the stains set.

"What happened when they arrived?" Elena asked as she ran water into a small tub. Friedrich stood by, his hands in his trouser pockets, watching Elena's ministrations.

"Ah, well, the minute they got into the lounge, Strauss was all over Eva like a rash. David thought that we might need to go out there sooner than we planned, but Eva managed to say the 'go' phrase. By then, David was already halfway through the bedroom door. The rest was easy." Friedrich paused a moment. "I don't understand her; she scares me sometimes."

"Who?"

"Eva," Friedrich replied. "She's so tall and she intimidates me," he said, embarrassed by the admission.

"You're kidding, right?" Elena said, drying her hands on a towel.

"No," Friedrich replied, shaking his head. "When I first met them, I couldn't figure them out. Zoe was the firebrand and Eva the quiet one; it's usually the quiet ones that you need to watch out for."

"Eva is one of the most gentle women I have ever met, sweetheart. I don't know her as well as I would like because she is a very private person, but she absolutely worships Zoe and would do anything for her friends. I should know. It does take a little time for her to warm up to you, but she was trying at the barbeque yesterday."

Elena handed Friedrich one of his shirts that she had washed some time ago. She let a small smile play across her face while she watched Friedrich put the garment on.

"Yes, I know. Maybe it's because she's so tall," Friedrich said.

Elena could tell that he was not serious, and she smiled. "Well, I don't think she can help that." The two of them strolled out onto the balcony.

"Hmm," Friedrich leaned on the balcony railing with a smile on his lips. "So do I get a kiss?"

"You want a kiss?" Elena teased. "Just a kiss?"

"A cuddle would be nice as well," Friedrich replied, opening his arms to her. Elena snuggled up against his chest and closed her eyes.

Alberta looked around the disheveled apartment and began to clean up, putting things back to normal. Earl had volunteered to cook them all dinner. He was busy in the kitchen, while her husband was getting Mrs. Jenkins' feathers unruffled once again.

She quietly opened the bedroom door and winced when it squeaked a bit. Alberta hoped the noise had not awakened Eva and Zoe from their rest. The room was in semi-darkness and both women were in bed. Zoe had a protective arm around Eva's body and slept. Alberta thought Eva was also asleep until she was about to leave.

"Ally?" came Eva's sleepy voice from the bed.

Alberta turned back around to find a pair of very exhausted looking blue eyes looking at her. "Oh, sorry I woke you," Alberta said quietly so as to not disturb Zoe.

"No, that's okay."

"How are you feeling?"

"Tired," Eva admitted. "Relieved, I think, and tired. I can't get to sleep. My mind is galloping a mile a minute."

"You're still over-excited. Do you want me to call Dr. Theophanous to give you something to help you sleep? I'm sure he'll be happy to prescribe a sedative."

Eva shook her head. "No, it's okay. I'm just going to try and rest. How's Father?"

"Well he's trying to soothe things over. I don't think this building has seen this much excitement since Mr. Jenkins' toupee went flying in last week's wind storm," Alberta joked. The mental image of their landlady's husband, trying to hold on to his toupee in the Sydney southerly winds that were common during summertime, was quite funny. She went on, "Once the excitement dies down, everyone will be happy. Now, young lady, I want you to rest. Earl is cooking up a storm in the kitchen, so if you feel up to it later, come out and have a bite. I think it would be good for both of you to eat something. I know Zoe hasn't eaten all day."

Eva said, "I couldn't eat either; my stomach was in knots."

"I don't doubt it, but you have to eat something later."

"I will, thanks, Ally."

"You're welcome. We'll talk later. Get some rest." Alberta tiptoed inside, leaned down and kissed her stepdaughter on the head, tucking the sheet around her.

Eva watched Alberta leave, closing the door carefully behind her. She looked down at the woman she held in her arms and found a tiny smile on Zoe's face. She murmured something that Eva could not make out and burrowed deeper in Eva's embrace.

Eva closed her eyes, wanting to catch up on the sleep she lost the previous night. She was too restless to sleep, her mind too active.

"You're thinking too loud again," Zoe murmured.

"Sorry, did my loud thinking wake you?"

"No, but I'm glad I woke up. I had this most wonderful dream."

"What were you dreaming about? Us on a deserted island, no Nazis, no excitement?"

"No."

"No? Couldn't have been that nice a dream, then. I know that is my dream," Eva teased.

"Really?"

"Oh yes." Eva grinned. "What were you dreaming about?"

"Hmm, I was driving this huge American tank. You know how big they are. I couldn't see over the top, but I was driving it. Greta was standing on the road waving that blasted Nazi brooch of hers. I got so mad I ran her over a couple of times just to make sure, but the funniest thing was that I could hear *Hymn of Freedom* playing."

"Hey, musical dreams; that's different *and* patriotic." Eva chuckled. "I bet that stupid pin survived."

"Nah, I made sure it got pummeled," Zoe replied, her head resting on Eva's chest.

"I wish life was like a good dream."

"It is," Eva replied. "Sometimes, it's even better."

"Aww, that's so romantic." Zoe grinned up at Eva.

"I'm just a romantic kind of gal," she replied, getting a giggle from Zoe. "I've been thinking of taking a few days off work. Would you like to go to the mountains?"

"Hmm, sounds good," Zoe said sleepily and patted Eva's belly. "But right now, you have to sleep. You've been awake for too long."

"Yes, *Mutti*," Eva teased and closed her eyes. Eva was certain that sleep would not come, but having Zoe in her arms was all she wanted.

Earl wiped his hands on a towel and draped it over his shoulder. Alberta had told him that the girls might be coming out for dinner, but it was late. He closed the doors to the balcony and shut off the lights before retiring to the spare bedroom. He turned to switch off the light of the lounge when the bedroom door opened and Zoe came out, her footsteps quiet.

"Hey, Wiggy," Zoe greeted him. "Come here, big guy, I want to give you a hug." Zoe put her arms around his waist and hugged him. "Are you okay?"

"Me? Oh yeah. How's Eva?"

"Tired. She didn't sleep at all yesterday."

"I have something to tell the both of you when she gets up," Earl said cryptically.

"What is it?"

"Can't tell you without Eva," Earl shook his head.

"Are you sure?"

"Quite sure," he said. "Now why are you up?"

"Do you remember you were telling me about that jeweler friend of yours?"

"Yeah, Bobby. He does some nice pieces."

"Do you think he can do something for me?"

"Sure, what is it?"

Zoe smiled. She took off her ring and handed it to Earl. "I want one like this for Eva."

Earl twirled the ring in his hand. "Exactly like it?"

"Yeah."

"Not a problem, Stretch. I'll see him tomorrow and give him the specs. This is for your anniversary this August, huh?" Earl asked as he returned the ring to Zoe. She replaced it on her finger.

"Yeah. I should be able to save for the costs in time, so be sure to have him give you an estimate as soon as possible before I have to pick it up."

"What are you two talking about?" Eva asked leaned against the doorframe, yawning.

"Why are you up?" Zoe asked.

"Wondering where you got to. I can't sleep without you. Why are you up?"

"Earl has something to tell us." Zoe easily sidestepped Eva's question and went to her side. "So, Wiggy, tell us?"

"You woke up because you knew Earl had something to tell us?" Eva asked.

"Not exactly." Zoe grinned and glanced at Earl, silently beseeching him to tell them his news so she could get escape Eva's questioning.

"I have decided to go back to teaching," Earl announced. He was nearly bowled over as both women came rushing forth and hugged him in their excitement. "I take it you like the idea?"

Eva grinned. "That's so exciting. Which school are you going to teach at? Are you going to teach History and English again? What—"

"Whoa, wait a minute," Earl put up a hand to stop Eva's questions. "I haven't taught in ten years."

"You taught Zoe and Elena."

"That's different, but it re-ignited the fire." Earl smiled. "I'm going back to university for a refresher course."

"You're going to become a student again, in order to become a teacher?" Zoe quipped.

"Yep. Now would the two of you please go back to bed?"

Eva leaned over and kissed him on the cheek.

"Not my fault," Earl said.

Eva laughed and shook her head. Without another word, Eva put her arm around Zoe's shoulders and led her back into the bedroom, leaving Earl alone in the lounge.

If there were ever two people who deserved to be happy, Earl thought, *it is those two*. It had been quite a few months with meeting Eva at the biscuit factory, meeting Zoe, then the time with Muller and Rhimes, and now this Greta woman. "I'm getting too old for all this excitement," Earl told himself, chuckling.

Epilogue

"Oh, Evy, don't stop!"

"You like?"

"Uh huh."

Eva smiled down at the young woman who was sprawled below her on the beach towel. Eva spread the warm suntan lotion over silken skin, massaging the liquid onto Zoe's back, eliciting moans of pure pleasure.

Zoe hummed as Eva's soft hands spread the warm liquid over her back. It was clear that she was feeling very relaxed and a little sleepy.

It was a hot and sultry Sydney day, the heat baking the sand. The beach was packed with sun worshippers in various states of undress. Young children played near the water's edge while their protective parents looked on. Eva glanced up from her enjoyable suntan lotion duty to see Earl coming towards them. He was dripping wet from the surf, holding his surfboard in one hand and a clump of seaweed in the other.

Earl put a finger to his lips to stop Eva from alerting Zoe that he was heading their way. Eva shook her head, grinning as Earl stuck his surfboard in the sand, came near, and dropped the wet seaweed on Zoe's back.

"Arghhhh!" Zoe screamed. She sat up and glared at Eva, then grabbed the offending seaweed and threw it at Earl.

"Hey, don't look at me!" Eva put her hands up in protest. She pointed to their friend who had wisely chosen to stand back.

"You are in big trouble, mister!" Zoe got up and chased Earl down to the surf, squealing when Earl stopped and easily picked her up, tossing her over one broad shoulder and walking purposefully into the sea while she wriggled and kicked in protest.

Eva watched the two of them having a mock fight in the water. Zoe's yelp at being dunked caused Eva to grin as she sat back on a low chair, extending her legs and digging her toes into the hot sand. Zoe had bought her a pale blue one-piece swimming costume, which she was wearing under a light cotton shirt. She put on a pair of sunglasses and sat back to enjoy the sun. It had been a few days since they had gone through one of their most traumatic times together. Eva had chosen to take a couple of days off from work to take care of Zoe, to reassure her of her love, and just be with her.

Eva picked up her book, intending to read, when she caught sight of Earl trying to teach Zoe how to swim. She fingered the light cotton shirt she wore and sighed. She thought back to how courageous Zoe had been when she was going to confront the woman who taunted her. *"I'm not going to let her think she's beaten me,"* Zoe had said.

Eva decided it was time to stop letting Muller dictate to her, time to stop being afraid. She put her book down, pulled off her cotton shirt, and put it with the rest of their clothes. After laying her sunglasses aside, she got up and walked towards the sea.

Earl brushed back his wet hair as he held Zoe, who was making a valiant attempt to float but kept squealing when Earl tried to let go of her. He glanced when Eva walked towards them. His mouth fell open in astonishment, which she knew was caused by the realization that she was not wearing her usual shirt, just the swimming costume.

Mimicking Earl's earlier gesture, Eva put a finger to her lips to prevent Earl from letting Zoe know she was there. Coming around Earl, she replaced the tall man's hands, keeping Zoe up with her own. When Earl was far enough away, she leaned down and whispered, "I've got you."

Zoe's eyes flew open. "Eva!"

"Hmm?"

Zoe touched bottom and turned to Eva, who was standing in the water next to her with a smirk. "Your shirt?" Zoe asked, referring to the ever-present shirt that covered the scarring on Eva's back.

"I left it with our other stuff." Eva grinned. "It's time I stopped being scared. I remembered what you said about not allowing Greta to think she'd beaten you. It made me think that I've allowed Muller to do that to me for too long."

"Oh, Evy!" Zoe cried, hugging her. More than anyone, Zoe would understand how much courage it took for Eva to expose her back. "You're going to get burnt now."

"Well, would you blow on my back to cool it down, if I do?" Eva asked, causing Zoe to look up at her with a sexy grin, nodding vigorously.

"Kiss me," Zoe demanded.

"Out here?" Eva asked, indicating all the people in the water and out on the shore.

"Yes," Zoe replied, jumping into Eva's embrace and wrapping her legs around Eva's waist. "I don't care what people think. I love you, and if I want to kiss you in the sea, then I'll kiss you in the sea."

"Zoe?"

"Hmm?"

"You talk too much." Eva kissed Zoe, letting her hands roam under the water and causing Zoe to moan.

"Oh, this is much better than learning to swim."

Eva laughed as she went into deeper water with Zoe still wrapped around her. She had not gone swimming in years and the feel of Zoe nuzzling her neck while they stood in the surf was making the experience all the more enjoyable. "Zoe, we're going to the mountains next week."

"Hmm, more climbing." Zoe waggled her eyebrows, earning herself a passionate growl from Eva.

Eva felt eyes on her back. She turned her head and saw Earl watching them from the shore, grinning broadly. He shook his head and, hefting the surfboard, turned to find a good place to catch some waves.